RISE OF THE
DRAGON SWORN

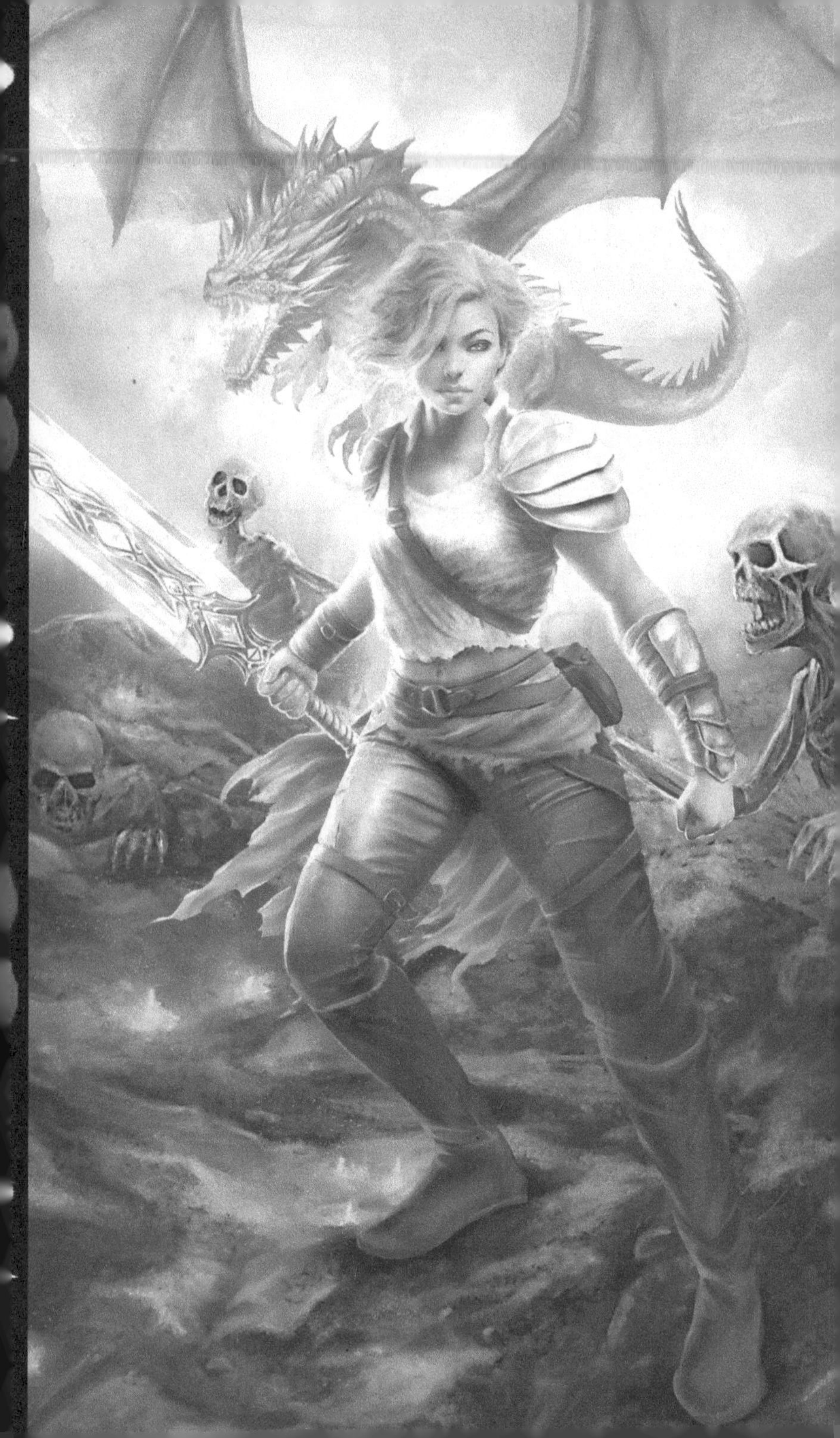

DEDICATED TO

All those who dream of a better world.

Shadow Dragon Saga

Curse of the Dragon Shadow

Legend of the Dragon Soul

Rise of the Dragon Sworn

Blood of the Dragon Throne

Reign of the Dragon Born

Secret of the Dragon Crown

First Edition
Published by Fairies and Fantasy Pty Ltd 2024

ISBN: 978-1-922390-91-2 (paperback)

www.selinafenech.com

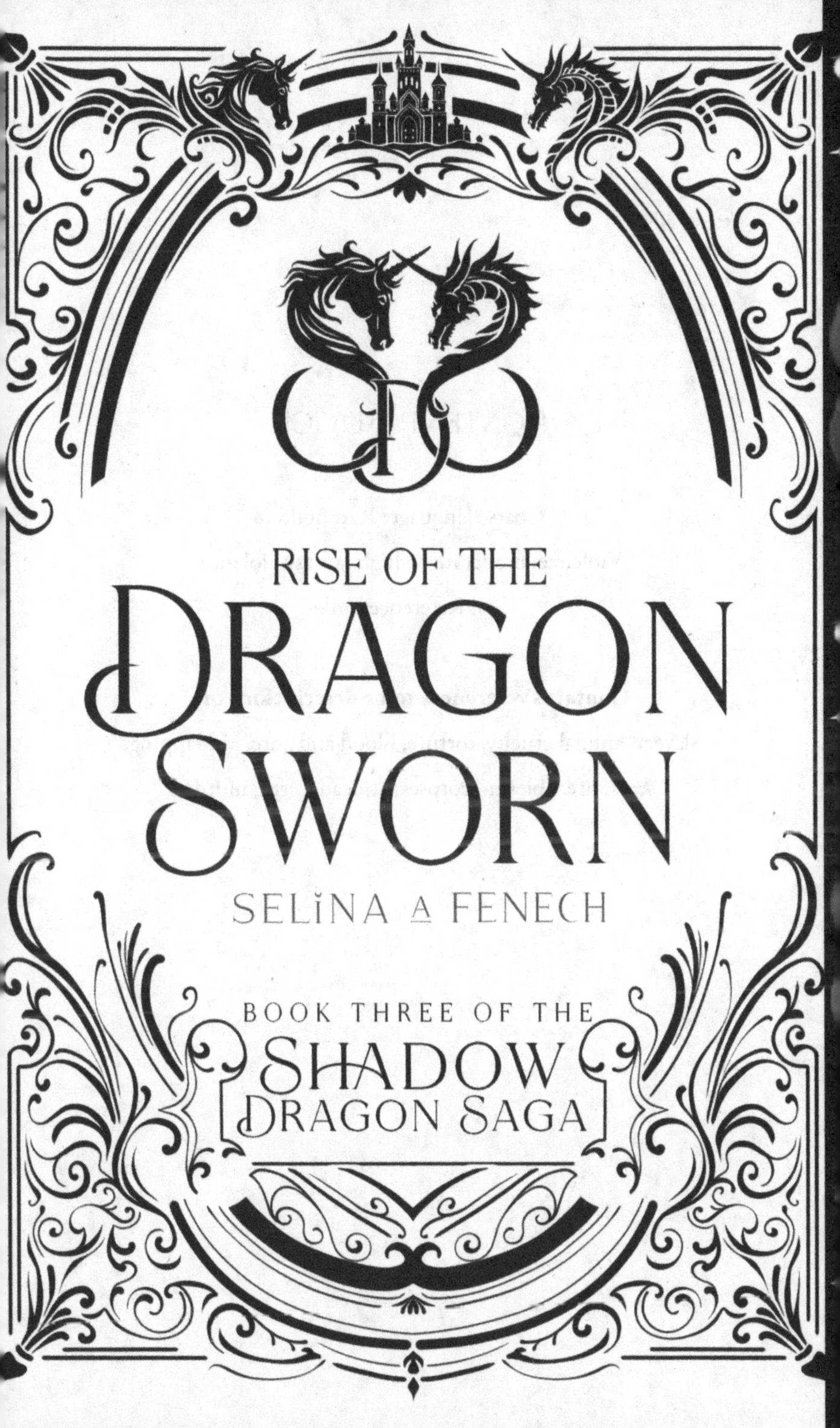

RISE OF THE DRAGON SWORN

SELINA A FENECH

BOOK THREE OF THE
SHADOW DRAGON SAGA

CONTENT ADVICE

Coarse language: Rare/mild

Violence: moderate-to-high fantasy violence

Sex: References only

Contains references to or descriptions of:

Slavery, animal cruelty, torture, blood and gore, kidnapping,
scars, fire, ableism, corpses/undead, birth, murder.

CONTENTS

ELUNDRAE
EIGHT WINDS OC
TAEN HIGHLANDS
Nord Halfort
Heithorn Estate
Tree Wi
Eldisun Grove
The Grea Wing
EYLE TAENESK
Vesland Plains
Unicorn
Dragon Keeps
1. Braigwenkeep (Trade Hub)
2. Nevrynkeep (Mining)
3. Ardahnkeep (Trade Harbor, Old Rolanian Capital)
4. Tjollaskeep (Mining)
5. Salixkeep (Fishing)
6. Ulfrenkeep (Mining)
7. Ylvakeep (Farming)
8. Leskakeep (Farming)
9. Pryshakeep (Farming)
10. Dastmyrkeep (Glass)
11. Tarrickeep (Mining)
12. Gerichkeep (Lumber)
13. Skaellakeep (Farming)
14. Idrakeep (Penal)
15. Hjelzahnkeep (Training)
16. Eslindekeep (Incomplete)
EYLE TAENUSH
Longtail River
Abandoned Quarries
(1)
Lorg Cornis
(11)
WESTERN ALDERKIN DEPTHS
(Ewess Deemfret)
Midsun Dale
Snowshimmer Ri
(2)
Yeonard's Passage
Vasthome Reach
Sturmfell Peaks
Lorg Blessu
Lorg Nisk
(12)
(10)
Tallesis Shores
(16)
Sut Myrr
EYERSUNN SEA

NORTHERN ALDERKIN DEPTHS
(Nerrun Deemfret)
Gris Hofen
(15)
Sunborn Range
Stonewing Crest
(4)
CENTRAL ALDERKIN DEPTHS
(Luns Deemfret)
Eishowl Peaks
(6)
Bovin Steppes
Unicorn Tears River
(13)
(5)
The Red Cliffs
Erst Hofen
SOUTHERN ALDERKIN DEPTHS
(Sous Deemfret)
Talon Bluffs
(8)
Lorg Sesstra
Nord Myrr
(9)
Lorg Eldstrom
Lorg Draeka
Draeskull Crags
Serpents Run
Starris River
(3)
(7)
Etherflame Plains
Grand Hofen
DRAEKHANHELM
EYLE NORDCREST
(14)
Seasong Shores
Mestra's Horn
EASTERN ALDERKIN DEPTHS
(Ilst Deemfret)
DRAEKHAN'S REST
SKYBREAK SEA

ALDERKIN DEPTHS
Relic Lower
Wet Descent
Whisperwin Passage
UPSLOPE
DragonMaw Descent
Stores
1.
Upper Flats
The Curtain
2.
12.
Relic Upper
9.
The Grand Arch
3.
11.
Flowstone Steps
Delver's Circuit
Crystalline Reservoir
STONESHIELD GATE
Livestock
Roc Farr

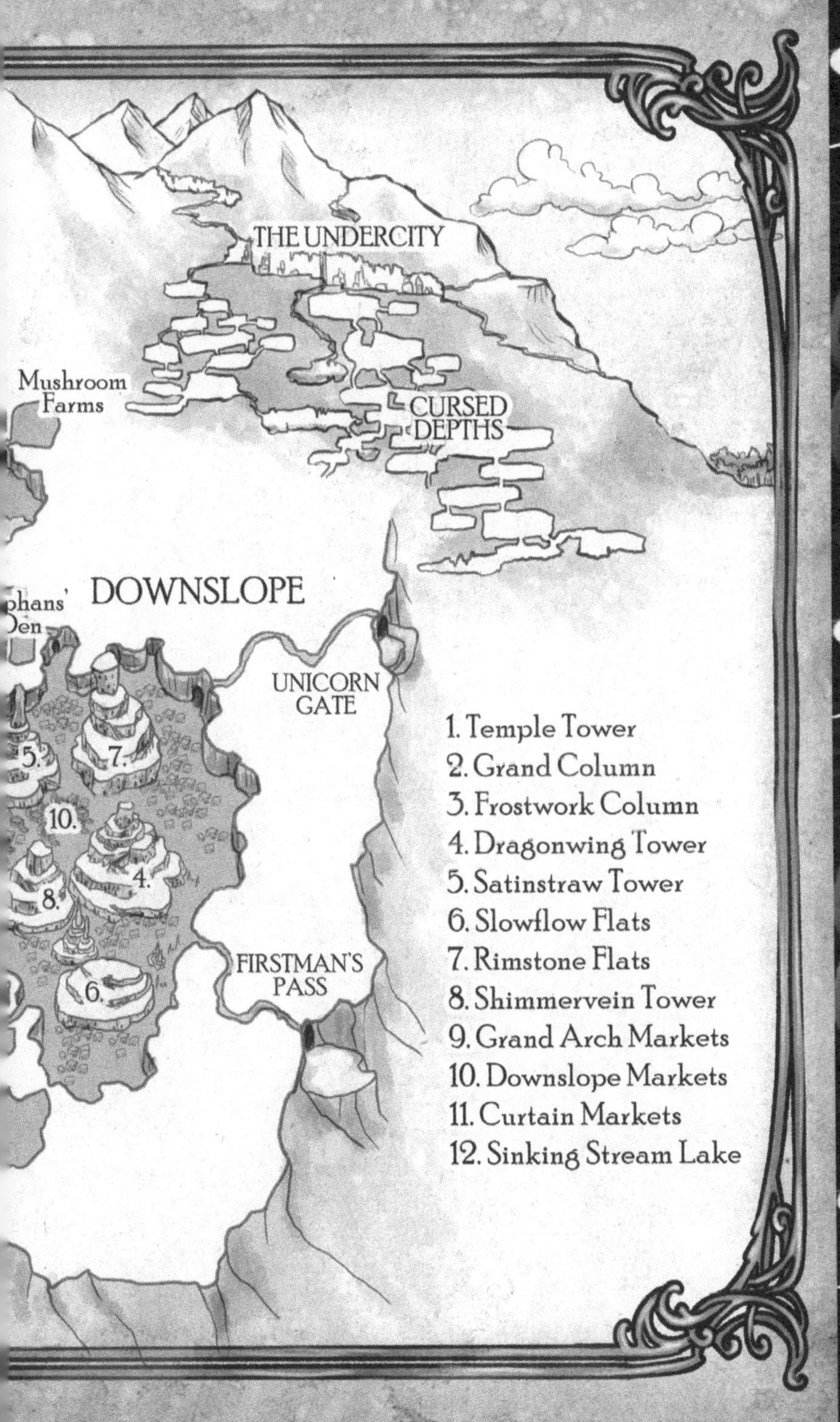

THE UNDERCITY
Mushroom Farms
CURSED DEPTHS
DOWNSLOPE
phans' Den
UNICORN GATE
FIRSTMAN'S PASS
5.
7.
10.
4.
8.
6.
1. Temple Tower
2. Grand Column
3. Frostwork Column
4. Dragonwing Tower
5. Satinstraw Tower
6. Slowflow Flats
7. Rimstone Flats
8. Shimmervein Tower
9. Grand Arch Markets
10. Downslope Markets
11. Curtain Markets
12. Sinking Stream Lake

ONE

Riony had thought the most perilous thing about living aboveground again would be the ravenous undead or the threat of Kess and Lady Hjelzahn hunting them or being caught up in indiscriminate burnings of dragonfire or attacks by ruthless lowlifes and slavers.

She never thought it would be Niskina's grief.

Although Riony had never imagined she would be traveling aboveground with Niskina and the two remaining Hjelzahn siblings in tow, all still grieving in their own ways. With Riony responsible for them all.

This was the third small sanctuary of life they had come across in the few weeks since leaving the undercity and the roughest of them all. Despite the relief of finding other humans to trade with for desperately needed supplies, they were in the locality equivalent of a rusty bear trap.

Riony's eyes darted in each direction, warily checking every ramshackle building and equally ramshackle inhabitant around her. Her fingers twitched, ready to draw the huge crystal sword strapped to her back. Aishena walked close beside her, her younger brother wedged between the two women.

"Where the stars did Niskina go? She was supposed to wait around the corner with the kids while we traded with that mockery of human sentience back there. Who skinned us for far more than we owed," Riony grumbled to Aishena while scanning down the dry dirt street for a sign of the other young woman.

Aishena's eyes remained on Benjin, as though if she could only stare at him long enough and hard enough, she could protect him from all harm.

She reached for Benjin's face, and he scowled and pulled back. Her voice was more worried than scolding as she said, "And you were supposed to be waiting with Lyrrin and Dracuni and Niskina, all out of sight and safe."

Riony looked toward where Lyrrin was keeping Dracuni distracted and hidden behind the broken walls of a crumbled building a couple of houses down. She couldn't see her sister or the growing hatchling, but at least that meant any eyes on the street wouldn't see them either. Still, she knew they were safe.

Catch. Catch good! Dracuni's cheerful narration of her game with Lyrrin was a constant, reassuring presence in Riony's mind.

The surrounding shambles might have once been a pretty village, but only three buildings remained intact, their walls blackened by fire. A few grizzly men, laden with scrappy, chipped weapons, sat leaning against a wall, gambling with dice. Despite their apparent engagement in their game, all eyes were on the newcomers.

"I followed Niskina to try to stop her. She went in there. Also, we're not just kids, and we don't need a babysitter." Benjin pointed to the largest building, a two-story structure of stone from which the sounds of rowdy carousing emerged, even though it was barely midday.

Riony turned her face up to the smoky sky and said a silent prayer. "Every time. Every sparking time."

If there was alcohol or a man anywhere within a dragon's flight, Niskina would find them and end up there, drowning her sorrows in both. Riony tried to be compassionate, but Niskina's behavior added exciting new risks to any run-ins with fellow humans, and Riony was feeling risked out.

"I didn't want to go in *there* after her," Benjin said.

"Smart choice." Riony juggled the ragged sack of food, waterskins, twine, and tools that she'd just traded for, eating up the last of the gold sovs that Aishena had

had in her pockets when they'd left their home for good.

Aishena hadn't said a word of protest about paying for everything. She had been so fast to follow Riony's orders and suggestions lately that Riony had become scared of how that power might corrupt her.

The men who were gambling stood quickly, making Riony twitch. Her eyes locked on them and theirs on her. She could see them sizing up her and the sword she carried, and she lifted her chin to them in a dare to try her.

They moved past, swaggering into the crude tavern, leaving Riony and her companions alone on the street.

"Aish, would you go in there and drag Niskina out before she drinks away everything we own or gets into some other trouble?"

Aishena straightened as though at attention and nodded once.

"That wasn't an order. If you want ..."

The silver-haired young woman had already turned and slinked away toward the tavern.

"I'll look after the kids then, I guess," Riony muttered.

"We don't need looking after." Benjin lifted his chin and extended himself to his full not-even-teenaged-yet height.

"Do you want to go back with the other ... *sss*." Riony caught herself before using the word *kids* again.

Benjin still scowled at her. "What did you get from the

trader? You should have let me come and haggle, since you did so badly at it."

He's sounding more and more like his brother every day. Hooray.

Riony raised her eyebrows at the boy. His short-cropped pale hair had grown into a thicker mat since leaving the undercity, sparkling in the grayed out light. The cool brown of his skin had warmed in their few weeks under the sun, even with its light filtering through ashy skies.

Riony's own skin was transforming too, from the ashy wan it had taken underground to a glowing sienna. Only Lyrrin seemed unaffected by their days aboveground, her pale tones denying the sun's influence.

"I got everything on our list except fishhooks, which they didn't have, and I did just fine with the bargain, thanks. This isn't the same as doing a trade at Curtain Market, little delver. Getting out of a trade with one of these lowlife overworld smugglers alive is the deal you aim for, and you should be grateful for anything else."

Every moment they lingered left Riony antsy. The sour scent of stewing meat emerged from a low building with half its walls lying on the ground in piles of loose stone, a makeshift stable and kitchen in one. Riony didn't want to know what they were cooking. She also planned to ignore any curiosity about the subject when eating the dried meat they had traded for.

Benjin grumbled, "Like you're an expert on living aboveground."

"Lived my whole life aboveground until two years ago, and not locked away behind dragonkeep walls like some."

Benjin flinched almost imperceptibly, and Riony regretted mentioning anything that related to his family and the past that had led him here.

"Weren't you kept by the Heithorns under their protection, too?" Benjin jabbed back. Aishena must have been telling him things.

It was Riony's turn to flinch. Anger rose like a boiling tide in her, and she willed it away. Her anger was all for Kess—not for Benjin. "Not since Lyrrin was born. We were on our own after that, for years, until we found somewhere relatively safe." *Until it wasn't safe either.*

Benjin harrumphed and reached for the sack, his face still a picture of disapproval. "Let me see what you got."

Riony handed it over with a sigh.

He riffled through, pulling out some of the dried meat and two of the waterskins and transferring them into his bags. He didn't take more than what would be his and Aishena's share, so Riony didn't argue.

They were still salvaging together enough supplies for survival on the run. They had been thrust out of the undercity without notice, with only what they'd had on their person. Riony, Niskina, and Aishena had their delving tools and armor—although Riony's chest armor had been left on Kess and lost.

Aishena had been disarmed of almost all her athames during her fight with her mother, but Lyrrin had sneakily picked up a couple of the dropped weapons amongst the chaos and returned them to Aishena afterward—something Aishena seemed very grateful for.

The twin blades taken from Lady Hjelzahn remained with Aishena too, although she refused to acknowledge or use them.

Aishena, in return, gave Lyrrin her spare glow stone. Lyrrin added it to her treasures with glee, along with the few random crystals Riony had snatched from the Alderkin warrior's tomb when she'd taken her sword.

She had a seeing stone like the one on Yoskar's staff, a small burn crucible, two matching stones that Lyrrin hadn't worked out the function of yet, and a crystal with a ten-stroke rune she couldn't activate, no matter the hours she'd been spending trying to crack the sequence.

After one night at the first shrine, they had moved on to the ruins of the slavers' camp to salvage what they could.

There wasn't much left amongst the charcoal remains— almost everything flammable was gone—but they had

found one crate that had escaped the dragonfire. Within it, a few blankets, which were treated as a treasure more precious than silvernix after a chilly night on the hard ground with nothing soft for comfort.

Lyrrin had also found a sling, and Niskina a metal-handled poleaxe. Riony tried to find some armor to replace her missing delver vest, but although lots of metal pieces remained, the leather straps were burned away. She took a couple of bracers anyway and had been working on drying leather to repair them as they traveled on.

They'd been heading west since.

Despite having spent time in this ruined aboveground world before, Riony had to admit it felt far worse now than it did then. At least then she'd had her parents with her.

Along the dusty road that cut through the ruins, shards of charred bone scattered the ground. The remains of revenants.

There were no high stone walls around this settlement as there were with the dragonkeeps, bringing safety to the population and keeping the revs out. Only a few scrounged together barricades huddled around each of the standing buildings themselves, the windows blocked and barred.

But even settlements with walls weren't always safe. Riony knew that too well.

During the weeks between using the strange Alderkin

gateway to flee from the murderous Hjelzahn mother, Riony and her friends had several brushes with revs themselves. But no more of the strange ashy ones.

Between Riony's beloved sword, Aishena's athames, and Yoskar's crystal-studded staff—now Benjin's—the odd lone rev was no longer much of a threat to them as long as it stayed dead.

Up the roadway, through the haze of old smoke and kicked-up dust, a cart rattled toward them.

It was drawn by a scrawny goat and led by a woman whose face was marred with dirt settled into worried wrinkles. Three other people rode behind, perched between bundled baggage.

The woman's eyes softened in relief as she brought the cart to a stop within a safe distance of Riony and Benjin.

"See? There are other children here," she called behind to her companions.

One of the three blanket-shrouded figures on the cart turned to look, revealing a small eager face. What should have been the puffy cheeks of youth were hollowed and the sockets of their eyes dark. Any visual signs of gender were lost to the ravages of hunger.

Riony's heart contracted as she moved forward, only a few steps separating them. "No, there aren't other children here. We're only passing through, as you should be too.

This isn't a settlement for families. This is a hive of hornets lured to nest by a sweet drink."

As though on cue, a rousing chorus went up from within the makeshift tavern. What was taking Aishena so long?

A shaggy man emerged from the kitchen-stables and leaned against the doorframe, picking his nails. His keen gaze scraped over every inch of the cart and what it carried. Riony saw what he saw. No weapons in sight.

"You need to keep moving," Riony told the woman in a low voice.

"Is there food here?" the woman asked, ignoring Riony's suggestion. "We had to leave Tarrickeep. Any Rolanian not serving a dragonlord is getting forced out. I thought another keep would take us, but ... We've been traveling, trying to find anything ..."

Riony knew hunger. She knew that when forced to choose between starvation and danger, safety could be dismissed over the chance to eat.

Riony reached over to Benjin and took back the sack, pulling from it three wrapped bundles of food. "Take this. Keep moving. There's a safe refuge below ground in the Eishowl Peaks. Try to get there."

Riony gave them hasty directions to the undercity as Benjin glared at her.

"We need that food," Benjin snapped.

"You've got yours. I'll sort something else out."

The woman's eyes turned red as she took the offering and handed it over to the boney arms reaching from the cart. She looked so very tired as she muttered her thanks. Her gaze flickered over Riony's sword and physique.

"Are you ... employable? For protection? Can you take us to this underground place safely?"

"I'm immensely flattered you think I'm some kind of hired muscle, but—"

"We can pay." Her voice was abrupt, desperate. She fumbled around the belt on her skirts and pulled a heavy coin pouch into view.

Riony slapped her hands onto it and hissed. "Careful! You want to get robbed?"

Riony checked the man who'd been watching and stepped to place herself between him and his view of the woman.

"But you ... you seem ..." She gestured to the food Riony had given them as explanation.

"Doesn't matter what I seem like. Everybody is looking after themselves out here. Don't forget that. And I've got enough to deal with looking after my own. I'm sorry." Not to mention that they couldn't be traveling with strangers—not without revealing Dracuni.

The unidragon had gone quiet, as though sensing

Riony's tension.

In a voice Riony hoped was loud enough for her and Lyrrin to hear, she said, "It's okay." And then in a quiet, growling rasp to the woman, she continued, "But you have to keep moving. *Now*."

The woman recoiled and her mouth curled as though to protest. But then she nodded and tugged the goat's leash, and the small cart rolled into motion again. Their figures grew smaller and smaller until they turned the corner behind a pile of rubble, out of sight.

The shaggy man at the stables moved as though to follow the family, but after a quelling glare from Riony he returned to loitering in the doorway. Benjin complained about the lost rations, and Dracuni returned to her game with Lyrrin.

Nobody but Riony could hear the unidragon's words, but still Dracuni chatted away happily as though they could.

Throw. Throw. Too high!

The door to the tavern burst open, and Aishena barged out, dragging Niskina behind her and bringing a swell of laughter and the scent of stale alcohol onto the street. Niskina stumbled as she was pulled down the building steps.

No wonder they'd taken so long. Riony should have known that a polite mention that it was time to leave wouldn't be enough to separate Niskina from her drink.

They arrived in front of Riony, and Niskina huffed, snatching her arm free. She tossed her tumble of chestnut hair from a face that was already reddening with alcohol and pouting fiercely.

Riony angled to get herself in line with Niskina's roaming, hazy eyes. "Niskina, with all kindness, could you please try not to drink dry every settlement we pass through within minutes of arriving?"

"Oh, they still had plenty." Niskina waved a floppy hand dismissively, as though that were the core of the problem.

Riony knew she was hurting. The death of her father was still so recent, but her behavior was a concern. Riony had worried at first that the feisty young woman might sell Dracuni out in her drunken state or in trade to fulfill some desire. But she, and the others, had all kept that secret close. So far.

A couple of men had gathered at the door of the tavern, pleading and jeering for Niskina to return to them. She grinned, turning back, and Aishena spun her around away from them again.

With a longing look over her shoulder, Niskina moaned, "Come on. Can't we just stay here one night? Or two?"

Aishena said coldly, "We're not risking all our lives so you can bed that lot."

Following the conversation, Benjin's eyes widened and

his cheeks went the same color as Niskina's.

"But they're sooo nice," Niskina slurred.

Riony raised her eyebrows. "Them? They aren't even men. They're red flags sewn together into creepy man-shaped puppets."

"So what? What does it matter what they are or what I do?"

"Because we need to move on."

"Why? Where are we even going, anyway? Move on, move on, that's all you keep saying. What's the point? Move on *to where*?" Niskina glared, waiting for the answer.

Aishena and Benjin also turned, looking to Riony for answers.

Riony still wasn't used to that. Frankly, it unnerved her, considering how much lower in the pecking order she'd felt in the past. But she hadn't lost her father or brother in the escape from the depths. She'd continue to take the lead while the others managed their grief.

Not that she had any answers.

She ventured her thoughts out loud. "There were other Alderkin depths around Elundrae. Maybe—"

"All destroyed in the war, from reports I've seen," Aishena said. "At least all the entry levels completely collapsed."

"What about getting into lower levels?"

Benjin said, "How would we get into them?"

"They might have magical gateways too, like the one we found."

"The one we found only went between it and the shrine we'd been to before," Aishena said. "That might be it, for all we know."

Riony wasn't sure about that. The oval geode structures existed in shrines all over the land. They must act as gateways too. But Aishena was right that there seemed to be no signs of other gateways being functional. At least, not *yet*.

The map Aishena had taken from the Alderkin chambers showed there was one nearby this settlement that Riony hoped to go to, to test some theories.

Niskina sighed a puff of spirits-scented air. "No way we can waltz up to a dragonkeep or some dragonlord-ruled estate with the bounty on you two."

Aishena paled.

"That's not our fault," Benjin growled.

"We couldn't do that anyway. Not with Dracuni," Riony added gently.

Benjin still turned on her, as though everything was her fault. "You said you lived for years up here, that you found somewhere safe. What about that place?"

Riony's throat dried up. "I said *relatively* safe."

"Relatively is still better than not at all, which is why my vote is still to stay right here." Niskina eyed the tavern again.

"Where was it? Could we go there?" Aishena asked over Niskina.

Riony scrunched a hand into her red hair, grimacing. "It was a secluded village in an abandoned strip mine. The town leaders figured that all the earth had been removed, so it should have been safe from the shadowdragon raising any revs there."

"That does make some sense," Benjin said.

"Yeah, and we all thought we were safe because the shadowdragon never came, and we thought it never came because there was nothing there for it to awaken. But then it did come, and there were still bones that answered its call." Riony's heart raced and her breath came quickly.

She swallowed the feelings down. "Not many people escaped alive. I don't even know ... It's probably abandoned."

"We should go there, then," Benjin said firmly, sounding so much like Yoskar that Riony jolted.

"I just said it wasn't safe after all."

"Back then. But if the shadowdragon raised everything already, and that was a couple of years ago, then there mightn't be any revs left there now. And if it is still abandoned, even better. We can set up a hideout there." Benjin's eyes glimmered as he presented his plan.

"I don't —"

"Aish, what do you think?" Benjin turned to his sister for backup.

"There could still be revenants, plus the bodies of the population ..."

Riony's breath juddered to a halt, and she had to force her lungs to work again.

Benjin scoffed. "Tell them we should go there."

"We should go there," Aishena repeated.

Across the road, the man remained at the doorway to the kitchen-stables, watching their debate with narrowed eyes. Urgent unease trickled like icy water through Riony.

"Fine, we can ... head in that direction." Better than continuing west, anyway, which would lead them toward Heithorn estate. They just had to aim farther south instead. Still, the idea of coming anywhere near either location left Riony feeling cold.

Dracuni had grown quiet again. A sensation of worry came from the unidragon into Riony's mind, washing over her own feelings.

Hurt? Scared? Dracuni inquired.

Whatever the bond between them, Riony hadn't been able to get Dracuni to hear her thoughts as she heard Dracuni's, but the hatchling seemed to sense her emotions well enough, which Riony would have preferred not to share.

She gritted her teeth and breathed through her nose

and put a smile on. "It's fine. Still, it's a long way to go. And I want to stop at that shrine nearby next."

She'd been itching to test out her theory about the Alderkin shrines since the morning after they had fled the undercity. She'd woken up to find that the cutting athame, used up the day before, was working again. Just as it had recharged during their journey to save Lyrrin and Benjin from the slavers.

It has to be the shrine recharging it somehow.

The bigger question was whether it was only that shrine. One of Benjin's glow stones had run out of charge during their weeks aboveground, so they could test that.

"The shrine isn't far, right? What if you all go and do that while I head back inside?" Niskina skipped a few steps away, out of Aishena's reach.

Riony ran to block her path, holding her arms wide like a barricade. "Nope, sorry, you've lost your do-things-alone privileges."

"Come on, Ri. I just want to have a bit of fun." Niskina slapped Riony's hand away, trying to step past.

Her sheer level of defiance made Riony grateful for Lyrrin's cheery contrariness. Sure, Niskina was hurting, but she was putting herself and the rest of them at risk.

"I don't know if you even care if you live or die right now, but I do, and I can't let you go back in there." Riony grabbed Niskina by the shoulders, stilling her.

Niskina's eyes washed over, glossy with tears. "If you really cared, you'd stop trying to tell me what to do with my life. Let me through and you can go and be boring somewhere else."

Anger flared in Riony, defeating her attempts at patience. "You're killing me here!"

Kill? Bad hurt? Dracuni's anxious call flooded Riony, then a cry from Lyrrin came from their hiding place.

Riony was ready to run for them when she saw Dracuni racing toward her.

"Come back!" Lyrrin whisper-yelled from behind the bounding unidragon.

Dracuni had grown enough in the weeks aboveground that she could no longer be carried. Not by Lyrrin, anyway. She was now the size of a large dog, and even stronger. If Dracuni wanted to go somewhere, it was hard to stop her.

Dracuni's frantic run slowed as she approached Riony, lilac eyes blinking. Her head tilted, horn shimmering in the glary light. ***Not hurt?***

Riony groaned. "I was exaggerating!"

Dracuni didn't have any grasp on hyperbole or sarcasm though, and now there she was, standing right in the middle of the dusty street.

The tavern door had closed again, but the man at the

stables remained. He straightened up, moving a couple of steps closer as he sucked air through his teeth. "Is that a dragonling you've got there? What is that weird thing?"

"It's your ass on a plate if you keep asking questions," Riony shot back at him with a leveled glare, daring him to try anything.

Lyrrin caught up after Dracuni. Her face crumpled. "I'm sorry. She just ran out."

Riony half nodded a response, but she kept her gaze locked on the man. He rubbed at his patchy beard, and Riony could see the calculations working through his head as his eyes narrowed and nose twitched.

Ownership of any kind of dragon was valuable.

Only three young women and two children stood between him and that value.

But one of them had a very, very big sword.

The man's chances of taking Dracuni depended upon whether he was willing to split that value with others or not.

As he lifted his chin and opened his mouth, turning as though to call for backup, Riony realized he'd decided. She reached for the buckles that strapped her sword to her back. "Get ready to run."

But before a sound emerged from the man's throat, something flew into it. It jabbed through the flesh, jutting out, bright white against the flush of blood that emerged around it. A slim dagger, carved from bone.

The man dropped.

Dracuni skittered behind Riony, who spun on the spot, looking for the source of that dagger, already knowing who she'd see.

A huge gray wolf prowled toward them down the dusty street. Atop Griskin, almost lost behind the thickness of his fur, rode Kess, more daggers already in her grasp.

"Pony," she drawled, her lips twisted in a sly grin. "Were you really about to let somebody else steal what is mine?"

TWO

S*he found us.* Fury ignited inside Riony, aching in her chest at the sight of the traitorous goblin. The audacity of Kess to show her face again after turning on them, let alone continue to hunt them, was something else.

Dracuni peered out at Kess from between Riony's legs. **Is friend?**

"Her? No. She isn't our friend," Riony muttered back.

But I helped?

"I know. I'm sorry. You can't trust her."

A wave of deep sadness and confusion channeled from the unidragon and she crouched lower behind Riony.

Riony had risked her own life, and Dracuni's, to save Kess from the revenant conglomerate. Dracuni had given her blood to save Kess. And Kess had betrayed them.

Riony still didn't know what had made her run back into that cavern.

She wished she hadn't. She should have just continued on and never seen Kess again, then maybe she could have helped the others beat Lady Hjelzahn. Maybe Brishan wouldn't have died. Maybe they'd all still be delvers, together, living safely underground.

But she had gone back for Kess.

Somewhere, in the depths of her mind, the way Kess had screamed her name—her *name*, not Pony or some other insult—still echoed, raising goosebumps over her skin.

It had felt as though Riony had seen Kess with everything stripped away by fear, and in that moment, Kess had cried out *her name*.

And then went right back to being an irredeemable, selfish assface directly afterward.

And she was still wearing Riony's delver armor!

Rude.

"When you say that guy was going to steal what's yours, did you mean a violent death at the end of my sword?" Riony questioned.

"Oh, stop your ridiculous posturing. Just hand over the dragonling, and I'll even let you and your ..." Kess looked over the rest of them—two defiant children, Niskina wavering on her feet, Aishena wavering in indecision. "Wow. Maybe I shouldn't let you all go. Seems like it would be a mercy to put this lot down."

"Sounds like something your brother would say." Riony's hand moved toward her sword.

Kess raised a dagger in warning. "Except I'm trying to do the right thing. Let me take Dracuni. You really think you and this lot can keep the creature safe? Look at you! You almost just let that scumbag call every lowlife here to see what you have, and what then? What happens when they find out what she is?"

"As though she'd be safe with you with a stake through her brain! You're outnumbered, Kess. You can't have her. Either you leave or you die, here and now. Either way, sounds like a good time to me."

"You want to take her on?" Aishena whispered from her side.

Riony nodded. "We can beat her and the wolf. I'm sure of it."

"But Niskina is ... and the kids ... Kess dropped that man with one hit." Aishena cast worried eyes over the rest of them.

She had a point, but Riony and Aishena together should be able to win this. And every part of her wanted to fight. "We take Kess out now, and that's one less thing we have to worry about hunting us. We're doing this."

Doubt flickered in Aishena's eyes but she nodded anyway.

"You're really going to try to *kill* her?" Lyrrin stared at Riony, her bright-blue eyes wide, sparkling under the shadow of her hood. "Right here? And what about Griskin? You're not going to kill the poor pup too, are you?"

Riony huffed out a grunt. None of this was *ideal*. But what else could she do? "We have to do this. *I* have to do this."

Kess watched with a shrewd, amused expression, toying with her throwing knife. "You really do want me dead, don't you? And how many of your little group here are you willing to lose before you get to me? Hand over the creature, or you're about to find out."

Before Riony could tell Kess she was about to find out what having a fist down her throat felt like, the door to the tavern swung open, and two men stumbled out.

"Told you she's still here," a tall man with an eyepatch said, then his gaze landed on the dead body.

Riony pointed at Kess. "It was her. She did it."

The second man, wearing an impressive array of mismatched armor and age-worn weapons, glared at Kess and Riony and every newcomer standing over the body of someone that might have been a friend to him, or at least some kind of shady acquaintance.

"You killed Aldo." Then he yelled into the tavern,

louder again, "Oi! These churls killed Aldo!"

"Not *Aldo*!" More than a few voices wailed back from inside.

Okay, maybe the thugs are closer friends than I gave them credit for.

There was a scuffle of movement from within the building.

Kess stared at Riony, and Riony stared back.

Riony's feet cramped with the tension of wanting to spring forward. Her arms burned with the desire to swing. Her teeth ground against each other with the swirl of emotions driving her to fight, fight, fight, to inflict pain upon Kess to match the hurt of her betrayal.

But more men spilled out, drawn by the call.

Riony ground out her command. "Run. To the shrine. Go!"

Aishena was the first to move, snatching Benjin by the arm and dragging him with her. "This way!"

Niskina broke into a dash after them, herding Lyrrin and Dracuni in front of her. The unidragon bounded in a glittering streak along the dusty road and around the side of the kitchen-stables. She could move fast now. Riony hoped it would be fast enough.

The tavern emptied, the rough men and women rushing out onto the street between Riony and Kess, yelling and drawing weapons.

After sending one final screw-you glare at Kess, Riony ran too.

The side street was in even worse repair than the rubble of the main road, with dead bushes and tumbleweeds tangling the way. Riony leaped and dodged around them.

Behind her, there was the growl of a wolf, the clink of metal, and the sound of one body falling, then another. More yelling, harsh and incensed, was followed by the pounding of feet.

Maybe the community of smugglers, thieves, and slavers would finish Kess off for them. That idea didn't bring Riony the happiness she'd hoped for.

She was even less pleased when she felt the sharp chink of a thrown dagger as it hit her sword, right near the back of her neck.

She didn't need to risk a glance behind her to know Kess was in pursuit.

Griskin was fast, but there was a score of pursuers after Kess as well, harrying her as she tried to reach her target.

Riony reached the edge of the ruined village, running right over the flattened remains of a cottage toward the tangle of burned forest ahead. She'd caught up with Lyrrin now, the others all farther away.

As though challenged by Riony's presence, the small girl put on another burst of speed, sprinting ahead again. They scrambled through an overgrown field then into the sparse woods.

A sear of pain along her upper arm made Riony catch her breath as another dagger sliced along it. Even with half a town chasing them, Kess wasn't letting up.

"Are you seriously still throwing knives at me right now?" she yelled back.

"This is your fault, Pony! You should have given me Dracuni!" There was a cry and a stumble, and a crossbow bolt whizzed past Riony's head. She spared a second to glance back, seeing the mass of people chasing them through the blackened trees.

Sparks! The shrine better be there, and it better work!

The ground sloped down, forming a small gorge, and up ahead, Riony saw a standing stone marking the wide perimeter of the shrine.

She skidded down the slope to where a trickle of a creek ran toward the Alderkin ruins, where the main structure sat upon a mound amid the tiny flow of water.

Benjin and Aishena reached it first, still far ahead of the others. They ran into the small temple of crystalline stone, and a few seconds later, Aishena yelled out, "It's not working! It's not activating!"

"Try it again!" Riony yelled back.

She bit her lip as she ran. If the gateway wasn't working, they were running into a dead end. They could try to fight back from within the cover of the shrine, but they were hugely outnumbered, and who knew which side Kess would fall on.

No wait, I do know. Her own side.

Griskin let out another vicious growl, and a man cried out. Riony winced. She knew what a bite from that beast felt like. Kess could also still be heard, hurling insults along with her knives.

Between Riony and Lyrrin, and the shrine farther ahead, Niskina had stumbled, and Dracuni was circling around her in an anxious trot.

Friend get up?

"Keep running!" Riony yelled back, but Dracuni remained by Niskina as she rolled forward and into a sitting position, her shoulders shaking.

"Still nothing!" Aishena called out through the shrine doorway.

Okay. Maybe we're fighting our way out of this.

Riony reached Niskina and grabbed her, dragging her up and into a sprint again.

The huffing breath of the wolf sounded right behind them.

"Eyes!" Lyrrin cried, swinging her sling about in one hand.

Riony turned away from it, squinting her eyes closed as much as she dared while still running.

"You aren't getting us with that again!" Kess yelled.

There was the sound of skidding leaves and stones

behind them as Lyrrin's altered glow stone burst into a flash of blinding light. It was only a sliver of the larger crystal, cut down for smaller pieces in Lyrrin's experimentations.

The light it produced wasn't nearly as strong as ones she'd used before, but it was enough to make Kess stop for a moment to avoid it.

That gave Riony, Lyrrin, Niskina, and Dracuni the advantage they needed to break ahead of her again.

Dracuni moved the fastest, splashing through the trickling puddles and over smoothed rocks. The other three were right behind as they ran through the circle of standing stones, and a shiver of energy raised the hairs on Riony's neck.

"Try the gate again!" she yelled as she skidded to a stop at the shrine doorway.

Benjin was crouched at the base of the massive slice of jagged geode, and his fingers moved swiftly, tracing the rune there in the way Lyrrin had shown them all.

Symbols on the side of the crystal gateway brightened with the glow of magic. Benjin gasped loudly, "There's two! Two symbols have lit up!"

"Just pick one! We need to get out of here, now!" Riony turned her back on the approaching pursuers just in time for her crystal sword to shield her from another crossbow bolt.

"One of them is the same symbol as before," Lyrrin said, rushing in beside Benjin.

"Then do that one!" Riony looked back, as Kess and Griskin bounded toward them ahead of the army of Aldo's friends.

The circle of standing stones at the other shrine had kept a revenant out, and for a moment Riony hoped it would keep out all evil, heartless things. Unfortunately, Kess passed straight through.

A sparkling glow filled the shrine as the gateway activated, showing another place through the rippling air within it.

Benjin stood up straight beside Riony, Yoskar's staff held before him, the burn rune activated. "You all go through. I'll hold them off."

"I don't think so," Riony said, turning and giving him a push toward Aishena.

A knife plinked again off the wide sword shielding Riony's back, then Benjin yelped as it ricocheted into him, scratching across his cheek.

Aishena grabbed him bodily, and they were the first through the gateway.

Riony's head swiveled, watching her friends, her pursuers, her friends again.

Lyrrin went through with Dracuni. Niskina stumbled after. Griskin was within pouncing distance. Riony dove headfirst through the swirling magic.

She bit the dirt on the other side, rolling and yelling, "Close it!"

Lyrrin deactivated the portal.

For a long moment, the only sound was heavy breathing as they all drew breath back into overworked lungs.

Then Benjin turned a circle, scowling. "This is the shrine near the undercity. We're right back where we started again!"

Riony blinked at her surroundings, wiping dirt off her face. He was right.

"It was the same symbol as we used before, so it makes sense it's taken us to the same place." Lyrrin ran her fingers over the markings around the side of the geode slice.

There were dozens of symbols around it, some of them cracked.

With a dull voice, Niskina asked, "Do you think the other one was the gateway in the depths?"

"Maybe. Either way, we can't go back there." Riony looked at how big Dracuni was getting. There'd be no way to keep her hidden in the undercity for much longer. And if Aishena and Benjin returned, their mother would no doubt get news of it quickly enough. "I mean, Niskina could probably go back if she wanted."

"No. I don't want to see that place ever again." Niskina moved from a sitting position onto her hands and knees, crawled into the corner, and promptly vomited.

"You got hurt!" Aishena reached for Benjin's face and the fine red line marking his brown cheek.

"I'm fine. It's nothing."

"You can't go trying to take on enemies like that. You've got to keep yourself safe." Aishena turned to Riony. "Can we fix this? Can Dracuni heal him?"

Dracuni sniffed at the air, standing up on hind legs and looking at the cut.

Hurt. Should help?

"No, this isn't bad hurt." Riony winced as she leaned on her cut arm to bring herself upright.

Help you too? Dracuni tossed her chin upward at Riony.

"She seems to be happy to help," Aishena said.

"No! We're not bleeding her every time one of us gets a little scratch! Does that really sound okay to you?"

Aishena's eyes narrowed, and for a moment, Riony actually hoped for the return of the caustic, headstrong woman who seemed so absent now.

"I'm really fine," Benjin repeated, tugging Aishena's hand and making her look at him. "We aren't using Dracuni like that."

"Here." Riony got to her feet, rummaging in the pouches on her belt where she'd been collecting herbs on their travels. She handed over some short green sticks.

"Squeeze the sap from these and rub it on. It should stop the cut from turning bad."

Lyrrin appeared in front of Riony, hands out for some of the weftweed.

"Did you get hurt too?"

"Nope," Lyrrin said, then went over to Benjin and wiped his cheek with her gloved hands.

Her sister's kind ministrations didn't stop Benjin from glaring at Riony as she dabbed some of the sticky clear sap onto her arm. "We should have run earlier. You and your grudge against Kess are going to get us killed."

"Kess is the one chasing us. I was just trying to stop her." Riony's nose wrinkled at the pungent tang of the sap. "Would I have taken some pleasure in stopping her? That's up for debate."

"I can't believe she found us, that she's still chasing us," Lyrrin grumbled.

"That's Kess for you. Stubborn to her core. And knowing what Dracuni is, what her blood is, well ... Kess wouldn't be the only person who would chase us to the ends of the earth for that." Although it appeared more personal for Kess than simply wanting Dracuni for the value of her silvernix blood.

There was a deep, hurting anger hiding in Kess's expression. That Riony, her ex-slave, was running around with the thing Kess had always wanted and more ... it must be eating Kess alive. Riony was surprised Kess had been as restrained as she was, that Riony wasn't the one lying back on that dusty road with a knife in her throat.

She's never going to stop. I'm going to have to stop her.

The thought of actually ending Kess's life sent an uncontrollable shiver across Riony's shoulders.

She had only really taken one life before, the guard at Lyrrin's birth, and that was in self-defense. Dealing with Kess was a form of self-defense too, but she kept recoiling from the idea.

She knew she could possibly order Aishena to do it, but that wouldn't be fair.

If it's going to happen, it should be by my hand.

"You were really mean to her though," Lyrrin said, pouting toward Riony as she finished dabbing sap on Benjin's cheek.

"I'm sorry, what?"

"The very first thing you said was that you were going to kill her. How is that going to solve anything? If you'd been nicer, maybe we could have talked it through and explained that we really are looking after Dracuni. And maybe she could help us and not try to take her away or tame her. She seemed to understand that, sort of, back in the caves. We got along for a little while."

"Yeah, and how did that turn out? How did that end?

With her betraying us and siding with a murderer to get what she wanted."

Lyrrin inhaled in a way that scrunched up her nose, and she tossed the spent weftweed sticks into a corner of the shrine. "I just think there are lots of nasty things in this world already. You don't need to become one too."

Riony's shoulders slumped. She felt exhausted, worn thin physically and emotionally. "We can't make friends with everyone."

Lyrrin remained firm, staring up at Riony fiercely. "Doesn't mean we should make them enemies instead."

Riony broke eye contact first, turning her focus on the small weeds tufting through the cracks in the stone floor. Lyrrin didn't really understand how bad things could get, that Riony was doing everything she could to keep them safe. But then why did it feel like Riony was getting everything wrong?

Aishena fussed over Benjin, holding his chin to tilt his head and check what Lyrrin had done. She muttered, "We're just lucky that the gateway finally worked."

Niskina, who had cleaned herself up a little but still looked a shade paler than usual, rejoined them. "Why did it take so long?"

"It worked once Dracuni got closer to it," Riony said.

Me? Dracuni lopped across to Riony, leaning her chin on Riony's hand.

Riony's fingers scratched around the tufts of moonlight hair down the back of the unidragon's head. "I've been to other shrines before. There was one on the grounds of Heithorn estate. They've never felt like the ones I've been in when Dracuni has been with me. They've never had this feeling of energy and magic."

The others nodded their silent agreement that they felt it too. Niskina shivered visibly.

"Dracuni is the only difference. And I don't think it's the dragon part of her. I think it's the unicorn part of her." Riony pointed to the carvings that decorated the lichen-covered walls.

Five unicorns frolicked in a line, elegant and long legged, their manes and tails stylized into knotwork that swirled into the sculpted foliage around them.

Aishena moved closer to the beautiful relief, brushing a hand over it. "Unicorns gave the shrines magic?"

Am I unicorn? Like those? Dracuni looked between her scaly tail and the carvings.

"You're something else." Riony crouched down beside Dracuni, staring into her liquid lilac eyes. "And I'm just guessing. The Alderkin got their magic from somewhere. They must have had a way to recharge their crystal artifacts. All the gateway crystals across the land must have worked at some point."

"The magic could have been something else from the Alderkin themselves, maybe?" Lyrrin asked, her voice soft.

"It was since Dracuni came to this shrine that the gateway worked, and crystals recharge here. My cutting athame has recharged twice now. I think maybe the shrines were all working, back when there were more unicorns around."

"That would give the Alderkin another reason why they fought so hard to stop the unicorns from being killed," Aishena said.

"Like they needed more reasons than it was awful and wrong," Niskina cut in.

Aishena continued, ignoring the interruption. "If they needed unicorns to keep all their magic working, it would also make sense why the war turned so badly against them not long after the last unicorn was gone. They wouldn't have been able to recharge their war weapons."

"Pabba told me that once," Niskina said, eyelids low. "He said that they found glow stones and athames for utility and household items still with charge but rarely ever found any kind of weapon still charged."

"If Dracuni is making these shrines magical again, then we can keep all our things charged!" Benjin said brightly.

He pulled out the glow stone that had recently run out and activated it. It sputtered a little light, but they mustn't have been there long enough for it to be fully working again. Still, the small show of light encouraged Benjin's smile to grow.

"All the more reason that Dracuni is special. That she needs to be protected, no matter what." Riony turned to hold the gaze of each person around her as they nodded their agreement.

Special! Dracuni trilled.

"Do you think if we got some raw crystal and brought it to a shrine, whether it would work if I put a rune on it?" Lyrrin's eyes were sparkling now, too, with the same enthusiasm Benjin had.

"We should try to get some and give it a go!" Benjin replied.

Lyrrin had already been spending most evenings with her crystal experiments, Benjin watching along with rapt attention. She'd broken a glow stone down into half a dozen smaller slices but was disappointed when she realized that they all still seemed to be set to the light rune, even if they didn't have the rune directly on them anymore.

Lyrrin had said something about it being attuned to the first rune activated on it, as far as she could tell, so all the shards had to become light shards again, plus the addition of other runes that Lyrrin knew the effects of.

"We could use the Alderkin map to travel around to

all the shrines and recharge them with Dracumi," Lyrrin said. "That way none of our crystals will run out of charge, and if we can get all the gateways working, we'd be able to travel all over Elundrae!"

"That's not a bad idea, actually," Niskina said. "You said that you stayed here once and a revenant couldn't get in?"

Aishena grimaced. "The thing was right across from us, howling and clawing at the air."

"But it didn't get in," Riony added.

"Then we've got a map that shows us places we can go that are safe from revs. We should aim for them as we head toward Riony's old village. Let's have a look. We can plan our route."

"The shrines won't keep us safe from Kess or ... Lady Hjelzahn," Aishena said as she extracted and unfolded the map. She held it flat between them.

"Kess is three weeks' travel from us now, even if she works out where we went," Benjin said, pointing to where they had last been and drawing a line with his finger to where they were now.

"Doesn't mean we can let our guards down. I get the feeling that both Kess and your mother are very much the 'strike when you're least expecting it' types," Riony muttered.

"Whereabouts was that village of yours?" Niskina asked.

Riony looked at the map, trying to get her bearings, remembering how they'd traveled there the first time, how they'd fled from there the last time.

She pointed and shrugged. "Somewhere around there."

"There's what, seven or eight shrines between here and there? More if we take a more roundabout route."

"A roundabout route sounds good," Riony replied. Her words stuck in her dry mouth, and she had to swallow mid-sentence.

Benjin took control of the map then, planning out a path for them, arguing with Niskina and demanding backup from Aishena.

Riony turned away from them, moving to the doorway for fresh air. They needed a plan to keep them all together and moving on, but the thought of their destination left a cold sweat across her back and a chill in her stomach.

Traveling around the shrines would be good. It would draw out their journey to her old home. Because Riony wasn't sure if she was ready to face those memories.

THREE

The magical glow emanating from the crystal circle went dark just as Kess and Griskin reached it, cutting her off from her target.

With slight pressure from her fingers, Kess brought Griskin to a stop, whirling him around to take them back out of the enclosed shrine before they were cornered.

Razing, cursed Alderkin magic! Her eyes burned with caustic frustration, and she shrieked wildly. The rough men and women of the settlement that were pursuing her slowed down, recoiling from her outburst.

Then another close call with a crossbow bolt proved they hadn't yet given up their vengeance on Kess for the death of one of their friends.

That man had to die though. Kess couldn't allow him to take Dracuni or find out Dracuni's true value.

If Pony had been brighter, she'd have done the same thing too. But it was clear Pony wasn't capable of doing what was needed to keep the creature out of the wrong hands. And the rest of the group seemed to be even more of a useless mess.

Which was why Kess needed to get the unidragon for herself.

Kess wasn't sure she had even communicated her intention to Griskin when he burst into movement again, whether she'd shifted her body or pressed her fingers through his fur as a signal without realizing.

They were so often of the same mind, on where to go, and how to protect themselves and each other, that the wolf acted as she wished with no need for commands.

"Let's dust these chumps," Kess whispered, leaning low into Griskin's back.

He loosed a low growl, kicking out around the entrance of the shrine, then broke into a long, loping sprint through the burned forest. Clouds of ashy dirt flew up behind them.

He didn't run as fast or as straight as usual, and tension tightened the muscles under the pads of Kess's fingertips tangled in his fur.

"Come on. We've almost lost them."

They ran up the low gorge slope, over the rise, and

down another valley where the trickle of water met them again, flowing into a larger creek. Kess held the saddle tight as Griskin jumped over the muddy stream. They landed on the other side, and one of her legs shook free of the stirrups and straps holding her in place.

She leaned around to bring it back into position with her hands, and her breath stuck in her throat. A crossbow bolt was lodged in Griskin's thigh. Blood made the fur around it dark and glossy.

Kess growled as rough and low as her wolf. "Those unblessed monsters!"

Back on the other side of the small creek, a man with a crossbow had stopped and worked on reloading.

Kess slipped the smooth, sharpened bone of one of her knives into her hand, exhaled, then sent the knife flying.

Her lips curled crookedly as the blade landed true, right into the man's eye. A cold, melancholy satisfaction shivered through her as he fell.

More yelling and curses came from behind her as she pushed Griskin on again, dashing along the side of the stream.

Kess winced with Griskin's every step at the rasp and whine of his breath. He was hurting. But they would both be dead if he stopped.

"It's okay. It's okay. Just a bit farther."

The forest grew thicker, less burned and dry and more

a riot of fresh, tangling growth, vivid green and tender, sprouted from a hard black core.

The stream, too, grew clearer. The water there filtered into icy clarity over reeds and polished stones.

When Kess could no longer hear the murderous yells of her pursuers, she kept Griskin going until *he* could no longer hear those cries.

He slowed then, the tension easing in the muscles of his haunches.

Pulling at straps and buckles, Kess dropped the saddlebags and packs onto the ground. Then with a lean to the side, Kess urged Griskin toward the water.

Griskin whined and huffed.

"Don't be a baby. I know you hate baths, but we have to wash your wound." She pushed again.

After one more soft growl, Griskin relented, wading into the softly flowing stream. It came halfway up his legs, and the bolt was lodged in much higher.

With further urging from Kess, Griskin lowered himself down into the water, lying stretched out on his belly. Water rippled and ran around Kess's ankles.

Kess turned to inspect the wound, but no matter how she twisted herself around in the saddle, she couldn't get a good view or a good angle on the bolt. So she unstrapped herself from the seat and slid into the water beside the wolf.

The water instantly soaked through her pants and shirt, tickling around her with icy splashes. Shuffling along the slippery stones, Kess brought herself close to Griskin's side. He dwarfed her when she was next to him like that, even one of his hind legs seemed twice her size.

She placed a palm over the bloodied fur and her other around the short shaft of the bolt.

"Hold still," she ordered, and then pulled.

Griskin keened, and his leg twitched, claws scraping against Kess's thigh. They didn't break through the leather of her pants, but it stung.

Kess bit her tongue, inhaled through her nose as the pain subsided, then began scooping water over Griskin's wound.

"I'm sorry," she whispered, barely a breath.

She worked her fingers gently through the fur, loosening where the already dried blood matted it. She continued to wash water over the area until the fur parted and she could see the injury clearly.

It was a clean, deep hole, like a spot of night sky between the tufts of charcoal fur. Blood welled, dripping out, staining Kess's hands.

She couldn't bandage this, not around that high part of his leg—it was more his rump than anything. The fabric she had would never be enough to loop around it.

She needed something else.

It grows everywhere. People think it's a useless, gangly weed, but they just don't appreciate it for what it can do.

Something-weed? Wilt? Wild? What was it?

That time ... Kess's face scrunched up at the memory.

Pony had tripped while carrying Kess through a field on the estate. They were never meant to be out that far, but Kess wanted to watch the dragonriders flying routines, and the southernmost paddock had the best view.

Riony tripped in a hidden ditch, and both of them had fallen hard, hit the low stone wall beside them, and come away bloody.

Riony just wiped herself off on her shirt, said it was nothing. But she'd seemed so worried about the deep graze on Kess's knee.

Probably because she knew what would await her if the lord and lady of the house saw her bring Kess home bloodied.

She'd found a twiggy green plant right beside them.

Kess had balked at the stinky, slimy sap it produced but finally allowed Pony to apply it. It didn't soothe the pain at all, but it slowed the bleeding and apparently helped avoid infection too.

Riony had been so careful with Kess's wound.

And when they'd returned to the estate, Riony was whipped that afternoon anyway. Because she'd allowed Kess to look dusty and unkempt. They hadn't cared about

Kess's injury at all.

Kess scowled, and a hot feeling grew behind her eyes.

She shook it off. "There's got to be some around here somewhere."

Shuffling through the water, Kess brought herself up onto the bank in a section between the tall reeds and called for Griskin to follow.

The low shore of muddy soil was thick with growth, blades of thin, lime-green grass, patches of moss and clover, and thicker bushes of rangy weeds.

Griskin moved past her up onto more solid ground where the bags had been dropped, and his body exploded into a shiver, sending water droplets flying all around Kess.

"Careful!" She wiped them off her face. "You'll hurt yourself."

Griskin whimpered at her tone, sat in a curled position, and began licking at the bleeding area.

Kess scanned over the wild garden surrounding her, hoping to identify the plant from memory. It didn't take long to see something that might have been right. It had the same firm green stems and apparent disinterest in growing leaves.

Kess snapped off a section, and a clear sap spilled quickly from the break. The smell that hit her nose, an offensive, tart stench, was what made her sure she'd found the right thing. There was no forgetting that scent.

It took a great amount of shuffling to crawl up the marshy embankment to where Griskin had settled, but Kess didn't call him to her.

She pushed his licking muzzle away from the wound and squeezed the sap onto the area. Even if it didn't help much, maybe the offensive odor would stop Griskin from bothering it.

The bolt hadn't been in too deep, but even small wounds could turn a whole body bad quickly. Kess shivered, cold from her saturated clothing. She drew in closer to Griskin, tucking herself next to his warm fur.

They weren't going anywhere right now anyway, not unless the drunken thugs from the settlement had more persistence than she would credit them with.

After wiping the last of the sap off her fingers, Kess gave Griskin a scratch between his eyes.

"Don't worry. If Ri—" Kess's throat went dry. "If Pony's stupid weeds don't work, we'll fix you up some other way."

Kess still had silvernix, after all. If there was any sign of the wound turning bad, she'd use it.

Silvernix was required for a taming ceremony, but she'd never get to that stage if she lost Griskin first.

For a moment, she wondered—if she were forced to

choose between Griskin and a dragon, which would she pick? But that was ridiculous to question. She would not choose. She would have both.

If she had to start again from scratch, she could obtain unicorn blood again. It might even be possible to use Dracuni's own blood. Would that work? Would the spike even stay in the creature? It seemed to heal quite quickly itself.

Maybe Dracuni didn't need to be tamed at all. Riony had managed to keep the thing under control without taming. But Kess had to admit there was some sort of bond between the two of them.

If someone took Griskin away from me and then expected him to behave for them in the same way, I'd call them a fool.

She didn't doubt Dracuni would be the same. Loyal to Riony at this point.

It would have to be tamed.

From this higher point on the bank, Kess looked over the unruly stretch of green to the stream below. It might be worth finding some swampland to harvest more morass mercy from too. It could come in handy.

It was a risk traveling into areas where it grew, as people had been known to succumb to the sedative scent and fall asleep there, drowning in the mud. She'd become dangerously woozy gathering what she'd needed the last time.

Maybe she could find a trader selling some instead.

Traders out in the wastes were unscrupulous types that sold all sorts of terrible things. Finding some morass mercy should be easy enough.

And she had plenty of land to cover before finding Pony and the unidragon again, if her hunch about where they were was correct.

Kess pulled one of her bags closer, digging around in it for some food. She'd bought a couple of jars of pickled fish the last time she was on the coast before following the mother dragon inland to the mountain. She'd thought at the time she'd save them until she had her own dragon, to share as a meal with her first tamed hatchling.

"No hunting tonight. Let's rest." She cracked the seal on one of the glass jars. Using a large leaf as a plate, she tipped the contents onto it in front of Griskin.

Griskin slurped and inhaled the soft fish, bones and all, before Kess had even opened the second jar for herself.

She dipped her fingers in, picking at the flakes of pink flesh. It was buttery and salty on her tongue.

Closing her eyes for a moment, she tried to remember what she saw as Pony and the others had gone through the magical gateway. Riony's 'sister' had tapped a lit symbol on the side, the same symbol as when they'd escaped from the Alderkin depths.

Are they selecting where to go?

Why would they go back to the same place again? That was what it had looked like to Kess. But only two symbols had been lit up, so maybe they didn't have a choice, really, from what they were yelling. Maybe they could only go to places they had previously been.

That wouldn't help Kess get back to them faster though.

"If it weren't for those intolerable gateways, we would have had them. Twice, we would have had them! How are they doing it? How is that blighted Alderkin magic even working for them?"

Griskin replied with a soft whine as he sniffed at the jar in Kess's fingers, brine sloshing over the edges as her hands trembled.

Kess dumped the remains of her jar, barely picked at, onto Griskin's leaf-plate. Then she leaned back into him, closed her eyes, and worked on formulating their next steps.

Kess had been lucky the first time, coming across their scent at the shrine just down the hill from the undercity. She'd also found there the muzzle and some of her daggers snapped in half. There was no doubt Pony and the others had spent the night in that location. She'd been able to get Griskin to follow their scent from there, only a few days behind.

But now, if they'd gone back to that first shrine again, it would take weeks to hike back there, giving Pony a few weeks head start. It would be harder to follow their scent. And if they found another gateway from there, Kess could lose them for good.

There's no way I can keep up with them, let alone catch them, like this.

She needed something more. A faster way to travel.

She was going to have to get help. And it was going to hurt to ask.

FOUR

The sky was almost blue, and the sun was almost warm, and Riony almost felt a sense of calm until the howl of a wolf set her teeth on edge.

"Back to me!" she yelled to her friends who had drifted away from her through the abandoned village they'd stumbled upon.

A rabbit bolted from between tall tufts of grass ahead, and Lyrrin's voice carried through the air, swearing roughly. "You ruined my shot!"

Danger?

Dracuni's head popped up from within the ratty remains of what might have once been a neat hedge. Egg yolk dripped down her chin and she crunched bits of shell in her mouth.

"That sounded like a wolf!" Riony yelled back.

It had been a few weeks since Kess's ambush, but Riony had been on alert for the wolf riding gremlin to catch up to them again.

Only Niskina was nearby. She couldn't see Lyrrin or Benjin and Aishena. Last she'd seen, they were all together up ahead, sneaking about in a small hunting group. Lyrrin's voice had come from behind the broken stone wall of a ruined cottage.

Dracuni pushed through the twiggy, untended bushes and ran to cower around Riony's legs, almost bowling Riony over.

There were a few more mutterings before Lyrrin and Benjin stepped out into view. Aishena lurked behind them, scanning all around the weed-woven ruins with her dark eyes.

Niskina strolled toward Riony at an unbothered pace. "Relax. That wasn't your psychotic ex-girlfriend."

Riony flushed red with a riot of unpleasant reactions. Her words ground out. "She. Is. NOT—"

"Not dumb enough to go spoiling her ambush by letting her wolf howl at us along the way." Niskina wandered over to where a feral urchin cucumber, brown and half dead, hung from the roof of the cottage. She examined the misshapen, spiky fruit with a pout on her round face.

"Yeah, I suppose you have a point. But ..." Riony looked over her shoulder, checking for an ambush.

Farther along the overgrown path, Benjin pointed up to the sky. "Besides, it wasn't even a wolf. It was that carrion bird. Used to get a lot of them back home. They sound like that."

Riony turned her face to the sky to see the wide-winged silhouette of the monstrous bird circling above. Her face spasmed involuntarily. All the wild chickens running around between the broken buildings and overgrown fields were bad enough.

"What was that?" Niskina asked softly with a knowing grin.

Riony shrugged and cricked her neck. "What?"

"That look of utter terror I saw pass over you just then."

"I ... don't like birds. They creep me out," Riony whispered.

"Hold on, I'm sorry. Birds?" Niskina put a hand on her wide hips and looked Riony up and down as though seeing her for the first time. "Just the big ones?"

"Any birds. I don't like their beaks and beady eyes. I don't *hate* them—they just make me ..." Riony shivered uncontrollably again.

Niskina pouted and approached Riony with her arms wide. "Oh, sweetie. You fight revs as though it's playtime, but *birds* scare you? Let me give you a hug."

Riony sighed and stood stiffly as Niskina wrapped her soft body around her in a tight embrace. "Please don't tell the others."

"Never."

I like birds. Want to fly like birds. Dracuni fluttered her filmy wings.

Lyrrin walked over, Benjin close beside her like some kind of bodyguard. She handed a dead chicken, small and still warm, over to Riony.

"Did you get this with your sling?" Riony swallowed and hid her disgust as she took it.

"Yeah." Lyrrin didn't seem happy about it, looking at the chicken sadly.

She gave it a soft pat, gloved hands trailing through the feathers. "It'll be good to have some more meat since there's a lot to catch here. I'm going to try to get a few more for Dracuni."

"You're becoming a good shot," Riony said, and Lyrrin's expression brightened.

The unidragon sniffed at the bird. Her jaw opened, revealing a row of small but sharp teeth, and she inched toward the chicken until Riony lifted it higher out of reach again.

"We'll eat soon."

But hungry!

"You were just feasting on chicken eggs," Riony said.

Hungry, always hungry! Want meat but can't catch!

Lyrrin frowned at the conversation she was only half aware of. "Can we go back to hunting now without interruptions?"

"We've still got to be careful. Stay close and stay alert."

"We *are*," Benjin said. "Besides, we haven't seen the wolf rider for ages. We've lost them."

"No. We can't become complacent. Kess will never give up."

"She could. She might change," Lyrrin said.

Riony barked a laugh. "I know you like Griskin, but just because you made friends with him doesn't mean you can make friends with all ferocious beasts—especially Kess. And Kess is the one in control—don't forget that. Griskin is loyal to her."

Riony still hadn't forgotten the feeling of the wolf's teeth around her leg, how Kess had aimed for her heart. She shook her head, unable to look Lyrrin in the eye. "I'm sorry. Not everything in this world can be solved by being nice."

Lyrrin glowered, muttered under her breath, then marched away, Benjin close behind.

"Don't go too far!" Riony grunted. "Sparks."

Niskina sighed breathily. "Do you need another hug?"

"As much as I'll kick myself later for ever refusing a good hug, I am *not* in the mood."

Niskina watched with laughing eyes as Riony held the chicken by a claw between her thumb and forefinger. Riony thrust it into Niskina's hands and left it to be her problem.

Dracuni snuffled at the out-of-reach hen as though insulted, then a couple more chickens ran by, clucking, and she bounded after them. She hadn't been able to catch anything herself yet on their travels, despite trying.

She was growing fast and awkward on limbs that seemed bigger than she was used to dealing with. She still couldn't fly, her wings diaphanous and flimsy, and she hadn't breathed fire either.

Would she ever be able to do either, given what she was? Would she ever be able to look after herself if she had to?

There was a great clucking and flutter of feathers as Dracuni's pounce missed her target again.

Sparks!

Riony's eyes widened. *Between Lyrrin and Dracuni, maybe I need to be watching my language more.*

Turning back to her own task, Riony stepped over a low metal gate into a field to continue seeking herbs to dye Lyrrin's hair with. And Aishena's too, it was decided, after a bounty hunter had recognized her a few days ago.

The bounty on the Hjelzahn siblings was still active,

their mother still seeking them. And the steel-bright hair of the dragon king's lineage was drawing too much attention to them.

Stepping between the tangles of weeds, Riony's foot came down on something brittle and crunchy. A quick look sent a shudder right up her spine. Chicken bones.

It wasn't the first animal carcass she'd seen in the village, and between that and the multitude of overgrown plants, it was clear the area hadn't been burned in a long time. Riony hated to think what could rise there if the shadowdragon landed.

Don't think about undead chickens. Don't think about undead chickens.

A few hasty steps away, Riony found the bronze-leafed herb she sought.

"Stars, it's all so depressing." Niskina sighed the words. She sat on the low stone wall of the field, watching as Riony pinched off the fresh growth of the hennan.

"You'll have to be more specific."

"All this." Niskina waved both arms around her. "This would have been such a beautiful village once. Now it's a ghost town. And everyone who lived here once, loved here once, are probably all dead."

"They could have made it to a dragonkeep."

Niskina snorted.

"Or the undercity."

Niskina tsked. "Don't we deserve to live under the sun and outside of walls?"

"We are." Riony spotted something shiny between the brushy leaves and bent to pick up the steel shoulder guard there. Yet another piece of the common trash leftover from the Alderkin war.

"Running for our lives from shrine to shrine, hiding from revs and our own families and your ex-girl—"

"Only finish that sentence if you're prepared for the consequences." Riony thrust the metal armor at her like a weapon.

Niskina rolled her eyes. "This isn't really living though, is it? It feels as though the whole world is already dead and we just haven't realized it yet. Why are we even still trying? Why bother going on?"

Riony stared at the steel in her hands, forged by dragon breath, cheap and flimsy. Disposable fodder in a war that only ended when two races were exterminated entirely. Unicorns and Alderkin, and with them, the magic of the world.

She dusted the dirt off it, tested the crackled leather straps, then began buckling it onto her shoulder, adding it to her growing collection of armor. She didn't want to let it go to waste. She didn't want to give up on the world just yet.

"We keep going for Lyrrin and Benjin and Dracuni," she said.

Niskina looked at her with such deep sympathy it almost broke her. "I wish we could make things better for them too. But it seems impossible. Everything ... everything is broken. Stars, I could do with a drink!"

"Yeah, because that's going to fix anything."

Niskina glared back, a red flush tinting her eyelids and golden irises flashing.

Tucking the harvested herbs away in a belt pouch, Riony strode over to sit beside Niskina on the wall.

"You're a grown woman and you can make your own choices." Riony adjusted the shoulder guard, fidgeting with it instead of looking at Niskina directly.

The metal was dented and sat unevenly, pinching her biceps. "But I don't think throwing yourself at every bottle and every man we come across is going to make it hurt any less."

"What would you know? Give it a try and you might change your mind."

Riony gave a shrug and smirked. "Not even the end of the world is going to find me throwing myself at men. And unfortunately, the women I've thrown myself at equally aren't interested in return."

"Sincerest apologies for my part in that disappointment,

although I never really knew if you were being serious anyway."

"Me? Not serious? How could you have gotten such an impression? If you ever decide girls are for you, I'll show you how serious I can be." Riony waggled her eyebrows and gave a bright smile.

Niskina elbowed her softly.

Riony's grin faded quickly. "At least yours isn't a personal rejection. Meanwhile, I have no clue what to think about Aishena."

Niskina's eyes narrowed conspiratorially, and she glanced over her shoulder to check they were alone. "She did date a fellow delver once. Male."

"Oh."

"Broke it off very quickly. And dated a girl right after."

"Oh?"

Niskina chuckled, shaking her head. "Again, briefly. Despite *much* wooing and desperate attempts to re-win her favor from both sides. You should have heard Pabba scolding ..."

Her shoulders slumped, and her lips turned down, and she swallowed hard.

High above, the carrion bird keened again, the wolflike cry echoing through air that smelled and tasted of old smoke.

Riony leaned in, pressing her arm up against Niskina's. "I'm sorry. I'm sorry about Brishan. I wanted to help.

I thought we were coming to save you from Aishena's mother. Then I didn't do anything. I didn't get to help anyone because I brought a traitor back with me."

Anger turned Riony's breath ragged, shaking out her nose as she worked to unclench her teeth. Because of Kess, because she'd saved Kess, they'd lost Brishan. Niskina had lost her father. And Riony had lost her chance at the life she'd wanted for so long.

To be a delver, to be somebody who could earn a good life for Lyrrin and Dracuni and the caramel little rat they'd left behind, Sir Butterfur Spelunkychunks, and any other pets Lyrrin brought in. It had all been lost because of Kess.

"It's not your fault. That he died. It's mine. It's mine, and it was *his*." Niskina snapped her mouth harshly around the last word.

Her head bowed, a tumble of chestnut curls hiding her face. "I wanted to help too, and if he'd just let me do what I wanted, if he'd trusted me to do what I could, maybe I could have made a difference."

Riony's heart kicked against her rib cage and she relived the horror of watching Brishan turn away from his deadly combatant to push Niskina out of the fray. And the price he'd paid for that.

"But he didn't trust me. And then he was gone. And now we're here, doing nothing but ticking off another day we've remained alive. So yes, now, *now* I'm going to do whatever I want. Including all the ale and dubious men I can find."

Niskina's skin trembled between where their arms touched. Riony was about to ask about that hug again, or offer one herself, when Aishena appeared silently beside them like a ghost from the shadows.

"Sparks! Give us a little warning sometimes!" Riony gasped.

Aishena just shook her head and pointed across the village. "You have to come and see this. Now."

FIVE

Lyrrin took a step closer, enthralled by the view before her.

Benjin snatched her arm and tugged her back a step. "Careful. The stones are loose."

She nodded vaguely in return, eyes still stuck on the landscape before her.

From the rocky outcrop they'd found at the edge of the village, the valley dipped below them, winding between low mountains like the furrows of a messy blanket. A strange, dark area marred a point in the distance, but that wasn't what had attracted Lyrrin to the scene.

It was the unique pointed arch of the mountain to the left, the clearly defined jutting stones of the hillock beside it backdropping that dark area.

She'd seen this landscape before. She'd locked the shapes in her mind.

Dracuni made a sad trilling noise and sat beside Lyrrin, licking her fingers. Lyrrin wished she could hear Dracuni's thoughts but didn't need to know her words to know her intention. This was a very sad place, and Dracuni could feel it too.

A commotion of pounding feet and snapping foliage came from behind.

"What is it? What's wrong?" Riony ran up beside her, puffing deep breaths.

Niskina and Aishena followed close after, pushing through the branches that stretched across the goat track.

Lyrrin brushed off Riony's concerned hands. "Look. Do you recognize it?"

Riony looked all around them, a frown of confusion over worried eyes. "No? Recognize what?"

"This is it. This is where the first taming happened." Lyrrin pointed to the shapes in the landscape. "It's exactly the same as the mural in the Alderkin depths."

Riony squinted at the horizon. "Oh yeah, the mural. Something with a dragon and a unicorn? It flashed by as I ran for my life."

Lyrrin's heart sunk. She wanted her sister to have seen

the full carving, to have seen the beauty and tragedy of what it showed, and to have seen the depictions of the Alderkin, with their gem-bright eyes and sharp, clawed hands.

She hadn't talked to Riony yet about it, how connected she'd felt, seeing those people who looked so much like her. She wasn't sure how to bring it up—not without Riony having seen it too. Maybe it had only ever been wishful thinking on Lyrrin's part that those people were like her. It seemed like a dream that felt dead before it even began.

Because even if, somehow, Lyrrin was part of the Alderkin race, what would it matter? It would only mean the same outcome that she already knew. That her family was dead and gone.

"We had a better look at the mural," Aishena said. "This is a pretty clear match for the landscape the Alderkin depicted."

"It would have been right down there." Niskina's voice was low and rough as she pointed to the dark area. "What do you think that is?"

Benjin brought Yoskar's staff up in front of his face and activated the seeing stone. The magnifying crystal flickered and cleared.

Peering through it, he hummed. "It's hard to see. It's just ... dark. But there are standing stones around there. I think it was a shrine."

"Can I see?" Lyrrin asked. She put away the sling that was still in her hands, looping and tying the ends around the strap of her backpack.

Benjin handed the staff over quickly, but there was a soft hesitation when she pulled it from his hands.

"There are also *a lot* of revs down there," Benjin said.

Lyrrin looked through the crystal, shining and clear, and it brought the distant landscape closer to her. It felt almost as though she could reach out and touch it.

The darkness surrounding the shrine spread as though night had fallen just in that area. All around and within those shadows, things moved. Skeletal, wasted undead from the tiniest rodent through to gigantic bovin and dreer shambled over blackened, cracked ground.

For a moment, Lyrrin thought she saw the shadow itself moving. She waited, looking harder, but saw no other signs that the shadow had life.

With a shiver, Lyrrin handed the staff back to Benjin. It slipped from her gloved hand before he had it and one end clattered to the ground. He snatched it up.

"Careful!" He pulled the staff close to his chest, clinging to it with both hands.

Niskina squinted at the view. "That means they were here, right? The Alderkin who made the mural. They were there. They saw the first taming."

"Doesn't mean the mural showed what really happened," Aishena said.

Lyrrin recalled the depiction of the shadowdragon emerging above the scene.

Riony put her hand out for a turn to look with the seeing stone, but Benjin ignored her.

Benjin continued. "I didn't see the mural. But the stories of the first taming shared by the dragonlords say that Yeonard Draekhan went to the Alderkin to heal his beloved, and they betrayed him, attacking him by calling a dragon with their magic. But he fought back mightily, and his spear struck the dragon between the eyes and tamed it."

"What about the unicorn, then?" Niskina asked. "The dragonking hid the truth for years, that his spear had silvernix on it. He tried to keep the secret of how to tame dragons to himself. Then it finally came out. So just think through the sequence of events. There had to have been a unicorn there. And he, at the very least, hurt it, if not killed it, like we saw in the mural."

"Why would he do that? Why kill it? If he was trying to save someone, he didn't need much silvernix." Lyrrin glanced down at Dracuni, and her stomach felt burbly and sore.

Aishena turned away from the view, staring at the ground instead. "Whatever happened with his attempt to have his first wife healed, I think it's safe to say it went wrong. All accounts say she died that day. There's a yearly day of mourning in the keeps on that date."

Riony counted on her fingers. "His girl doesn't get healed like he wants. So he straight-up murders a unicorn in return. Alderkin get angry and somehow summon a dragon—"

"Pabba said once there were rumors of Alderkin summoning wild dragons into battle during the war," Niskina interrupted.

Riony finished her thought. "Then he gets a lucky shot with his spear and tames his first dragon, then tells everyone what a big hero he was. Yeah, I could see that being the kind of unhinged thing a guy who has been keeping himself young off the blood of unicorns for eighty years might do."

"And making everyone call him *Draekhan*. Be for real," Niskina muttered.

The whole idea made Lyrrin's lips turn down. Killing another thing because something you loved died. It sounded awful.

She tried to imagine what she would do if Dracuni failed to, or chose not to, heal Benjin after he was hurt. Or if she refused to heal Riony if Riony was dying. Would Lyrrin lash out and hurt Dracuni in return? Kill her? Even

thinking it made her feel sick.

She tried to turn away from those dark thoughts and instead look again at the darkened landscape.

"Should we go down for a closer look?" Lyrrin asked.

The others gave her appalled looks. Lyrrin puckered her lips and turned away. She could see the swarming revenants as well as they could. But it had also been a place the Alderkin had found so important they'd created that imposing mural about it.

And there was a hollow within her that desperately wanted to be closer to anything that could answer her questions about them, and herself.

"Can I see the map again?" Riony asked, and Aishena quickly retrieved it.

Riony unfolded the map and hunched over the parchment. "Whatever happened down there, the place looks the very opposite of safe right now. We're not going to that shrine. But there's another one nearby, across the other side of the village."

"Odd that there are two so close together. We haven't come across any others like that yet," Aishena said.

"Maybe the Alderkin made a new one after whatever happened down there," Lyrrin said.

She squeezed in beside Riony to look at the map as well. The next shrine they went to would be their fifth, and they had marked them on the map as they went. They had been traveling from shrine to shrine, and at each one their presence, or most likely Dracuni's presence, reawakened the magic there.

Their Alderkin crystal items recharged, and the gateway, if it was still standing, was activated. The large geode slices at a couple of the shrines they had passed were smashed and broken, and they'd crossed them off on the map. You couldn't travel through a broken crystal.

"Yeah, I know. I can feel it too," Riony said.

Lyrrin had gotten used to her sister seemingly speaking at random, so she watched and waited. Dracuni had tucked herself in between Riony's legs and rested her chin on her front paws.

"Dracuni says the shrine down there feels really sad, and she doesn't like all the bad things."

"Dragons flying!" Aishena snapped.

Out across the horizon, two tiny dots soared. They were a long way off, but Aishena was already herding Benjin back into the thicker bushes and away from the clear outcrop.

Riony folded up the map and gave Lyrrin a soft nudge as well. "Better safe than sorry."

"It's not going to be Mami," Benjin groaned, pushing Aishena's grasp off, but he still continued away from the open area. "She doesn't ride her dragon anymore. Not since she changed."

"We can't rule it out. She might ride again. She would do anything to find us. We're lucky she doesn't have a wolf's nose to track us down or we'd be dead already."

Lyrrin followed her sister down the goat track back into the village along with the others. Even the mention of a wolf made Riony's shoulders lift and tension show in the lines of her neck.

They had backtracked a couple of times in their travels, going from a new gateway back to a previous one to make it harder for Kess and Griskin to track them, but still Riony behaved as though the wolf and rider would jump from the bushes at any moment.

Riony cast her eyes over the cluster of chickens hanging from Benjin's belt. "We've got plenty of food. We should get moving onto the next shrine and get there before it's dark."

As they stepped back out of the overgrown outskirts of the village, there was a rumble on the road beside them.

Carts, moving faster than seemed safe, were drawn by a range of creatures. The smaller two were pulled by a horse and a goat, and one sizable wagon was drawn by a bovin. Its large head bobbed, shaggy mane hanging over hooded eyes. Heavy hooved feet thudded as it dragged the wagon over the uneven ground.

A crowd of people moved around the carts and wagon, rushing back and forward to drag debris off the ragged road where it lay in their path, crying to each other to keep moving.

Riony stepped to the front of their own small group. The eyes of the approaching crowd were already on them, watching warily.

"Dracuni, back up," Lyrrin whispered.

Dracuni snorted softly and circled back around to hide under a bush.

A bent woman with wild gray hair moved to the front of the convoy. "Children! Hurry, hurry with us."

Riony called back, "Why the hurry?"

A man who was more bones than skin hobbled by, carrying a sniffling toddler at his chest. He gave a wild wail. "Revenants. Hundreds. An army of them!"

Lyrrin's heart pattered, and she stood on tiptoes to try to see behind the crowd, to see if the undead were within sight, but couldn't.

The wagons had reached them where they stood beside the remains of a cottage on the side of the road.

The procession didn't slow, but the bent woman did, stopping before them. Worry crinkled the pretty wrinkles lining her eyes. "We had to run. Our home ... we saw them coming. We can handle a few revs, but this ... The walls would not keep them out. We took what we could, but they are still behind us. They will be here soon."

Each cart and wagon was piled high, each animal towing what seemed to be an entire village packed into baskets and barrels. A few smaller children were loaded between the belongings, and around them, scores of people hurried along.

Within the crowd, another older lady glanced over, and her eyes met Lyrrin's with what felt like the shock of lightning. Her eyes were the color of flowers, a lilac brighter than Dracuni's. The woman turned away quickly, her hands tight around a child on both sides.

Lyrrin's heart beat faster again. She stepped forward, trying to get a better look at those hands.

Riony gripped her shoulder, pulling her back beside her.

"We'd better move too," Riony said. "We know where we're going. Let's get there fast."

"Good luck, then," the gray-crowned woman said, turning back to her own flock. A girl, older than Lyrrin but younger than Riony, wobbled past with a flushed face and huge belly, and the older woman put a hand on her lower back, urging her on.

"Let's go," Riony said.

"What about them?" Lyrrin asked.

Mid step, Riony paused, chewing her lip.

"We should let them know where they can be safe. We should take them with us," Lyrrin said, heart in her throat.

She still had nightmares about the few friends from the orphans' den that they hadn't taken with them from the slavers' camp, taken away in a cage by the dragonrider.

"What about Dracuni? They'll see her. They could ..." Riony shook her head.

"They'll just think she's a baby dragon. We'll keep her away from them as much as we can. But we can't just leave them all running from the revs. For how long?"

Niskina moved in beside Riony, tilting her head. "They're exhausted already. If the revs aren't far behind, they're already going to be moving faster than these people. If they don't go somewhere safe, they aren't going to make it."

"Sparks," Riony hissed. "I know. You're right. But is that going to be safe for us? For them?" Riony's eyes went over Lyrrin and Benjin and Dracuni, still tucked under the branches.

Aishena had a thoughtful scowl but said nothing.

"We'll find out. But we should try," Lyrrin pleaded.

"They're coming!" a child toward the back of the procession yelled, their voice high and cracked.

From the far end of the road, a skittering, rushing shape barreled toward them. First one, then another, then five more at once, bursting from the surrounding brush and charging their way.

"Stars save us!" the gray-haired woman cried, her hurried

gait turning uneven on wobbly legs.

Riony let out a long, low groan as Lyrrin kept her fixed in a glare.

"Fine. Okay. Yes." Jogging out into the path of the crowd, Riony waved her arms in the air. "Follow us. We know somewhere safe. This way, now! Leave what you can't carry and run!"

Six

*H*ome. *What a dreadfully depressing place to come back to.*

A home Kess hadn't returned to since the day she'd been unceremoniously jettisoned from it. She approached with caution, as though the place she had spent her childhood was a snake that could rise up and strike her without warning.

Coming to a crest, Kess paused to look down over Heithorn estate. The looming, fortified walls cradled the main cluster of buildings within. The grand central keep had the appearance of an old-fashioned stone castle, towering above the main hall, kitchens, stables, hatchery, gatehouse, and dormitories, with their newer, ceramic-tiled roofs and smooth, rendered walls.

"We came all this way. Let's see this through. Come on, Gris."

He moved with hesitation, as though he could sense her rising anxiety. His paws treaded softly, and he stalked, low and hunched, ears down, straight toward the estate.

Maybe she should enter through a back gate or a concealed entrance. Shouldn't she hide herself and her return with the shame her family would no doubt treat both?

No. I will not hide. There was no reason she shouldn't ride straight up the main road to the entrance gate. This was her home, her birthright. She was the daughter of the Heithorns, honorable dragonlords and riders. She wouldn't cower.

But she was also going to see family who had plotted her death once already.

Kess noticed the quiet first. An eerie silence, without any sound of human life making Griskin's ears swivel toward it. No smoke came from chimneys. No slaves worked the fields around the walls.

Strange. But the only person who needed to be there was her brother, with his dragon. That was who she was going to get help from, one way or another.

And it was without doubt going to be the most intolerable experience of her life, but Kess couldn't see how she was going to catch Dracuni without a dragon, and Kife was her closest connection to a dragonrider.

It was a last resort to even consider asking Kife for help. Kess was certain the chances he would kill her on sight were far higher than him helping her—just one reason she'd never returned for help or to attempt to get herself a dragon from there before. But now she had leverage.

Now she could offer a share in the most precious creature in all the land. That should be enough to keep even Kife on her side.

As she got closer to the estate, she realized it wasn't going to matter how she approached. The place looked entirely empty.

The solid front gates stood ajar. Through them, once manicured gardens sprung with wild vines and unruly foliage, chasing each other up the walls of nearby buildings.

Abandoned? How long had the estate sat empty? Kess had been gone for five years. From the looks of it, it could have been an equally long time since anybody had lived there.

Kife had always said they only stayed at the isolated estate because of Kess. Had they left as soon as she wasn't a problem anymore? Had they left the very next day?

Maybe they threw a party first.

Kess mused that she should perhaps feel grief or anger to see her family home in this state of disrepair. But all she felt was a dull, heavy sorrow that she wasn't at all surprised.

Abandonment came easily to Heithorne.

It only hurt that she could imagine them now, living safely and richly in a dragonkeep, happy, as though she'd never existed.

Should I have come home sooner? Made my way straight back here from where Kife left me? Forced them to continue to suffer my existence?

A burning sob hit Kess's throat so fast that she almost toppled backward off Griskin in her attempt to breathe it away.

"Raze them all!" she rasped, then set her face like steel. "Let's see if they left anything valuable behind in their rush to be rid of the life I subjected them to."

Kess and Griskin circled the entrance courtyard. Everything was as Kess remembered it—the well with its woven metal roof, roses growing beside the portcullis, the whipping post—but with added layers of grime and weeds sprouting from every gap and corner.

Griskin didn't like going into buildings, but Kess still urged him up to the main hall, stroking his neck. "No one is going to catch you. Nobody's here."

The door was already open, and Griskin whined, sniffing at a lump of debris right behind it.

It took a moment for Kess's eyes to adjust to the dim interior light. Not just debris, but a body. Mostly bones and moldering remains of clothing. The bared teeth of the skull were open in a silent, endless scream. A couple of the limbs were farther away from the torso than they should have been.

Frowning, she turned back to glance over the walls and surroundings outside. No sign of burning. If there had been a revenant attack, Heithorn estate was protected by Kife and two other dragonriders. There would have been fire.

But now that she looked again with a keener eye, she saw the dull ochre of other old bones piled into corners, obscured beneath vines and grass.

Whatever had happened, there hadn't even been anyone around afterward to clean up.

A plague couldn't have taken everybody so quickly.

A bandit assault would have had less chance of getting past the dragonriders than revs.

A low growl echoed from one of the pathways between buildings outside, all too familiar.

I guess it was revs after all.

Kess watched from behind the door. The living skeleton of a horse wandered aimlessly into the courtyard, growled again in a way that a horse never should, then ambled away.

"What odds do you give that it's the only one?" Kess whispered to Griskin.

He lapped his tongue and huffed.

"Yeah, me too. Keep your ears open, and bolt if anything gets too close."

Kess and Griskin stalked silently through the main hall and up the carpeted stairs into the chambers above. Candelabras still lined the walls between paintings and tapestries. A few finger-sized bantam ferrets scattered in the distance, making Griskin twitch.

Lord Heithorn's office was open, and Kess led Griskin in. Papers and letters were spread on the desk, grayed by mold. Velvet upholstered chairs lay toppled to the side.

Two skeletal carcasses rotted in a jumble in the corner. Unlooted, untouched. The faded silver brocade dress on one body and the heavy gold chain on the other were all too familiar.

Mami. Fadda. Kess's lips curled, and she tried not to breathe in the dry scent of death wafting from them. *I guess you didn't leave after all.*

She hurt, unexpectedly, feeling their loss deep in her chest, and she hurt again feeling that she probably cared more for them in that moment than they ever cared for her. Sure, they had gone to great expense attempting to "heal" her, but Kess had never felt as though it came from a place of love.

It had come from a place of shame. From attempts to make their daughter worthy of the Heithorn name so that they would no longer have to stand the dishonor of having a child who wasn't a perfect physical specimen in a world where the rich should be able to heal anything.

Why had they stayed once Kess was gone? If she were the reason they'd lived far from the luxury of a dragonkeep, why were they still there? Had the attack come before they were able to leave?

And why hadn't the dragonriders fought the revs? Were her brother and the other riders killed before they could?

Kess blinked at her parents' remains, dry-eyed.

"I should burn them. That's the right thing to do." *And the safe thing as well.*

She couldn't bring herself to move closer to them. She couldn't imagine touching them, dragging them outside to burn on a pyre.

Whatever unkindness they had shown her, they were her parents. And now they were bones, and the sight of those bones shook something deep inside Kess until she had to turn away. Nobody should have to see their family that way.

Pretending her parents weren't lying dead in the corner, Kess took Griskin around the desk. She pulled the tattered curtains aside and peered out the window. There was movement below, at least three more revs, shambling aimlessly through the estate surrounds.

We're going to have to be careful getting out of here.

Revs didn't seem to target animals, only humans, and sometimes Kess remained unnoticed, hidden up on Griskin's back. But not always.

Maybe she should set fire to the entire place before she left.

But Kess wasn't leaving empty-handed. There had to be some value she could wring from these hollow walls first.

Bringing Griskin close beside the bookshelf lining the back wall, Kess reached in beside a heavy dragon-head bookend and pressed the lever there.

A soft click sounded from behind the wood and books, and Kess tugged on that section of shelf. It swung forward with a whine of old hinges to reveal the compact vault where her family stashed their wealth of silvernix.

She glared at it for a long moment before turning back to her parents' bones. She needed the key.

She almost turned and left without clearing any riches from that vault. She still had one vial of silvernix, and Griskin's leg was healing well so far.

But if there was any chance the lockbox held more, it was worth having. She had to toughen up and do what had to be done.

She brought Griskin beside the bodies and lowered him down onto his belly so she could lean over and reach within the clothing of her father's corpse.

The ragged fabric felt damp in a way that sent grotesque shudders through Kess's fingers, up her neck, and over her scalp.

When her hand closed around the key she wanted to jerk it back, but she held her mettle long enough to also take the gold chain and house crest beside it as well. Then she was able to turn away again and pretend the bodies weren't there.

She wiped her hands furiously on her saddle blanket.

Two turns of the key and the vault opened.

She reached in, rifling through a scattering of papers, opening a single velvet pouch which held fewer sovs than Kess carried on her. Not a single bottle, not a tiny vial, not a drop of silvernix.

Kess swallowed the acid in her throat.

All her family's wealth, gone. Her parents hadn't used it all on her. There had been a few dragons tamed, and a scattering of illnesses cured.

But Kess had counted at least five doses on her in the time she could remember, and no doubt there'd been more when she was younger, as soon as her parents realized she wasn't learning how to walk. As soon as they saw her legs didn't kick and move the way other babies' legs did.

How long had the Heithorns been out of silvernix?

Kess turned Griskin away. She didn't bother closing the vault or any doors behind her.

She still had her single drop of silvernix which she'd use for taming her dragon. As hard won as it was, she couldn't spare it on anything else.

She'd almost died for it, Griskin had almost died for it, and worse, she had killed for it.

After finding each other, it had taken a little while for Kess and Griskin to grow strong enough together to do more than simply survive.

Once they had, Kess had begun pursuing her goal of owning a dragon. She'd considered the ways she might obtain one and decided raising one from a wild dragon egg was her best option. And for that, she needed silvernix.

There were plenty of unscrupulous smugglers out in the wastes and Kess sought them out, looking for one that sold the precious liquid.

She'd been through almost a dozen smugglers, fleecing them of their gold and valuables after they'd lied to her about their ability to provide unicorn blood. It had satisfied her growing frustration and helped her to build her own considerable wealth.

But the news of the wolf-riding thief had spread, and when she finally found a supplier who really was trading silvernix, it turned out he already knew about her.

The guy was a monster. Kess had seen it from the moment she'd met him. From how he called himself *Shadowlord* to the decorations on his coat, made from fingers of those who'd crossed him. But Kess needed the silvernix, so she took his invite to meet at his hideout to make the trade. And walked right into his trap.

A literal pit trap that 'Shadowlord' had built into his den, dropping her and Griskin into a pit with the smuggler's own pet—a revenant wolf.

From the bodies down there, Kess knew she wasn't the first to have fallen victim to his trap. But she and Griskin were the first to fight their way out of it.

Kess had realized then that she should have killed all the smugglers from the start instead of letting them warn each other about her. She'd been too soft and almost paid the price. And so Shadowlord was the first she'd killed.

There had been many since then, but it never got easier. Her heart felt hatched with scars tallying all the lives she'd taken to survive. And voices spoke deep in her soul, voices that sounded like her family, telling her she didn't deserve to take lives to preserve her own.

Kess took the narrow servants' stairs down again and cut quickly across the courtyard to the hatchery. Heading in from the back like that, she passed one of the standing stones of the Alderkin shrine ruins that backed up right behind the hatchery building.

Heithorn estate was built almost directly over whatever the Alderkin had been doing with the land there before.

Her family hadn't bothered demolishing the shrine and instead had used it as additional storage during harvest months.

It didn't take long to see that the hatchery was empty. Kess had hoped there may have been a dormant egg or abandoned dragon, but there was no sign of either, alive or dead.

The ever-present pile of hay in the corner had mulched itself down almost flat and writhed with beetles and worms.

It had been behind those bales that Kife had hidden her the time he brought her down to see the baby dragons. When he'd tricked her into choosing his dragon for him.

Then he'd left her there, alone and cold in the night air that she wasn't supposed to be out in, too humiliated and upset to try to make her way back to her room herself.

Riony had found her crying on the dirt beside the one tamed hatchling and the burning bodies of the discarded options.

Without a word, she'd picked Kess up and carried her out. And then she'd roared, running and swooping, pretending to be a dragon. Through a growing smile, Kess had hissed at the fool to hush.

90

But it was too late, and they were heard, and Pony was blamed for taking Kess out of her rooms at night, and it was Pony whose back was opened yet again at the whipping post.

Only months ago, there had been such fire inside Kess, so much drive while hunting that mother dragon, for all the time tracking and waiting. How come all she could feel now was this dull, bland weight of sorrow? What was wrong with her?

It's Pony. Seeing her again, it's mixed up everything inside me, making all these intolerable memories come back. That's all.

And even if Pony had been the only person to ever be kind to her, she didn't *like* Kess, didn't care for her. Given the nature of their relationship, Riony could only ever know hatred for Kess.

But still, Riony was kind, mostly, and that was more than even her family had mustered. And that kindness had kindled a brittle ember inside Kess that had wanted more, had wanted that kindness to become liking and caring.

How could it, though, when it was Kess's ownership of Riony? When it was Kess's family and Kess's very existence that kept Riony in constant suffering and torture? So Pony hated Kess, and Kess made sure she hated Pony in return because nothing else would be tolerable.

And now Pony stood between Kess and what she needed. If she could have Dracuni, that wealth, that power, would it be enough to make people finally respect her? Would it be enough to make people find kindness for her, or more?

Kess wasn't sure. But she had to follow through.

I have to achieve my dream. Otherwise, what am I?

Kess only narrowly dodged a roaming revenant on the way into the keep. It was a big risk spending any more time in the rev-infested estate, but there was one last place she had to check.

The dragonriders' rooms. Kife's room. They were in the upper levels of the keep, since the dragons themselves were often kept roosted on the battlements up top.

She needed to find his body too, to know for sure that all her hopes had come to nothing, that she'd have to start planning anew again.

This was one part of the estate Kess had never been allowed in, never managed to sneak into. Only dragonriders were allowed.

She followed the polished marble stairs up as they circled around the tower, checking rooms as she went. Empty. Empty. And empty again.

Finally, an immense pyre of emotion ignited within Kess.

Empty? No bodies, no belongings, no anything.

They might have packed up and left after the revs got in, after Mami and Fadda died. Kess knew she was kidding herself. There were no signs of burning because the dragonriders were already gone. Kife was already gone.

Kess grasped at the only remaining furnishing, a Heithorn crest banner, and tore it from the wall.

He was supposed to protect the estate! That was his job, their job, as dragonriders. I would have done it!

Kess's breathing slowed again, and her eyes narrowed, glaring at the room before her, stripped of all belongings, all furniture, everything her brother could take with him.

He had abandoned Kess, and then he'd abandoned the entire estate.

But that also meant that Kife might still be alive out there somewhere.

Kess just had to find him.

SEVEN

R iony ran. She had the toddler that the malnourished man had carried in one arm and the man himself slung over her shoulders.

Aishena and Benjin led the way, navigating through a thicket of dry brambles and scratchy twigs. Lyrrin, Dracuni, and all the other children and refugees filled the space between. High-pitched yelps punctuated the pounding of feet as the army of revenants closed in.

"Almost there. I see the standing stones!" Aishena called back.

Riony had one good look at the massive number of revenants before they ran, and it almost paralyzed her with hopelessness. She ran anyway hoping the shrine would work and protect them. Otherwise, they were all in for a very unpleasant death under an ocean of undead.

Not all the army of revs seemed to be chasing the people. They were moving with some purpose of their own. Unfortunately, it seemed to be in the same direction the humans were going, and as soon as any of the revs caught sight of them, they raced ahead to attack.

They seemed to be coming in from all sides now and were almost upon them.

"Nisk! Take her!" Riony tossed the toddler across into Niskina's arms.

Niskina cradled the crying infant and kept running.

Riony bent to the side and put the man back on his feet. "Go! It's just up ahead!"

He nodded, hobbling unevenly away, one leg not working as well as the other.

And Riony unbuckled her sword.

She didn't get a chance to activate it before the first revenant hit. A haggard goat of rotting flesh rammed its head at her, jaws gnashing.

Riony got the sword between them, knocking it out of the way with a heavy blow that strained her arms. Then she ran her fingers over the float rune, and the sword lifted weightlessly in her hands.

Riony swung and clashed against the ferocious undead

as she jumped and jogged backward, holding them off from the remaining stragglers as they closed in on the shrine.

Sparks, it had better be safe. They'd had one other experience since the first time they sheltered at a shrine when a revenant hadn't been able to breach the invisible barrier. But that had been only one rev each time. Not dozens. Not hundreds.

Even activating the gateway and trying to flee that way would take long enough that the revs could take half the people there before they got through.

A full-grown dreer skeleton galloped toward her. All deer-like elegance it would have had in life was lost in the wild fury of its attack. It stood twice Riony's height, and its cloven hooves were cracked and sharpened by rot. It would only need to kick her as it passed by to have her saying goodbye to her intestines. And she really preferred that they stay where they were.

A glance over her shoulder showed the remaining refugees crossing the boundary of the standing stones. They huddled and pushed, trying to all fit within the shelter of the walled shrine within the ring of tall crystalline blocks.

Sister? Sister, hurry!

Riony turned her back on the approaching revs and sprinted for safe ground. A slithering bolt of patchy red fur hung over bones raced for Riony's feet. An undead fox, snapping and growling. Riony leaped, the float magic of her sword bringing her far higher than natural, and she came flying through the barrier between the standing stones.

She felt the small flutter of energy ripple over her skin, then landed firmly on both feet. Her eyes sought Lyrrin and Dracuni, finding them encircled by Niskina and the Hjelzahn siblings, backs to a wall.

Safe? Dracuni angled her head, watching behind Riony.

A great scream went up from almost every voice sheltering in the shrine as the wave of revenants crashed down upon them.

And then were held back, blocked by the invisible wall.

As the revenants clawed and roared from the boundary of the standing stones, people continued to scream and sob, but slowly, as eyes opened and they saw the revenants couldn't reach them, the cries dwindled.

"What is this? How is this possible?" The elderly woman who had given them warning before walked boldly right up to the invisible barrier, staring the gnashing revenants in the eye like a grandmother scolding a child for stealing dessert too early.

"We don't know for sure how it's happening, but we noticed some other shrines kept the revs out. Not all the shrines, though." Riony glanced again at Dracuni.

She didn't want them making any link between the

unidragon and the magic of the shrines. But she also didn't want them assuming all shrines would be safe.

The woman turned again, assessing Riony with her gaze. She lifted a finger imperiously in the air. "Will it hold?"

Her accent was strongly Rolanian, and there were a few streaks of red hair amongst the gray.

"For now." Riony honestly wasn't sure how long the magic keeping the revs out would last, especially if and when Dracuni wasn't there anymore. For all she knew, it only worked when Dracuni was at the shrine since that was all she'd experienced.

The older woman gave Riony and her glowing sword one long, hard look, then lifted both arms in the air, tattered shawls hanging from them like wings, and she strode into the crowd, speaking in hurried words to this person and that as she went.

The people, a few dozen of them, murmured in low tones between themselves. They unloaded whatever filled their arms—baskets, bundles, babies—onto cleared space on the ground.

Riony deactivated her sword and leaned it against the wall beside Lyrrin, then dumped her packs beside it.

"Is this everyone? Did everyone make it?" her sister asked.

"I didn't see anyone behind me that wasn't made of bones and rot. Are you all okay?"

There were nods all around, and then Lyrrin sighed into a smile. "We won! We won against *them*."

Her blue eyes flicked to the revenants amassing around the barrier. Her small face tensed. Her lips trembled, then returned to the smile again.

"Not really a battle, which is good because we would not have come out of that with all our insides still on the inside. But sure, I'll count it as a win," Riony said.

But safe? Safe here?

Riony sought Dracuni, who was curled between Lyrrin and Benjin's legs, face tucked under the hanging hems of Lyrrin's long coat.

Riony realized she'd never answered her before. "Yeah, the bad things can't get in."

Also safe from others?

Dracuni was looking behind Riony at the crowd of refugees. They had calmed now, a relieved energy spreading as they laid out cooking supplies and rugs on the ground.

Others are not-friends. Dracuni's emotions were a muddle of sadness and confusion.

"They aren't Kess. She's the not-friend. These people ..." Riony didn't know.

These people were desperate, and if they knew what Dracuni really was ... Riony hated the thought of having to protect Dracuni from them. But she would.

She patted Dracuni on the snout. "Just stay out of the way, okay? I won't let them hurt you."

"We aren't going to hurt any of you, child." The older woman approached them again, stopping a respectful distance away from their cluster. "But we would like the same guarantee."

Riony stepped up to meet her. "Because we lured you to safety here from the revs just so we could beat you up ourselves? Sounds exhausting."

"Plenty of folk in this world who offer safety provide harm instead."

"Can't argue with that. But no, we're not planning on hurting anyone." Riony held her hands up in a gesture of peace.

"And what is that creature you have with you?"

Lyrrin tucked Dracuni's head farther under her coat.

"Just a baby dragon," Riony replied.

Something else. Dracuni snorted softly but remained still as though tamed.

"And what are you? Dragonlords? Dragonriders?" Her words cut sharply from her mouth as she eyed their weapons, Aishena's steel-bright dragonlord-born hair, Niskina's mixed features.

"No, just travelers. The dragon is ... a rescue."

The woman's eyes roamed over all of them, the irises pale against her dark skin. She smirked when she saw

Niskina, still clutching one of their children.

"Just a group of rescuers, then. Well, keep the dragon away from us. We've no love for the things."

A soft sigh of sadness blew from Dracuni. ***Not-friends.***

Riony couldn't reply then; nor did she know what to say. She wished it were safe for Dracuni to make friends, that the very blood in her veins didn't make her a target.

The woman tapped two fingers on her chest. "I'm Myrwa."

Riony introduced herself but left the others anonymous. She took a couple of steps toward the shrine entrance, seeing that the gateway there was still in one piece. "Listen, we'll keep to ourselves—"

Myrwa waved a hand. "I didn't say that. Just keep the beast away. The rest of you are welcome to join us. We're making some food and would like to share it with the people who saved our lives."

"Thank you, but what I wanted to say was we can split paths. You don't have to stay here. Amongst all of this." Riony pointed at the swarms of revs building around the barrier.

Their growls reverberated through the cooling afternoon air.

Riony hid a shiver. "Inside the shrine, there's a sort of magic doorway. We know how to make it work. You can travel straight to the Alderkin undercity, where it's safe."

"I'd scoff at such a thing, but I'm not quite blind enough to miss that giant glowing sword you were heaving around. Alderkin magic if I ever saw it. And I've heard of the undercity refuge. Let me speak with the others. Until then, come and join us."

Riony lifted a shoulder to her companions, questioning.

Niskina offered a halfhearted shrug in return and strode off to find someone to hand the sniffling infant to. And probably something to drink.

Aishena seemed less comfortable.

Myrwa was already heading away, so Riony asked the delver quietly, "Was it okay for me to offer them passage through the gateway?"

Aishena's expression dropped. "I ... don't know. We couldn't send them *there*, could we?"

"Oh, oh no! Not to the gateway in the depths," Riony clarified, waving her hands to dismiss the idea.

None of them wanted to open the path back to where Brishan, Yoskar, and the other delvers had died. Where they may still lay, for all they knew.

"We'd send them to the one down the hill and give them directions from there. And we wouldn't show them how to use the gateway either—just send them through." Riony hoped her offer sounded at all sensible.

Aishena chewed her lip thoughtfully.

Lyrrin spoke up instead. "I think it's a good thing. We're helping them. That's important."

"As long as it doesn't bite us back," Benjin added in a flat tone that sounded like his brother. "We should take Dracuni now and leave in case any of them get curious."

"We don't know whether this place stays safe without Dracuni here though. What if we pop away through the gateway and the revs come crashing through onto these people?" Riony flicked an arm at the growling wall of desiccated bodies around them.

Benjin's jaw worked. "Maybe one night will be okay."

With less confidence than before, Lyrrin asked, "If we're staying, can I ... go and meet them?"

Riony looked over the group of refugees. There were mostly families, all quietly settling in, trying to get comfortable with what they had managed to bring with them.

Niskina had found the thin, older man who'd carried the toddler before and another younger man with him who greeted the child and Niskina happily. Niskina leaned her curves into the conversation as she laughed at something the young man said. Riony found herself envious of how the girl could make the most of any situation.

There seemed to be no imminent threat from the people around them.

"Sure. Just be careful, and stay away from the hordes

of ravenous undead. You know, the usual rules."

I stay, Dracuni huffed. She circled the ground, then sat and leaned against the wall of the shrine.

"I'll stay with Dracuni," Aishena offered and gave Benjin a look that told him he would too.

A large cooking fire was soon roaring, brightening the area as dusk fell with a soft blanket of fog.

The army of revenants had mostly lost interest in the humans they couldn't reach, but continued to stream past, parting the mist like ghosts. Riony shivered. Despite being safe within the shrine, it was super creepy. Where were they all going? And why?

Riony settled down at a clear spot near the fire and collected her harvest of hennan, setting it out to prepare for drying and grinding to make hair dye. It had to be processed properly before the soft leaves spoiled.

Pots burbled beside her and Lyrrin stood across the flames, offering one of her chickens to the refugees. There was a strange expression on her face, both timid and fierce at the same time, as she stared at the young woman she'd approached.

As that woman turned to the fire, taking a seat to pluck the hen, Riony noticed her eyes. Bright lilac.

"Know some of the old crafts, I see?" Myrwa took a seat beside Riony, nodding to Riony's fingers picking away

gently at the leaves of their own accord. "Got some good skill there, not bruising the leaves at all."

Riony smiled softly. "This was how Amma taught me."

"Using it for dyeing?"

"Mm-hmm."

"Did she teach you that if you mix in a little shillgrue, the color will hold longer?"

Riony's fingers stilled. "No, she didn't. She wasn't around for long enough to teach me everything."

Myrwa nodded solemnly. "Well, now you know. Even with all my years, I still feel like I haven't done enough, haven't taught enough."

Riony put down the sprig of hennan she was working on and looked at the ground for a long moment. "Does that feeling ever change? I never feel like I'm doing enough ... Like I should be doing more. For my family, friends, people like you, for the whole sparking world. But what can I do? What can any of us do in the face of so much wrong?"

Riony pointed with her chin at the slow marching horde of undead surrounding them. Endless, undying horror. Relentless. Uncaring. Unyielding. The very sight of them seemed to drain the hope from Riony like water burbling down a drain.

She dropped her voice to a whisper, as though ashamed of the words coming out. But still they spilled. With

Niskina intending to do whatever she wanted to do right up until the end she thought was nigh and Aishena unable to form a single opinion of her own, Riony had been feeling utterly alone in the burden of her responsibilities.

Faced with this woman, with kind, wrinkled eyes, and a willingness to share knowledge of herbs that felt so much like home, Riony's heart seemed to crack open and flood her mouth with words and worries.

"Things are getting worse. I've never seen anything like these numbers of revs before. If this is what the world is now ... what future could we have? What future will the kids have?"

Riony sought Lyrrin in the crowd, still awkwardly trying to strike up a conversation with the purple-eyed woman. Nearby, the pregnant teenager winced as she paced. Benjin sat beside Dracuni, meticulously cleaning Yoskar's staff. The toddler in the ragged man's arms pinched at his beard.

"I've been fighting and fighting just to keep us all alive. But for what, in the long run?" Riony whispered, unable to speak her worries any louder.

Myrwa picked up the work that Riony had laid down, carefully plucking the small leaves from the stems. "You don't look to me like the type who gives up. You're doing just fine. And more than that, you are making change."

Riony huffed. "We've lost our home more than once.

Lost family. All the changes in our lives recently haven't exactly been positive."

"I mean for us. Look what you did for us!" Myrwa tilted her head to the people around them. "You got us here. You brought us to safety. You saved our lives. Every single life here. And you've given us hope."

"You'll go to the undercity?"

A man approached and handed Myrwa a bowl of steaming food. She took it, then passed it along to Riony.

"No. I spoke with the others. They're tired. Tired of running. Tired of hiding. So we thank you for your offer, but we've decided that we are going to stay here."

"Here?" Riony raised her eyebrows at the ruined stones, scraggy bushes, and growling undead circling them.

"The revenants will pass by, and we're safe here from them anyway. We could start again. Go back and see if anything on the wagons is salvageable, reclaim our belongings. We could build something here." Myrwa waved to a girl across the fire then pressed her hand to her heart, keeping it there as she returned her focus to Riony.

"Safe from revs. Not reliant on dragonriders"—she paused and spat on the ground—"to protect us. No longer running. Free and aboveground. This place, it's the hope we've been looking for."

"That ... sounds nice." Riony's fingers warmed around

the bowl she'd been given, and she sniffed at the food.

Rice, with a little carrowmy making it fragrant and golden. She hadn't had rice in years. It wasn't something that could be grown underground. But it had been a staple in the village they'd raised Lyrrin in. A rush of nostalgia hit her like a sword to the chest.

"You could stay here with us," Myrwa offered.

"I don't think that would work out." Riony didn't want to explain the multitude of ways they were being hunted or why.

"Think on it. Your little one seems very taken with Naya." Myrwa nodded over to where Lyrrin watched the young woman preparing the chicken to cook.

Lyrrin stared at Naya's working fingers, a small frown of disappointment on her face.

Naya's eyes had a brightness to them like Lyrrin's, but her hands had no sharp, clawed nails. Riony couldn't see any sign her hair, a mousy brown, had been dyed either. Larger than usual ears poked from that hair, pointed, with tufts of hair at the ends.

She broached the subject carefully. "Naya, her eyes ..."

Myrwa tsked. "Unicorn blood used while she was in the womb. She has the usual silvernix-birth changes. Lilac eyes, ear shape, a bit of fur here and there."

"Those are the usual changes? No changes to hands?

Hair color?"

"Not that I've seen. There were a lot when I was young and before people knew better. Not sure the story with Naya's mother, why and how she used the cursed stuff, but Naya ended up with us when the family didn't want her."

"Cursed stuff? You don't like silvernix?"

Another bowl of food arrived for Myrwa, and she took a mouthful with pinched fingers. "Don't like where it came from. We are siblings to all life, and when we take life to sustain our own, we must do so with respect."

Riony nodded. That was how she'd been raised too, in Rolanian customs.

Myrwa continued, "There was no respect in the slaughter of the unicorns. To utterly destroy our eldest siblings, first born to Amma moon ... What person with a heart and soul would approve?"

Riony glanced over at Dracuni, snuggled up onto Aishena's lap despite getting too large to fit now, tail and back legs dangling off. "That leaves a lot of heartless and soulless people out there. Nobody seemed to care where it came from or who they hurt to get it if they could profit from it."

"Some of us cared. Back when people were running hunts, trying to catch and bleed every unicorn they could get. Some of us tried to stop it."

Riony stared at her food. She hadn't been able to bring herself to taste the rice, as though she would be eating memories. "I thought only the Alderkin fought to stop the hunting of unicorns?"

"Taens believe they are above all other life in our world—not a part of it. But many Rolanians were against it."

"Really?"

Myrwa shrugged, picking at her rice. "More people cared than you know since those who caught those unicorns then became dragonlords and shaped the world in their favor, pretending they had every right, that we were all on their side. But we protested, and when our protests were ignored, we fought. We were labeled extremists, traitors, and worse. But we tried anyway."

It warmed Riony inside to know that there were people who cared more about the creatures being harmed than the value that could be gained from them. She wondered what they would think if they knew about Dracuni. Whether they would still hold strong to their past principles.

She wasn't about to test that theory, but there was a subtle release of tension in her shoulders.

"Was it worth it?" she asked. "Fighting. When faced against so much? When fighting a losing battle?"

Myrwa put her bowl down and stared deep into Riony's eyes. "It was. Even if we didn't win. If only for the reason

that when our children ask us what we did in the face of something terrible happening, at least we don't have to say *nothing*."

Riony looked over the somber procession of corpses slowly marching by. This world, with magic all but gone and undead dominating the land ... Was this the price all humans had to pay for the greedy few who'd glutted themselves on the deaths of unicorns?

Riony had only seen the mural of the murdered unicorn in the depths briefly as she'd fled past, but the others had described it to her. How it seemed to suggest the shadowdragon had been around since that first unicorn died, not since the end of the war as a final curse from the Alderkin.

But unicorns had been gone for more than thirty years, and Alderkin gone now too, so why was the undead plague only getting worse? More and more revenants, revenants that didn't die when burned, revenants that came back again and again. Revenants marching together with some united cause.

How was the shadowdragon getting stronger and stronger?

There was one other important moment depicted in the mural of the unicorn's death.

A human tamed a dragon for the first time.

And more and more and more dragons had been tamed ever since.

Despite the heat of the fire brushing a warm glow over her face, Riony shivered.

"Do you think the Alderkin cursed us with the shadow-dragon?" Riony asked Myrwa.

Myrwa scooped the last few grains of rice from her bowl. "I don't think they needed to. I think we cursed ourselves." She stood with a soft groan and brushed off her skirts. "Eat your food before it gets cold. I have people to see to. I think maybe you do too."

Riony followed her gaze across the fire where Niskina had a half-empty bottle in her hands and was sitting between two young men.

They were laughing boisterously, and despite them feigning hushed whispers, Riony could hear their game of 'bed, wed, or behead' carry across to her. Just in time for Niskina to put Riony up for consideration to her new friends.

"If you declare your intention for any of those three to me, you'll be getting bed, wed, and beheaded by my sword instead," Riony snapped back.

"Oh, would you relax? It's just a game!" Niskina pouted.

She stood and gave Riony a challenging glare before pulling the two men up to their feet as well. Before she

could lead them away, a whimpering moan broke over the soft chatters of the camp.

"Myrwa?" a young girl's voice called.

Riony traced it to the pregnant teen.

The girl's round-cheeked face was both pale and blotchy red, and she buckled forward, clutching her bulging stomach. "I think it's happening!"

EIGHT

Riony found herself on her feet as Myrwa chatted to the young woman in hushed tones. The old woman brushed the blond curls away from the girl's warm sienna face, then pressed a hand to her swollen belly. Wetness soaked through her skirt.

"Yes, love, I'd say it is definitely happening now."

"What is it?" The commotion had been enough for Niskina to abandon her potential partners and join Riony, craning to see.

"I think she's gone into labor," Riony replied.

There was a fluster and worry on Myrwa's face at odds with how commanding she'd been before. She ushered the pregnant girl away from the main group, eyes seeking, bringing her by Riony on the way.

"Is everything okay?" Riony asked.

Myrwa said softly, "We lost our midwife a few months back. Kellae is our first birth without one."

"Riony can help!" Lyrrin almost shouted in reply, having appeared in between Riony and Niskina.

Myrwa frowned at the ramshackle collection of armor covering the bulk of Riony's arms. "You're a midwife?"

Riony took a step back. "Oh no! No. Not really. I mean, I trained to be one. But only until I was sixteen. And I haven't even been at a birth in years. And I never did one on my own—only ever as an assistant. It's really ... I couldn't ..."

Kellae grunted out a scream, bending in pain so suddenly she slipped from Myrwa's supportive grasp. Riony lunged forward and grabbed the girl.

Gently lifting her back to her feet, she bit her lip as the girl met her gaze, her expression wildly pleading.

"If the pains are coming so close together now, it won't be long. This should be quick for you." Riony tried to sound reassuring and remove herself from her position of support, but the girl gripped back on to her fiercely.

"Amma died. She died giving birth. I don't want to. I don't want to do this."

You and me both, Riony thought, blood rushing from her face.

"Come on. We don't have anybody else," Myrwa said, grasping both Riony and Kellae and pushing them on.

They stumbled together like that around the side of the shrine where Aishena, Benjin, and Dracuni had stayed.

It was the quietest, most private area, as the refugees had given the unidragon space on the otherwise crowded safe ground.

Her hurt? Dracuni lifted her head.

"Her have baby. Sparks, I mean, *she*." Riony cleared her throat, pretending she was talking to Aishena. "She's having a baby."

A couple of other refugees, older women mostly, brought some blankets over but quickly stepped back again, hovering at a distance. Riony sent Lyrrin to the campfire for hot water.

"Niskina, swap with me?" Riony said, prying herself from Kellae's clutches.

The flush of alcohol seemed to have vanished from Niskina's face, and she wore a wide-eyed, awed look of terror, at war with her attempts to school it into something calm and confident.

She gave a wobbly smile to the groaning girl. "Hi. You can call me Nisk. Do you have any family you'd like brought over?"

Held up by Niskina on one side and Myrwa on the other, Kellae shook her head roughly, sobbing through

her pain. "A brother. But he's ... a long way away. Slavers got him."

"Lower her," Riony said, and they brought Kellae down into a squatting position.

Lyrrin returned, sloshing a large steaming pot. Riony gave her hands a brisk scrub in the hot water, then checked on how far along the labor was.

Her finger shook, and she muttered about a million apologies, feeling clumsy and awkward, but her own mother's voice came through in her mind, reminding her, guiding her as it had when she was younger.

"You're really close. I'm going to ask you to push soon. Do you think you can do that?"

"How? How? It's too much. I can't do this!" There was a high edge of panic in Kellae's voice, and she was crumpling in Niskina and Myrwa's arms.

Riony was worried the girl was about to lose it entirely. "Listen, okay? Nobody likes to admit it, and it's going to sound gross, but it's the truth. You're going to push, just like you're doing the biggest poo of your life."

"Riony!" Niskina scolded.

Kellae's eyes widened, and then she coughed out something between a sob and a laugh.

"You can do that, right?" Riony gave her a casual smile.

Kellae brought herself a little more upright and nodded.

"Yeah, you can do this. You're already doing amazingly," Niskina added.

Riony showed the girl how to breathe with the pain, but the fear was still heavy in her eyes. Her breaths came out shuddering and soaked in tears.

Niskina drew her attention again, smiling encouragement. "Is the father around?"

Kellae bared her teeth and growled through another wave of pain.

Myrwa shook her head. "The father is a dragonrider. He ... took payment from Kellae for saving our village once. Two revs he burned, and half our winter stores as well, and still demanded *payment*."

A stone formed in Riony's throat.

"I'm so sorry." Niskina leaned in, holding Kellae closer and rubbing her back.

The fear had left Kellae's eyes, and they burned bright with anger. "They think they own everything!"

"Okay, I need you to push now!" Riony urged.

Kellae's hands fisted closed around Niskina's and Myrwa's, and her whole body tensed as she bellowed. "They won't own my baby. They won't. They won't!"

"Again, push again!" Riony's hands were slick, cradling the tiny head. She prayed silent wishes to the stars that the shoulders would follow, that the babe would breathe, and

that Kellae would stop bleeding.

Kellae's legs shook violently, and she threw her head back in a wailing cry.

Riony caught the baby in her trembling hands.

And the baby breathed.

As the army of the undead growled and shambled at her back, Riony rubbed the baby down, marveling at the tiny hands, gasping lips, and the lift and fall of the chest, then handed the newborn to the mother.

She helped Kellae settle the baby down into her shirt, up against her skin, tucked in there almost the same as how Riony had carried Dracuni home from the ice cave.

Niskina and Myrwa lowered Kellae again, letting her lie down and rest as Riony cleaned up. Once the afterbirth had passed, the bleeding stopped as well, and Riony let out a long sigh of relief.

"Good work," Myrwa said, catching Riony's eye as Riony washed her hands again.

"I honestly didn't do a thing. It was one of the easiest births I've ever seen."

Myrwa's expression turned sad. "You do far more than you realize."

Kellae stared down at the new life on her chest in utter amazement, as though she couldn't comprehend where it had come from.

"How are you so beautiful?" she whispered.

Riony stood and wiped her hands dry on her pants.

Niskina rose as well and stared at the new mother and child for a long moment, then turned her eyes to the revenants surrounding them. She murmured, "That was ... that was something."

There was a brightness in her eyes for a moment, but then her face crumpled and she stormed off, swiping tears from her cheeks.

Riony picked up the pot of water, turning to empty it farther away.

"Wait! What do I do now?" Kellae called out. "I don't know how to look after a baby."

Riony tipped out the bloodied water and huffed a wry laugh. "You know, I was ten when I ended up with a baby to look after."

Myrwa seemed to do the math, looking over at Lyrrin, but Kellae's eyes remained on her baby.

"I didn't have to do it alone though, because my amma and pabba were with me, at least for a while. And you don't have to do it alone either." Riony nodded to Myrwa and then tilted her head to the other women hovering a few more steps away.

One of them was just finishing knitting some tiny clothing.

Myrwa gave Riony a long, knowing look, her pale eyes glossy.

Riony nodded to her, then strode on wobbly, tired legs over to the wall beside Dracuni and Lyrrin.

There was a bright, happy sense of amazement humming from Dracuni. She had her neck stretched long, straight up, watching over Kellae and the baby.

Riony settled down next to her, thumping onto the stone paving as the rush of energy within her waned.

Made baby! Dracuni thought. ***Her make baby!***

"You liked that, did you?" Riony asked.

Dracuni's body shivered in a strange, excited dance. ***New life, new life!***

"It was kind of more gross than I thought it would be," Lyrrin replied. "And I already thought it would be pretty gross."

"Yeah," Benjin agreed, cheeks gone ashy pale.

Riony rolled her eyes. "I think Dracuni gets it. It was kind of magical."

Baby! Baby life! Dracuni trotted forward on excited paws, but then backed up again after a wary look from Kellae and Myrwa.

Lyrrin moved in closer and tucked herself under Riony's arm. Since traveling with Niskina, Aishena, and Benjin, she hadn't cuddled up to Riony as much as she used to. Wanting to seem as grown and tough as everyone else, Riony figured.

"Was it like that when I was born?" Lyrrin asked.

"Not really. Your mother was in labor for far, far longer."

Lyrrin's eyes widened. "Like that? But longer? How long? An *hour*?"

"All night and then some. She was really strong."

Lyrrin was silent for a moment, then asked, "Do you remember anything else about her?"

"Just that she had this haughty audacity I admired. Serious attitude goals."

Lyrrin smiled, close-lipped. "Do you think now we're aboveground, maybe we could look for her?"

Riony's heart gave a lurch. "I never even knew her name. I don't even know where we'd start. We can't go back and ask the Heithorns. They'd kill us."

"Do you think ... she might be looking for me?"

"If she knew you were alive, I'm sure she would. She seemed to me like the type that would stop at nothing to get you back. But ... she was told you didn't survive."

"So she won't ever look for me, and I'll never know ... who she is."

Riony tried to pull Lyrrin in tighter, but Lyrrin pushed her away and sat up, moving back over to where she'd put her bag and blanket on the ground beside Benjin's.

A hot ache built behind Riony's eyes, and she closed them for a long moment.

She got it. She could understand entirely why Lyrrin wanted to know about her birth parents, but it also hurt. Riony had done everything she could to be there for Lyrrin, to be her family. Because they were the only family they had. Riony's own parents were gone. And they were never going to come back, could never be tracked down and found again.

Riony looked away from Lyrrin as well, only to be met with Aishena's cold, dark eyes beside her.

"You did a good job with the birth," she said.

"Yeah, I really sat there and waited for the baby to come out like a champion."

Aishena tilted her head. "I'm not coddling you. I wouldn't say it if I didn't mean it. You took control and helped the girl through."

"Well, you can go ahead and take control whenever you like too. And I don't mean in a sexy way. Although I wouldn't say no."

Aishena leaned forward, her mouth twisted in offense and eyebrows furrowed. Then that moment of fire vanished, and she backed down, staring at the ground. "I can't."

Riony sighed and rubbed her face with her hands. "Almost thought I had you back for a second there. I miss the old Aishena."

"The old Aishena got her family killed." She jolted up onto her feet, then stalked away, moving to the other side of Lyrrin and Benjin, closest to him.

Dracuni had settled down, her head laying on Riony's lap, still watching the mother and child curled up on their blanket across the ground.

Riony rubbed her soft ears. "Just you and me, then."

Dracuni trilled.

Although her bags and sword lay just nearby, Riony didn't unpack or even pull out a blanket. All her limbs felt like stone and her heart seemed to be solidifying to join them.

She leaned her head back against the shrine wall behind her, chest heaving with breaths to try to ease the pain in there.

More than anything, more than she had in a long time, she wished her amma was there with her.

She felt like she was doing everything for everyone and was exhausted through to her core and worried she still wasn't doing enough.

It felt good to have helped save the people there, helped bring the new life into the world, but it also felt so futile. How much longer would any of this last?

Does that even matter? We did good here and now. That's what's important.

And Riony liked the idea of doing more, of working toward a world that could be safe for Lyrrin and Dracuni and all the other people in her life and this land.

If I can just keep us alive, one more day, then another, and another.

Riony knew she'd keep trying. She wouldn't stop trying. She just didn't know whether she'd break first.

Nine

Kess and the city wall guard stared each other down at the entrance to Skaellakeep.

"Are you going to let me in or what?"

She sat atop Griskin before the solid iron gate, and on either side the dragonkeep walls rose boldly from the earth, towering into the sky and encircling the entire city.

The gigantic barrier was crafted from weathered stone that bore the scars of dragon fire and scraping claws, overlaid with sleek steel plating like protective scales, designed to keep the undead hordes out. Although scratched and mottled, the metal plates caught the smoke-filtered afternoon sunlight, flashing orange-gold like fire.

The face that had peered at her through the peephole

in the gate turned away. "I don't know, Borab. Some wild-looking girl. She's riding on a wolf! You have a look."

The face disappeared and another replaced it, staring down his long nose at Kess. "What do you want?"

"I want to come *in*, obviously."

"For what?"

"To be inside?"

The guard slurped air through his teeth. "We're all full up. Not taking any more refugees and thieving scum. You'll have to find somewhere else."

"Do I look—?" Actually, Kess realized how she must look. Keeping her hair untangled hadn't been much of a priority in recent years. She was covered in ashy grime, and her clothing was a patchwork of mismatched leathers. Pony's delver armor, although too large, was the nicest thing she owned. It was too well made to waste.

Pulling the gold chain and family crest she'd taken from her father's corpse, she held it up high for them to see. "*Regardless* of how I look, I am a dragonlord, daughter of the Heithorn line, and I demand to be let in."

"How'd we know you didn't steal that from someone? Never met a dragonlord that travels by ground. Don't get much of anyone coming in by ground anymore. Either people travel by dragon or don't travel at all."

"Then congratulations, you've only ever met cowards.

Listen, I've been told that my brother, Kife Heithorn, is in this keep, and he does have a dragon and would be happy to show it to you up close if you don't let his little sister in."

An embellishment of the truth, but they didn't need to know that.

The voice of the other man came muffled from behind the gate. "I've heard of that guy. He's with the city watch riders. Maybe we should let her in."

So the info she'd tracked down was true. Kife was here. She'd finally found him, after months of searching.

The face in the peephole grimaced. "I'm not sure …"

"Standing there and opening the gate for anything that is still alive is literally your one job, you gutless bovin. And if you don't, I'll still find my own way in, and we can have words about your inability to do simple tasks while my wolf uses your balls as a chew toy."

"Okay, maybe we shouldn't let her in," the guy behind the door said.

"You just said we should!"

"Maybe we should check with the captain."

"I'm not bringing her into this! Look, I'm letting the girl through and she can go be someone else's problem!"

The peephole closed and gears ground, clunking and clattering, swinging the heavy gate open.

As she waited, Kess ran her fingers along the cool,

smooth metal, craning her neck to absorb the full majesty of the keep's protective barrier.

It took Kess's breath away. She'd only been to one of these marvelous fortresses a couple of times in her childhood, when her parents were chasing down leads on a potential cure for her, some promise of new medical innovation that had proven to be a lie every time.

But she'd been as much in awe then as she was now. The sheer height of the dragonkeep cast an imposing silhouette against the horizon. The union of stone and steel, a marriage of tradition and innovation, formed an impenetrable bulwark, a solemn promise to the city's inhabitants that within those walls was a haven that the blight of undead could not touch.

And far above, majestic dragon silhouettes soared in the ashy sky, and Kess's chest felt both full to bursting and hollow at the same time.

The rattling ceased, the way forward open.

Griskin sniffed the air and growled softly but moved forward when urged. Kess gave a cold, hard smile to the two guards as she rode by. Then she was in darkness, the long tunnel spanning the thickness of the walls.

Even before she'd exited out the other side, she could hear the sounds and smells of the bustling city coming in with the beaming light.

The dragonkeep held every facet of human life cradled inside. Even the farms and factories were packed within the high walls. The road from the gate wound up through high-fenced fields with bovin packed shoulder to shoulder, braying in the sweltering heat. Their purpose was twofold—to sustain the dragon workforce and feed the ever-growing human population.

Kess smiled at the idea of buying a good meaty bone to treat Griskin with once they reached the city proper and the markets there. Even she hadn't had much more than rabbit or mouse deer in a long while.

The smell from the stockyards was intense and the heat far worse than it was outside the gates where a small breeze had been blowing freely.

Farther along, Rolanian slaves filled buckets of water from a tanker dragged into the fields by a tamed treedart dragon, sitting vegetatively as it waited its next command. Their crops looked dry, and an overseer yelled at them as though his volume could save the failed harvest.

In the distance, dragon-run factories belched plumes of smoke into the sky, forging steel, glass, and all the modern luxuries desired and deserved by those who kept the land safe. A fine ash fell in the air all around from some fire on the horizon.

Reaching the pinnacle of the road, Kess caught a view

of Grand Hofen, the water a rich blue against the browns and grays of the city that butted up against it. White sails of ships shimmered bright in the glary afternoon glow, and a steamer, run by dragonfire, puffed past.

All of this. All this majesty Kess could have if she owned her own dragon. And how much more she could have if she owned the only creature in the land with silvernix blood.

As she and Griskin stalked into the more built-up areas, the keep wasn't quite as majestic as she remembered others being.

The precisely paved streets teemed with homeless refugees, gathered on blankets in the corners like debris blown in the wind. Some huddled in the small shadows of palatial residences, trying to find relief from the heat.

And those doors were adorned with an excess of locks that spoke of growing unease.

The skyline was a blend of bygone grandeur and contemporary innovation. Stone fortresses, their turrets and spires reaching skyward with a timeless grace, stood amidst modern structures crafted from steel and glass that glittered in the sunlight, reflecting more of that burned orange heat down onto the world.

The silhouettes of dragons crowned many of the buildings, sitting motionless, tame and unthinking, awaiting their master's next command.

The people Kess passed were wary of her and Griskin, but Kess didn't feel the need to hide. Let them see her. Let them see who she was, and let them remember her when she returned once more, triumphant, and more powerful than any eyes that currently watched her with fear or disgust.

I just need to find Kife. And make him help me.

It didn't feel like an easy goal, but that had never deterred Kess before.

Kess stopped by a street vendor, buying a few kebabs of bovin meat for herself and Griskin. She dropped an extra gold sov into the man's hand for directions to where the city watch dragonriders spent their evenings.

As the man rattled off the lefts and rights of the pathway ahead, Kess looked over the streets. A death cleaner moved by, sweeping up a dead rat from a corner. He lifted the canvas corner of his cart and threw it in. Kess glimpsed the fingers of a human hand in the shadows contained within before he covered it over again.

Nothing dead could linger within the city walls. Everything was destined for the pyres that burned ceaselessly.

The street to the tavern the vendor had suggested took Kess near a building with elaborately carved unicorn horns flanking the entrance. The scent of desperation was thick as sickly figures surrounded the building, lying in the street. A woman in stark white robes overlaid with an excess of silver jewelry strode among them, followed by two heavily armored men.

They're all sick. The beggars reached for the white-robed woman, pleading and crying.

Kess tried to make out what they were saying in the cacophony of wails. Were they asking for silvernix? She'd heard of silvernix charities, but never seen one.

The robed woman pointed to a Rolanian child, lying limp between surrounding family. The guards picked the girl up, none too gently, and took her away. The family cried their thanks and praise as the doors to the building closed between them and the child.

Kess frowned, uneasy. The child had bright-red hair in a tone that was too familiar. That was all that was making her feel on edge. They were going to help her, weren't they?

"Come on. I want to get out of this heat." Kess nudged Griskin on.

They had to divert from the provided directions when they stumbled upon a riot. A dozen Rolanian slaves threw stones, clashing with armored Taen guards.

What razing madness is this?

Kess and Griskin went around, looping the block, until the tavern was in sight. A lamppost burned bright beside a swinging sign with a draconic emblem on it.

Griskin lifted his snout, and a shiver rustled through his fur beneath Kess's fingers.

"You have a scent?"

He chirped a short bark. He'd had a good sniff around Kife's emptied rooms at the estate. He knew what Kife smelled like.

"Lead the way."

Griskin followed his nose down a side alley of potted flowers and barred windows until he reached the doorway of a tall apartment, ornate with carved stone and faux crenellations along the rooftop, four stories up.

The door was as overburdened by locks and bars as all the other fine buildings Kess had passed.

She considered knocking but didn't want there to be any chance of being turned away, especially in her current state of dishevelment.

A balcony on the top floor had bay doors standing open.

"Let's go see if brother is home."

The narrow side street was almost empty, and the only person wandering through, a gentleman wearing a ridiculous turquoise suit, gave Kess a fearful look, then hurried away.

She spurred Griskin toward the challenging climb. The wolf's powerful hind legs propelled them effortlessly from the ground up onto the bars of the pregnant window, the metal shaped into a bulging protrusion to allow those inside to lean out.

Kess tucked herself in close to Griskin's back, his fur tickling her cheeks as she hugged around his shoulders, making her body part of his. Kess's eyes, sharp and focused, scanned the architecture for the perfect trajectory, guiding Griskin with the gentle pressing of her fingers.

His paws barely whispered against the uneven stone walls as he pushed off again, twisting mid-leap to land upon the neighbor's lower rooftop. The wind tousled Kess's hair in a moment of suspension that made gravity seem a myth.

With a final bound, Griskin soared across the gap between buildings to the targeted balcony. They landed with a whispered thump between the open doors.

"What in the sunless shit?" a woman's voice cried.

There was the scrabble of moving bodies, and Kess raised herself up on Griskin's back, staring into the gaudily furnished living room.

A young woman, her finely braided hair tinted wine purple, had fallen backward off her chair. A man with the physique of an ancient statue, wearing only the bottom half of dragonrider armor, dropped a bottle on the floor. And a third, glass in one hand, fumbled to reach his sword with the other.

Kife.

"*Kessara?*" he yelped.

"It's a razing wolf!" The topless man seemed torn between grabbing a weapon too and righting the dropped bottle that was spilling out onto the fur rug. "Kife, why is there an entire living wolf in your house right now?"

Her brother had the humility to look shocked for a whole few seconds before he started laughing and leaned back on the lounge. He wiped some spilled liquid off the plush fabric beside him.

"Bryn, Vori, meet my baby sister."

Getting to her feet, Bryn tottered sideways as she attempted to seat herself back in the armchair. "Really? This thing on this wolf—this is for real? I thought you'd spiked my drink for a minute there."

"With how much you drink I don't need to." Kife chuckled.

Kess narrowed her eyes, fury growing inside her.

He laughed.

He'd left her to die, and now, seeing her again, he sat there, laughing.

He hadn't changed a whole lot in the years since she'd last seen him flying away on his dragon. Being six years older than her, he'd always appeared grown-up, and the addition of some neatly shaped stubble seemed the only difference.

His charcoal hair was even kept in the same style of

braid he'd always worn, a thick central plait interwoven with smaller strands brought up from the sides, then hanging long down his back.

He wore full dragonrider armor decorated in the same colors as the flag that flew over Skaellakeep—blue and red.

Kess kept her anger in check. It wouldn't serve her. "I need to talk to you. Privately."

"Pssh, you just got here! Come and join the party! I'll find you a cup." Vori searched the table where flying goggles lay amongst empty bottles and plates piled haphazardly.

"I want to meet Kife's sister, the wolf-riding feral! You never even told us about her!"

"It's been a while since she's been around," Kife said, neatly leaving out why. He turned back and assessed Kess, then poured himself another drink from the mostly spilled bottle. "Did you come here to get revenge? Or just to embarrass me in front of my friends?"

Kess's reply was a rasp of hot air. "Embarrass you?"

Kife turned his sly smile to Bryn. "Blessed sun, Kess, we can smell you from here!"

Bryn chuckled in return, then pushed him away when he went in for a kiss.

The rage in Kess broke the dam, unable to be contained. "Don't you have *anything* you want to say to me?"

Kife raised his glass in a mocking toast. "I'm shocked

and impressed you survived!"

"What did she survive?" Bryn asked, as though it were a fun tidbit of gossip.

"He left me in the wastes to die," Kess shot back.

Vori actually looked scandalized. "Your little sister! Kife!"

A smirk settled cruelly around Kife's lips. "Family, right?"

All three of them laughed.

"But why is she *riding a wolf*?" Bryn asked, as though waiting for a punchline.

"Those legs still not working for you, Kess?" Kife threw the question to her.

Vori looked Kess up and down. "I thought she was just trying to be cool and tough with her pet. Not that she was, you know ..."

Vori made a face that was an awful mix of disgust and pity.

Covering the cruel smile on her mouth, Bryn leaned away, as though Kess's condition was catching.

Freezing her own expression into stone, Kess kept her eyes on her brother, determined to prove that she wasn't hurt at all. "Kife. You will come and speak with me. In private. Right now. Or I will drag you out of here with my wolf."

Her tone must have conveyed how deadly serious Kess was because the laughter stopped, and Vori and Bryn both drew their swords.

Kife lifted one hand, finished his drink, and stood. "Relax, relax! I'll go and have a little chat with the baby sis and her pet. Then we can go back to having fun."

He beckoned for her to follow him, and they exited down a short hallway to a grand bedroom. Griskin padded in, head low and wary in the enclosed space. Kife shut the door behind them. The solid wood muffled the conversation and laughter from the others almost entirely. Private enough for what had to be said.

Kess's mouth went dry at the thought of telling Kife what she wanted, what she needed, and why, no matter how many times she'd rehearsed the moment in her head. Her hands absently ran through Griskin's fur as she tried to regain her voice.

Kife turned on her, his expression flat and annoyed. "What are you doing here?"

"I've come to ask you ... to join me in a mission of great value."

Kife's eyes widened, and he blinked a few times. "Wow, you're here asking me for *help*?"

Kess sneered. "No, to join me, in an offer that will make you richer than you ever imagined."

"Sure, very plausible. How about you run off to whatever filthy den you and this creature came from? You don't even have the honor to try to get your revenge on me." Moving over to the bed, Kife began working on unbuckling his armor. The shining blue and red plates of dragonscale shimmered in the soft light of oil lamps burning on the bedsides.

Kess brought the throwing knives in her bracer up to display. "You aren't scared that I would? That I could kill you right now if I wanted?"

"Not really. You never had the guts for something like that." Kife tossed his chest plate uncaringly onto the end of the bed. He glanced back at Kess again, shaking his head. "How you even survived ... *you*. And that you'd come ... I want to say 'crawling back,' but, well, wolf."

Kess stared at him for a long while. Maybe she should just leave, find some other way forward. But as much of a heartless jerk as Kife was, she knew him. She could make this work.

"Are you going to listen to me, or should I find some other dragonrider who wants to win their weight in silvernix?"

Kife paused mid buckle, eyes snapping up to Kess. "Who are you planning on robbing? Not many but Yeonard Draekhan and the firsts have that much silvernix left in stores."

"Not in stores. Alive."

"Sorry, what?"

"What do you think I need a dragon and its rider for? This is a hunt for a living creature with silvernix blood."

"A unicorn? You've found one?"

Kess made a noncommittal grunt. She knew it was a risk telling him about Dracuni at all, that he could easily leave her for dead and hunt on his own, so she would keep some details to herself for now. Still, she had to tell him enough to get him invested.

"Is this some kind of joke or trick? This can't be real." Kife had laughter in his voice, but the way he assessed her with keen eyes showed there was also eagerness there. He was interested.

Kess consciously let her emotion into her voice, baiting the hook again. "Do you really think I would have come here, come to you for help, if this wasn't real? If it didn't mean *everything*?"

"It *is* clear that you're desperate," Kife admitted with a smirk. "Okay, I'll hear you out and join your little mission. I want to see how it pans out. I want to see this unicorn."

"Good. Get your friends to leave. You can't tell anyone else about this."

Kife cracked the door open again. "I'm not an idiot! Bad enough we're splitting the prize."

Strolling out into the living area, he barked, "Okay, clear out! We've got family business!"

Kess watched from the shadows of the hallway as his two dragonrider friends grumbled, collected their belongings, and left.

Would I have friends like that one day? Kess snorted softly. Hopefully she'd earn better quality companions than them with the wealth and power Dracuni would provide.

Kife took a seat on the plush upholstered lounge again and patted a spot next to him.

Kess brought Griskin around, letting him sit in the breeze of the open doors where he could see the sky, and remained on him. "Speaking of family business, I'm not sure if you've heard, but our home in the west is in ruins and our parents dead."

Kife blinked once, then sniffed. "That ass-end-of-the-world place wasn't my home. This is where I belong—in a dragonkeep with other dragonlords, where the honor and the action are."

He leaned forward, jabbing a finger toward Kess over the cluttered table. Then he pointed around at the overly furnished chambers. "Couldn't even afford a nice place with what was left after our parents blew all their wealth on you."

Kess realized she'd shrunken smaller in her saddle, and she straightened herself up. "Were you there when—"

"I already heard about it, reports of their death. It's old news." Kife leaned back, arms extended on either side along the back of the lounge. "Tell me more about this unicorn and how we're going to catch it."

Across the room, a door opened, startling Kess. Not the main entrance, but a smaller side access. A boney Rolanian woman in a plain servants' dress stepped in, a metal cleaning bucket dangling from one hand.

"Not now. Go away," Kife snapped.

He still keeps slaves? Of course he does.

Kess waited for her to leave before continuing. "There's a group of intolerable fools protecting the creature, keeping it with them. And they are using the Alderkin shrines, using magic there to travel around the land. We'll need to start by locating all the shrines."

"No, we won't. We have that info already. They're marked on dragonrider maps from back during the war," Kife said.

Hope crept anxiously through Kess. "Does it show their unique symbols?"

"Symbols? No, just locations."

"Then we still need to visit and identify them." Kess reached for a roll of paper in her side pack and unfurled it to show the glyphs she'd drawn on it in charcoal. "I've seen how they are using the shrines to travel and how each gateway has a unique symbol. I think we can track them that way."

Kife didn't seem too sure. "You think we can track where they'll end up if they make their escape through one of these gateways?"

"Yes. That's how we'll catch them." Kess nodded firmly, despite her doubts.

It was only a theory so far, but it had to work. It was all she had left to try. Surely, on dragon wings, they would be fast enough to catch their prey.

But if she was wrong, she'd just sold out the most precious creature in the world to the man who had thrown his little sister to the wolves for less.

TEN

Kess dreamed of her brother stabbing her in the back, right through the heart.

She gasped awake, arms seeking Griskin, and panicking again when she didn't find him close.

It took a couple of moments to remember where she was. That she was lying on the bed in her brother's guest room. That Griskin had refused the strange, soft fabric and instead slept away from her for the first time, underneath an open window.

Kess pushed herself into a sitting position. The covers of the bed lay undisturbed beneath her. It had felt too unfamiliar to tuck herself into that comfort, and the room was already warmer than the cold ground she was used to.

Only a cool, dim glow came through the open window, the sun not yet fully risen, and there were no other sounds from the door to the rest of the apartment.

Kess tried to get comfortable again so she could be well rested for the day ahead and the beginning of the hunt. The mattress was the softest thing Kess had touched in years.

But Kess tossed and turned. She probably just wasn't used to this sort of luxury. But she had been once. She'd grown up with fluffy beds and full plates and clean clothes. It was so much more than many people had or she had experienced since.

So why was I never happy?

Sitting up again, Kess rubbed her face. Despite a solid night of sleep, she felt exhausted, her eyes dry and her chest heavy.

Stretching her arms wide, Kess got a whiff of herself. She really did smell.

She reached for the jug on the nightstand and poured water into the basin. Even the washcloth she used to scrub herself with was plush and velvety.

To live like this again ... Kess's shoulders slumped. She could. She could give up her hunt and just stay in the dragonkeep, find a home there with the gold she'd accumulated over the years and her Heithorn name. It would be easier, wouldn't it?

Kess wrung the cloth tight in her fists. She couldn't forget the way Kife's friends had looked at her. She knew the way dragonlords treated anyone with physical weakness. No, it wouldn't be easier.

She could never fit in among their ranks, never get the respect she deserved if she didn't have her own dragon and more.

That was why she was doing this—all of this. She'd never been happy back home and could never be happy until she was in a position that would command respect. And then ... then maybe even friendship. Or love.

She couldn't give up.

Besides, now Kife knows about Dracuni, there'll be no stopping him.

Kess was about as clean as she could get herself. She had no fresh clothing to change into and wasn't prepared to take Griskin into the bathroom with her and subject him to running water spouts. He'd never forgive her.

But her face was no longer smeared with ash and her fingernails no longer black-rimmed.

The dragonglass mirror over the nightstand gave her a view of herself in startling clarity, and Kess frowned at the tangle of her hair. She raked her fingers through it, breaking up some of the larger braids and redoing them. But she'd never been good at braiding her own hair. It had

always been one of the slaves, or Pony, who did that for her.

In the end, despite her efforts, Kess felt just as scruffy as before—wild and disgraceful compared to the city nobles.

After calling Griskin over to the side of the bed, Kess slipped into the saddle, and they prowled out into the living area. The sun reached in, golden and warm through the open balcony, and the mess of the night before had been cleared away by silent hands during the night.

Why isn't Kife up yet? He's not taking this seriously at all.

As she glared at his bedroom door, it cracked open. The same boney servant woman from the night before slid out through the narrow gap and closed it again behind her. Her head was bowed, ebony hair falling around her face in waves. Her dress hung undone, and she worked to hurriedly button it as she skittered down the hall.

Kess's heart pumped into a riot and her skin went cold.

He'd done that back at Heithorn estate too, forcing any slave he wanted into his bedchambers. Kess hated it. But it had taken him showing an interest in Riony for her to take action.

I can't believe he's still doing that. Or maybe I can.

No matter that Kess had lodged a fine steel throwing dagger into the collar of his shirt, pinning him to a door. No matter that it was the only time she'd ever drawn his blood in one of their sibling scuffles.

Kife had wiped the nick on his neck and laughed. "There are plenty of better options than that boyish beast of *yours*."

That was the moment Kess had realized Riony didn't feel like she was *hers*. That despite the awful ownership involved, there was no connection between them. Not in the way Kess wanted.

All Kess had achieved that day was keeping Kife away from Riony, not restraining his conduct or teaching him any lesson. And Kife had quickly taken his revenge in return.

Maybe Kess's mistake that day was throwing a warning shot. She could have finished him, then and there. But she was pretty sure that would have been the last straw in her parents' tolerance of her.

Now, Kess wondered if it would have been worth it. She should have stood up to Kife sooner, not just because he was interested in the person closest to Kess, but for everyone he'd hurt.

A hot flood of shame overtook her face as the servant reached the exit.

"Hey!" Kess called out, her voice rasping. "Come here."

The girl's whole body jarred to a stop, but she obeyed the command in a dull, unflinching manner.

"I mean ... please, wait a moment." Kess nudged Griskin forward, closing the gap between her and the servant.

Large eyes of sunset amber stared more at the wolf than at Kess, but the servant stood calmly before Kess as though ready and willing to be eaten alive.

One sleeve still hung from a shoulder, and soft pink scars crept over her dark skin. Fresh lash marks.

"Kife isn't going to be home for a while." Kess pulled her coin pouch from her belt. Most of her gold was tucked deep in Griskin's saddlebags, stitched into hidden pockets, but the pouch held more than enough. "Take this. Buy your way to somewhere else. Find work under a dragonlord who doesn't ... do what Kife does."

Were there any? Kess didn't know.

There was a skepticism in the young woman's eyes that reflected Kess's thoughts. If the servant hadn't been drawn thin from hunger, she would have been startlingly beautiful. No doubt Kife had bought her for that very reason. There was a stillness to her, a resigned submissiveness born of self-preservation.

She didn't immediately reach for the offered coins.

Footsteps and the clink of porcelain came from Kife's room.

Kess thrust the bag toward the servant again. "Just take it. Go somewhere else, or don't. Do whatever you want with it. I don't care."

The slave met Kess's gaze for barely a second. Then

thin, long fingers snatched the coin pouch, and she hurried to the exit, not looking back once.

Kess watched the back of the door for a long time, trying to ease the turmoil in her gut.

"Good morning, little sister!" Kife strode out into the living area, buckling the straps of his armor at the wrists. He looked around the room, especially at the bare table. "Where's breakfast? Olan should have had it set out by now."

"We're skipping breakfast," Kess snapped, worried the girl may have gone that way herself on the way out.

"I'm not going on a unicorn hunt hungry."

"We've already wasted enough time with you sleeping off your booze! We should have gone last night."

"I at least need to grab some food from the kitchen."

Kess prowled Griskin up toward him. "There is a creature alive out there, with silvernix blood. How long until its existence is discovered by someone else? How long before we miss our chance? We leave now."

"You really expect me to head out, chasing around the wastes without any food?"

"I managed it when you left me for dead. Do you really think you'll fare worse than your poor little sister did?"

Kife's mouth pulled closed into a tight pucker. "Fine. We'll go."

He picked up his sword and goggles from where they'd

been left on the lounge the night before.

"Do you have any spare?" Kess asked as he pulled the flight goggles over his braided hair.

"No."

Kess pressed her teeth together. That was going to make flying unpleasant.

Kife made a sharp beckoning gesture, then opened a door leading to a spiral staircase rising between the stone walls. The steps were narrow, and Griskin gave a breathy whine at the enclosed space. But he followed Kife in, and they wound around and around until they pushed through another door and out into the harsh sunlight scorching the flat rooftop.

Lying on the hot stone, a chain around his neck and food trough by his side, was the purple dragon Kess had once wished could be hers.

"You still have him," Kess said flatly.

"Oh yeah, it's been a fantastic beast. You picked well, sis." Kife strode up and unlocked the chain.

The etherdart's scales weren't as bright as Kess remembered. Now, they were a dull, smoky purple.

"Did you end up naming him?"

Kife scoffed. "Why would I name it?"

As the heavy chain released from the steel collar, the dragon didn't move. The padlocked chain was a ward against theft rather than to stop the dragon liberating itself. It blinked once, its wedge-shaped head lying on the ground, as large as Griskin from snout to jaw.

The saddle was already in place, scales beneath it worn and smoothed from the rub of ever-present leather over the dragon's shoulders.

Kife gave a soft whistle, and it lowered its wings to allow a clear way to climb up to the seat. Kicking his feet into the thick scales, Kife jumped up into the saddle in two swift steps.

Turning back to Kess, he gestured at her and Griskin. "What are we doing about this situation? Are we leaving the overgrown dog behind?"

"No!" Tempering her tone, Kess added, "We're not leaving him. I'll need him when we're not flying."

"I suppose I can get the dragon to carry the wolf."

"In ... his claws?" Kess looked at the talons, long and curved like scythes.

Kife made a grabby motion with both hands. "Your pet isn't going to get squished. The dragon is entirely under my control, sis."

Yeah, that's what scares me.

She couldn't trust Kife—not really. But at this point she wasn't sure what other choice she had. "It's going to be okay, Gris."

She urged him closer.

"How are you even going to be able to get up to the saddle?" Kife asked, one corner of his mouth lifting.

"Just fine." Kess brought Griskin sidelong against the dragon's neck, then gripped the angular scales running in a ridge over the dragon's shoulders and pulled herself out of Griskin's saddle.

Her arms were wiry but strong, and she could climb better than most. It wasn't the elegant mount Kess wished for, but she was up and seated behind Kife fast enough.

There was a moment when Kess considered pushing Kife off the dragon and claiming it for herself. But Kess only knew dragon riding in theory—not practice. She wasn't certain she could control the creature on her own.

And Kife already had the dragon moving, scooping Griskin up in its front claws. Griskin howled a high whine that pierced right into Kess's heart. She angled for a view of him and heard him whimper again. Scared, but unhurt.

But she took the message. She knew if she tried anything, Griskin would suffer first, and her suffering would follow on swift wings.

The dragon lifted from the ground. A strong surge upward almost threw Kess off its back, and Kife chuckled as she scrambled to hold herself in position.

Grabbing a spare belt from her waist, Kess used the steel

loops on the delver vest to buckle herself safely to Kife's saddle. She wasn't going to fall or be pushed. She wouldn't be left behind, and neither would Griskin.

The dragonkeep spread out below them, growing smaller and smaller as they rose into the air. Wind rushed around them, stinging Kess's eyes, but she refused to close them. The world below was burned and gray, stone and steel, smoke and dust.

She hadn't flown for years. She hadn't flown since the last time Kife took her out on his dragon and never took her home.

Kess had made friends with death that day. Had fixed her one desperate goal onto her heart with the stab of a sharp blade—that she would become someone that no one would dare abandon.

Now, flying alongside her brother, she only hoped she could get what she wanted from Kife before he decided to leave her to the wolves again.

ELEVEN

Riony wasn't sure her father's motto of *big dreams, bold deeds* was ever meant to include brazen attacks on dragonlord properties.

"Are we really, literally, seriously, actually going to do this?" she asked.

In the shadows of a rocky outcrop, Riony squinted through Lyrrin's seeing stone, scanning the ore mine sprawled below. The gritty scent of dust hung in the air, drying Riony's tongue, and her words were punctuated by the faint clinks of metal echoing from the excavation site.

Aishena remained silent as though she wasn't the person Riony was most seeking advice from, and Niskina sharpened her poleaxe as though already decided.

Lyrrin snatched the clear crystal back. "That's Avri and Tamas down there."

Benjin nodded. "It's definitely them."

Riony squinted at the now much smaller children sitting on a mound of muddy rocks, sorting through the muck with their bare hands.

"We didn't save them when the slavers took them from the orphans' den. This is where they ended up. And all those other kids too. We owe it to them to help out now. We've got to save them." Lyrrin punched her small, gloved fist into the palm of her other hand.

"Okay, little spitfire, don't go charging in yet." Riony remembered the terrified faces in the cage the dragonrider had carried away, the one she and Lyrrin had jumped from.

Children she hadn't been able to take with her. She hadn't known them personally. But Lyrrin did.

And whether she knew them or not, whether she owed them or not for having failed to save them the first time, she wasn't sure she could see them kept there as slaves and then turn away.

She just didn't like the idea of risking her family to save them.

Every part of her existence had become about weighing lives against each other, and she hated it.

Dracuni lay low on her belly beside Riony, snout

resting on the rocks as she looked down at the mine. Her lilac eyes were focused and bright as they followed all the movement far below.

Want to help.

Riony sensed her anticipation, both fear and excitement. Dracuni had grown so much in recent months, too big for even Riony to carry with any ease. But both flying and flaming were still absent among her skills.

"Even if we go ahead with this, you're staying out of it," Riony replied.

Air puffed from Dracuni's nostrils, disturbing the surrounding dust. ***Still want.***

She had learned more in their travels about *friends* and *not-friends* and why they had to be so careful nobody found out what she could do—what her blood could do.

That had scared her at first, but she'd also grown bolder. They had come across more groups of refugees as they'd traveled and had helped those people find safety at the shrines, too, or sent them to the undercity. And each group of people they met who didn't capture and bleed Dracuni only made her more excited to meet and help the next.

Even Myrwa's small community had come to accept Dracuni after a couple more visits. Dracuni hadn't yet called them *friends* but had started calling them *not-not-friends*.

Riony now thought of them as friends though. Seeing

Kellae's baby grow happy and strong within the safety of the shrine had made their visits back there worth it. The shrines seemed to stay safe at least for a while without Dracuni's presence, but without knowing how long that lasted, their group tried to get back there regularly, bringing the magic with them.

And Myrwa always had a hot bowl of carrowmy rice available for Riony whenever they did.

Riony felt good about the people they had helped.

But this was the first time they'd considered outright attacking a dragonlord property.

Aishena, who had been sharing the seeing stone on Yoskar's staff with Benjin, continued to stare at the field of rocks and rubble below, chewing over her thoughts but not sharing any.

The dye Riony had prepared at Myrwa's camp and used for Lyrrin, Aishena, and Benjin's hair had run out in the weeks since, and Aishena's long locks had faded almost back to their normal silver. Just a hint of earthy red tinted the silky lengths.

Niskina didn't bother to get a better look with the magical Alderkin crystals. "Come on. Let's do this! This is it—our chance to help people, to be more than just idiots on the run. We can make change, like in the *Rebel Riders*."

"Those are just stories," Riony said.

Stories she'd missed since leaving the undercity. There were no chapter vendors in the wastes of the aboveground world. She doubted any of the overseers below would read that sort of fiction either, so turning up some booklets wasn't likely to be a fun surprise bonus to their guerilla ambush.

In the last chapter Riony had read, Rider Zeina had just kissed her true love on the Cradle Archway before being ambushed and Riony might *never* find out what happened next.

Niskina huffed. "They could be real. We've heard plenty of stories from people about some dragonriders fighting back against the dragonlords."

"Rumors. And a few outlaws making trouble isn't the same as it is in the books. It's not all honorable saviors and glistening chests."

Niskina stared longingly into the distance for a moment as though she were missing the chapters as well. "Stories or not, I don't care. There's still truth in stories."

"How often do the Rebel Riders win in those stories? How often are they triumphant in making the world a better place?"

"Most of the time."

Gesturing to the ashy sky and burned remains of bones lying in the dirt around them and the slaves down the hill, Riony scoffed. "Yeah, lots of truth."

Niskina rolled her eyes. "I'm doing something whether you're too cowardly to help or not."

Riony turned to her other side, putting her back to Niskina. "Aish, what do you think?"

"The plan is solid enough. I'll do as instructed."

"Our plan of walking in and hoping for the best? Yep, it's up there with the greatest moments in tactical history." Riony tugged at her tangled pigtail.

Her hair had grown and fell over her face. She undid the short braid, pulled her hair back, and retied it again. Still, a wavy red strand flopped across her eyes.

Lyrrin said, "The plan *is* good. We've seen the cargo dragons leave and return already, and we know we've got a couple of hours once they go again. We know how many overseers there are—one in the front watchtower, four down in the mines, and four up top. That's less than two each."

"I think you're miscounting because part of the plan was also that you and Benjin are staying out of the way with Dracuni."

"You, Aishena, and Niskina only have five to deal with before the ones in the mines come out, so my math is still good," Lyrrin shot back. "We've got to help them."

Riony couldn't say she hated the odds. Two against one felt like a treat compared to being chased by hordes of revs.

Benjin looked eagerly at Lyrrin, but then a frown came over him. "I think, if Yoskar was here, he'd say it's too risky."

"The cargo dragons are almost done being loaded," Aishena said.

"It would be less risky if you let us help," Benjin added.

"No," Aishena and Riony said together.

Riony leaned over to look down at the mine again. Slaves ranging from scrawny children to elderly men were bowed under the weight of baskets that they brought and dumped into canvas containers in front of the dragons.

Two seasongs, one green and black, one green and silver. Both tamed. They reminded Riony of Dracuni's mother. Although not as large as her, they were still some of the largest dragons she'd ever seen.

Behind them, toward the back of the mine, was another small tower that looked only half-completed, the top section draped in dark cloth.

The men on the dragons gave a signal and the canvas containers were lashed closed and attached with hooks to the industrial harnesses over the dragons' backs. The great leathery expanses of their wings stretched out, almost as wide across as the mine itself and the fortress wall encircling it.

The beating of those wings echoed like distant thunder as they worked to lift their burdens into the sky.

"Now or never," Lyrrin whispered in a rush.

Riony took in her sister's determined expression with a frown. "More like 'now or maybe another time soon after we've thought about it a bit more.' I'm still not sure this is a great idea. We would be putting targets on our backs."

Lyrrin raised one shoulder. "Well, Niskina is already gone, sooo ..."

"Sparks!" Riony jumped to her feet.

Niskina was gone, beyond the scree-strewn slope and approaching the mine gates.

"You three, stay here!" Riony gave her best, most commanding glare at Lyrrin, Dracuni, and Benjin. Then she took off.

She'd already removed her bags and left them with the kids, but the weight of the sword on her back made the stumble down the steep hill an exercise in stubbed toes and scratched hands. She cursed Niskina for adding this rush to their risks.

Niskina was almost at the gates when Riony caught up to her, panting and cursing.

"You were really going to walk in there on your own?" Riony scolded.

Niskina smiled sweetly back. "What do you mean? I knew you'd come and help me. You're too much of a softy."

"And thank you, so much, for exploiting that."

A male voice called from the stone watchtower beside the gate, "Someone approaches!"

"Revs?" another voice replied. They sounded right on the other side of the steel-plated door.

The man with pale skin and neatly braided black hair leaned out of the watchtower to take in the two women.

They both waved back politely.

"More visitors," shouted the watchtower guard uncertainly.

"Busy day. Let them in then. Let's see what these ones will pay us."

Riony whispered to Niskina, "Busy, do they get traders or something through often?"

"Yes, just hoping to trade," Niskina called back to the guard in her sweetest voice.

The solid gate swung smoothly aside, and as Riony marched across the threshold, she unstrapped her sword and brought it before her in her hands.

Niskina tucked her tumble of hair away from her face and drew her poleaxe.

All four aboveground overseers had come toward the entrance to see who the visitors were. They each wore clean and neat leather armor, painted gray and green. Only their boots showed any sign of the muddy conditions.

Two of the men had salt-and-pepper hair that matched their uniforms, but the other two were closer to Riony's

age. All had lashes carried on their belts.

Heat rose through Riony, prickling over the scars on her back. Maybe she did want to fight these guys after all.

Her and Niskina's approach was met with a ripple of chuckles.

"What is this supposed to be? The feeblest ambush in history?" one of the older men waved a hand dismissively at them.

Riony put her sword tip down and leaned on the hilt casually. "This is your warning to get yourselves out of here. You're all going to run. Run back to whatever dragonlord owns this place and tell them the mine was lost to revs. That there were no survivors. You can run and tell them that, or you can stay and experience the 'no survivors' part yourself."

The four of them stared back, still chuckling.

The older man spoke again, his tone friendly and distinguished. "Don't be silly, child. If you want to trade, we can trade without violence. We have plenty in our stores, and I'm sure you two can find some way you can pay us."

The chuckles rose to laughter.

"And what would a stain on humankind like yourself charge to allow us to walk out of here with every slave?" Riony gestured to the children sorting ore from waste amongst the lode pile.

The overseer frowned at that. "More than any value you have, girl. If you refuse to be respectful about this, then we are done."

He lifted a hand in the air, flicking a finger at Riony. He held his hand like that for a long moment, then flicked it again, looking up toward the watchtower at Riony's back with confusion.

Riony turned as well, seeing the direct line from the window down to her and Niskina. There was movement within, a flash of glowing yellow, and a crossbow clattered out of the window and landed on the ground.

A moment later, the overseer in the watchtower followed it, groaning as he hit the mud below.

"How dare you attack us like this!" One of the younger men, someone Niskina no doubt would have been flirting with under better conditions, turned wildly around.

He looked to all the walls and shadows as though they had brought an army against them. "This mine belongs to Ulfren the First! We're supplying all of Ulfrenkeep and most of Elundrae with copper. They need this metal."

Riony lifted her sword again, activating the rune so that it lit up purple. "If they need it so much, tell them to come and mine it themselves."

The door in the base of the watchtower squeaked as it opened, and Aishena strolled out, cutting athame

glowing bright.

"What is that she's carrying?" the other young overseer asked, his eyes wide.

"Alderkin magic." The old one spat on the ground. "These rats side with what isn't even human."

Niskina gasped. "Watch out! There's another guard."

Riony followed her gaze toward the covered tower. The man was up the long ladder on the side and tugged a rope. In a swish of fabric, a large, glittery disc was revealed.

A signaler. Riony hadn't seen one of those since the night her parents had died.

The guard began cranking handles beside the plate covered in facets of mirror, adjusting the angle.

"No, we do not want that." Riony ran for him.

Her sword made her footsteps light and she glided across the scrappy dirt and puddles. She prepared to leap up to the man, but it was too late.

The signaler caught the weak sun, magnifying it into a beam that lit up a patch on the blanket of slate-colored clouds above.

The older overseer said, "Let's see which side has no survivors when the dragons arrive."

Riony adjusted her hold on her crystal sword and continued toward the structure. "Not if I bring that whole thing down before anyone sees it."

The man up on the signal tower pulled a crossbow from his back, aiming it down at Riony. "Don't even—"

There was a soft *thunk*, and he stilled, then fell. A heavy pebble tumbled down with him.

Good aim!

Dracuni's thoughts came through clear, sounding close, much closer than where she'd left her. And she'd bet good money that stone had flown from Lyrrin's sling.

Riony couldn't see where they were and didn't have time to look. She had to deal with the signaler first, still angled and burning into the sky above them.

If the dragonriders on the cargo dragons turned back and saw, or any other nearby dragonriders caught sight of it, they'd be in big trouble. The nearest shrine to escape through was a half hour run from there.

Riony rolled her shoulders and lifted the huge Alderkin blade. Taking in the support structure beneath the signaler, she chose her target and brought her body around in a full spin.

The sword struck right in the joint between the metal struts. The impact jarred Riony's muscles, but the sword cracked through, separating the rivets and bending the structure. It toppled to the side. The disc separated from its supports, cracking with the screech of metal and rolling down onto the ground.

Shards of glass mirror clattered and chinked as the metal disc whined to a stop.

The slaves working aboveground scattered. The four overseers huddled closer together as they looked at Riony and her sword again with newly born fear.

But from a hut beside the mine entrance, four more men appeared, shouting at the destroyed signaler and their cornered colleagues.

"More of them? I thought we'd accounted for them all." Riony rejoined Niskina and Aishena.

The overseers drew weapons—lashes and swords—and squared up against the women.

Niskina muttered back, "Night shift maybe? They didn't come out all morning! I didn't know they were there!"

Riony rolled her eyes. "Maybe another good reason to have spent more than a few hours watching the place before we rushed in! Honestly, if you're relying on me being the voice of reason, maybe consider things aren't going well."

Drawing another athame which lit up burning red, Aishena looked from the mine entrance to the eight men before them. "We can't be sure the others in the mine didn't hear all this noise. They may be on their way too. The dragons might have also seen the signal and will return as well."

Riony sniffed and cricked her neck, gripping the hilt

of her sword strongly in both hands. A dark, violent mood arose within her, and a desire to break the face of every man with a lash in his hand.

"Go," she growled. "You two go and get the slaves out of the mine as fast as you can, and I'll hold back the ones up here. And hopefully we'll all get out of this place in one piece."

Aishena gave Riony a concerned look but followed orders with a swift nod. She and Niskina made a dash for it and disappeared through the black square entrance into the earth.

Riony hoped Aishena and Niskina could deal with the four overseers in the mines. She hoped that once the slaves worked out what her friends were trying to do, they would join the fight, and the numbers would turn to their side.

She also hoped that, wherever Lyrrin and Dracuni were, they weren't planning on getting any closer.

But as the eight men edged around, encircling her and testing her boundaries, Riony suddenly felt very alone.

Twelve

All the air rushed out of Lyrrin's chest as the eight men surrounded her sister.

There weren't meant to be that many. Riony, Niskina, and Aishena were supposed to work together to incapacitate the guards up top before going down into the mines together.

But instead, it was her sister versus eight. Her sister, grinning and goading the men as though any one of their swords couldn't end her.

Lyrrin grunted fiercely. "I'm going down there."

"We're supposed to stay here," Benjin said. "Well, really, we were supposed to stay up there."

He tilted his head toward the slope and the higher vantage point in the rocky crags they'd left behind.

As soon as Riony and Aishena had hurried after Niskina, Lyrrin had followed to be close enough to gather up any fleeing slaves if they ran out the open gate so they could be led to safety. And close enough to be able to hear snippets of the conversation and know what was happening.

They were tucked on a small ledge behind some jagged rocks just outside the gate, a perch tall enough that they could see over the stone walls encircling the mine.

"I'm going anyway," Lyrrin said, sliding down the rocky edge on her bottom. "You stay here with Dracuni."

Dracuni snorted and stretched her front paws, revealing the talons there, then shifted forward.

Lyrrin raised a hand, putting it in front of Dracuni's snout. "No, you stay here. Stay with Benjin."

"Who said I was staying?" Benjin leaned on Yoskar's staff, using it like an extra limb to navigate down between the stones.

Dracuni opened her mouth and snapped it closed again, then pushed against Lyrrin's hand, moving past her and down the angular boulders.

Lyrrin wished she understood what Dracuni was saying the way Riony did.

"Well, they can't be angry at us for not sticking to the plan anyway," Lyrrin said as she jumped the last section to the road below. "They didn't either."

And Lyrrin was angry too. Angry at her sister for always acting like it didn't matter what happened to her, like she didn't need help.

The three of them ran for the open gate.

Through the entrance, the fight was a swirl of circling bodies, swords and lashes swinging.

Riony stood defiant at the entrance to the mine, wielding her massive sword to ward off the men. But even with the float rune activated, the crystal gleaming with otherworldly luminescence, the swings were slow. Powerful, but slow.

Especially compared to the eight guards with their slim steel blades and flicking leather, who dodged in and out, taking turns trying to skewer Riony. She caught the strike of one blade against the steel of her shoulder guard only to be met with a fist in the back of her ribs.

Riony roared as she hammered the sword in a horizontal sweep, catching up one man with the flat and flinging him across the yard into a pile of muddy stones.

Lyrrin gasped, and Dracuni trilled a whimper when the flick of a lash landed across Riony's face. They ran faster, through the gate, almost there.

Riony's breaths came in ragged bursts, and blood poured from her brow, but she didn't slow down, didn't yield. Steel clashed with crystal, reverberating within the stone-walled space.

Dracuni was ahead of the kids now, galloping in long, leaping strides.

"Dragon!" one of the guards yelled.

"What in the unblessed ..." Another turned as well, the two of them aiming swords at the unidragon.

"What are you doing? Get out of here!" Riony snapped in between blows.

Dracuni growled and gave her head a violent shake. She raised up on her back legs, chest heaving like bellows.

Is she going to flame?

Lyrrin skidded to a stop outside of the main fight beside piles of sorted stone, ore, and coal. She scooped a rock up into the cradle of her sling. She swung the leather straps in circles, taking her aim.

Dracuni's shoulders strained, and her neck shivered. Her mouth opened wide. The men scrambled to get clear.

Nothing came out.

"Get it! Get that thing!" one yelled as they ran back toward her.

Dracuni opened her mouth again, roaring with the hint of a whimper.

She dropped back onto all fours and lowered her head, her single horn angled right back at the guard's threatening weapons. She skittered left and right, jumping and pouncing toward the men, then backing away again, and nipping at

their legs.

Lyrrin loosed her first stone, but it flew right behind a guard's back when he stepped forward in a lunge. She loaded another.

"Back off!" Benjin ran up beside Dracuni, Yoskar's staff alight with a burn rune.

The flaming red crystal left streaks of heat in the air as he swung it, scaring back the men trying to hit Dracuni.

Lyrrin sent a shot again, and again she missed. Everyone was moving too fast, dodging in and out unpredictably. Standard stones weren't going to knock any of them down—not if she couldn't hit them.

"Eyes!" Lyrrin shouted as she activated a flash stone.

She only had two left, and no one would let her slice up their remaining glow stones to make more. One left now as she sent the stone soaring into the fray. It landed at Riony's feet.

Dracuni tucked her face under a wing, and Riony and Benjin threw an arm up over their eyes as the burst of light went off. The guards stumbled and swore.

Riony held her sword before her like a shield against the blind swings of their weapons and barreled through them, stopping in front of Dracuni. "Go. You're clear—get out of here! What do you mean, 'make me!?' We are *having a talk* after this!"

The guards wiped at their eyes, slowing their assault as

they regrouped. The flash stone had only bought them a moment. The men circled around the three of them, taking a few breaths, and stared at the new threats. The strange, snappy little dragon. The fiery blazing staff.

That red glow seemed to be holding their attention the most.

Lyrrin had also sliced the small crucible Riony had found her in the Alderkin depths into smaller shards. But all they had on them were burn runes, which wouldn't do much if she couldn't hit her target.

But maybe she could make them do more.

Lyrrin tugged one of her gloves off, shoved it in a pocket, and scrambled over to the pile of coal, grasping a large chunk. She quickly pressed one of her sharp-tipped nails into the stone, slicing a gash.

Activating one of the burn shards, she wedged it in. The black mineral sparked and smoldered, glowing from within. She dropped it into her sling and sent it flying.

It caught alight midair, soaring like a miniature meteor into the middle of the fight.

It hit a guard in the ankles, making him dodge back from the crackling stone, taking him out of a melee with Benjin. The guard's thick leather armor didn't catch, nor did the coal seem to hurt him, but he swore and stared into the sky as though it had begun raining fire.

Lyrrin prepared another, as large as she could throw with her sling. It came flaming down through the sky between two guards and her sister, making them scatter.

More accustomed to Lyrrin's explosive experiments than her opponents, Riony recovered fastest, pressing the men back with a slicing arc of her sword.

As Lyrrin continued to rain the field with fire, one man turned and fled, running into a nearby building and slamming the door behind him.

Riony had another guard on his back, and Dracuni and Benjin kept their attackers at bay with nipping teeth and burning crystal.

From the dark entrance to the mine, a clamor of voices and slapping feet emerged.

Niskina stepped out into the light, poleaxe in hand, herding a group of children ahead of her. "Straight out the gate, run!"

As the fleeing slaves streamed across the yard, more faces peered out from behind huts and rubble.

Lyrrin waved her hands above her head. "Come on! We're getting you out!"

Her friends from the orphans' den turned toward her, their eyes widening. Avri, Tamas, and a few others came running in a huddle, taking a wide loop around the clash of combat still centering on Riony.

A group of four young men came out of the mine after Niskina, guiding some of the younger kids and older slaves. They remained near the entrance, helping people through and sending them toward the gate.

The faces of those who came out of the mines were fearful, eyes bulging and cheeks hollow. Bare hands and arms were pale from spatters of dried mud, their feet and legs the same. They all looked one color, their skin, clothes, and hair all the shade of dust and stone.

One child who tottered past looked barely four years old.

"Get back to your stations! Don't you dare leave!" the older man who had led the conversation before rushed at the fleeing slaves, smacking his lash in the air. "We will find you! You'll all be dragged back and punished!"

A slash of Riony's sword forced his retreat.

"I think that's all of them!" Aishena stepped out of the mine with her athames glowing.

The group of four men nodded to her, grouping around her as they joined the others running for the gate.

"Lead them out, I'll be right behind you," Riony said.

Niskina nodded from up front, taking the first group through the exit.

Lyrrin raced across the muddy ground to Benjin and Dracuni just as Aishena reached them too.

Aishena gave Benjin a deathly cold glare. "Take Dracuni

and get to the front with Niskina."

A guard swung his sword in a slash toward Aishena's chest. Without even seeming to look, she raised her cutting athame in a block and sliced the sword clean in half. The man stumbled back, swearing.

"We're done here. Go!" She grabbed Benjin by the shoulder and brought him into a run with her.

Two guards gasped in the mud, and one other had fled. The five remainders gathered close, arguing between themselves, wary of the slaves rushing around them freely.

Dracuni showed no sign of leaving Riony's side.

Lyrrin grabbed one of Riony's belt loops and tugged. "Come on. Let's go!"

"NO!" Riony barked.

Her arm was sliced raw from lash bites, and she swung it accusingly at the guards. Blood ran down the side of her face, dripping from her chin, and her expression was wild, ruthless, and anguished all at once.

"I can't let them go. Not after everything they've done. I can't forgive them for this! They don't deserve to live!"

The quiver of fury in Riony's voice terrified Lyrrin. "Come on, please. You're hurt. You can't keep fighting."

Dracuni whined a low whimper, circling closer around Riony's legs and nudging her with her cheek.

"I can, and I will!" Riony's eyes were red-rimmed and

glossy, her words hissing out between bared teeth. "They kept them, all of them, as slaves. These children. They whipped them and beat them!"

"It's okay—the kids are out. They're going to be safe. We can go." Lyrrin tugged again.

"We're just doing our jobs!" one guard yelled back, spittle flying.

Riony roared wordlessly at the men, raising her sword high.

She's going to kill them. If she stays, she's going to kill someone.

She couldn't let Riony keep fighting and fighting and fighting. She was going to end up with blood on her hands, and Lyrrin didn't want that for her sister. Not again. Not for her or anyone.

No, I'm not going to let you do this to yourself.

With her breath held, Lyrrin stepped between Riony and the men.

"Stop!" She raised her hands up, one at her sister, and one at the guards.

Riony's chest pulsed with panting breaths, her attack frozen. "What are you doing?"

Lyrrin's face scrunched up with the sting of emotions, and she blinked tears.

Lyrrin turned to the guards, pleading. "This is your last chance. Run. Just run!"

THIRTEEN

Blood roared in Riony's ears like the rumble of an angry sea. She wiped her face with the palm of her hand, and it came away slick and red. A dull ache spread around her eye from an elbow that had connected with it during the scuffle.

Hurt?

"I'm fine!" She sucked at the air that hissed the words out, trying to bring them back in, soothe them.

Hot liquid trickled down her temple and cheekbone, and she swiped it away again. A tentative touch of the area revealed a wide split across her eyebrow.

At least it's going to leave an awesome scar.

"I'm fine," she said a second time, her voice softer, barely audible over the raging beat in her chest that wouldn't ease, no matter that they were no longer running. "Don't worry."

Dracuni looked up from beside her hip, her lilac eyes narrowed. ***Not fine. Do worry.***

The light of the shrine gateway spilled across the faces of all the people who had escaped the mine. From children to very old, almost all were Rolanian, but some of the young men had Taenish features. They looked at the gateway with shivering expressions and determined, thinly pulled mouths.

The first brave few had already stepped through to the other side.

"It's safe, see?" Lyrrin and one of her friends from the orphans' den did a pass through the gateway and back again.

She held the boy's hand—Tamas?—and as they came back to the starting side, his eyes lit up and a smile split his dusty face.

Letting go of her hand, he ran into the gateway and back once more, barking a laugh of wonder as he grabbed another friend for the next round trip.

"We do want to get everyone to the *other* side as quickly as we can, please," Riony called over the crowd.

She gave the kids a little push to suggest they stay where they end up.

She wasn't sure how much time they had before they

were followed, before search parties were formed and dragons filled the sky, as they had done when Riony and her parents fled the Heithorns.

The guards at the mine had laid down weapons when faced with Lyrrin's ultimatum and Riony's fury. They'd left the men tied up, but it wouldn't be much longer before the carrier dragons returned and found the whole mine cleared out.

The freed slaves moved more confidently into the gateway after the children's demonstration. They knew they couldn't stay there, and as much as the Alderkin magic scared them, being recaptured was less preferable.

Niskina and Benjin had gone through with the first of the group, and Aishena remained beside the gateway, reassuring those as they stepped into the window of magic that would take them across Elundrae.

As the last few passed through the gateway, Aishena gave Riony a nod and followed. With a final glance at the sky, Riony pushed Lyrrin and Dracuni in front of her through the shimmering light.

Lyrrin deactivated the gateway on the other side and beamed up at Riony. "We did it! We helped them all get out!"

With her eyes on the crowd of both new arrivals and people from Myrwa's enclave, Riony spoke low. "*We* weren't all supposed to have been there. You shouldn't have come in! Those guards have seen Dracuni now.”

"They didn't know she was anything other than a baby dragon," Lyrrin whispered back.

"Which we shouldn't even have! You think they aren't going to be telling the dragonlords they work for that there was a baby dragon running around with the people who are freeing slaves? What do you think they will want to do about that?”

Not little sister's fault. I choose. I go! Fight like big sister!

Dracuni stood tall on straight legs, her neck up and chin high.

She was getting big now but was still a baby compared to any of the massive, tamed beasts the dragonriders would hunt her with if they realized what she was.

Riony said to both Dracuni and Lyrrin, "What aren't you understanding about how dangerous that was?”

Danger for you also.

"I couldn't stop her, and I told her not to, and you were the one trying to take on eight guards at once! I could see just how dangerous that was. Could you?”

"I could have taken them!”

Lyrrin's mouth closed, and her lips and cheeks puffed out with air. "At what cost?”

Benjin came over from where Aishena had been fussing

over him, and gave Lyrrin a big grin as though this was all their victory.

"Not at the cost of any of you three." Riony gave them all the hardest glare she could offer.

Lyrrin gasped, open-mouthed and insulted. "What about you?"

Benjin shrugged. "Aish is being like this too. As though I was going to stay out of it. I have to look after Aishena too because family looks after family."

Myrwa swept in beside them then, pulling Riony into a hug that shut her mouth and turned her from the three stubborn children.

"You've doubled our numbers, my friend," Myrwa said into her ear, then let her go, patting her shoulder and staring at her bloodied and bruising face. "We welcome these people. But I do wish you'd given us some warning."

"Some of them we will take to the undercity," Riony replied. "That's where they came from. We just wanted to get everyone somewhere safe, fast. Sorry."

Myrwa waved off the suggestion. "They can go if they want to, but they are welcome. Look, look who you brought!"

A mid-teen boy was on his knees in front of Kellae who was also kneeling and leaning into an embrace with him, her child pressed between them. Their faces were wet with tears and stretched with smiles.

Kellae leaned back, using one of the baby's rags to wipe the dust and saltwater from the boy's face, her mouth moving, saying so much so fast.

Riony tried to remember the night of the birth, the questions about Kellae and her family. "Her brother?"

Myrwa smiled in return. "All of these people are family now."

Outside the shrine building, all around, Myrwa's people brought the new arrivals in, and they in turn were coming back to life with relief.

The space had changed again since Riony's last visit, with small huts crafted from rugs and old, charred timber filling the space within the standing stone ring.

At least a couple of the huts were starting to look almost solid, as newly salvaged material was added to the structures. Patches of garden beds sprung with vibrant seedlings. Clean laundry hung in a line between two of the larger standing stones.

Pieces of broken pillar had been rolled into a ring around a central fire pit, where a sputtering collection of pots hissed the scents of roasting vegetables and stewed mushrooms into the dulling day. Seats were given to the newcomers and food doled out.

A warm glow fell through the surrounding woods as the sun dropped away, and as the light faded, voices grew

louder with released joy.

Slowly, finally, the churning in Riony's chest wound down to a soft, anxious thud.

She sat with Dracuni at the edge of the celebrating people. She cleaned her wounds as she watched Lyrrin and Benjin play with their lost friends, doing some strange wide-legged dance with their arms in the air.

She ate a bowl of rice as one of the older women of the shrine enclave rolled a barrel out from one of the huts.

There was a short argument about whether it was ready or not before the barrel was unstoppered and drinks were poured.

Niskina made a face and coughed as she had her first mouthful, and the four young men with her teased her before mirroring her reaction to the drink. They dragged Aishena, scowling, into their cluster and cheered as she downed a cup without flinching.

Riony wiped mud from her sword and boots as Kellae introduced her brother to Dracuni, their voices lost beneath the growingly boisterous crowd. The young boy reached a timid hand to pat the unidragon but snatched it back when Dracuni raised her snout to meet him. Kellae hugged her baby and laughed.

"What is it?" the boy asked, his eyes too large in his skinny face.

"Just a baby dragon," Kellae responded, giving the same reply Riony had always given them.

"I've never seen a baby one before."

"They normally raise them in factories until they are big enough to work. But this is how they look." Riony tried to give her words the weight of someone who knew everything about dragons and couldn't be questioned. Having grown up around Kess, it was easy enough to channel.

"Is it ... tame?" The boy reached a hand again, clearly wary of how Dracuni tracked his movement and sniffed at his fingers.

No matter how Riony had tried to get the dragonling to act still and calm like a tamed dragon, she had become bold around people she knew.

Riony nodded. "The taming spike is under the horn. It's ... decorative."

Most of Myrwa's people and the new group kept well away from Dracuni still, as Riony preferred it, but Kellae had taken to the unidragon and would give her small strips of meat and other treats when they visited.

The young men with Niskina were keeping their eyes on Riony and the unidragon as they toasted again.

Kellae and her brother wandered back to join the others.

Riony winced as she rubbed some weftweed sap over the cut on her eyebrow.

"Took a nasty hit there." One of Niskina's four young men sat down beside Riony.

Bronze-skinned and amber-haired, he looked as if he'd been dipped in honey. He gave her a smile that almost entirely hid his eyes.

She shrugged. "Me and lashes are old acquaintances."

"And what's this little fellow? Treedart?" He leaned forward, directing his gaze at Dracuni, on Riony's other side.

Riony leaned forward as well to block the man's view. "Yeah, treedart. Runt of the litter. Just a rescue we picked up."

The man whistled low. "Just a rescue, she says, as though having a dragon of her own is nothing. Pretty impressive, I'd say."

Riony placed a hand on Dracuni's neck, hoping she took the hint. Dracuni made herself small and still, behaving the most like a tamed dragon that Riony had ever seen.

You worry?

"Gotta do what we can to stay safe out here," Riony said, answering them both.

The man leaned back, smiling again. He was cleaner than most of the other slaves from the mine, in rough leather pants that had been scuffed and resewn in places.

"Riiiiiiiiiiiiiii!" Niskina squealed as though forgetting the rest of her name.

She dumped herself down on the ground in front of

Riony in a burst of tumbling hair and flushed cheeks. Two more young men sat somewhat more gracefully on either side of her.

"We did it, Ri! Look what we did!" Niskina leaned over her legs and squeezed Riony's boot.

"Found some new friends?" Riony tried to raise her eyebrows, but it hurt.

"Oh! This is Renshy." She gestured to the man beside Riony. "And this is—"

"Eydon." A sandy-skinned man with dark hair pulled back into a long ponytail leaned forward to shake Riony's hand.

"Layle," said the man on Niskina's other side. All mousy-colored, his eyes kept darting, alert and wary.

"And Stets," Niskina said, looking behind her. When he wasn't immediately at her back, she propped herself up higher. "There he is. Stets!"

From over beside the crowd, a wall-shaped slab of man looked over the heads of others and nodded back. He returned to conversation with Aishena, an intense focus on her face and lips.

Good luck, friend, Riony thought as Aishena gave the man a glance up and down once, then maintained her usual, skeptical scowl.

"These lovely men helped us take down the guards in the tunnels," Niskina said, leaning into Eydon's shoulder.

Riony could smell the tart, bright tang of unaged wine on her breath.

"Happy to help out," Renshy said, taking a sip from his cup. "I mean, you were freeing us, after all."

"Been there long?" Riony said, eyeing their clothing, not caked in mud and dust the way the other slaves were.

There were weapons on their belts too, but they could have been taken from guards on the way out.

"Only just got brought in an hour before you lot showed up," Layle said with a hushed voice.

"Barely long enough for us to start plotting our own escape." Renshy laughed. "So we're very grateful that you dealt with that for us, because planning is not one of our strengths."

"Can't say it's ours either," Riony said. She gently pushed away an offering of Renshy's cup.

Niskina slapped both her hands down onto the ground. "I have a plan, though. That we keep doing this!"

"Drinking and flirting with more men than you have orifices?" Riony said.

Renshy spit his drink, choking.

Niskina only gave her a daring grin in return. "Saving people! We were like the Rebel Riders today. Fighting back, making change!"

Riony's mouth moved in small twitching shapes. "Okay.

It was pretty great. Maybe not as great as the stories. But we all made it out alive."

Niskina's whole body seemed to soften, sighing out the fire of battle it held. "I used to hate it, you know, hiding underground in the depths. I never wanted to be there, forced into that awful greedy work that killed my mother."

Riony offered a sympathetic look. Niskina had told her once about the lively Rolanian woman who had won a grayglim's heart. It sounded so grandly romantic, how they ran away together, only to end in tragedy during a delving accident.

Niskina poked the dirt in front of her with one finger. "I've wanted to be up here, doing something good for the world, for as long as I could remember. I'm just sorry it took my father dying to get me out."

"I'm so sorry," Eydon said, leaning closer to her again.

Niskina's eyes glistened for a moment, but she shook her melancholy off, maintaining her smile. "It's not like how I thought it would be, up here. I had been so idealistic! But today ... today makes me feel as though we can help make the world into something better."

"Our lives are certainly improved," Renshy said and lifted his cup in a toast.

Music started up near the main fire, and Niskina grabbed the hands of the two men beside her. She rose to her feet, dragging them with her. "Come on. Let's dance!"

Renshy offered a hand to Riony. "I'd love to dance with you."

"Oh. Um. No, thanks. Not really in the mood."

"For dancing? I can stay here with you if you'd like some company?" he replied.

Riony rubbed the back of her head. "Depends on how you define company."

"I told you she wouldn't be interested." Niskina gave her a sly smile. "What she might be interested in is that lovely doe-eyed maiden over by the smokehouse that has been ogling her since we got here."

Riony looked, catching the young woman's gaze. Dark round eyes were rimmed in thick lashes that fluttered down over her cheeks, then rose again to hold Riony's stare. The hint of a smile, bottom lip pressed between teeth. Riony had noticed her on a previous visit. Totally, sweat-inducingly gorgeous.

Heat rushed up Riony's neck.

"Somebody needs to stay sober and on watch." Her voice broke over the words. She swallowed hard and looked at the ground.

The gasp Niskina drew in sounded like it could have exploded her chest. "What is this? All the flirting and lecherous proposals that tumble from your mouth, and when presented with an opportunity for a *real* tumble, you're going shy?"

"It's not that. I just ... I'm—"

"Riony," Niskina rasped, scandalized. "Have you ever even kissed someone before?"

The hot, squirming embrace of shame tangled around Riony's chest as she remembered. "Of course. Plenty."

Her first kiss ... she couldn't forget that.

But since then? She'd never really gotten a chance to do much of anything since taking care of Lyrrin. It wasn't that she didn't want to—she just knew it would be too hard. Too hard to have a relationship like she really wanted.

Instead, she vented that with her big mouth, and when that turned people away? They wouldn't have wanted her anyway. She couldn't have been with them even if they did. It didn't matter.

And now she had Dracuni too. She couldn't think beyond caring for her charges.

"Plenty? I mean *real* kissing. Just like this." Niskina grasped Eydon's collar, tugging him in to meet her mouth.

He leaned into the kiss for a few passionate heartbeats, then both of them chuckled as they pulled away, eyes on each other.

"I'm perfectly aware of what kissing is. It's what you can all do to my ass."

Niskina tsked and tugged at the hands of the two men beside her, gesturing at Renshy to follow them as well. "Come on. Let's go have some fun."

Renshy stood up and offered his cup to Riony one more time before following the others away.

"Nisk?" Riony called out. "Just be careful, okay?"

Niskina blew a raspberry in return and skipped crookedly into the dancing crowd.

Riony leaned back against the wall, watching her go.

It was nice to see some fire in Niskina again, a reawakening of who she'd been before. But she was still being too reckless for Riony's liking. They'd gotten lucky today, in many ways. Things could have gone much, much worse.

But Riony wasn't thinking about the mine anymore.

She closed her eyes, trying to block out the words, the vision, the feelings. She didn't want to remember, but the memory had wedged itself into her head like an axe.

Sitting together on Kess's bed, staring out the window at one of the estate's dragonriders who was kissing a kitchen maid up against a shadowy wall in the courtyard. The way their bodies had moved and entwined with each other ...

Mouth dry, Riony had asked, "What do you think it's like?"

"What?" Kess replied.

"Kissing someone?"

"It sounds gross. Kife said they put their tongues in the other person's mouth. Intolerably disgusting."

"Hmm." Riony leaned on her folded arms, eyes fixed on the couple below, her heart beating fast in her small chest as though thumping a signal drum she wished someone would answer. Not yet ten years old and only guessing at the new feelings within her.

Kess lowered herself from the window ledge back to the bed, leaning on the wall.

There was a pink blush, high on her cheeks, under the constellation of dark spots sprayed across one cheekbone.

She muttered, "But we could ... I don't know ... try it. If you *have* to know."

"I'm not going to kiss you even if you order me to. Even if you whip me." Riony ducked back down too, thumping onto the mattress in a way that made Kess bounce and scowl.

"I'm not ordering you! I was just offering, you ungrateful wretch—something *you* seemed to want. I don't *want* to kiss you!"

"And I don't want to kiss you! You're just trying to trick me, then tell on me to your parents!"

"Forget I offered!"

"You never meant it anyway!" Riony leaned forward, anger flushing her face.

Kess leaned in too, poking Riony with a pointed finger. "Neither did you!"

"Oh, really?"

"Yeah, really!"

"Fine! Kiss me then." Riony dared, heart in her throat, nose brushing Kess's.

And Kess did.

And for a startling, brief moment, it felt warm, and right, and aching.

And then Kess kicked Riony out of her room in a fit of tears and screams.

And then for a week she told all staff that she'd fallen ill and let nobody into her chambers.

And Riony didn't get whipped that week, and she had no idea what she'd done wrong.

Kess's usual psychological torture.

The furious beating in Riony's chest kicked up again, as achingly fast as it had been when fighting the men with lashes. There was nothing quite the same as the burning sting of a lash.

Dracuni had fallen asleep next to Riony when Aishena appeared like a ghost at her side in a swish of silky hair.

She looked at Riony with heavy eyelids. "Did we do the right thing today?"

Riony frowned at the cloying fragrance of alcohol

that had arrived with the woman. It wasn't like Aishena to drink. "The plan didn't exactly play out right, but we all made it out."

"I mean doing that at all, attacking the mine."

"It was risky, but I think we made a lot of people happy." Riony gestured to the partying crowd.

Aishena slipped as she sat down beside Riony, falling against Riony's shoulder and staying there. "I'm not sure … I don't know if we did the right thing. I'm not sure it's what Yoskar would have done."

Her voice hiccupped over her brother's name. The flash of fire reflected on flat glass and the thin bend of wire held tight in Aishena's hand. Glasses. Yoskar's glasses.

Riony didn't have the heart to bring up that Yoskar didn't always choose the right thing over what served him and his family first.

"Are you okay? What did they have in that barrel?" Riony shifted to bring her arm out from between them and straighten Aishena up, and as she did, Aishena leaned into her more, bringing her face close.

"I heard Niskina telling one of the women that you were looking for someone to kiss."

"Okay, firstly, that's Niskina deciding what I want and who I want. And secondly, Niskina is going to be telling everyone the tale of how badly I beat her ass if she doesn't quit it."

Aishena's gaze remained lowered, not looking Riony in the face. "What do you want? Do you still want to kiss me? I know you did once."

A breath shook out of Riony's mouth. "Honestly? I'd given up on having anything more than begrudging mutual tolerance from you."

Aishena flinched. "I'm following commands. I'm trying to do the right thing and do what I'm told. That's what I'm supposed to do. You don't want that? You don't want me?"

"There's wanting. Trust me, there's wanting. But I kind of like seeing that there's some wanting in return, you know?" Riony tucked a finger under Aishena's chin, tilting it up to look into the young woman's eyes to see if there was anything there other than pain.

Gaze still turned away, Aishena lifted herself toward Riony's lips.

Riony gently pushed her away. "Whoa. Hey. I don't think this is the right time to turn any wanting into doing, okay?"

Aishena's face crumpled. "What do I do? Just tell me. I have to get it right. I have to do what I'm told. What do I do? Tell me what to do, and I'll do it."

Riony had never seen Aishena like this, her words slurring and eyes unfocused, chest heaving into inconsolable sobbing. Niskina had always been the one for breaking down into drunken tears and venting all her grief and fury. Aishena had remained solemn and guarded in her mourning as she did in all things.

Where their bags had been piled together near the wall, the glint of metal showed, poking out the top of Aishena's. Her mother's twin blades, that had ended so many lives, that Aishena carried the weight of.

"Nothing." Riony looped her arm around Aishena, bringing her close to her chest and holding her as her body shook. "You don't have to do anything."

Grief poured from Aishena in waves of whispered wails and shuddering sobs, and Riony held her, watching the night and the fire and the dancers and the dusty children and the sleeping baby dragon and the stars far overhead who were watching them in return.

As the heaviness of Aishena's grief soaked into her, Riony's eyes filled too. Which of the stars overhead were her own parents? Her own family lost?

Against the ebony blanket of sky, a bright spark burst, shimmering and flying like a falling star but bright and close.

Blinking her eyes clear, Riony tried to make sense of what she'd seen, but it had already passed.

She wanted to believe it was some message in the sky from her ancestors, but her heart only knew messages of fear and loss, and raged within her again like a cornered animal.

FOURTEEN

"We lied to you." Renshy's expression was flat, guarded, as he and his three friends stood squared off with Riony, Niskina, and Aishena.

Aishena's hand drifted to the athames on her belt, and Riony brushed her arm with her fingers in a message of patience.

"Lied about what?" Riony asked.

Her eyes were still bleary from a restless night, but despite waking to this confrontation, she could still spot Lyrrin, Benjin, and Dracuni nearby, and all seemed well around Myrwa's camp.

"About why we were at the mine, about who we are. We're sorry, but we needed to know we could trust you first."

Niskina's eyes sparkled, and she pulled her lips in, sealing her mouth tight.

"I didn't think you looked much like the others at the mine." Riony again catalogued their weapons, trying to gauge whether she should be drawing hers. "And do you trust us enough now to stop being vague weirdos?"

Stets, the big one, laughed in a deep rumble.

Renshy smiled in that way that hid his eyes and gestured to the refugees and liberated people resting in the cool morning air. "I think we know enough about you now."

"Come on. Tell them," Niskina hissed.

"Do you know what they are talking about?" Riony asked.

Renshy grew solemn again. "We were in the mines on a reconnaissance mission, for the rebellion. And we want to invite you to join us."

Letting out a squeal, Niskina bounced on the spot. "They told me last night!"

"Rebellion, like ... the Rebel Riders?" Riony asked, trying to imagine the men in front of her like the characters in those stories without blushing.

Three of the men looked back blankly, but Layle replied softly, "Not quite. No dragons. Not so much romance. We just organize and do things like what you and your friends pulled off yesterday."

"And with your help, we could do more," Eydon said,

snaking his arm around Niskina's waist.

The way she giggled and cast lazy, longing looks over his mouth made Riony wonder what they'd gotten up to the night before.

Riony's neck still felt sticky from Aishena's dried tears.

Aishena had awoken that morning to her usual cold, bristly self. And had refused to do anything more than apologize for her 'misdirected outburst' then ask that they never speak of it again.

Riony got it. She knew Aishena was just seeking comfort. That she needed it. After so long holding it together. She needed someone there for her when she broke.

She hadn't wanted Riony. Not really.

Sighing, Riony tried to focus on what the men were saying. It seemed important, after all. Riony just felt like there were too many important things to keep track of.

"Sorry, what are you asking? Are you inviting us to join your rebel group?"

Renshy lifted his hands. "It's not our group. We're just a part of something bigger. But we can give you an introduction to people that run the show. They have a base not far from here, in the old glass factory."

Niskina grabbed both of Riony's hands in hers. "This is it! This is our chance to help more people, to really change things!"

Aishena took a step back, bringing herself close by Riony's shoulder.

In a hushed voice, she said, "Our actions yesterday will have drawn attention. I'm not sure if seeking more rebellious associations is a good idea. We have too many enemies after us already."

"I haven't forgotten," Riony replied.

She still flinched at anything that sounded like a wolf howl, even though it had been half a year since they'd last seen Kess.

Aishena's voice was firmer than it had been for a long while. "Then we should lay low. At least for a while. Maybe it's time we finally go to our planned destination."

Their planned destination—Riony's old village. A shiver tugged at her flesh as though it were trying to drag her forward, make her run. That was the feeling she always got when thinking about that place. Even the thought of it made her want to run the other way.

Niskina gave Riony a pleading look.

Shaking her head, Riony said, "It's just a meeting. We should at least go and hear what they have to say. Maybe they can help us stay hidden better, have somewhere even safer for us to go."

Aishena opened her mouth, seemed to think again, then nodded. "As you say."

"Yay!" Niskina cheered.

Renshy clapped his hands together. "Fantastic. Gather up your things, and we'll take you after breakfast."

It didn't take long to pack as none of them had really unpacked after the party the night before.

Myrwa joined Riony to discuss plans for the new arrivals as she chewed on some day-old flatbread. They stood together, looking over the small community within the ring of standing stones.

Children lay wrapped in blankets on the ground in small clusters, but some of the older newly freed were up and talking with the settlers, helping with cleaning and cooking.

"They've all decided to stay," Myrwa said.

"Even the undercity kids?" Riony replied, trying to identify them amongst the sleeping children, but they were all identical dusty-haired bundles of fabric and limbs.

But then a flash of Lyrrin running by drew her gaze to a few children who were awake and playing near the makeshift huts. There were hugs shared and waves of goodbye-for-now, then the children went back to their game, crawling around on the ground.

"They said they don't have anyone waiting for them underground. They want to be in the sunlight again."

Riony could see it in their faces as they wriggled on their bellies like worms, touching the grass that sprung

up around the paving with giggling awe. There was joy there and hope, like she'd never seen on their faces when in the orphans' den.

"Is that okay for you? I didn't mean to have you look after everyone."

"I'm not. We all look after each other here. And it's only for now. Some seemed excited by the idea that other shrines are safe and settled as well. That they could travel and start their life again at the closest shrine to their original homes. But we can help people move around more on your next visit, yes? I can see you're off again already."

"Yeah." Riony frowned as she adjusted the pack on her back and the sword strapped beside it. "Do you know anything about an old glass factory nearby?"

Myrwa nodded. "A couple of braver types have been there when out foraging. Good place for it. It's not far."

"Haven't seen anyone else around that area?"

"I haven't been myself. My legs don't run fast enough to risk getting caught outside the shrine. But no, nobody has mentioned anything."

When Riony told this to Niskina on their way out of camp, Niskina just scoffed. "It's a hidden rebel base. They're going to stay hidden if they don't know the people poking around."

"I guess so."

Myrwa's group had been at the shrine for months now. If these rebels were good people, wouldn't they have made some effort to introduce themselves, being so close by? Maybe do something to help the new settlement grow and stay safe? Or even trade with them?

Or maybe Niskina was right and they just needed to remain secretive to protect themselves and what they did. Still, Riony checked her access to her sword, undoing one of the straps so she could draw it faster if needed.

They had only been walking a short time when the forest ended abruptly, replaced with low scrub that had recently been burned, leaving it brittle and blackened. And ahead, beside a quarry scraped clean to the bones of the earth, was the remains of the factory.

Renshy led the way toward it. "The entrance is inside the main building there."

A couple of smaller side houses seemed to cower in the shade of the larger one. They leaned against the massive walls of metal beams and charred masonry that formed the main building, like ducklings beneath their mother.

Almost the entire top half of the largest structure was made of glass, but those windows were high and fogged with soot. The walls were solid and unbroken, and Riony couldn't see inside.

Their steps crunched through the tangle of twisted

roots and scattered leaves, kicking up the scent of smoke and sulfur.

An uneasy tension knotted in her gut. Her footsteps faltered as she gazed at the tall steel door, standing ajar before her.

Aishena made a small sucking breath sound.

"What is it?" Riony whispered to the woman at her shoulder.

Aishena met her gaze, her eyes worried. But then she shook her head. "Nothing."

"You don't like this either, huh?" Riony had hoped it was just her being paranoid. But as much as Aishena refused to admit it, she'd had excellent instincts in the past.

"The kids and dragon should wait out here," Riony said.

Whatever they were walking into, she didn't need to bring them with her on the off chance this was going to be safe. She didn't want whoever was in there to see Dracuni yet either.

As long as Renshy was telling the truth that they didn't have any dragons, then Riony and Aishena could deal with a few thugs if they were about to get robbed.

Lyrrin pouted. "You're leaving us out again!"

Dracuni, who had continued doing her best ever performance of playing tame, rose up tall as well. *Not want to stay.*

"This is just going to be a boring grown-up chat, okay? Stay out here and keep watch for us. That will be more exciting."

Benjin stamped Yoskar's staff on the ground in front of him. "We should get to meet the rebels too. We should get to have a say in what's going on."

Renshy held the door open as Niskina and Eydon went in. "I'm sure it's fine for us all to go in. The people we're meeting don't mind having kids around."

Riony held her little sister's glare, pleading with her to acquiesce. "The kids and dragon stay out here. That's final, or we're turning around right now and Niskina will never get to live her dreams."

"Fine. It looks smelly in there anyway," Lyrrin said, sneering at the moldy darkness around the base of the walls.

"Layle," Renshy said. "Stay out here with them. Make sure they stay safe."

The man gave a casual salute, alert and stern as he turned to watch over the children and Dracuni.

Aishena gave Riony a grateful nod, then stepped with her into the building, with Stets at their back.

Riony's eyes adjusted to the gloomy interior.

The huge space was divided in two by a half-length partition wall, and the area they entered first had rows of cages along one side, lined up and aimed toward domed furnaces.

Checking them with a focused stare for signs of prisoners or signs that those cages were their intended destination, Riony realized they had been cages for dragons.

A couple of the narrow stocks still held the lifeless bodies of the dragons who'd worked there, squeezed into the space and draped in chains. The desiccated corpses didn't look very old, scales and draped skin clinging tight over their bones.

Were the dragons just left there to die when this place closed down?

Riony shivered. The whole building seemed to have been left to ruin without any care for what had been left behind. It should have at least been burned, to get rid of the corpses that the shadowdragon could raise.

The carelessness infuriated her. But she'd seen it before. It infuriated her *because* she'd seen it before.

Stacked across the other side, piles of old wooden tools and baskets burst with the rippling shapes and round caps of fungus in vibrant oranges and dull browns. The air was thick with their cloying, earthy scent.

The skitter of movement caught Riony's alert eyes. Dozens of tiny mouse deer grazed amongst the fungus on their stick-thin, dainty hooves. A few startled at the presence of humans, dashing away into a maze of rotting crates and barrels. Others sniffed the air, then put their

slender heads down again.

Shattered glass refuse littered the floor, glittering and sharp like all the stars had fallen out of the sky. Above them, the ceiling was all glass, a few panels broken, but that didn't account for all the shards.

It must have been wastage from the factory itself. Jagged edges dug through the soles of Riony's boots as she stepped inside.

Stets closed the door behind them.

"This is it," Renshy called out.

"Where's the entrance?" Niskina asked. "Are they going to come out and meet us?"

There was a long, soft sliding sound from behind the partition. Something large, in motion. Shadows shifted and glass crunched and from behind the wall, the head of a huge, purple dragon emerged, snarling at them, fire flickering between its teeth.

And beside that dragon, Kess rode in on her wolf.

FIFTEEN

Basic thugs, Riony could handle. A secret rebel group who might have decided they weren't on the same side, she could handle.

But Kess, with a dragon? Kess, and the person who was *on* that dragon?

A clammy, chilled sweat rushed over Riony.

Movement fluttered all around as the little mouse deer made themselves vanish into any nook available.

"What's going on?" Niskina asked, turning to Eydon beside her, as though he might say this was some mistake, that he didn't know these wolf-and-dragon-riding ambushers.

Instead, he lunged forward, grabbing her arms and pinning them behind her.

There was a scuffle to Riony's left as Renshy grabbed Aishena.

Riony's hand was halfway to her sword when Stets had her pinned as well, locked in his massive arms.

"What are you doing?" Niskina cried, struggling and wrenching against her captor.

"We're getting one hell of a bounty," Eydon said, close to her ear but loud enough for everyone to hear. "We were looking for someone else in the mines, then you lot landed in our lap—in more ways than one."

Niskina stilled and went pale. "You left. You left during the night. Is this where you went? To plan this? How could you!"

"Pretty easily, actually," Eydon replied. "It didn't take much to get you away from the Alderkin gateway to somewhere we could grab you. Rebels, ha!"

Renshy swore, and there was a flurry of limbs as Aishena broke free from his grasp.

"Give it up before I burn you on the spot." Kife leaned forward in the saddle of his dragon, and the beast directed its mouth her way.

Kife. His presence made Riony's stomach churn.

Riony had always wished that he wasn't still plaguing the world with his presence, that some deadly accident had befallen him on a dragonrider mission long before now.

But there he was, still alive, looking far too excited by the idea of burning a human alive.

What had Kess told her twisted brother? About Dracuni? About her blood? Keeping away from Kess and Griskin was one thing, but now that she'd teamed up with a psychotic dragonrider, it was going to be so much harder.

Riony cursed herself. They'd gotten too complacent. Things had been going so well and they hadn't seen Kess for so long, hadn't had bounty hunters recognize the Hjelzahn siblings for so long. Riony had walked into the factory half expecting trouble but believing she could handle it.

And then there was Kess, bringing a dragon to a knife fight.

Aishena stilled, lifting her hands back off the hilts of her athames.

"You can't burn this one." Renshy yanked the coil of cave silk rope from Aishena's belt and pulled her hands behind her back to bind them. "Remember the deal."

"You made a deal with *these two*?" Riony laughed at him. "And I thought I was dumb."

"Nobody is disputing that, Pony." Kess had the kind of triumphant look on her face that made Riony's hand itch to slap it.

"After all this time without you around, I thought you'd given up, Kessara." Riony tested Stets's hold on her,

214

finding no give. "Is this what you've been keeping busy with? Selling us out to *him*?"

Riony flicked her chin at Kife, who simply seemed amused by the scene.

Then she gave Kess the most shaming look she could muster. "I mean, you've done a whole load of dumb and evil things in the past, but this is on a whole new level of idiotic malice. Congratulations on the personal best, but you know he's going to kill you, right?"

Griskin gave a grumbling moan, his eyes and nose weeping. Kess leaned forward and petted him casually. "And wouldn't you be happy if he did? Saves you the trouble."

Renshy finished tying Aishena, cut the rope, and threw it across to Stets. The bulky man began wrapping Riony's wrists behind her back.

She kept her chin up, an uneven smirk across her bared teeth. "I've got the feeling I'd be dead by that point and unfortunately wouldn't be able to celebrate. This is the guy who tried to kill you already. What are you thinking?"

Despite the triumphant sneer on Kess's face, somehow she seemed smaller than usual. She hunched close to Griskin, almost hidden in his fur. "Don't pretend you care. I told you I'd do anything to get what I wanted off you, and so here we are."

Kife clapped his hands together, the slap echoing

through the large space. "All right, now where is this creature she's supposed to have?"

Still outside. Still with a chance to get away. Riony hoped Dracuni and the kids had heard Niskina's earlier cries and were already gone, but she could still sense Dracuni nearby. There were no spikes of fear yet, just a low edge of concern, as though she was picking up on Riony's stress.

Riony breathed deep to belt out a warning.

Stets slapped a meaty hand over her mouth and pressed a sharp length of metal to her throat.

Riony stilled. With her pack and sword still strapped on her back, her arms were bent at a painful angle to where her wrists were tied together. She tried to shift them and rub the rope against the blade, but she couldn't get the angle right.

"Don't worry," Renshy said as he pulled a leather pouch from his pocket. "Your critter is just out there with a couple of kids. Layle can handle it. You'll have your bounty in a moment."

"Those kids are little savages," Kess replied. "Don't underestimate them."

"I'll go and help bring them in," Eydon said, finishing off the knot around Niskina's hands.

Her shoulders were slumped, but she turned toward him fiercely when he let her go. She kicked him in the back of the knee as he walked away, making him stumble.

"Watch yourself!" he growled back as he steadied himself. "We've got no bounty to collect on you, so we can go either way on whether we keep you or not!"

"Bounty hunters? Is that all you are? I should have known you were such cowards. You handle a woman's body like one." Niskina leaned into the words, spitting them in fury, but there were tears on her cheeks.

Sparks, she wanted this to be real so badly. And now we're all screwed.

Aishena, hands tied and held tight in Renshy's grip, said, "Whatever bounty is out on me and my brother, I'll pay more. We can work it out. We—"

Renshy pressed the pouch he was holding over her mouth and nose. Aishena gasped and wheezed, fighting for a moment before her eyes rolled and she slumped, leaning into Renshy's hold. Her legs buckled beneath her.

Morass mercy? Riony glared daggers at Kess. Had she given it to them?

Renshy juggled his grip on Aishena, keeping her pinned to his chest like a precious trophy. He grinned at Kife. "All right now. We brought you the redhead with the strange dragonling, all as agreed last night. I'd like to see that payment we also agreed on now."

"Get out there and get us the dragonling first!" Kess

ordered. "I'd do it myself but I have to keep my eyes on this one. She's trouble."

Riony winked at her over Stets's hand.

Kife narrowed his eyes as he looked between the two of them. "Relax, little sis. We can deal with these three, then go grab the others ourselves. It's a couple of kids and a hatchling. What are they going to do? Even if they run, we can catch them. It'll make it more fun too."

"It's *not tamed*, brother. Have you ever met an untamed dragon before?"

"Hold up. It's not tamed?" Renshy barked. "Eydon, leave that one and go help Layle bring the others in."

Seeming hesitant to let go of Niskina again, Eydon sneered then stepped back from her quickly, dodging the boot she stomped at his shin.

"Come on. Let's wrap this up," Kife said, pulling a jingling pouch from the bags on the dragon's saddle. "You'll get this when we have the dragonling. And you can keep the Hjelzahns too, for whatever they are worth. The other three can be disposed of."

"Eydon seems to have a soft spot for the pretty one," Renshy said, and Eydon gave a noncommittal grunt as he crunched across toward the door. "But might as well get rid of the big one now. Do it, Stets."

Riony winced as Stets's grip around her mouth tightened

and he rumbled a low chuckle.

Run. Run. RUN! She closed her eyes and screamed inside her head as loud as she could, hoping Dracuni could hear, trying to pierce the distance with her thoughts.

There was a shimmer of feeling in return, a ripple of confusion and worry.

Then Stets shoved Riony hard from behind, toppling her forward.

She landed on her knees and gasped as shards of glass jabbed through the thick leather of her delver pants. The tip of her sword, strapped to her back, hit the ground too, sending her forward again. She went down, hands tied, unable to stop the face-first fall onto the glass-barbed ground.

She turned her chin and gritted her teeth as she landed. Sharp points of agony sprang up all across her chest and cheek. Riony tried to bite off her cry, to not give Kess or Kife any pleasure in seeing her hurt, but it felt as though she'd been struck by a hundred daggers, slicing and needling their way into her skin.

She whimpered, and the opening of her mouth scraped more shards over her chin and lips as she worked hard to draw breath.

"Riony!" Niskina yelled and charged forward, shouldering Stets.

He brushed Niskina off, sending her stumbling, careening sideways in an effort to not fall into the glass herself.

"I like that one's spirit," Kife said, jingling the coin pouch. "Maybe I'll buy her too."

"You couldn't afford me!" Niskina spat back, setting her feet firmly and looking ready to charge.

Behind them, Eydon hovered near the door, seeming unsure whether he needed to get Niskina under control again or continue outside as ordered.

Riony squirmed, trying to get her knees under her and push up off the biting ground, and every movement cut her more. Before she could even twist onto her side, Stets's foot struck out, cracking into her ribs. He worked the point of his toes between her and her backpack and pressed down.

Glass fractured beneath Riony, grinding through her shirt into her skin. A racking wail of pain came unstoppable from her chest.

"Come on, Stets. Stop mucking around," Renshy said.

"Hmm, fine." He grunted.

The boot was removed, then was replaced by the crushing weight of Stets's entire body as he straddled Riony's back, sitting on her backpack. He leaned over her, chuckling softly every time his movements made the glass beneath them crackle.

Fingers wrapped into the hair on the back of Riony's scalp, then squeezed tight, wrenching her head off the ground in a painful arc.

Niskina gasped, a flurry of cries and prayers coming from her mouth. She stepped forward again, but a turn of the dragon's head toward her kept her in place.

Slivers of glass clattered as they fell from Riony's face, stinging as the heavier pieces slid free. Blood dripped into Riony's eye and she tried to blink it out. She stared across the ground, wanting to scream at Kess, to spit and spite her, to say something so devastating that it could take some of this victory away from her. But Riony couldn't even breathe.

Kess stared back as Stets pressed his dagger again to Riony's throat.

Then Kess flinched and averted her eyes.

It was the smallest thing. The briefest flicker of humanity, the kind of slip Kess never usually made, like screaming *Riony* back in that revenant-filled cave. It was the closest thing to a kindness Riony would ever know from her.

And she tried to accept that in the moment before she died. But it didn't feel like enough.

"Wait!" Kife snapped. His eyes weren't on Riony but on Kess. He smiled, and there was no kindness in his expression.

Stets remained in his crushing position. Riony desperately tried to drag in some air around the blade at her neck.

"This is no good," Kife said. He leaned back in his saddle, folding his arms. "We can't let some random thug kill an Uf'Heithorn. It just doesn't feel right, don't you think, sis?"

"What are you talking about?" Kess replied in a jittery, scathing tone.

Riony felt no comfort from Kife's words. Whatever he was planning, it wasn't going to save her. He was going to find a way to make this hurt even more.

"I mean, she was your pet, after all." Kife's eyes glittered mischievously, and he gave Kess a mocking, doting look. "*You* should be the one who gets to put her down."

SIXTEEN

Lyrrin thought she heard something from inside the building. A crunching sound, a cry.

"Did you hear that?" she asked.

Benjin turned his eyes upward. A carrion bird circled high above and warbled a howl, echoing the sound.

"Ugh." Lyrrin squinted into the morning light at it, willing it to leave so that its wolflike howls didn't set Riony off into overprotective mode again.

Although she's still leaving us out anyway.

Dracuni sat still and calm, watching Layle pace in front of them, with only a flick of her tufted tail betraying her impatience.

Lyrrin ran a hand over one of her soft ears. "Shouldn't

be much longer. They'll probably come and get us once they decide it's safe."

Dracuni huffed softly.

Benjin stood with his back to the building, Yoskar's staff held before him, staring out across the scrub toward the forest, at least making an effort to be on guard. But Lyrrin knew Riony had only left them outside to keep them safe.

It made sense. They shouldn't be letting too many people see Dracuni, if they could help it. But it still annoyed her that if something wasn't safe to start with, why was Riony going in at all? Or why go in with fewer people to help?

A rough snort came from Dracuni, and she rose in a start onto her hind legs, eyes wide.

"Hey! What's your dragon doing? What are you telling it to do?" Layle said. "Move away from it!"

He put a hand on Lyrrin's shoulder, giving her a shove to the side so he was between her, Benjin, and the dragonling. "I don't want to get burned by kids mucking around with a dragon."

"She's not going to hurt you." *Unless you deserve it,* Lyrrin thought, cringing at the place the man had touched her, pushing her like she was a piece of furniture. "I think she's worried about something."

A cry, muffled by the wall of the building, came from behind them.

It was Riony. Lyrrin knew it. And Riony never screamed like that. Not unless she was really, really hurt. Lyrrin's heart raced into a gallop.

"What's—?" Benjin's mouth clamped closed again, his question answered before he asked it.

The mousy man had drawn his sword in a swish of steel. His ever-roaming eyes narrowed, darting between Benjin and Lyrrin. "Come on then. Time to head in with the others. Go on, you two."

"What about our dragon?" Lyrrin said, refusing to move. "What are you going to do with her?"

Layle didn't even glance back at Dracuni. "It will come along as commanded too. Does it do voice commands yet? Tell it to go inside."

"I'm not telling her to do anything for you." Lyrrin glared at the man from under her hood.

The man tsked and stepped toward her, sword raised. "We don't need you, girl. Only the Hjelzahn boy and the dragonling. I'll work out how to make the tame-brained thing move without you."

Lyrrin pulled a face at him and said, "Except that our dragon isn't tamed."

Layle only had a moment for realization to hit him, to try to turn back and put his eyes on the dangerous creature behind him, but it was too late.

Dracuni snapped her jaw closed around one of his ankles. He cried out, hopping and trying to pull away.

With a flick of her snout, Dracuni tossed the man onto the ground in a puff of soot and dust.

Wood and sparkling crystal swung through the air and Benjin thunked the end of Yoskar's staff into the man's head where he lay. Layle lolled to the side, unmoving, but still breathing.

Dracuni growled, giving her head a shake before letting the man's ankle go.

"Sparks, these guys *were* leading us into a trap!" Benjin grumbled. "Aish thought so. She told me on the way, but I didn't believe her."

"Come on. We need to see what's going on in there." Lyrrin scanned the area.

They couldn't go through the front door without immediately being seen. Beckoning Benjin and Dracuni to follow her, she ran over and climbed up a couple of old wooden crates and onto the roof of one of the small buildings leaning against the large factory.

They were at the level of the first row of sooty windows there, and Lyrrin hurried to the first broken one and peered through.

The first thing she saw was the dragon. It was huge. Bigger than the ones who had come to the slavers' camp

and tried to carry her away in a cage. A heavy purple beast with a wide chest and dark wings.

It had a rider, propped casually on top, and beside them was Kess on her wolf.

Benjin leaned next to her. "This is bad. Really bad."

"They always leave us out, and then we have to go and save them anyway!" Lyrrin replied.

One of the young men who had brought them there was holding Aishena, only partially upright, in his arms.

Niskina had her wrists tied, standing off to the side, cringing away from the sharp teeth of the dragon's maw hovering near her.

And in the middle, the biggest man leaned over Lyrrin's sister. He grabbed her by the back of the head and her bound hands, lifting her up off the ground, then dropping her onto her knees.

He kept one hand clasped at the back of her head, holding her up by the hair like a puppet and making her face Kess, who stalked toward them on Griskin.

The wolf had leather wrappings around his four paws, protecting him from the glass that was spread all across the floor. They'd clearly had plenty of time to plan this ambush.

Even from a distance Lyrrin could see blood, and lots of it, dripping from Riony's arms and face and soaking the front of her shirt.

Dracuni let out a quiet whine.

Lyrrin felt it, too. She wanted to moan and scream and run in there throwing fists, but there was a *dragon*, a full-grown dragon and rider. She put a hand on Dracuni's neck to still them both.

Kess pulled a throwing knife, and her voice echoed up from the expanse below. "I'll finish it fast for you. Where do you want it—eye, neck, or heart?"

"You left out the best option," Riony replied. "Up your own ass."

The third man was near the exit, pausing to watch for a moment, his hands on the door.

"We've got to do something, fast." Benjin leaned forward, checking the gap between the jagged pieces of the broken window as though seeing if he would fit. More crates were stacked up and covered in fungus just beneath them.

Lyrrin nodded but backed away from the window.

She whispered, "What can we do? There's a dragon in there! I only have one flash stone left, and it's really small. I could maybe hit Kess or the guy holding Riony, but that doesn't deal with the dragon."

"You don't have to take out the dragon," Benjin said. "It's tamed. You only have to take out the rider!"

Lyrrin looked again, taking in the high walls and glass ceiling and Kess pulling her arm back to throw the blade

that would kill her sister. They needed a distraction and a way to disable the dragon.

Lyrrin got her sling into her hand, a stone from her pocket loaded into it, then she slid forward on her belly through the broken window so her whole top half was hanging out into the air.

She spun the sling and let the shot fly.

A sheet of glass above the dragon shattered, cracking like sharp thunder, then falling in a jingle of bells.

Her aim was slightly off. The shards hailed down over the dragon's tail.

"What in the razed earth?" The rider turned in his seat, sheltering his eyes with a hand as fragments bounced near him. He craned his neck up, searching for the cause.

"Watch out!" Kess held her throw as Griskin sniffed the air, his nose wet and snuffly.

Lyrrin had another shot on its way, and it landed true, directly above the dragonrider.

Glass fell like crystal daggers. The rider dove from his saddle and tumbled under a wing to take shelter.

The dragon didn't flinch, didn't move as glass plinked and scattered from its scales. No longer controlled, it sat numb and dazed.

"That's it!" Benjin cheered. He grabbed Lyrrin's hand as she turned around on the windowsill and lowered onto

the crates below. "Go!"

Lyrrin landed in a puff of spores and dust, stinging her eyes and nose, but she kept moving, climbing down the stacked boxes and barrels.

There were two thumps behind her as Benjin and Dracuni followed, wobbling the rotting wood.

Without the threat of being bitten in half, Niskina was first to move, charging the big man holding Riony. She crashed into his side, hard.

His grip on Riony must have slipped because in a roar, she thrust up onto her feet.

Turning back from watching the falling glass and de-seated rider, Kess swore and sent her knife whipping through the air.

Riony bent at the waist, ducking low as the knife flew toward her neck.

In a soft thud, it stuck deep into the flesh of the man behind her, right below his Adam's apple.

Blood spurted, and the man clawed blindly for the blade, tried to press against the freely flowing blood and hold it all in. He dropped down onto one knee, then toppled like a felled tree onto the ground in a crunch.

"Stets!" The man holding Aishena almost dropped her as he fumbled for his sword.

Benjin came in swinging, Yoskar's staff lit up red with

a burn rune. "Let my sister go!"

The staff cracked against the sword, sparks flying in the dim, dusty light.

Niskina was at his side, hands still bound behind her back. The man who had been going outside must have seen that the reasons he was going out were all inside now anyway and rushed toward Niskina with his own sword drawn.

Lyrrin reached Riony's side. A curved sliver of glass jutted from Riony's cheek, and all over her chest and shoulders, fragments glittered between flowing crimson. Lyrrin shuddered and her eyes went hot. She scrunched up her nose to fight off tears.

"Cutting athame!" Riony hissed.

"This is faster!" Lyrrin already had a glove off and clawed one of her sharp nails down through the rope around her sister's hands. It tore and snapped, the frayed, blood-stained sections falling free.

With a moaning sigh, Riony stretched her arms. She tried to reach for her sword, but Kess already had more daggers drawn.

Then Kess lifted her head in a scream. "You wild monster! Get off me!"

Dracuni was there, snout snapped shut around Kess's toes.

Griskin circled, trying to turn back and bite the dragonling circling around behind him, teeth locked on Kess's boot.

"Dracuni!" Lyrrin cried.

"Free the others." Riony gave Lyrrin a short, worried glance before she ran headlong at the wolf and his rider.

She cleared the distance and leaped forward as Kess aimed a dagger at the unidragon, tackling Kess off Griskin's back and sliding across the floor in a jangle of glass shards.

"I should have killed you the second you stepped into this building!" Kess screamed, gurgling with fury.

Riony had her pinned, straddled over her, hands holding her arms down. "Then why wait for your sadistic brother to order you to do it?"

Lyrrin hurried to Niskina and Benjin, who warded the two men there away with Yoskar's staff.

There was a snarl and a growl as Griskin pounced, trying to get to Kess, and Dracuni blocked his way. The glass beneath Dracuni's claws shimmering with spots of opalescent blood. Lyrrin bit her lip and it trembled between her teeth.

The dragonrider remained under the dragon's wing, picking shards off his armor almost casually. He made no effort to rush back into his saddle, a moment Lyrrin was hurrying to beat as she sliced Niskina's bonds as well.

Instead, the rider glared out over the combatants and shouted, "Fire!"

The dragon's purple jaw dropped open, its chest heaved,

and golden light burst from its throat.

A ball of fire shot out, roaring across the room. The dragon hadn't aimed, hadn't turned its head toward a target—just loosed the fireball directly the moment it was ordered. It flew past Lyrrin and Niskina, barely an arm's reach away. The searing heat was gone in an instant before it collided with the row of cages across the other side of the room.

It hit like an explosion, setting fire to everything around it. A stampede of tiny deerlike animals emerged from hiding places and rushed for a way out.

"Sparks! He's going to kill everybody!" Riony rolled off Kess and onto her feet.

She glared between the rider and his dragon, as though trying to gauge how to take either of them down while also keeping watch of Kess, gasping for breath where she'd been left.

Riony drew her sword, activated it, and stood over Kess, and for a moment, Lyrrin was sure she was going to bring that sword down and finish off the wolf rider once and for all.

Then Dracuni was there too, looping around Riony's legs and mewling.

"I have to!" Riony barked back. "If we run now, they're only going to keep chasing us! Forever!"

With a powerful huff, Dracuni rose up on her hind legs and pushed Riony back with her front paws.

As the dragonling's iridescent silvery claws touched to Riony's chest, she gasped, "No!"

And then she lit up. As though flooded with moonlight from within, Riony glowed.

Everybody stilled, drawn to the strange sight.

There was a *tink*, *tink*, *tink* of glass shards sliding free from her healing skin and dropping to the floor. Freely bleeding gashes closed. Riony stared back at the dragonrider and the young men who'd brought them there with a terrified fury.

"Raze it all, Kess. You were telling the truth!" the dragonrider crowed, wide-eyed as he raked his gaze over Riony and Dracuni.

"That thing, it bleeds silvernix?" Renshy's head was shaking as he looked at the trail of immeasurable wealth Dracuni's bleeding claws had left behind her. "Eydon! Come on!"

Renshy let Aishena fall limp from his grasp. Whatever she had been worth to him before was nothing compared to Dracuni.

Niskina rushed in and managed to catch Aishena's ragdoll body before she hit the glass too.

"You're not getting anything from us!" Benjin growled,

swinging the staff at the men as they tried to push past him.

Renshy brought his own sword clashing down against it, striking hard, no longer trying to capture Benjin, no longer playing it safe. Eydon dodged through beside them, running toward Dracuni.

They knew about Dracuni's blood now. All of them. The rider, these men. They would all want the unidragon. A knot of cold fear tangled in Lyrrin's chest. Kess was back on Griskin and the rider was redirecting his dragon's head with taps on its jaw.

Panic crept like frost over Lyrrin's skin. They needed something, something big to get out of there.

Lyrrin shouted, "Eyes!"

Benjin stepped back, covering his face as Lyrrin's final flash stone landed in front of him and went off.

Renshy swore and stumbled back, still swinging his sword wildly.

"Give me Yoskar's staff," Lyrrin cried, arms reaching out.

"What? What for?" Benjin pulled it back closer to himself.

"Fire!" the dragonrider shouted again.

A crackling sphere of fire hurtled right toward them.

Lyrrin and Benjin threw themselves down in a crouch. Eydon, between them and the dragon, wasn't fast enough, and the flame passed right through him. He screamed for only a moment, then fell, still burning.

Benjin hissed as one side of his head caught alight, the short hair getting singed. Lyrrin patted it out with her gloved hand, gasping at the acrid smoke.

"Please, the staff," Lyrrin said again. "Trust me. We have to do something to stop the dragon and rider long enough to get away from here."

Benjin, frowning and teary, handed Yoskar's staff to her.

With one hand still ungloved, Lyrrin worked quickly, scratching additional runes over the ones already there in the crystals embedded in the wood. She added burn onto light, and burst onto burn, and return onto cut, using every combination she'd tried before and many she hadn't, and activating every sigil as she went.

The staff hummed with power as half a dozen crystals activated at once with even more runes.

Getting back to her feet, Lyrrin hurled the staff across the room.

"What are you doing?" Benjin gasped.

Lyrrin's heart pounded as she watched the staff clatter to a stop at the feet of the dragon. "Saving us, I hope, or blowing everything up. Come on. Run!"

The first explosion was bigger than Lyrrin had expected. There was a whomping boom that seemed to lift and throw everything in the room for a split second, then a gust of air rushed all around as Lyrrin and Benjin ran for the door.

A flurry of curse words came from the dragonrider as the staff shot up into the air, popping and flashing and zipping around, and then another larger burst went off, loud as a lightning strike.

Above the dragon, every window shattered and fell.

The dragonrider and Kess, on Griskin, ran for cover beneath the dragon's chest. As the shining slivers rained down, carnage cascaded across the ceiling, section after section breaking and falling, chasing Riony and Dracuni across the room.

Riony caught up with Niskina and took Aishena from her, scooping her into her arms as they ran.

Lyrrin pushed the door, holding the heavy metal open. "Come on!"

Dracuni ran out, followed by the others.

Benjin turned back, his face red and twisted as he watched the staff crackle and snap into pieces, burning and blasting apart, then he ran out too.

Out in the burned scrub, they kept running, feet pounding until they hit the forest.

Benjin stopped there, breathing so hard his body shook all over.

"You destroyed it! Yoskar's staff, it's gone!" Benjin yelled at Lyrrin.

"I ... I'm sorry." Lyrrin's mouth went dry. She had; she'd destroyed Yoskar's staff. She hadn't really thought about what that meant, in the heat of the moment, only that it might save them. But Benjin looked at her with such fury it cut right to her heart.

"We have to keep going. We have to get to the shrine!" Riony shouted back.

Aishena hung heavy and still in her arms.

Niskina gasped, her eyes on the glass factory behind them.

Lyrrin turned to see Kess and Griskin emerge from the door. The wolf and rider raced their way.

SEVENTEEN

Kess pulled a splinter of dark blue glass from the leather of her bracer as Griskin navigated them through the woods at a caning pace.

She was lucky it hadn't gone through to her skin.

She'd seen exactly how ripped up someone could be by those broken shards.

There was so much blood—so much blood on her.

Kess saw flashes of Riony—Pony—kneeling on that glittering ground, swathed in red. Then of her lying on the frozen floor in the cave, washed in a scarlet sea. Flashes of her bloodied back, struck by a lash.

The intolerable woman treated suffering as a sport.

And when the dragonling had pressed her bleeding

paws to Riony, she hadn't ordered it, hadn't asked for it—instead she'd said *no*. Was she not using the creature for healing? What kind of unblessed fool was she?

And what kind of fool am I for not putting Pony out of her misery sooner?

Why, when Riony knelt on the floor in front of her, cut through with agony and even still defiant, why did Kess's heart achingly contract? She had no room to feel anything—not pity, not compassion, not doubt—when it would block her from her destiny.

Still more fragments of glass scratched against Kess's back, caught in the thick vest armor. She'd have to deal with them, and her traitorous emotions, later.

Now, she had to catch her prey. They were just ahead of her through the trees, but they'd almost reached the shrine settlement.

She'd stalked around the edges of it the evening before but couldn't see a way to get in and take Dracuni with so many people around, partying through the night. So instead, she and the bounty hunters had made a plan to lure those they wanted out.

A rock whizzed past Kess's head, slung from Pony's "sister." Where had Pony picked up that little feral?

With the standing stones in sight, a cry went up amongst the settlers at the incoming chase. Some fled and hid, but

more stood their ground, bringing Pony's group into them.

Pony skidded to a stop before the wall of people. The Hjelzahn girl was cradled in her arms the way she had once carried Kess. Kess shuddered at the memory of those same arms around her, and she sneered.

"Help her through." Riony handed the limp weight of the woman to a person in the crowd.

Then Pony turned to face Kess, glowing sword ready to swing.

Griskin came to a halt too, growling at the crowd blocking the way.

"Want to rumble, Kess?" Pony asked with a smirk, angling her sword so it glinted in the late morning sunlight. "I'll have you on your back again in no time."

"Not before I stick you with my knives." Kess prepared to throw one of the thin bone blades, but an older woman stepped in front of the monstrous redhead.

She said over her shoulder to Pony, "Leave, child. Be safe."

Through a gap in the people Kess saw the gateway light up. She cursed, angling to get a better view of the glowing symbols.

Pony gave her one more look, lips twitching, then disappeared through the crowd as well.

"Coward!" Kess screamed, her voice breaking over the word.

Another rock clattered down beside Griskin's booted paws. Not from Lyrrin's sling, but from a different child, hurling it with their hand.

"Go on, girl. Get out of here. Whatever your reason for chasing them, you won't find understanding here." The old woman stood boldly before Griskin, the shawl over her arms swaying as she made a shooing motion.

Another rock landed close. Barely a pebble but enough to make Kess flinch.

The way they were looking at her, glaring shame with piercing eyes ... as though *she* were the bad guy.

They never could understand. They didn't know she was doing everything, anything she had to do to become someone who could do good for the world. So she could be a dragonrider, to help save people just like them.

She was doing what she had to in order to become a hero. Wasn't she?

Kess couldn't think of anything she could say to make them understand that, not fast enough. Not when they were already on Pony's side for some unblessed reason.

They didn't know Kess was trying to do the right thing. Yes, she wanted to be a dragonlord again, and a dragonrider, for respect, but also to do the good work that dragonriders do.

The light of the gateway within the shrine went out.

Pony and the dragonling had escaped again.

But Kess smiled. Because she heard the approach of beating wings.

Now these people would see that she was on the side of a dragonrider! That she was on the right side, the good side.

Faces turned upward as the sound grew clearer, and Kess watched them to see the awe in their expressions she felt when she saw a dragonrider fly.

But as the dragon's shadow passed over the people, they shrieked and ran. Some fled into the flimsy huts, others into the stone structure of the shrine, and a few out into the dangerous woods. Only a handful remained rooted in place, terror on their faces fighting with a furious determination.

"He's on your side," Kess whispered, more to herself, as she gaped at their reaction.

Why were they running? Why were they scared of a person who had probably saved hundreds of people just like them from the revenant plague?

Weren't they grateful?

Kife brought his dragon down. There wasn't enough clear space to land on the ground so he perched up on the arched roof of stone and crystal covering the shrine. The stone creaked and crumbled under the dragon's weight, and the people inside wailed.

"Where are they?" Kife called down.

"Already gone. But I saw where," Kess replied.

Kife punched the front of his saddle. "This was a mess! And the last time we're going with one of your awful plans."

Kess said nothing in reply, tonguing the inside of her teeth to keep from biting back.

"Hurry up, then!" Kife snapped. "Let's go so we can catch them at the next stop."

He turned away, fuming, as Kess jumped Griskin up onto the shrine roof beside the dragon. She had to run the wolf past some of the braver people to get there, getting an eyeful of the older woman's utter disdain on the way.

Kife pressed his hands to his dragon's neck as Kess climbed up behind him. "We should blast this place. Destroy the portal and stop them using this one again."

His dragon's flame crackled around his teeth.

"There are people in there." Kess buckled herself to the saddle behind her brother.

"So? They're protecting criminals. We should start destroying all the shrines as we go, get rid of all escape routes."

"We won't let you!" the old woman called up from below.

The numbers around her had grown again, others coming back to join her, daring the dragon and its riders with their expressions.

Kife laughed. "And what do you think you could do

to stop me?"

A rock flew from the old woman's hand, glancing off Kife's leg. He swore and directed his dragon's head to aim at her. "I'll burn the lot of you!"

"Kife, stop it." Kess shoved him in the shoulder.

He glared back, and despite the rushing turmoil inside making her shake, Kess gave him the dullest eye roll of sibling contempt possible. "You'd really dishonor yourself with something as low as burning a pathetic old woman who hurt your feelings?"

Kife twitched the shoulder she'd shoved, as though cringing off her touch belatedly.

"We're wasting time," he said, and the dragon's wings flicked out in a clap of leather.

They lifted from the shrine rooftop as a hail of pebbles and jeers chased them from below.

Griskin gave a soft whine. He'd gotten used to being carried in the dragon's talons, but he didn't like it. Kess didn't blame him. She hoped none of the stones reached him.

Kess checked their map, identifying the symbol she'd seen lit up on the gateway against the ones they'd recorded, then pointed a heading. The dragon's wings beat hard, pushing them fast through the air.

It wasn't far. They would be on their target again in no time with the swift flight of the purple etherdart.

She looked back at the shrine disappearing in the distance. Her face heated, shame at her brother's behavior like poison burning her skin. But that was just Kife. He'd always been awful. Other dragonriders weren't like him. Surely.

"A sun-razed glass factory," Kife scoffed, his voice barely carrying over the roar of wind around him. "What were you thinking?"

"It was the only building big enough nearby," Kess yelled back. The only place to lure Pony where they could hide Kife's dragon inside until they could spring their trap. "It would have worked if those bounty hunters had brought everyone in at once and believed me when I said not to underestimate the kids."

"What would have worked was not having a saddle full of glass I had to clear off before making chase. Anywhere else and I could have caught them."

"Is that what took you so long? Scared of a few bits of glass?"

"Not scared—just not stupid enough to cut my ass into pieces." Kife made a show of dusting off the saddle again. "That and making sure those bounty hunters were done. Couldn't have any of them surviving after learning about that little silvernix dragonling."

Kess had to admit that was important. They had seen Dracuni's blood with their own eyes. She should have

thought of that too, should have done something about it before chasing off. Was she slipping so much?

Maybe she'd just hoped she could have caught Dracuni without any more blood on her hands.

"You screwed that up in every way, Kessara."

"I did? You're the one who delayed things. You should have let the bounty hunter finish off ..."

Pony. The slave. Riony. Her pet.

Every word felt wrong now on Kess's lips. "Finish *her* off. It should have been fast and easy, and her death would have broken her group and let us take the dragonling."

Even if the fungus-filled space had made Griskin sniffly again, Her plan should have worked. Even with the shattered glass all around, it should have worked.

But Kife always had to bring cruelty into everything. He could never allow something to be easy when it could be cruel instead.

"It was a gift to you, sister." He seemed taken aback, hurt she hadn't appreciated it. "You're the one who took too long dealing the death blow."

She couldn't deny it. A shiver ran over her, the chilled wind blasting through her leather garments. Riony kneeling, covered in blood. It should have been fast. It should have been easy.

Getting Dracuni was everything Kess had ever wanted,

wasn't it? At any cost?

Kife turned in his seat, glaring down at Kess from behind his flight goggles. "I shouldn't have let you take the lead on that plan. My contribution has been the only thing that has worked so far. Getting those signal flares out to bounty hunters across the land. *You* have been useless."

His shifted angle brought a gust of smoky wind over Kess, and she grasped the buckles holding her in place, checking they were connected tight. A fire burned below, and Kess imagined herself falling, falling into that burning forest, pushed from her seat. But her brother didn't try to kill her. Not then. Not yet.

And the flares had been a good move, but she wouldn't concede that aloud. The time and expense it had taken to get those flares out to as many bounty hunters as they could had delayed the hunt, but seeing one light the sky the night before had made it all worth it.

Having the extra eyes on the ground looking for Pony and the dragonling had paid off, and the flare had worked as intended, getting to them fast.

They didn't want the bounty hunters trying to capture the bounty on their own and discovering what Dracuni was.

Kife sniffed. "That weed you gave the bounty hunters to subdue the grayglim-in-training worked well though. We should get more of it, use it on the lot of them next

time. Was it the same thing you used on me that time you slipped something into my soup?"

"It was Pony who did that," Kess replied fast.

"Sure it was. The pet acting without the master's command. You never did train the wild beast well. Learning about this sedation herb is the one thing she was ever good for."

A dreadful desire to defend Riony caught in Kess's throat. But it was just a symptom of wanting to defy her brother. Whatever he said, she felt the urge to argue. He could say the sun was hot and she'd feel the urge to debate that it was made of ice. That was how they'd always been and had nothing to do with Pony, or what she had or hadn't been good for.

Still, Kess found she had to say something. "You and our parents seemed to think she was plenty good at being whipped."

Kife laughed, huffing in time to the dragon's wings. "The kid deserved it every time! That whole family were mad. We should have gotten rid of the lot of them before they decided to murder a dragonguard and steal a baby."

"Sorry, what?" She was unsure she'd heard him over the deafening rumble of flight. "A baby?"

"The baby. The guest's baby. Those criminals stole it."

Kess straightened in the saddle, her mind rushing over what she'd remembered of when Riony had abandoned

her and fled. All she'd been told was that they'd killed someone and run.

But it did line up to the time when the guest, that mysterious young woman who had haunted their estate like a ghost during her pregnancy, had also left. No longer pregnant. But without a child. After Riony and her mother had been at the birth.

"I thought the newborn died?"

"That's officially what happened. Our parents didn't want anyone knowing what their slaves had done. But they were seen with the baby during their escape. I was told since I was part of the main hunting party for them." Kife seemed to take pleasure rubbing those words in.

That he had information Kess wasn't privy to. That he always had a higher standing than Kess ever had, ignored and locked away most of her life.

But she knew something he didn't. She knew that Riony called one of the kids she traveled with 'sister,' despite it being clear that she wasn't. And the child was just the right age to be the stolen baby.

It didn't mean much—not to her hunt for Dracuni. But it did mean that somehow, for some reason, Pony and her family had stolen that baby and raised her as their own, and Riony called her sister and was loving and protective of her in a way she'd never been to Kess.

"Do you know who the guest was?" Kess asked.

"Some dragonlord lady," Kife said confidently, providing that he knew no more about the woman than Kess did. "Not someone I've ever met since—not at Skaellakeep. I haven't exactly been able to rub shoulders with the upper class as I should, with the Heithorn name as tarnished as it is. Thanks to you."

"Of course," Kess replied flatly. Of course that would be her fault. Everything was.

"Chin up, little sis." Kife reached back and squeezed her roughly on the knee. "Once we have this silvernix beast, all will be forgiven. Incredible how you were able to find such a unique creature. I can't even fathom it!"

"I didn't know what it was when I first found the eggs. I had only hoped for a dragon of my own to ride." A weight was filling Kess's chest, like a slow trickle of molten lead.

Visions of blood. A stolen sister loved more than a Heithorn daughter. She turned away from staring at her brother's back and squinted narrowed eyes at the huge expanse of the dragon's wings keeping them in the sky, and her heart hurt.

"And how were you even going to raise a dragon? Or tame it?" Kife scoffed. "You never could think things through."

"I was ready!" Kess snapped. "I have what's needed."

"Really?" Kife drawled the word, as though it were a sound of triumph. "Where under the sun did you get silvernix from? Our family had been out for so long."

"There was a lot that our family was lacking," was all Kess offered in explanation.

Kife's words drew cold, stabbing like icicles. "And you know why. You know why we moved into isolation, why I was taken away from the life and honor I deserved. And even after you were gone, nothing changed!"

After I was gone. After you left me to die. "Is that what you'd hoped to achieve? By getting rid of me?"

"Don't take it personally, Kess. I'm sorry about what I had to do, but it was for the best for *our family*. For the Heithorn name! But nobody understood, and your damage had already been done. Our parents refused to leave the estate, mourning their poor lost daughter."

"Did they—?" Kess's voice was small and lost in the wind.

"That's what they told everyone. But really, they were too embarrassed to move back to a keep because of how poor we'd become."

They hadn't mourned her. Nobody had missed her at all. Abandoned by everybody. Kess wasn't surprised.

Rushing air pummeled Kess's eyes, making them water. She closed them for a moment, trying to give them some relief, but they continued to burn and sting.

Kife continued, pummeling her with words as hard as the wind. "I refused to let that be the fate of the Heithorn name, fading out of history in squalor. I took the other dragonriders with me to get work at Skaellakeep, to regain some of the wealth and honor you took from us. And while I was gone, revenants overtook the estate."

There wasn't a hint of remorse in his tone. "I lost my parents because of you, little sister. Because you broke them. Because they couldn't face the world in their shame, they remained trapped in that place to die."

Kess shook her head, wanting to argue. Wanting to say that it was Kife who had abandoned his family, left them unguarded. But it did all come back to her. Her very existence, and how nobody could just accept her as she was, had cursed their family into its demise.

And now the only person who had ever been kind to her was the life she had to end to gain the acceptance she'd never had.

The heaviness in her chest had filled right up into her neck and behind her eyes, wanting to burst out between her ribs in an ugly flood. Everything had been easier before Pony came back into her life. Everything had been clear. Get a dragon. Become a rider. One dream, strong and honorable and inevitable.

And now, here she was, letting her hateful brother's

words slide like knives under her skin as cruelly as the glass had sliced Riony. She was having rocks hurled at her like a common criminal and questioning how far she could go for her dream.

I should be stronger than this.

"I think I should hold on to the silvernix, sis," Kife said. "That and the taming spike. You can't be trusted to handle anything. You ruined the ambush—ruined our family. I don't want you to ruin the taming of this creature too."

Kess felt for the pouch at her side that held the items for the taming ritual. She'd taken them off Griskin to keep close when she thought they'd have Dracuni that morning.

Her voice was weak. "I can do this."

"Have you ever tamed a dragon before? No. I have. I know what to do."

Kess's hand reached into the pouch and closed around the parcel. "Fine. Take it."

She thrust the leatherbound treasures forward.

"Raze it, Kess! Not now!" Kife snatched the parcel quickly, securing it in front of him. "You could have dropped it! Absolutely hopeless."

Kess only blinked the water from her eyes and moved to buckle her pouch closed again. A thin length of leather flapped at the closure, caught in the wind. She narrowed her eyes and tugged the thonging free, revealing the acorn

dangling at the end.

That stupid, simple pendant that she'd found in the icy cave when she'd returned after leaving Riony to die from her injuries. When she'd gone back and found her missing, only her frozen blood and the pendant remaining.

It must have been tangled around the other items when she'd taken them from Griskin's bags and ended up in her belt pouch.

Kess squeezed it in her hand and tucked it into a pocket in her vest. A token to keep her focused on her target. To keep her on track to achieve her goal.

But the focus didn't come. She felt more confused than ever. She knew she was losing all her cards to Kife, but somehow she couldn't seem to care.

All she could think of was the way Riony had looked at her when she'd seen Kess standing beside her brother. Not with fear. Not even anger, really. But concern.

Riony knew as well as Kess that it was only a matter of time before Kess was abandoned again.

EIGHTEEN

Kess had a dragon. She had a dragon to chase them with now and with that dragon came Kife.

"Oh sparks, we are so screwed." Riony let the words drop like an unwanted weight from her mouth.

She knelt on the stone floor of the shrine they had arrived at, old leaves and vines tangling beneath her. There was no roof left on this Alderkin ruin, and dark pieces of ash drifted down like snow from a nearby fire.

The air was thick and tangy with smoke. Riony filled her chest with it anyway, dragging deep gulps and letting the acrid sting on her tongue reassure her body it was still alive.

Stars, it was so close.

Riony had been sure for a few moments that it was the

end. She could still feel the ghostly pressure of the knife to her throat. The sensation of glass under her skin. How Kess had turned away. Riony's shirt was still saturated in sticky blood.

Yup. She was definitely having nightmares tonight.

I can't believe Kess brought her sadistic brother and his dragon into this. What was she thinking?

Still, thanks not at all to Riony herself, she and all her loved ones had escaped. Having Dracuni, Lyrrin, Aishena, Niskina, and Benjin all there and mostly unharmed helped the air return to her tight lungs.

Then the relief Riony felt at having escaped curdled inside her. Myrwa and the others ... Kess wouldn't hurt them, would she? Would Kife?

Riony scrambled to stand. The floor of this shrine was cracked and sunken, tilted to one side, making Riony feel unstable on her feet.

Should she go back? Myrwa had told her to leave. As long as Riony wasn't there, there should be no reason for Myrwa's people to be harmed. But Kife loved to do cruel things for no reason.

"Are you okay?" Lyrrin looked up from under her hood, blue eyes bright and wide. Dracuni stood beside her, tail flicking.

Riony wavered, caught between pacing toward the

gateway and worry for those with her there. Her sword was still in one hand, glowing and light as a cloud but feeling like a weight regardless. "Are you?"

You answer. You answer little sister. Dracuni's eye ridges lowered, and her nostrils flared.

Riony shook her head, whether as the answer itself or the refusal of one, she wasn't sure. It didn't matter. She dropped the sword without deactivating it. She didn't have to worry about it running out of charge. Not here.

She checked Lyrrin with her hands, tsking at the singed edges on her gloves. "You weren't hurt?"

"We're fine."

Big sister hurt most.

Riony reached for one of Dracuni's front paws, lifting it to check under the claws and finding it already healed, no sign of glass splinters.

But Dracuni had still bled. "That was so reckless, coming in like that!"

Lyrrin's face scrunched up fiercely and her lips popped, ready to argue, when Riony grabbed her, pulling her close to her belly and squeezing her tight. "You saved me, Lil Moon. You saved us."

Helped too, Dracuni huffed.

"All three of you," Riony added, nodding acknowledgment to Benjin.

"Effess um emmums arress agth," Lyrrin said, muffled.

"Huh?" Riony gave her some space.

Lyrrin said again, "I guess you making us stay outside helped. I mean, if we'd all gone inside at the same time, we'd all have been trapped by that dragon."

Riony wanted to smile but it didn't come. She crouched down to Lyrrin's height. "I'm so sorry I'm stuffing everything up. You should never have had to do any of that."

"Should never have destroyed Yoskar's staff," Benjin said, scowling. The brown skin across one side of his head was an angry, dark plum, the hair scorched away.

He knelt next to his sister who lay on the cracked paving, haloed in dry leaves. He watched her with a worried frown as she stirred but didn't wake.

Niskina knelt opposite. "We should never have been there at all. I was so stupid to think I could ever do something more. To ever trust this blighted world."

She pressed her palms hard into her eyes and screamed once, long and strangled.

Aishena's arm twitched, lashing out clumsily to grab an athame from her belt. Her eyes peeled open, fluttered. "What ... what happened?"

"It's okay. We're okay," Benjin replied.

After one false start, Aishena bent at the waist, leaning smoothly up into a sitting position. Her mouth opened in

pain, and she grasped her forehead in both hands for a moment before her expression returned to its usual steely calm.

"Careful. The morass mercy has a nasty hangover." And probably didn't mix well with the actual hangover Aishena had done amazingly well at hiding that morning, Riony thought, but didn't pile on.

Aishena kept an admirably composed expression, but her words came slowly. "We were ambushed ... Kess. And ... that was her brother, wasn't it? On the dragon? I could see, for a while, but I couldn't move."

Aishena had told Riony about how she'd met Kess, only once, at Hjelzahnkeep. But once had been enough to make an impression. There weren't many dragonlords with disabled children.

And Riony's experience with Lyrrin's birth had taught her why. Children who were born different often didn't survive their first day.

She didn't know Aishena had met Kife too, but the way she said *her brother* made Riony think he'd made an impression as well.

Riony replied, "Yup. Kess, Kife, and a dragon. We're absolutely boned in the worst possible way."

Aishena had turned her attention to Benjin, fussing over the singed area across his temple.

"I'm fine. It's just soot." He pushed her hands away.

"The fireball barely touched me."

"*Fireball?* That Heithorn set dragonfire upon children?" Aishena's eyes glinted with the desire for murder. "Why were you in there? You came in, didn't you? You should have followed orders and stayed out!"

"Maybe you should have not followed orders and followed your instincts for once and none of you would have walked into that ambush." He growled back. "And maybe Yoskar's staff wouldn't be gone. It's gone forever now!"

"I'm sorry," Lyrrin said softly.

"Gone?" Aishena clutched at a pocket on her chest. "But we got away. Somehow. Somehow, we got away?"

"For now," Riony said. "Map?"

Aishena nodded and drew the folded parchment out.

Riony took the map and laid it flat on the ground. "We're here, the gateway we activated before going to the village where we met Myrwa."

Aishena's eyes narrowed. "You couldn't have moved us farther from our now-airborne hunters?"

"Sorry, that was me. I just hit the first symbol that I could," Lyrrin said.

"Maybe you should have thought for a second before doing it, then," Benjin hissed.

Riony held up a warning hand. "It's fine. We're safe here for the moment. I'm just worried about how close that

fire is. And whether it's going to flush any revs our way. We should pick our next location and move on from there."

Niskina, who had been watching everything with dull eyes since her scream, flicked the corner of the map. "Move on where? Why?"

"To safety," Riony replied.

Niskina scoffed and turned away.

Riony gave her a long, hard look. Niskina seemed completely crushed, but Riony didn't know how to manage that right then. Immediate risks of danger had to be dealt with first.

"Aish, what do you think about where we should go? If you were a couple of raging monsters with a dragon and scent hound, where would you *not* go looking for your prey?"

Aishena frowned, bending over the map as well. Her fingers traced a few locations, then she mumbled, "I don't know."

Drawing a sharp breath, Riony cricked her neck, then let the air out slowly in an effort not to hit something.

Behind her back, there was a rasping whisper from Benjin again. "I can't believe you did that. You told me to trust you, and you destroyed the last thing I had of my brother."

Lyrrin's voice had the high, growling edge it took on when she was trying not to cry. "I didn't think—I'm sorry.

I just needed something, fast."

"It was Yoskar's! And you blew it up without even caring!"

There was a strangled shriek and the stomp of a foot. "I *saved* us!"

"Did you have to do it that way?" Benjin stalked away to the shrine entrance, glaring out at the smoke-gray surrounds.

Riony was halfway turned to call Lyrrin over to try to calm her down when the light of the gateway illuminated the hazy space.

She whipped around fast, expecting another ambush, that somehow Kess had unlocked the activation of the gateway rune. She couldn't have—she had no idea how to use even basic runes. And they hadn't taught Myrwa or any of the others how to do it either.

Instead, she saw Lyrrin there, stepping away through the light.

Sister? Dracuni galloped toward her, and Riony scrambled to her feet, chasing after.

"Lyrrin!"

But the light went out. And Lyrrin was gone.

"Did anyone see where she went?" Riony ran to the tall slice of crystal geode, scrambling to trace the sigil.

"I didn't see," Aishena said, brow furrowed and lips thin.

Benjin moved in stumbling steps toward his sister, staring at the empty space where Lyrrin had disappeared.

"I didn't mean ... I didn't want her to go."

"Nobody saw which symbol she used?" Riony growled, frantic as the rune sequence finished.

Around the edge, all the location markers that they had been to before lit up. Between them were the ones they had not yet visited, and the ones which had cracks through them.

There was silence behind Riony and she grunted louder again, smacking her hand on the closest symbol to Lyrrin's height.

The gateway lit, sparkling with the vision of the shrine near the rough smugglers' settlement. Riony half stepped through, looked, called, came back.

She deactivated the rune, fingers shaking, then tried again.

Their first shrine, back near the undercity outskirts. Nothing.

"Sparks! Why would she do that? Where is she?" Riony closed the gateway again.

Dracuni stood close to where Riony crouched over the Alderkin carving. **Sister coming back?**

Riony's fingers slipped over the rune, tracing the wrong line, ruining the sequence. She clenched her hand into a fist and choked on her breath.

And the gateway lit up again on its own.

Lyrrin appeared before Riony, her face firm and determined.

In a scooping step, Riony grabbed and lifted her as she got to her feet. "What was that? Where did you go? Don't do that to me!"

Lyrrin jangled in her arms, pokey and pointy lumps pressing between them as Riony squeezed her. With a stern snap, she said, "I went for supplies."

Sister came back! Dracuni circled around Riony's legs and Lyrrin's dangling feet.

Riony put Lyrrin down again before the three of them tangled up and fell.

The 'supplies' Lyrrin had gone for were sticking out of every one of her pockets and balanced in a clinking pile in her folded arms. Calcite spikes and spars, glassy and shimmering.

"You got crystals?" There was only one place Riony knew from their shrine locations where she could have gotten them.

From the looks on the faces all around her, they knew it too.

Lyrrin nodded. "I'm going to make a new staff for Benjin. I needed these. I had to go."

Somewhere none of the rest of them had been willing to return to. Riony's throat went dry, and all the strength

seemed to leave her body. She leaned against the crystal of the gateway.

"You went back to the Alderkin depths," Niskina said, stepping forward. Her chin was up, and her chest heaved visibly up and down. "Was ... What was it like?"

Lyrrin's head tilted, and she spoke gently. "It's been cleared. Ropes and pulleys set up. There were large candles, melted down where ... where your family were."

Aishena put a hand on Niskina's back, turning her so they faced each other. "The delvers have seen to them. They've been honored. They've had their final light."

Niskina sobbed and pulled Aishena into an embrace, crying into her shoulder. "But we weren't there. We weren't there for it."

Benjin swiped the back of his hand across his cheek and nose, still staring at Lyrrin.

"Did you see anyone?" Riony asked.

"There was no one there. Almost everything was taken, but they must have left all these behind since they were unruned." Lyrrin shuffled the crystals in her arms to steady them.

Raw crystals. They would have been useless to any delvers, but Lyrrin might be able to work with them. Riony just shook her head, unable to think through the rights and wrongs and risks and fears, and Lyrrin in trouble, and

Lyrrin gone, and was any of this worth it?

"You're really going to make something with those? For me?" Benjin asked, mostly to the stone floor.

"I'm going to try. I know it's not a replacement, that nothing can replace what is gone. But it's the best I can do since it was my fault."

Benjin took some of the crystals from Lyrrin, helping her empty her full arms. "It's okay. You did save us. And Yoskar ... Yoskar's gone. Keeping his staff safe seemed so important before, as though I was keeping part of him alive. But it was more important that you saved everyone still here."

Lyrrin sighed, silent but visible in the deep droop of her shoulders. She and Benjin started sorting the crystals from her hands and pockets into bags.

Niskina still sobbed, arms wrapped around Aishena, who stood considerately still but didn't return the embrace. In the delver's hand, Yoskar's glasses were held tight.

Riony hadn't really seen how much Aishena was hurting. Not until last night. But she should have known. She should have known how much all of them were hurting, having lost their family and their home.

Riony had felt it all herself before. She still felt it every day.

She let her back slide down the gateway crystal until

she hit the ground and sat there, staring over her small, sorry group. All broken. And Riony doing her best to keep them together but making all the wrong decisions and nobody listening to her anyway.

And horribly, at that moment, the person that Riony most wished would listen to her, would just hear reason for the first time in her life, was Kess.

The dreadful gremlin was obsessed. Obsessed with getting a dragon, and now obsessed with getting Dracuni. That was all she'd ever cared about.

Riony knew that, but still, the lengths Kess had gone to left her rattled.

Back at Heithorn estate, Kife had taken and enjoyed his share of whipping duty, when Kess's own parents or the estate master delegated out the torture. Riony knew Kess didn't care about that, but she should care that her brother had also been the cruelest of everyone to Kess as well.

Had she forgotten? Had she forgotten that he was the one who'd taken her from her home and left her to die?

Kess and Riony had almost, *almost* been friends at times. And still Kess had chosen to betray Riony without a second thought and turn to her ruthless brother instead. It felt like a knife to the heart, and Riony was furious she even cared.

She was also keenly aware she could have had a real

knife in her heart, one that Kess didn't throw.

Kess had plenty of time to skewer her in the glass factory. But still … had there been hesitation? Riony shook her head and rubbed her aching eyes.

Big sister is bad hurt. Dracuni bumped her arm with the tip of her snout.

"I'm fine. You healed me already. This is old blood." Riony wiped her cheek clean, showing the smooth, repaired skin beneath.

Bad inside hurt.

Wetness rushed over Riony's eyes, and she blinked it away. "The smoke is making my eyes sting."

Dracuni huffed but sat down without any more thought words accusing Riony inside her own brain.

Riony remained resting there, trying to slow the race of her heart, still raging from her visit to death's door and following escape. Trying to make Dracuni sense that her insides weren't bruised or battered by everything that had happened.

She waited while Niskina cried and Benjin and Lyrrin made plans for their crystals, and Dracuni curled up beside her and said nothing more in her thoughts but thrummed a soft, purring sound.

Yet even after some time, Riony's pulse still beat in her ears and it only seemed to be getting louder.

"What is that?" Aishena asked, pressing Yoskar's glasses

away into the pocket of her vest.

Dracuni stood on her hind legs, ears twitching toward the open ceiling of the shrine. **Dragon. Flying dragon.**

"Dragon!" Riony repeated aloud for the others. She scrambled forward and grabbed the map, still lying on the ground. She folded it roughly, patting down the misaligned mess. She was panicking for no reason.

Dragons were fast—*even etherdarts, although they're built more for combat than speed.* Kess's voice offered the information through a memory—but it couldn't be them. How would they know to come for them here?

"I see it," Aishena said, standing alert and staring skyward.

The faint silhouette of a serpentine body and wide, flapping wings was grayed out between gusts of smoke blowing through the sky. It tilted and dove straight toward them.

"Go. Get the gateway open!" Riony barked.

"To where?" Lyrrin asked, crouching over the activation rune at the base.

"As far away as possible!"

Air rushed around them as the leathery expanse of wings seemed to wrap the shrine itself right above them. A dull purple. Front talons carrying a wolf.

Riony scooped up her sword and pushed Dracuni

first through the lit gateway. The others followed in a rush, Riony at the back as the dragon landed behind her, snapping at the space she'd just vacated.

The gateway closed, cutting them off from their pursuers.

"Sparks, how did they get to us so fast?" Riony glanced again over her shoulder, scared that they might still somehow come through behind her.

There was a cracking rumble like a mountain collapsing on itself. On the side of the geode gateway, the symbol for the shrine they'd just been at split through the middle, fine fractures spidering out.

"You don't think …?" Lyrrin asked.

"They destroyed it," Riony rasped.

Getting away through the shrine gateways was one of the few advantages Riony had to keep herself and her loved ones safe.

But their hunters had found them and had been fast enough in the skies to reach them before they'd even had time to recover.

And if they destroyed the shrines, there would be nowhere left to run.

NINETEEN

"Careful!" Kess scolded as Griskin whined and bucked in the dragon's claws.

The blowback from the fireball that had destroyed the shrine was uncomfortably hot even up on the dragon's back. Kess leaned as far out from the saddle as she could to check her wolf's fur wasn't singed. He looked back up with deep, mournful eyes.

I'm sorry, Gris. Not much longer now. I hope.

"What are you complaining about?" Kife pressed his hands and weight against the dragon's neck in a combination of motions, similar to how Kess moved when riding Griskin.

The dragon responded, stretching its wings again to fly. "That's one less place for those rats to scurry to next time. Did you see where they went?"

"Yeah, but it's a long way off." Kess showed him on their map.

"Nah, no problem at all. We'll be on them again before dark."

And the dragon lurched quickly into the sky in a motion that left Kess's stomach behind.

She wanted to enjoy flying, to relish these moments in the sky, being where she always dreamed that she'd belonged.

But she was with Kife. On Kife's dragon.

And all it did was make her remember the first time they'd flown together.

"If this is for my birthday, you missed it by a week," Kess had said from where she'd sat on her bed, picking at food that seemed flavorless.

It had been a few years since Pony had abandoned her, and although there had been other slaves that managed Kess's everyday needs, there was no one who'd replaced Riony. Kess spent most of her time in bed.

Kife ushered a large servant in and had him pick Kess up without even asking first. "A week ago? Yes, I'm very sorry about that. That's why I wanted to make it up to you."

Kess tried to get comfortable in the slave's hold of her. He wasn't at all used to carrying her, not the way Pony had

been. He pinched and squeezed her legs too tight.

"Just what is this surprise you have for me?" Kess was skeptical it could be anything good.

She checked for her pair of steel throwing knives she always kept on her, worried that her parents, finally sick of their bedridden daughter, would smother her in her sleep. They were tucked neatly away under the tight sleeves of her velvet dress.

They stepped out into the courtyard, and there was Kife's purple dragon, awaiting patiently, mindlessly.

Kife waved his arm at it. "I wanted to take you flying. I know you've always wanted to."

All the air left Kess's chest, and she devoured the shining scales and elegant wings of the beast with hungry eyes.

She spoke breathlessly. "Mami and Fadda won't allow it."

"Do we care what they will or won't allow?" Kife climbed up into the saddle in a couple of long, acrobatic steps.

He reached down as the slave lifted Kess up and Kife pulled her onto the saddle in front of him, passing her around like a parcel.

Small for her age and not yet a woman, thirteen-year-old Kess was speechless with awe as she ran her hands over the dragon's neck.

"Watch it!" Kife said, smacking her away. "It's trained to take orders from touch. You could set it off to burn this

whole place down."

"Sorry." Kess sat back again, pulling her hands in and tucking them folded around her middle.

She should have known. She'd studied the entire theory. But she'd never been on a dragon in the rider's position before. And it was overwhelming and magnificent. It felt right.

And when they took off, Kess thought her heart was flying as well.

Rushing air tugged at Kess's finely embroidered day dress and lifted her hair, and she suppressed the rising giggles of pure joy. Heithorns didn't giggle.

Although Kife controlled the dragon, Kess felt every sweep of its wings and all the strength of its grace as though she were one with it. And below her, everything seemed so small. A land and its people wrought into a distant painting, insignificant.

All that existed was Kess and the sky and the beat of powerful wings. It was everything she'd ever wanted.

They had been in the air so long that Kess's back and stomach hurt from the effort of keeping upright and stable against the gusts of wind, and her uncovered eyes stung and watered, yet she could have stayed up there forever.

But it had been a long time, hadn't it? Why were they traveling so far?

The dragon descended, circling on still wings and

lowering toward a forest clearing below. A blackened patch amongst the green, where something had recently been burned.

Were they near home? Maybe Kess hadn't realized they'd turned around at some point. She scanned the area for landmarks or signs of the estate buildings but saw nothing she recognized.

"Why are we landing?"

"The dragon needs a short rest. We'll be done and home soon."

It was as they landed that Kess couldn't suppress the short trill of a giggle at how purely beautiful the creature beneath them was, how incredible its motions as it carried them. She turned, willing in that moment of happiness to sincerely thank her brother for this gift, when his hands grasped her shoulders and threw her from the saddle.

The fall to the ground was swift and shattering.

Every part of Kess turned cold and heavy from brutal shock. Brittle ashes crunched beneath her, wafting a bitter scent all around. She winced at the bend in her wrist and the crunch of her hip she'd landed hardest on.

"What was that for? You idiot!"

Kife wasn't smirking or laughing through cruelly twisted lips as he usually did when he pulled such pranks on her. He rolled his jaw, sniffed once, and said, "Goodbye, Kessara."

"Goodbye?" Kess laughed, bemused.

"It's time our family moves on. Without you. You've held us back long enough."

He turned from her and flew away without another word. Kess screamed at the empty sky until her voice was gone.

In that clearing of leafless, thorny brambles and burned bones, Kess remained, staring at the sky until the sunset. It had to be a prank. Or even if not, he'd change his mind. He'd come back. Someone at the estate would find her missing, and her parents would be informed, and people would come looking.

Her first night alone was spent in tears and sobs made silent through fear and aching cramps from a hungry belly. She curled up, right where she'd been left. Waiting. Waiting for someone to find her and take her home. Waiting for *something* to find her and end her suffering.

She awoke with leaves stuck in her hair, her dress wet from dew, and shivers raking through her due to the cold she had no protection from. And by the time the sun had risen high enough in the sky to warm the life back into her, Kess knew nobody was coming for her.

She wanted to scream again but her throat was already torn and dry.

So she cursed her brother silently. If he'd wanted to kill her, he could have at least done it quickly. She might

not have even fought him.

But now, now she was angry.

She must have survived on fury alone for her first few days.

Although the trees of the forest had some green shoots in the canopies, the understory had recently been burned. Kess crawled through the ashes, finding no berries, no game, not even the common weedy grass shoots that Pony had shown her could be pulled up whole and the sweet inner stems chewed on.

Kess drank from muddy puddles, and she ached with hunger and her mind felt foggy and almost gone when she finally saw a lone soot-darkened rabbit.

Low to the ground as she was, it hadn't seen her yet.

Kess's hands shook around her throwing knife. On a good day, she'd hit it no problem. But this wasn't a good day, and if she missed, she doubted she'd have the strength to ever throw a blade again.

The knife flew straight, and with a short piercing cry, the rabbit stilled.

She collected her kill, leaned her back against a tree trunk, and fought back the bile in her throat as she held the still warm, velvet-furred body.

The initial swell of triumph Kess felt at the successful hunt was swiftly quashed. She didn't know how to dress

a rabbit. She didn't know how to start a fire. She didn't know how to cook.

Turning her eyes up and away from the blood on her hands, she saw two eyes shining back at her from behind thin, charred scrub.

Kess froze, rabbitlike herself in the face of the massive predator.

A low, rumbling growl reverberated, the wolf lowering its head.

It didn't approach, but it didn't leave either.

Kess remained still, not wanting to provoke it, wondering whether her small daggers would do anything against the giant lupine.

They remained motionless, locked in each other's gaze for so long that Kess grew bold. She growled back at the creature, frustrated. "Why aren't you trying to eat me?"

No reply—not that she expected one.

She dared to move closer, crawling around it in a wide arc. She took her rabbit with her, worried the wolf was just waiting for her to leave it so it could steal her catch. Not that she knew what to do with her kill anyway. Her arms shook beneath her as she pulled herself over the rough ground, weak and exhausted.

The full length of the wolf came into view as Kess moved around the dead bushes. It still didn't move. It

couldn't. It was caught in a trap.

A tangle of snare wire wore bloody lines around the wolf's front leg and neck. It was ragged, the charcoal-dark fur matted, and body thin beneath.

Kess shifted closer. The wolf tried to back away, but the wire tugged against it, and it twitched and whined, stilling again.

In the soft dirt all around the trapped creature were dozens of other footprints, matching the tracks pressed into the ground beneath the bound animal. Wolf prints, of all different shapes and sizes, circled around the area.

Kess listened, waiting to be set upon by the pack, but nothing came. How long had this wolf been stuck there? She checked the tracks again, seeing them trail away.

"Your pack abandoned you?" Kess was no tracker, but even she could see the prints surrounding them were old, softened with rain and wind. "Of course they did."

Kess wondered for a moment if she could kill and eat the wolf. But she didn't even know what to do with the small rabbit she'd dragged over with her. She knew she would only waste the wolf's life in her failed attempts to preserve her own.

And if either of the two of them should be put out of their misery, Kess wasn't sure it was the wolf.

The shadowy animal licked its lips as the gamey scent

of blood wafted around them.

In a fit of hopelessness, she flung the rabbit toward the wolf's head.

"Go on. You have it." She shuffled closer, knife in hand.

It remained still as stone, eyes on her as she cut the thin snare wire free. "You can eat me too for all I care."

The last section of twined metal snapped and Kess sat back, staring into the face that would end her. Those icy blue eyes regarded her. The jaws snapped.

The wolf snatched the rabbit in its teeth and ran.

A rough, hysterical laugh burbled from Kess's empty chest. Maybe she always was destined for a slow and painful death.

She tried once to move on again, but her arms crumpled beneath her.

Lying in the remains of the snare wire and wolf prints, Kess wondered how long it would take for her to die.

It wasn't within the next few hours, as she watched the sun pass overhead, stinging her dry eyes and cracking her lips. She was still alive when she heard the faint sounds of padding paws approach.

She lifted herself up to see the shaggy dark wolf return. "What are you doing back? Couldn't find your family? I told you, they left you to die!"

It moved closer, head low and wary.

"Come to fill yourself on more meat? Go on then!"

The wolf opened its snout, giving a soft, grumbling *oorf*. It turned, flanking her, then began moving away again.

"Are you going to eat me or what? I'm done! I can't ..." Tears spilled in a rush from Kess's eyes.

The wolf paused, looked back, took another step, and waited—almost as though it wanted her to follow it.

Kess crumpled, dropping to her elbows and pressing her forehead on the ground. "I can't."

The press of warm fur at her side made her cringe, but she didn't fight it. There was a scrabble of paws, and Kess wobbled as the wolf burrowed its head beneath her chest. Then she was being lifted into the air.

She grabbed tight, hands clutched around fur in surprise, as the wolf got underneath her and stood with her draped over its back.

It was awkward and uncomfortable and the wolf smelled of old meat and rot, and Kess pulled herself closer to it and held it tight and cried.

And the two of them survived. Together.

"Stupid beast!" Kife snapped, bringing Kess back into the present. "We aren't going to make it by sundown."

"You flew your dragon hard already on the last stretch. It's tired."

"It's not working hard enough! Dumb thing is getting

old. I'd have replaced it by now if I could afford it." Kife adjusted his seating and the dragon began its descent. "Today has been a complete mess. We're making camp. We'll pick up the trail again tomorrow."

The dragon settled them down in an old field, more rubble than weeds. Kess would have never chosen such an exposed place to camp when traveling alone with Griskin, but the threat of revenants attacking in the night was less with a dragon around.

Back on the ground, and back on Griskin, Kess hunted their dinner and cleaned the game and set the fire as Kife lay on his blanket, picking his nails.

On her way to her own bed, Kess passed by the purple etherdart and paused. She had been so enamored by the creature once. But after having spent so long tracking the wild seasong mother dragon, after having met Dracuni, there was something so sad and pathetic about this tamed creature now.

The thing she'd always longed for, and it just seemed ... broken.

She reached a hand up to the scales of its cheek. It remained stone still beneath her touch, neither flinching away nor leaning into her hand. There was no brightness of life in its eyes as there was in Dracuni's, so alert and emotive. Only a dull stupor.

Its head was lowered, and Kess stared at the steel diamond of the taming spike, stuck there between its eyes. The imprint of the hammer on the end was still visible.

"Get away from my dragon," Kife muttered.

Kess did because it was his dragon, and she couldn't bear to look at it any longer. She and Griskin curled up on their blanket together as they always did.

He was the only one who'd ever really cared for her. The only one she could trust.

There was a moment, in the depths of those unblessed caves, when Kess had wondered if maybe she could have trusted Riony too. Riony, who had come back for her. Who hadn't let her die.

But it was a mirage of hope. A shimmer in the distance that Kess hadn't dared look at lest she crawl toward it only to be left dead for wanting what it didn't provide.

And even if there was a real chance it had existed, Kess had then broken any trust with Riony in a way that could never be fixed. It wasn't worth considering.

Kess glared across the fire at where her brother snorted and grumbled in his sleep, her eyes on the pouch by his side where he'd put the silvernix and taming spike.

She couldn't trust anybody. She was alone. Always.

TWENTY

Griskin nipped at Riony's heel, teeth gliding over the leather of her boot. Riony lunged away. She wheeled around, sword drawn.

The gateway closed, blinking out before her eyes and leaving them adjusting to the absence of light. Another close call, one of many.

The beat of dragon wings echoed like a nightmare in Riony's head—a sound she was now constantly on guard for and heard far too often.

The shrine they'd arrived at was dark, empty. Cyan light flared as Aishena activated her glow stone.

Watching the symbols around the geode gateway, Riony held her breath. There were refugees sheltering at the shrine they'd just fled, as there were around many of the Alderkin ruins now.

The symbol didn't crack. Riony let the breath out slowly through pursed lips. Hopefully it meant nobody there had suffered Kife or Kess's wrath at their escape.

Riony was honestly surprised that, so far, they hadn't destroyed any of the shrines where people had settled. Or destroyed those people. They only destroyed shrines without communities around them, which there'd been a few of.

Maybe Kess was reining in Kife. As far as the lesser of two evils went, at least Kess was never one for wanton destruction. She was more about personalized cruelty and psychological torment. She knew her strengths and stuck to them.

They'll probably destroy this shrine when they get here and don't find anyone.

It was the first time they'd been to this location since activating it, due to it being high up craggy mountains that were a pain to travel around on foot.

But they wouldn't be leaving on foot again. They couldn't risk getting more than a short sprint away from a shrine anymore. If they were caught out by the dragon with nowhere to run, it would be over, and with Griskin able to track them traveling on foot, it left few options.

Aishena already had their map out and was muttering

calculations softly. After weeks of relentless pursuit they had a good idea of how fast Kife's dragon was now.

"If they head straight here, we have about two hours."

It was mostly guesswork, since they didn't have a timepiece with them, but 'two hours' translated roughly to 'enough time to catch our breaths and get comfortable before having to run again.'

Lyrrin groaned, dumping her backpack on the ground, then dumping herself down onto that. "I want to sleeeeeeeep! You said we could sleep!"

Riony winced, exhausted too. "Sorry. They don't normally keep coming at night. I thought it would be okay to stop for the day."

Benjin held a blanket, hurriedly gathered in his arms. They had just been preparing to settle in for the night when their hunters caught up to them again.

He had the same thoughtful look that his brother often wore. "They must be getting desperate."

"Or just pissed off from this stupid game of dragon-and-mouse," Niskina said.

"Either way," Benjin continued, "they're choosing to prioritize the chase over getting a good night's sleep or resting their dragon, like they did before."

"Maybe they just didn't feel sleepy tonight?" Riony shrugged.

Benjin rolled his eyes. "Or maybe they thought changing up their actions would catch us off guard, and it almost did. It's time we start changing things up too. We should be fighting back! Setting a trap! Finding some way to stop them coming after us."

Dracuni, eyes wide and sending shoots of excited anxiety through to Riony, pounced backward and forward on her claws.

Fight back! I can bite!

"Not going to happen." Riony gave the unidragon a quelling glare.

Although around the same size as Kess's huge wolf, Dracuni's scales were still soft compared to a normal dragon's, and her teeth not as long, and her talons not as hooked, no matter how fierce she'd been acting lately.

Aishena pulled Benjin protectively to her side as though he were about to leap into combat right then. "It's too dangerous. We just have to keep away from them."

"We should fight. Yoskar would have done anything, *anything*, to keep his family safe," Benjin said.

Aishena put a hand to her chest as though clutching at her heart and it came to rest over the pocket which held her brother's glasses. "That's what I'm trying to do for you—trying to keep you safe."

"That's not enough!" His words cut hard, landing in

a swell of silence like an ocean.

The words slapped Riony in the cheek, even though they weren't directed at her.

It *wasn't* enough. Running and hiding and barely living, existing in a way that could hardly be considered life—it wasn't enough. Not for Lyrrin, not for Dracuni, not for any of the people in her care. And she couldn't work out how to make it better.

Aishena's face flushed, and although her lips formed shapes, she didn't reply.

With a sigh, Benjin said, "It's not enough because our family is bigger than just you and me now. It's everyone here."

Aishena brushed a hand over the place where Benjin's hair had been singed by dragonfire. One of the burns had gotten weepy and still wasn't fully healed. She nodded but didn't seem entirely convinced.

The words didn't comfort Riony either. It was a nice sentiment, but her shoulders sagged as though an additional weight had been laid upon them. Because he was right. They were all family now, and Riony was responsible for all of them.

Lyrrin and Dracuni and Benjin all stared up at their elders with fiery gazes, as though they really thought they could take on a full-grown dragon.

"We can discuss war plans later," Riony said, mostly

to placate them. "For now, we take a moment here before we move on again, and hopefully we can sleep at the next stop. We'll go before they get here so they don't see where we end up. That will buy us maybe a day. But first, rest."

That seemed to settle things, and bags were unloaded, and seats taken on the dirty floor. Niskina shared flatbread, still warm from the fires of the settlement they'd just left. She didn't keep any for herself, and instead unstoppered a brown bottle she must have also received and took a long, steady swig.

Aishena remained on her feet, moving to take a guarding position at the door, and the two kids laid out Lyrrin's blanket, then lined up Lyrrin's remaining collection of crystals on it. Dracuni crouched with her chin on the ground, watching as Lyrrin tested and worked on the shining stones.

Everyone looked exhausted. They'd realized early on that Kess and Kife must also know where all the shrines were. And had somehow worked out how to tell which gateway Riony and her friends were traveling to if the terrible siblings caught a glimpse of the symbol activated.

How do they know which symbol takes us where? Knowing Kess, she's probably mapped every shrine in Elundrae, even ones we couldn't have reached and activated yet, just to rub in how much better she is at strategy than us.

Riony didn't bother unpacking anything. She just sat

on the cold cracked tiles of the ruined shrine.

They'd worked out a few tricks to buy time, jumping back and forth between multiple gateways so their hunters wouldn't know which one they were at. But having refugees at the shrines was a blessing and a curse.

More than once the settlers had been threatened into revealing what symbol had been illuminated. None of Riony's tactics had delayed the swift dragon long. And there were only so many shrines activated, all fairly close together since they'd had to get to them all on foot the first time.

Maybe Benjin is right. We need a plan. And we need someone better to come up with that plan than me.

"That's the last one," Lyrrin said, holding the newly carved staff close to her face and flicking at the crystal embedded there, as though checking it wasn't going to fly out.

"It's amazing!" Benjin beamed, gave Lyrrin a quick hug, and then moved away to show Aishena the finished staff.

All of Lyrrin's new crystals had been expended upon that staff, except for one that she'd turned into a cutting athame for Aishena, since they all agreed that might come in handy in case they were captured again.

Some of the crystals broke in the making, simply too fragile or flawed to stand up to carving, but everyone

remained in awe that any of the crystals carved fresh by Lyrrin had worked at all.

All Lyrrin had left were the two matching stones and the crystal with a ten-stroke rune from the Alderkin tomb Riony had taken along with her sword.

Dracuni shuffled closer to them until her front claws were touching the shining stones. **Rocks pretty.**

"Still haven't worked those ones out?" Riony asked.

Lyrrin huffed, wiggling a finger in the air in frustrated motions. "Ten strokes! I just can't keep them straight in my mind. I've tried marking them down, but after about five strokes, I don't feel the crystal singing as strongly, can't tell if I'm still on the right track. And these ones ..."

Lyrrin picked up the matching stones, shaking them in paired fists. "They activate, but they don't seem to do anything!"

Riony reached a hand to take one of the crystals from her. It was a flat slice of hexagonal calcite that fit in the palm of her hand. "You don't have to work every one of them out. You've already done amazing things. If we were still in the undercity ..."

Riony's throat dried up and she swallowed to fix it but her words had dried up too.

Dracuni's sadness also reached her. **I miss brother Butterfur.**

Yeah, I miss the slithery rat too. Riony tilted her head toward Dracuni, but didn't say anything aloud, since any mention of the cave otter made her sister burst into tears.

Unaware, Lyrrin continued, "But this could be it! One of these crystals could be what we need to keep ourselves safe." Lyrrin ran her finger, ungloved, over the rune on the paired stone. A soft rosy-pink light glowed.

Dracuni lifted her head. **Pretty, pretty rocks!**

And the slice of crystal in Riony's hand pulsed. "This seems to be doing something. I don't know what, but something."

"What?" Lyrrin took it back, staring. "It's not doing anything. It's not even activated."

"It did something. I felt it. Yours didn't do anything?" Riony swapped to take the activated rosy stone.

Lyrrin's eyes went wide. "What? I can feel something. It hasn't done that before! It feels like a heartbeat."

"Activate that one too," Riony said. Lyrrin traced the sigil in a liquid motion. And the same pulsing beat she'd felt before thrummed under Riony's fingers.

It *was* like a heartbeat. Small and faster than her own, a heartbeat she knew well from years curled up sleeping together. "It's your heartbeat."

"Do you think so?" Lyrrin shuffled in and pressed her ear toward Riony's chest as she held her own crystal.

She gasped. "This one matches yours! In time and everything!"

"Have you ever had someone else hold one before?"

"No, I just tried one on its own. I just thought they were two of the same. I didn't think they were paired together like this."

"Dracuni, hold still for a moment," Riony said.

She balanced her crystal onto Dracuni's snout.

"It changed!" Lyrrin said, passing her stone over to Riony again to feel.

It had changed to a heavy, solid pulse, slow and rumbling.

Nose tickles, Dracuni sniffed, eyes smiling.

The incredible magic the Alderkin had, and to have created something like this with it, left Riony's own heartbeat stuttering.

She said a silent apology to the person whose grave she'd stolen these from. At the time, she hadn't thought of them *as* a person who had a past and experiences and loves and hopes. She'd only seen treasure that she could take.

But that warrior who'd lain there with their sword and their belongings, and these stones ... had they taken one into battle with them so a loved one back home could feel that their heart was still beating?

How far away from each other did these work? If the gateways could take people all the way across Elundrae,

Riony wouldn't be surprised if these stones allowed them to feel their lover's heartbeat all the way across the world.

"Heartbeats ... this is the most romantic thing I've ever seen," Riony whispered, pouting.

"Ew," Lyrrin grunted. "They're useless! I doubt I could even make them explode if I tried!"

She took back the crystals and deactivated them with a huff.

"Not everything has to explode to be valuable," Riony said.

Lyrrin replied with an eye roll.

"Says the woman who thinks hitting things with her sword is always the best answer," Niskina grumbled.

She sat cross-legged, the bottle on the ground in front of her and gripped in both hands.

"Shush, I'm trying to make this a learning moment!" Riony replied.

"You know what I've learned? That we should never have tried to be heroes." Niskina pushed the bottle out of her hands and it rolled, clinking and empty across the uneven tiles. "That stupid stunt at the mine ... thinking we could actually be rebels ..."

"We still did the right thing though?" Lyrrin's voice went up at the end, as though she asked a question.

Aishena turned as though to say something but remained silent.

"We helped a heap of people. That was something." Benjin returned to sit beside Lyrrin. He sounded tired, questioning as well.

Niskina leaned back against the wall, rolling her head from side to side. "And *we* paid for it. We got betrayed. We're the ones being hunted."

"Bad people screwing things up doesn't negate that we did do a good thing," Riony said, trying to sound confident and comforting and failing.

"We never should have tried to change anything. We should have just gone straight to that secluded village of yours and hidden from the world as long as we could." Niskina locked her gaze on Riony, and it was cold and brutal. "But you've clearly been avoiding taking us there. Why? Does this place even exist?"

"It's not like that. I just ..."

Aishena's back straightened just as her face fell. "Does it exist? You haven't been lying to us, have you? Just to give us a place to hope for?"

Everybody looked to Riony then, a sea of tired and broken faces. Even Lyrrin, who knew the place they'd grown up in was real, seemed confused, worried, as though maybe that life had all been a long-lost dream.

This family Riony had gathered were all looking to her.

She firmed her insides, pushing down the fear and

doubt. "It's real. And we can go there. We will go there. But now, without being able to get too far away from the shrines, I don't know how. It doesn't have a shrine very close by. We could be tracked and found too easily."

"More excuses," Niskina muttered, turning away.

"I think I have an idea about that," Lyrrin said, patting Dracuni beside her. "I think we can shake off Griskin's scent so he can't track us on foot."

"Really?" Riony's pitch rose weirdly as she tried to hide her disappointment.

Excuses, Niskina's voice echoed in her head.

Because Niskina was right.

She had been avoiding going back to the place where she'd watched her parents die. And all her excuses were running out.

TWENTY-ONE

Lyrrin had felt good coming up with a plan. Like she was clever and contributing as much as the bigger kids. But then everybody's lives depended on her plan working, and that left Lyrrin in a constant anxious sweat.

It was a big responsibility, no matter how much Riony encouraged her that it was a great plan, that it was working.

It's been weeks since Kife and Kess have found us. It's going to be okay. It's going to be okay.

After collecting what they needed, they covered every gateway they had activated with fungus from the glass factory, they'd headed off on foot as stealthily as they could. They'd started from a shrine where there were no witnesses to point their hunters in the right direction, even if it was farther away from where they were going than others.

They didn't go straight to the village. They zigzagged, activating a couple more shrines along the way but not using the gateways, including, finally, one that was only a couple of hours walk away from their old home.

Our home.

Lyrrin didn't remember a lot from her time growing up there. And those memories were warm, fuzzy, sunlit fragments of smiling faces and games with dolls.

The sloping, crunchy ground of slate and rugged boulders was familiar in a way that felt like she belonged there. The warm orange tones of the rocks and the trees with fresh-scented, needlelike leaves brought Lyrrin a nostalgic joy she hardly understood.

But she knew it meant they were close now. Would she remember more when she was there? Would she know which home was hers if it were still standing? Would she remember her parents' faces again?

Riony hissed, holding up a hand, and everyone stilled. Lyrrin couldn't hear or see anything, and after a moment of silent, stone-still waiting, Riony shook herself and gestured them forward again.

There was one sound—the low burble of water from ahead.

"The river!" Lyrrin gasped.

She hurried to the head of the group, leading the

way. The modest stream came into view, tumbling along over flat slabs of stone. "Is this the right one? Where's the waterfall? Wasn't there a waterfall?"

"This is it." Riony nodded, her face as hard and level as those rocks. "The waterfall is over on the other side of the village."

Wasn't she excited, too, to see their home again?

Dracuni stopped for a drink, and they all filled empty waterskins, bobbing and keeping watch like deer, then they followed the stream out of the thick woods.

A wide, empty stretch of rock lay ahead—a canyon stripped bare to hard, orange stone glowing in the warm afternoon light. Concentric tiers looped around the flat base, carved into the surrounding slope like giant steps.

And in the middle, tall, spiked-log palisades were ringed around a clutch of cottages.

Lyrrin pulled her seeing stone and Benjin lifted his staff, activating his own as well.

"I can't see any movement inside," Benjin confirmed first.

Lyrrin looked a little longer, her eyes raking over the buildings. Stone walls and straw-thatched roofs were drooping and green with weeds. Raised garden beds spotted the solid stone ground, some in thin rows, and some wider rice paddies layered in tiers, all overgrown and brown.

It was there, hazy in her mind, the memory of all these things. Like watching a play performed of a story she'd once been told. It resonated within her, like a fairy tale coming to life.

But the way her sister looked at those houses reminded Lyrrin that it was a dark kind of fable—one that had ended in horrible death.

"Seems clear to me too," Lyrrin said.

Riony looked up at the last fluffy tree shading them overhead. "Maybe we should wait a little while undercover before—"

"I'm going to check it out," Niskina said, marching forward.

Benjin and Aishena followed. Lyrrin took a step, then turned back, waiting for her sister.

With a small nod, Riony walked with Lyrrin toward their old home, Dracuni at their heels.

The gated entrance hung open, the orange stone beneath it stained and dark. As everyone walked ahead, right through, Lyrrin noticed Riony frowned and walked around the darkest patches.

"No bodies," she said, barely a mumble.

"Maybe there were some survivors? Maybe the bodies were burned before the last people abandoned this place?" Lyrrin offered.

They ambled farther into the walled-in village, but there were no remains of pyres—only one large scorch mark beside a mostly destroyed town hall.

"Or maybe the shadowdragon visited again," Riony replied, her lips thin.

Riony didn't need to finish her thought—that all the humans who had died there had gotten up and walked away. Lyrrin shivered.

From up ahead, Benjin said, "There are no signs of revs. Unless they're all hiding in buildings, but that's not like them."

Aishena moved from door to door, pushing them open and peering inside, checking just in case.

"Stick with me," Riony said to Lyrrin and Dracuni.

The unidragon ruffled her wings, the thin, iridescent film over them shimmering.

"Because it could be dangerous still."

There was another gap of silence as Dracuni stared up at Riony.

"I know we came here to be safe, but we have to check it *is* safe first."

Lyrrin tried not to be jealous of the conversation she couldn't really be part of, but it didn't work.

Riony strode with purpose, beelining for a building ahead. The high thatched roof was punctuated with a solid stone chimney. Was that home? It didn't seem familiar

to Lyrrin, no more than any other cottage around them.

"Stay back," Riony said. Taking one deep breath at the already ajar door, she pushed it open.

Lyrrin watched her sister's face, the flickers of emotion over it unreadable.

"What is it?" Lyrrin asked.

"Nothing. There's nothing here." Riony stepped away, wobbly for a moment. She put a hand against the wall before rolling her shoulders and moving on.

Frowning, Lyrrin peeked in to see what Riony was looking for. Inside the dark space, a heavy anvil and barrels lay toppled on the floor. Half-formed weapons and bars of steel lay scattered amongst pliers and hammers.

What was it about this building that had drawn Riony to it? What didn't she find?

Lyrrin looked up, following a shaft of light that shone in through a hole in the ceiling, making dust motes dance.

High above the messed-up workspace, solid wooden beams created triangles and struts, holding up the high roof around the large central furnace.

The flicker of memory tugged at Lyrrin, and a pain filled her chest.

She'd been up in those rafters. Hiding. Crying. She didn't remember much though. Her eyes had been covered the entire time.

She'd only been told afterward that her parents were gone. Was this where they died? Right on this stone floor?

Lyrrin didn't want to look too closely for fear she'd see the stains of their blood.

Dracuni trilled, a questioning sound, then circled behind Lyrrin, herding her away from the haunted space.

She moved on, following the others through the ghost town.

Two more houses along, and Lyrrin's heart jumped into her throat.

That was it—their home.

She didn't need to see Riony freezing before the modest cottage to know. Her sister reached up to her neck, clasping around her collarbone for the acorn pendant that was no longer there.

Does she even realize she still does that all the time?

Lyrrin knew Riony missed their parents so much more than Lyrrin did. Lyrrin missed the absence of *parents*, of having an amma and pabba, and the few clear memories she held close. A lullaby sung at night. A grazed knee wiped clean by Amma. Wrestling with Pabba on the soft rug of their living room as stew bubbled away on the hearth.

Riony must have so many more memories. So much more of them to miss.

"Should we go in?" Lyrrin asked.

"Sure. Why not?" Riony replied flatly.

Riony went through first, pushing the heavy door. It groaned loudly, scraping a protest across the floor. The three of them winced, but after a moment where nothing rushed them from the shadows within, they stepped inside.

Dracuni sneezed softly at the dust stirred up by their entrance.

"It's our ... it's where we grew up," Riony said, as though in reply.

Dracuni's head rose up, eyes wide and curious. She trotted over the rug, mildewed and moth-eaten and barely there. Lyrrin tried to remember what colors it once was. She'd been six the last time she'd seen it. She felt like she should remember more, but so much felt locked away.

Through the side door, Lyrrin found their bedroom.

Two small beds, side by side, lay flat on the ground without frames. The mattresses were split and spilling old straw turned to sawdust by beetles and rodents.

"That one was yours. Do you remember?" Riony pointed.

There were no headboards, but the stone wall that butted up to the heads of the beds had rough carvings of flowers and stars scratched into it.

"Oh!" Lyrrin's chest swelled, happy and sad all at once. "I remember! I got in so much trouble for doing that!"

A couple of time-grayed blankets remained strewn across Lyrrin's bed, and on the pillow lay a straw doll.

Lyrrin gently picked it up, but it still cracked in her fingers, as though the straw and tiny woven clothes would turn to dust in her hands. It matched the one that she'd taken with her into the undercity, right down to the bow tied around its waist.

She rubbed her thumb over the ribbon. Blue.

The one they had left behind in the undercity was red.

More memories stirred. "I always thought ... I thought my doll had a blue ribbon. But you said I was mistaken. You said it was red. Always was red."

"I ... I'm sorry. I lied." Riony stared at the ground.

"Why? Why did you trick me?"

"I didn't have time to take both dolls. We had one each. Matching except for the ribbons. But that night ... I only grabbed one."

"You grabbed yours."

Riony nodded.

"And then you told me it was mine. You gave your doll to me."

Riony finally lifted her gaze to meet her sisters. "It was just a doll ... I didn't need it. And you'd lost so much ... I'm sorry I tricked you. I'm sorry I didn't get your doll."

Lyrrin put the toy down again. It belonged right there, left behind in this home they'd fled like the other doll remained back in the undercity. Was it still there, in their rooms?

Two homes lost.

It felt like reawakening bones in a grave, being there amongst these long-lost moments, disturbing them, returning to reclaim them.

No wonder Riony didn't want to come back.

Flinging herself around her sister's waist, Lyrrin clung tight. "It's okay. It was just a doll."

Dracuni circled around their legs in the dim, dusty light until finally, their embrace broke.

Riony's nose wrinkled, and she stared up at the ceiling. "Come on. Let's check on the others."

Back outside, Benjin ran up to meet them.

"Everything seems to have been left behind, untouched. There's so much stuff," Benjin said in awe, gazing greedily over the houses filled with belongings.

Lyrrin tried to imagine living there, in the houses people had left behind, with their belongings. There would be plenty of what they'd need.

At the lowest point of the quarry, a dam of deep blue water created a reservoir, filled by rain. Some of the garden beds had the wild remains of vegetables, growing in tumbling messes, reseeded randomly wherever there was dirt to grow. There was even the faint cluck of a chicken from behind a building.

Despite being overrun with weeds, and ghostly in the

absence of life, it was almost pretty there. It felt peaceful. Maybe it would work out.

"Wasn't there ... did we have a swing?" Lyrrin asked.

A faint smile came to Riony's lips. "Yeah, there was. Just down here."

There were no trees within the quarry boundaries, not enough soil anywhere to sustain plant life beyond the raised garden beds. But down closer to the water, a frame of logs had been built, with a row of swings hanging along it.

Lyrrin ran over and tested the frayed ropes with a strong tug before lowering her weight into the flat plank seat.

She wobbled her body to and fro, but the swing didn't move more than a jiggle.

Benjin grabbed the one beside her. "You've got to do it like this."

After a couple of sways of his body, the swing picked up.

"You never did learn how to get going on your own." Riony chuckled and gave Lyrrin a push from behind.

The hood blew back off Lyrrin's head as she swung through the air.

That was another familiar feeling—the rush and dip of her stomach and press of warm hands on her back. Her eyes prickled with tears and her mouth split in a grin.

Dracuni ran beside her, nipping playfully at her legs as they pointed skyward.

There was a crash of sound from nearby, and Riony grabbed the rope, stilling the swing in an instant.

Niskina leaned halfway through the shutters of a building nearby, feet dangling out behind her. "Yeah, there's heaps inside. Bottles, barrels, food and drink for days!"

"As long as it hasn't all gone bad by now," Aishena said from her side of the wall.

"Be careful over there," Riony called, flinching as Niskina shimmied back out of the small, high window, knocking one of the shutters down with her.

The crash echoed softly through the rocky walls of the surrounding canyon.

"Relax!" Niskina called back, far louder than Riony had dared. "This place is deserted."

"It won't matter if you're loud enough to draw in everything from the horizon!" Riony had tried to push the palisade gate closed again, but it was only propped up in place.

"Come on. Use your athame to cut the lock," Niskina told Aishena, her voice like an order.

With a brusque nod, Aishena had the glowing yellow blade in her hand.

"You don't have to do what she says!" Riony began marching toward them.

Aishena cut through the locked handle of the door,

and Niskina pushed the heavy wood, and the entire door fell inward, flat onto the stone within.

The crack that sounded was like a boulder split by lightning. It echoed around the quarry, reverberations swirling for long moments before vanishing to silence again.

Even the surface of the water rippled at the sound.

Lyrrin stood up from the still swing, staring at that deep, dark blue.

Something was moving beneath the surface. Rising pale-yellow domes dripping with strands of rot emerged. Skulls. Dark, hollow eyes. Melting, waterlogged flesh.

"Revs!" Benjin shouted first.

Five of them, all human.

"We can take them," Niskina yelled. "It's not too many. We should just take them out, then we can stay here."

Lyrrin nodded. It made sense. If there were only five of them, they could handle it. They had before.

But Riony wasn't answering. She wasn't drawing her sword. She wasn't running. She wasn't moving at all, other than with great shudders that shook her body.

She was staring at the rev in the middle.

Afternoon light glinted off the rev's skeletal hands beneath the drape of ragged sleeves.

Silver rings. Four of them, one across each finger.

Amma.

TWENTY-TWO

Amma. Riony knew she should move. She needed to get to Lyrrin and Dracuni. She needed to keep them safe. She couldn't move. Her whole body felt encased in suffocating ice.

Four silver bands. They stood out, glistening against fingers that were dark with decay. Mottled, leathery skin was wrought tight against the bones beneath.

But those were her mother's hands.

Amma.

Nothing else about the body was familiar. There were no green eyes left within the sockets to search for comfort within. There were no lips to cover teeth that used to only show when her daughters made her smile. Now those teeth were laid bare, a gnashing cage for the growls in her throat.

The wine-red woolen gown that matched her hair was a blackened, torn net. Bones were visible where once there'd been soft skin.

It was her. It wasn't her. Amma. She was dead and gone. She was there.

Amma and four other revenants crawled free of the blue-tinted reservoir, locked eyes on their prey, and rushed into attack.

Down near the swings, Lyrrin, Benjin, and Dracuni were the closest.

Get to the kids. Get to the kids. GET TO THE KIDS.

Words screamed through Riony's head. Maybe she even screamed them out loud because Aishena and Niskina bolted past her on either side, running in to meet the ravenous attackers.

But still, Riony's body remained stuck in place, turned to stone. Shattered, cracking stone, falling to pieces. If she couldn't hold herself together, there would be nothing left.

Amma.

The last time Riony had seen her mother, she'd lain twitching on the floor, flesh pulled free from all the soft parts of her and eyes staring blankly upward to where Riony clutched Lyrrin, hiding in the rafters. Amma had already been dead then. Riony hoped she'd already been dead then.

Either way, it had taken longer for her to die than Pabba. The revs had left him alone once he was still, but Amma still twitched, driving the undead into a frenzy. Why wouldn't she stop moving? Wouldn't it ever end?

It had lasted forever, until the stars had fallen from the sky and Riony's hands had grown ancient and cold, covering Lyrrin's eyes and ears, and Riony had forgotten how to breathe from holding in her screams. Had she died too? Why wouldn't Amma stop twitching?

Even now, her corpse refused to lay still.

Riony's breath was coming too hard, too fast, burning through her body and clouding her head. Her eyes dimmed at the edges as a deep, painful terror overwhelmed her.

With athames glowing in red and yellow, Aishena downed one rev with deadly precision as she moved herself in front of Benjin. There was a squabble as he tried to push back in front again, barely missed by a clawing hand.

Niskina had her poleaxe out, taking strong swings at the rev closest to her as Lyrrin and Dracuni both dodged back, trying to create some distance between them and the undead.

Move. Move. Move, Riony pleaded with her bones, teeth gritted and eyes watering.

With a strangled grunt of effort, she drew her sword. Her fingers trembled uselessly across the rune, rattling beyond control, unable to activate it.

One rev split free from the brawl near the water, knocked aside by a blow from Benjin's staff. Scrambling up from the ground, it caught sight of Riony.

A rev with silver rings. Her rotted jaw unhinged with the ferociousness of her howl. She charged, arms and legs flicking in a hideous, convulsing gallop.

Amma.

Riony couldn't move. She could only hold her heavy—too heavy—sword in front of her.

The rotting corpse of her mother smashed into that sword like a ball against a bat. But it wasn't the ball that gave way, flying off again. It was Riony that crumbled.

She landed flat on her back, sword crushing down over her chest and cheek, and the squelching, putrid flesh of the revenant—*Amma*—landed on top.

All the air left Riony's chest in a *whuff*. Even if she could draw breath, she didn't have time before the body on top of her flailed again into attack.

Those fingers with those rings had once been a source of comfort. Those hands that had once balmed her back when she'd been whipped, that had tucked her unruly hair behind her ear. Those fingers with those rings, one for each generation of midwife in their line, that were one day meant to be passed down again.

Those fingers scraped across Riony's scalp, pulling free a fistful of hair.

"Ri? We need you and your big-ass sword! What are you doing?"

Those fingers dug into uncovered arms between bracers and shoulder guards, squeezing and cutting deep between the muscles.

Riony's mouth opened, gasping, but she couldn't even scream.

Amma. Please.

Teeth gnashed and growled above the sword and Riony's face, turned and pressed into the hard ground beneath.

"Riony!"

"Someone get over there!"

Pain lanced into Riony's stomach, a skeletal finger, sharp like a dagger, pushing deep. Her breaths were frantic, bellowing. She was sobbing, out of control. She couldn't move, couldn't move, couldn't lift one finger gripped white-knuckled around the hilt of the sword she couldn't raise in defense.

Sister!

"I can't get away from this one!"

"Lyrrin, look out!"

Boney knees and long-nailed toes scrambled over Riony's legs, shredding through leather pants to the skin

of her thighs.

Amma. Stop.

The finger in her stomach curled like a hook, pulling free with a bloody pop before stabbing in again.

Stop hurt! Stop, bad thing!

Pale, iridescent scales danced across the ground in front of Riony's paralyzed face.

Dracuni's jaws snapped, closing on air as the revenant continued its clawing frenzy, arms and legs lashing faster than Dracuni could bite.

Stop.

Stop.

Her thoughts and Dracuni's thoughts overlapped.

The shadowdragon-risen body of Amma ignored the unidragon entirely. It only cared to extract its vengeance upon humans. It only wanted Riony's blood and was taking plenty of it.

Maybe there was something of her mother still in there too, seeking revenge for having been allowed to die, to die so painfully, as her daughter did nothing but watch.

I'm sorry. I'm sorry. Amma, please.

Dracuni snapped again, moving in closer, her feet beside Riony's face. The small dragon bucked and growled, and the rotting body bucked and growled in return, trying to reach past the stabbing horn to the soft human.

A finger dragged across Riony's ribs and finally a scream emerged, rattling from her throat. On the inside, Riony no longer pleaded to make herself move. She just pleaded for it to be over.

"Why isn't she moving?"

"This rev won't stay down! I can't ..."

The bang of an exploding crystal cracked through the quarry.

Amma's fingers raked down the side of Riony's neck and collarbone, almost a tender motion, drawn too deep into the skin. Riony twitched with agony. She couldn't even move enough to curl up into a ball—only jolt and jerk at each stabbing nail into her flesh.

This is how she must have felt. This is how Amma felt as she died.

Stop, creature, stop!

Dracuni fretted, dancing on her talons. Her snapping jaws and jabbing horn only slowed the tearing apart of Riony's body and soul. Both felt shredded to ribbons.

With one big push from Dracuni, the revenant rolled off Riony. There wasn't even a second before the living corpse turned to attack again.

With a high, desperate roar, Dracuni rose up on her hind legs. Her chest swelled. Her mouth opened. Rows of short, ivory teeth glistened.

And she breathed.

A bright, shimmering flame gusted out of the unidragon's throat. It didn't touch Riony as it passed over her, catching the revenant right in the face. Flames like wafting moonlight rippled over the rev.

And it didn't burn. But it did change.

Spine arching and limbs twitching, the revenant of Riony's mother rolled onto its back. The silver flames flickered all around its bones and rotting skin, and beneath that bright light, flesh reformed.

Soft and pink at first, then deepening to bronze, muscle and tissue grew over yellowed bones. The revenant gurgled and howled as the empty section at her stomach closed over, organs plumping out beneath the skin. She curled up, then stretched out as though in agony, raising up onto her knees, knees that were now whole again.

She was being healed. Every part of her was changing beneath the iridescent flames from corpse to living flesh.

Deep-red hair sprouted from her scalp and eyes bulged wet within sockets, and as the throat regrew, Amma gave the most dreadful human scream Riony had ever heard.

"Amma?" Riony rasped, her chest convulsing with ragged breaths.

Finally, she moved, without any order given to her limbs, without deciding first to do so, one hand detached

from the hilt of her sword and reached for her mother.

Her mother, there, made whole again.

Could it be? Was she healed? Riony shifted, her sword sliding off her to the ground. Her body moved, responding to the sight of her mother, trying to draw her closer.

"Amma?" The shrill, desperate cry didn't come from Riony.

Her mother's scream juddered out to nothing. She hung there, kneeling on the ground, face turned up and arms dangling, and there was no more movement. No rise and fall of her chest. No pulse at her neck.

The body—*Amma, Amma!*—went still then fell in a slump.

"Amma? No, no. No*!" Not again. Not again!*

Riony couldn't bear it. She wished the revenant's clawing hands had ended her because she couldn't take seeing her mother there before her, watching her die a second time. She crawled, sobbing over the body, perfectly healed and untouched, and perfectly lifeless.

She wrapped her arms around the body of her mother and screamed wordlessly.

The body before her, as whole as it looked, as beautiful as it looked, was empty. All the flesh had healed, all the blood and bone and nail and hair restored. But not her soul—that had fled into the stars long ago. Not her life.

There were footsteps all around Riony now, rushing, cursing bodies.

"Sparks, what was that? Did you see that?" Benjin gasped.

"Amma?" Lyrrin's voice was broken by sobs. "It was ... it was ..."

"Help her up. Get her away from ... that." Aishena's hands came underneath Riony's armpits, dragging her off the body.

Riony tried to fight her, tried to hold the body of her mother just a little longer. But all her strength was gone.

She was up on wobbly legs, pressed between two people.

"Oh no, oh no, Riony. Are you okay? Hey, can you hear us?" Niskina moved close to Riony's face.

Dracuni remained silent.

Aishena's voice was hushed. "What do we do?"

Riony blinked, trying to regain her vision through thick, sticky tears. Blood dripped down her arms and from the tips of her fingers, over her stomach, pooling at the hem of her pants.

She couldn't. She couldn't do this. She couldn't do anything. She wasn't okay. She didn't know what to do.

She thrust the clinging hands off her, and she ran.

TWENTY-THREE

Kife hurled a stick into the campfire, making it spark up. "Another dead end! This was your last chance, Kess. And there was nothing here."

Kess dodged away from the flying cinders. She'd just kindled those flames and she scowled at the scattered embers, struggling to stay lit. They'd set down in the clearing around midday after finding no sign of Riony in the village within the quarry, and from how Kife had settled in, it didn't seem like they were moving on anytime soon if they even knew where to go next.

"It was worth checking. It matched what Riony said about where she lived after leaving the estate. But there could be other similar villages. Maybe it's not the right one, or maybe they haven't arrived—"

Kife lay back on his blanket again, as he had been for hours, hands folded behind his head. "Or maybe they're hiding underground somewhere like rodents and we're never going to find them flying from one side of Elundrae and back again every day! You've ruined all our hopes of capturing them. You and your dumb dog have lost the trail."

Kess petted Griskin on the ear. "The fungus stuffs up his nose. He can't help it. I didn't know those fools would be smart enough to use that against us."

She remembered the parcel of herbs wrapped in a handkerchief that someone had tucked into Griskin's collar when in the caves. She should have worked out what was in it before discarding it. But she'd never imagined Pony would use the fungus as a way to mask their trail.

"So you're both useless then."

"And what have you done?"

"If it weren't for me and my dragon, we never would have even gotten close to catching them the few times we did." He rubbed his temples. "I need a break to clear my head, work out a new plan. Somewhere that's not a filthy patch of ground!"

Go home then. Kess seethed.

She regretted bringing her brother into this at all. And she'd always known she would, but she'd thought any suffering he inflicted upon her would at least be balanced by how useful he and his dragon were. But they were no closer, at all, to her goal. And she still needed his wings.

She said, "It will be dark soon enough, so this filthy patch of ground will have to do for the night."

Kife grunted. He grabbed a leather pail from the stack of bags beside him and threw it at Kess. "Go and get some water for my dragon."

Kess caught the bucket made of thick hide, riveted together. She wanted to tell him to do something for himself for once, but at least heading down to the river would give her a reason to be away from him for a while.

"Try to keep the fire going," she said and turned Griskin away.

They meandered through the dense forest, weaving between the towering trees shrouded in slivers of gray-green foliage. The earthy scent of damp soil mingled with the crisp, refreshing aroma of needlelike leaves scattering the ground, crushed under Griskin's paws.

The river ran close to the village, and the distant murmur of flowing water grew louder until Kess could see the whitewater rush of it over the sharp-edged boulders.

Before they stepped free of the tree line, Griskin's ears pricked up. His nose twitched.

"What is it?" Kess whispered.

Tension prickled through the muscles down the back of Griskin's neck beneath her hands. She turned her own face toward the light breeze blowing over the water from upstream.

The wolf released a rumbling growl.

Kess tightened her grip and pulled herself low into his fur, a surge of anticipation coursing through her veins as she urged him to follow the scent.

Keeping to the long afternoon shadows of the thick trunks, Griskin skulked swiftly on silent paws, chasing his nose. Kess wasn't sure what had gotten him so riled up, whether he was leading her to their dinner or something else.

But nothing could have prepared Kess for what she saw as they rounded a bend in the river.

A thin waterfall sprayed down between tall rocks into a round pool below, gurgling and glugging. On the shore, pieces of armor and clothing lay strewn, and a bloodied, bare body stood in the stream of water. Strands of vibrant red hair looked like fire within the flowing water.

Pony?

Kess flinched and pulled Griskin back behind the bushes that ringed the tumbling stream, making sure they weren't seen.

She took a breath and dared to look again.

It's her.

Kess's heart kicked into a racing beat. She was right. They had come here. It was the right village. She'd found them.

And there was Riony, alone, defenseless, not even the clothes on her scarred back to protect her.

Kess's face flushed hot, and she almost turned away again, ashamed of looking. But this was who she'd been hunting. Her prey—that was all. Just an obstruction between Kess and what Kess really wanted.

There were no signs of anyone else, and Griskin sniffed the air a couple of times but didn't direct her onward.

Where are the others? Where's Dracuni? What happened?

A softer, more feminine sound echoed amongst the splashes of the waterfall.

Kess listened closer and heard it again.

Deep, gulping sobs mixed with the burbling of water. Riony's body twisted to the side, and the water flowing over her ran red.

The breath in Kess's throat caught.

She was injured. Badly injured. Even the constant spray of water wasn't clearing away the blood that continued to flow freely from long scratches and punctured holes across her arms, stomach, neck.

Riony's back curved and shook with the intensity of her grief, and she clutched the rocks beside her in support but still fell onto her knees.

Kess had never seen her like this. Never. Not after being cut by whips or glass or daggers or swords. She wasn't sure she'd ever seen Riony cry.

And this wasn't just crying. This was a soul-deep, broken wail.

She wasn't even trying to stand anymore and had curled against the back wall of the falls, letting the water hammer over her.

Kess's own eyes suddenly felt wet, and she widened them in horror and refusal of the sympathetic urge.

Turning away quickly, Kess tried to slow the furious pace of her breaths.

Whatever had happened, whatever was happening, it was wrong to be a spectator there. Even her enemy deserved privacy in such a vulnerable moment. It wouldn't be honorable to take advantage of it.

Even if it would have been a good idea, even if it got her so much closer to claiming Dracuni as her own, the thought of doing anything to Riony then caused an aching pressure in Kess's chest.

Kess led Griskin silently back down the river. She filled the bucket, wondering whether that water held Riony's blood, and her hands shivered. She returned to camp.

The fire was out. She scowled, dropping the bucket with a splash beside her brother.

"Watch it! What took you so long?" Kife sat up, flicking droplets off his chest.

"Nothing." Kess lowered herself off Griskin to her blanket and thumped down on her side. Her pulse and breathing were still frantic.

"Why do you look so flushed?"

"It's nothing!" Griskin lay down beside her, and Kess turned her face away from her brother, hiding it in the wolf's fur.

"Did something happen?" There wasn't any concern in Kife's words—only the edge of blame.

"No. Shut up. I'm going to sleep."

"It's not even dark yet. And the fire is out. And you haven't hunted."

"Then do it yourself if you aren't too dumb to manage it!"

Kife grumbled, kicking around behind her in a drawn-out show of annoyance as he worked on the fire.

Kess curled up tighter, trying to calm the raging pounding in her chest. She closed her eyes but only saw the body, the blood, the water.

What had happened? Why was Riony alone? Had she lost the others? Had she lost Dracuni? A stab of coldness dug into Kess's gut at the thought that the little dragon had been hurt somehow, that Riony hadn't been able to protect it.

No. Riony had told Kess she'd die before letting something happen to Dracuni, and Kess believed her.

But if the unidragon was still around, why didn't Riony use it to heal herself? Even in the glass factory, she'd tried to refuse the healing blood. Did she care so much about the creature that she'd suffer herself rather than harm it?

Kess could feel the truth of the answer. She knew Riony well enough that she couldn't deny it.

She always had been the kind of person who put her suffering last.

Kess closed her eyes again, haunted this time by a different vision. A thin line of blood across a cheek. A lash in her hands. Fingers around her throat.

It had been Kife's revenge.

The evening after Kess had warned him off Riony, with a dagger thrown close to his neck, Kife had sat at dinner and proudly told their parents just how excellent Kess had gotten with her aim.

"Really?" Her mother wiped her downturned mouth with a napkin.

"Wouldn't it be fun to have a demonstration?" Kife asked, eyes twinkling.

Her father placed his metal goblet on the table. "Yes, I would like to see this myself."

He muttered the words as though he couldn't believe

his daughter could be good at anything.

Kess's lips twitched, and she pushed the food around on her plate. "My aim is coming along just fine, but it would be crass to draw weapons at dinner."

"No, let's!" Her mother clapped her hands together. "A throwing demonstration it is. I want to see my daughter's excellence as well."

All three of them beamed sly smiles, like predators whose prey was her humiliation.

"Hmm, how shall we do this?" Kife picked a small apple from the overflowing fruit bowl, tossing it and catching it a couple of times.

He stared over Kess's head to where Riony stood still behind her chair. "Come here, you."

"Kife!" Kess hissed a warning.

He only smiled as Riony rounded the table to stand in front of him. He gestured for her to bend down to his seated level, then jammed the apple in her mouth.

"Go on now, back over against the wall. All the way. That's it." Kife leaned back in his chair, grinning at Kess. "You can hit that target, can't you, sister?"

"*Easily*," Kess rasped.

The blushed red of the apple matched Riony's hair as she stood stock-still, eyes on Kess without reprimand or judgment. Only waiting. Only a terrible feeling of

acknowledgment that both of them were the victim in that situation.

Kess turned away, glaring at the family portrait above her father that only showed three people. "You should have picked a harder target for me. Shall I show you how I can hit right through your eye in our family portrait there?"

"The apple, Kess. Go on," Lord Heithorn said. "No need to destroy artwork."

Kess looked down at the table, not wanting to look again at the target. Her fingers trembled as she closed them around a dull serving knife.

"No, no. One of your fine throwing knives. They're so lovely and sharp," Kife said.

Everyone stared at her, waiting. Could she refuse? She would be humiliated either way, whether she took the shot or not. Riony would be punished whether she took the shot or not. The only way out was to throw the blade and throw it well.

She shifted around in her chair, drew one of her thin steel blades, and tried to steady her hand and breath.

She could do it. She could hit such a target. But normally her targets weren't so very close to the eyes and lips and cheeks of someone ... someone she ...

If she missed ... *if she missed*.

She wouldn't miss. She sent the dagger flying.

Riony didn't even flinch.

The knife stuck into the apple, inelegantly, askew.

Kess stifled a shuddering sigh. "Done. Happy now?"

"She's bleeding!" Lady Heithorn sounded scandalized but a smile still bared her teeth. "Your pet is bleeding, Kessara. Poor form."

Turning back, Kess saw it too, a thin trickle of blood from where the knife and apple and lips all met in the corner of Riony's mouth.

With a hard, glimmering sneer, Kife stood and patted Kess on the shoulder. "Aw, better luck next time. Looks like you need more practice."

Her father said nothing at all. Just sniffed and left the table. Lady Heithorn and the serving staff followed him out.

Kife gave Kess's shoulder another tight, rough squeeze before leaving as well.

Nothing was said as Riony removed the apple and wiped her mouth with the back of her hand. It only smeared the blood, making it seem even redder. She picked Kess up and carried her back to her room.

Kess stared at her bloody chin the entire way back, unable to look away. An uncontrollable, awful turmoil of anger and shame curdled her stomach and burned her ears.

As gently as ever, Riony set Kess down on the side of her bed. On the bedstand lay a lash, gifted by the lord and lady in case Kess wanted to discipline her slave herself. She never had. She glared at that thick fringe of knotted leather.

"Do you ... need anything else tonight?" There was a softness in Riony's voice that infuriated Kess.

"You moved!" she snapped, her eyes stinging. "You moved and ruined my shot!"

Riony shrugged. "It's okay. The cut isn't bad. The kind of thing that might make your blight-born brother cry, but I've had worse."

The anger in Kess expanded in a rush, like flames under bellows. Was the tame-brained slave actually trying to comfort her? Trying to make her feel better?

How dare she? How dare she be the one, standing there bleeding, and still she pities me? How dare she be the one who is hurt over and over and still she pities me?

"Turn around!" Kess barked.

"What? Why?" Riony did anyway.

"Get on your knees!" Her voice was a broken shriek, and her hand wrapped around the handle of the lash.

She knelt. "What are you ...?"

Kess struck, bringing the lash across the thin fabric between Riony's shoulders.

The girl hissed, spine arching. She sounded more surprised than anything. "Kess!"

"You humiliate me! Every day!" She struck again,

harder. Blood welled through the pale cloth. "Your very existence shames me!"

Riony's shoulders rose and fell as each stroke cut her skin, her breath snorting and ragged, and then with an animalistic cry, she thrust back to her feet and flew at Kess, knocking the lash from her hand with the sweep of an arm. Her face was red and wild with ferocious emotions, skin stretched around bared teeth, still marked with blood.

They both screamed and clawed and Kess fell back onto the bed, and then Riony was upon her, fingers closing around Kess's neck. The grip was vicious but not enough to crush, and already softening as Riony's eyes widened, searched, as though she were coming back to herself.

"Do it!" Kess scraped the words free. Sobs clogged her throat as much as the squeeze of Riony's hands. "Do it! Get rid of me and be better for it! Get rid of me!"

Riony released her grip, stumbling backward.

"You want me dead! I know you do. Do it! Nobody will care if I'm gone!"

Kess had never forgotten the look of horror on Riony's face as she fled, leaving Kess alone with her guilt and her tears.

The girl she tormented had refused to grant her mercy, even if that mercy was for both of them.

And still, even now, it felt like every drop of Riony's blood spilled was Kess's fault, that Kess's presence still caused her suffering, and it no longer seemed to matter that it was for the cause of something greater.

Kess had always justified every cruelty. She'd needed her Pony to get around. She'd needed to get herself a dragon and would go through anybody to get it. She needed to capture Dracuni, and it didn't matter who was hurt in doing so.

But Kess could feel the truth worming through her veins like hot wire. She could no longer ignore it, no longer lie to herself.

It did matter.

Now Kess just needed to work out what that meant for what she did next.

Twenty-Four

Riony wasn't sure how long she cried beneath the waterfall. It was definitely at least one eternity, maybe two.

She cried until her bones ached and her throat was raw, and every time she tried to pull herself together—because how could she have *run away?*—she only cried harder again.

No longer could she tell the difference between the sobs shaking her body and the water pounding down over it. She curled up on a smooth worn stone beneath the cascade. Maybe the water would wear her down too, wash her away to nothing, and it wouldn't hurt anymore.

At least her wounds would be clean. The thought of those putrid hands, her mother's hands, digging into her flesh had driven her to strip off and stumble into the falls. She wanted to wash everything away.

Despite the crimson threads still spilling from her lacerations, they didn't bother her. She could handle physical pain. It was the only thing she'd ever really been good at. What a talent to have.

But she couldn't handle loss. She couldn't handle seeing those she loved die, or want to die, or come back from the dead only to die again. How could she survive that? It was clear that she couldn't.

It's too hard. Everything is too hard.

And even then, she knew the others still needed her, and she'd abandoned them. How could she go back, where they were, into the village where she'd lost her mother twice?

I'm not strong enough.

Everything felt broken, and Riony knew it could never return to how it was before. Everything she'd lost was gone forever. Everything had changed. Even this waterfall felt so much smaller than she remembered.

She'd lost so much, and she was so tired.

Her heart ached for her friends, knowing how much they had lost too. She had to pull herself together, for them.

Lifting her head under the spray of water, she let it rush over her eyelids and cheeks for a moment, cooling them before she stood and opened her eyes. She flicked wet hair off her face.

Over at the tree line, a rustling of leaves caught her attention. She made herself small and still behind a boulder. Nothing leaped out at her after a couple of moments waiting.

"Lyrrin? Aish?" she called softly, not wanting to draw attention to herself.

There was no reply.

"Niskina?"

It wasn't Dracuni either. She couldn't sense the unidragon nearby. She could barely sense her at all now that her own mind had stilled enough to listen.

In a rush, Riony squeezed her pants back on over wet legs. Her shirt went over her head in a tangle of torn and sticky fabric, and she scooped up her armor and boots. The metal clattered in her arms as she scurried over the rocks to where she'd seen the movement.

Scanning through the surrounding forest, she couldn't see any sign of motion beyond the dappled, late afternoon light streaming through the swaying trees and the odd bird flitting about.

Then she looked down. Tracks. Imprinted into the soft soil, leading up to this position and away again. The prints of a large wolf.

"No, sparking *no*!"

Riony ran. Barefooted over sharp sticks and bristling

leaves, flashes of branches and trunks either side, she hurled herself at a breakneck pace through the forest.

The air rushed across the torn parts of her skin, stinging the scratches as they dried and puckered. The deeper holes spurted blood with each pounding step, and Riony pressed a hand tight over her stomach in an attempt to hold it in.

Ducking through the broken gap in the palisade she had escaped through, she scraped her back and dropped a shoulder guard but didn't slow down.

Up ahead, Lyrrin sat on the flat stone ground, right where Riony had left her. Her sister had Dracuni beside her, the dragonling's head lying limply across her lap.

Riony came skidding to a stop beside them. Dracuni didn't stir.

"What happened? What did Kess do?" Riony dropped her remaining armor and reached for Dracuni.

"Riony! You're back!" Lyrrin said at the same time. Then, "Kess? What do you mean?"

"She ..." Riony looked all around them.

There were no sounds of fighting.

There were no revs left, no ... bodies nearby. Benjin rustled around in a garden bed, and Niskina and Aishena were down near the water, stacking logs and sticks.

There was no sign of Kess or Kife or his dragon. "I saw tracks ... wolf tracks. I thought Kess had found us."

"We haven't seen her."

"Then what's wrong with Dracuni?" Riony scooped a hand under the unidragon's chin, lifting her heavy head.

Dracuni blinked lazily. Her thoughts were soft and muted. ***Very tired.***

Just tired? Not wounded or sedated by morass mercy. Riony shook her head in disbelief.

They had been wolf tracks, hadn't they? Riony had only looked at them for a moment before running. Even if they were, and not some other animal, it could have been a different wild wolf.

It couldn't have been Kess.

If it were Kess, Riony would have been floating in the river with a knife through her back. If it were Kess, the Heithorns would have been here by now, stealing Dracuni away.

Riony's skin was clammy and a shiver ran down her back. She was still expecting the wolf-riding monster to burst out from between the cottages.

Lyrrin patted Dracuni's neck. "She just seems to be feeling weak."

Released from Riony's hand, Dracuni's head flopped back down on Lyrrin's lap, and her eyelids fluttered closed again.

"Aishena said it can happen with young dragons when they are learning to flame. She said a dragon's flame uses up their blood—that she didn't realize what that meant

for Dracuni until ..." Lyrrin choked up.

Until Dracuni breathed healing fire.

But the body she'd healed was one already long dead.

Leaning over Dracuni, Riony pulled Lyrrin into a hug. "I'm sorry. I'm sorry you saw that. I should have made it all stop sooner. I couldn't move. I—"

"No. It's not your fault. You didn't want to come back here. We all made you. We made that happen to you." Lyrrin squeezed Riony and sniffled. "I was so scared for you."

Riony winced at the pressure against her wounds but didn't let go.

Lyrrin seemed to notice though and pulled away, eyes on the smears of blood. "Were you hurt badly?"

"Not at all," Riony whispered.

Lyrrin gave her a dry, knowing glare. "You're allowed to say you got hurt. You're allowed to be scared sometimes too. You don't have to always pretend you're okay."

In the time since they'd left the undercity, Lyrrin had grown so much. Riony had felt protective of her ever since the moment the newborn was given a death sentence for looking different. And even more since Riony's parents had sent her and Lyrrin into the rafters to hide, telling her that she had to look after her sister.

It was her job, her responsibility alone. Because they were gone.

She'd never stopped to question who, then, would ever care for her in the times when she was broken. She'd just tried her best to never *be* broken, no matter what. Until everything came crumbling down.

And there was Lyrrin.

A soft, guttural sob escaped through Riony's aching throat, and she hung her head. "I'm not okay."

"Me either." Lyrrin reached for her hand, and they sat together in silence for a while, quiet tears running.

When she spoke again, Lyrrin's voice sounded younger than usual. "I thought, maybe for a moment, that we might have Amma back. Alive again."

Riony's chest sagged. "Yeah. Me too."

Dracuni's eyelids fluttered. ***Tried to burn. Tried to help. Didn't know who body was.***

"It's okay. You stopped *it* hurting me. It wasn't really our mother."

Still sorry. Still bad. Dracuni remained unmoving, her thoughts muffled. She seemed so very weak, barely able to move.

Running a hand over Dracuni's snout, Riony said, "I'm sorry I didn't come back sooner."

"She just needs rest. There was nothing you needed to do. Aishena and Niskina are handling everything." Lyrrin looked over Riony's shoulder.

"They are?" Turning, Riony saw then what the two other young women were doing with the branches and logs they'd dragged down near the water's edge.

They were building a pyre.

It wasn't neat, created from stacks of dried brambles and straw, overlaid with already half-burned timbers that had been part of the destroyed town hall. Lying on top was a body shrouded in blue cloth.

Aishena caught sight of Riony and strode up the quarry slope. There was a firmness to her steps that had been missing since they'd left the undercity, and despite the pained expression on her face, she stood tall.

"I only know Taenish funeral customs, but Niskina said she remembers blue was the color used for her mother."

Jogging up to join them, Niskina took a deep breath, wiped her eyes, and smiled. "I hope it's okay. We wanted this to be right for you."

"For me?" Riony swallowed.

"Lyrrin told us you didn't get to say goodbye properly last time. And it's hard ... not getting to say goodbye. It doesn't matter how long it has been," Aishena said.

She pulled Yoskar's glasses from her pocket and held them in a tight fist at her chest. "That doesn't excuse that we've been so caught up in our own grief that we have been making you carry us for so long."

Riony tried to reply, but her throat felt gummed closed.

Niskina knelt in front of her. "We're going to do better. I'm sorry. I've only been thinking about myself, and you're always so strong, I never saw your pain. But we're here for you."

Riony felt as though she should be mortified, humiliated that everyone was seeing her at her weakest. Instead, she felt warm and cared for and lighter than she had in a long time.

"Blue is perfect."

"These are the best I could find." Benjin ran over, flushed and panting with dried leaves stuck in his hair.

He handed Riony a bouquet of stringy stems, spotted with a rainbow of modest flowers.

"Thank you." A soft smile grew on Riony's lips.

It looked like he'd picked every flowering plant he could find, and in doing so had, he collected herbs and weeds that Riony had learned all the names and properties of from her mother. Placing flowers on a pyre was a Taenish custom, rather than Rolanian, but it seemed right.

"Are you ready?" Aishena asked, head bowed.

Riony groaned up to her feet. "We'll find out soon."

Lyrrin didn't follow. Her hood was off, and the bright blue of her natural hair sparkled along her hairline. Both of her gloves were off too, and Riony realized how comfortable she had gotten around the others, how nice it was that

Lyrrin could show herself to them and be accepted.

"Are you coming?"

Lyrrin shook her head. "I think I'll watch from here. I want to stay with Dracuni. Yes, I'm sure."

I rest. Dracuni whiffled.

It wasn't far to where the pyre was built, near the water's edge farther along from the swings. Lyrrin and Dracuni would still see everything, hear everything. Riony would have liked to have had Lyrrin by her side, but at the same time needed the space for herself.

Aishena said quietly, like an apology, "The others are in there too, underneath. So they can all be burned."

Riony nodded. That was important. The dead must be burned. She tried not to think of them as revs sharing in her mother's funeral. They were likely other people from her village. Riony hadn't looked at any of them long enough to try to identify them. She refused to speculate on who they were. But they'd all been people once. They all deserved a funeral too.

Riony placed the bouquet over the blue-draped body, and Aishena stepped forward. With a look to Riony for approval, she placed Yoskar's glasses atop the pyre.

Riony gave her a single firm nod, and Aishena let out a long breath.

Beside them, Benjin had the burn rune on his staff lit

and held it out, waiting for Riony to take it.

She hesitated, unsure whether they should light the pyre, whether it might attract attention. But fires were common in Elundrae, and she could see that she wasn't the only one who needed this funeral to move on.

Taking the staff, she thrust the brand-hot crystal into a tuft of straw and watched it light.

They all stood in silence as the flames licked around the edges of the blue fabric, growing stronger until the pyre was ablaze in brilliant heat.

"I don't remember enough from my mother's funeral to know what to say," Niskina whispered. "I could speak delver rights, if you like?"

"That's okay. I know what to say." Riony's mouth felt dry. She didn't remember the exact words, but she knew the meaning of what to express deep in her core.

Sunset had only begun to tint the horizon and the sky above had turned a deep cornflower blue. A single star pricked through the smoky expanse, shining down early.

Riony didn't have a candle to hold as she spoke, so she pulled a thin stick from the fire's edge, holding it upright so the small flame flickered before her.

"My love to those who rise to find their way home. The candles will guide you, the bright points in the sky, held by our ancestors, our family gone before. My love to you as you hold your own candle in the sky and wait for us, those you've left behind." Riony stuttered over the words and tears spilled from her eyes.

She looked into the light of the burning stick she held, then up into the sky. "Keep your candles burning bright. We will be together again."

"That was beautiful." Niskina sniffed and wrapped her arms around Riony.

Even within Niskina's tight embrace, Riony felt as though she was breathing easier than she had in a while.

They stood together for a long time as the fire roared and crackled and then stepped back as the heat grew too intense.

Aishena stood at attention, the flames reflected in her glistening dark eyes as she stared at the pyre.

She blinked slowly, then turned to Riony. "We thought we would stay here tonight, but we can move on again tomorrow if you want."

"Move on? Where?"

"Anywhere that's not here if you don't want to be here. We'd understand." Looking back up the slope to where Lyrrin cradled Dracuni, Aishena continued, "We could have left tonight if Dracuni was up to it, but she's too big to be carried now."

From the dreamy, calm sensations Riony was getting from Dracuni, she could tell the young dragon was already

asleep. And she clearly needed the rest.

Riony had a vague memory of Kess telling her how some types of dragon had flammable blood, and it was that blood they breathed, spraying and igniting from their mouths. It was why snowflames had such a short lifespan, with their concentrated liquid fire.

That worried Riony.

"We'll stay as long as Dracuni needs to recover fully. And then ..." Riony looked up over the cottages, the untended gardens spilling over their raised beds, the tall palisade walls.

There were painful memories there, both old and fresh, but also a sense that this was home. And maybe it could be again.

"We'll see if we can make a home here. There don't seem to be any other revs. We can fix the palisade. We could be safe."

"You don't have to stay here for us. Only if you're okay with it," Aishena insisted again.

Riony smirked. "I'd be more okay with it if you decided we could share a cottage together. Maybe a bed? I'm in tremendous need of comforting."

"And there she is again." Aishena rolled her eyes, but a small smile shifted her lips. "It's good to have you back."

Riony shrugged bashfully. "It's good to be back."

And for a moment, Riony felt it, that promise of safety, a place where they could stop running, a place that could be a home, and her heart itself seemed to sigh.

And then the sound of dragon wings filled the air.

TWENTY-FIVE

Riony closed her eyes for a single second, hoping it was only her imagination. Or the roar of fire. Distant thunder. An oversized bird. She'd even take the shadowdragon itself, although she knew its wings made no such sound.

Please let it be anything—anything other than that purple dragon.

She looked up, and there it was, swooping down toward them. Kife's dragon, holding two riders and the wolf in its front claws. Gusts from the dragon's wings stirred up the pyre, sending sparks skittering across the rocky ground.

It felt like a nightmare after having just woken up from one. They had nowhere to run. The nearest shrine was hours away. There were no trees to block the dragon from landing. And it was heading directly for Lyrrin and Dracuni, sitting together on the clear ground.

"How did they find us?" Niskina cried. She turned from side to side, searching as well for a sanctuary that wasn't there.

The wolf prints. It must have been Kess at the waterfall. But she would have had plenty of time and opportunity to have killed Riony then and come right here afterward. Why did it take so long?

Why would Kess choose not to take her advantage while Riony was so vulnerable?

She couldn't understand, but she could go crazy trying to understand that nasty girl's motivations. Maybe she chose not to end Riony then so that Riony could be witness to Kess's success in capturing Dracuni now. That didn't seem like Kess, though. She was driven, selfish, but not necessarily cruel.

Perhaps she'd spent too long with Kife, and he'd twisted away any humanity she had left.

Either way, they were there now, and they were going for Dracuni. Riony glared up at the tiny figures riding high upon the dragon's back, silhouetted against the dusk.

You don't have her yet.

They had nowhere to go. But they could still fight.

Scanning her eyes across the ground to the place where she'd dropped it, Riony couldn't see her weapon anywhere. "Where's my sword?"

"Beside the swings!" Aishena barked, breaking out her athames, her eyes on the approaching giant.

While it was still far higher than seemed safe, the dragon's front claws snapped open, releasing the wolf. He whined as he dropped through the air, and there was a cracking thump as he landed behind the overgrown gardens. Voices rose from the dragon's back, lost in the wind and thwumping beat of wings.

Riony found her sword with her eyes, leaning up against the triangular struts of the swings, and she ran for it as the dragon curved around in a tight banking turn, one wingtip touching the ground.

The purple beast straightened up again, claws out, diving at Dracuni and Lyrrin.

"Come on! Come on!" Lyrrin was on her feet now, bending over Dracuni with her arms around the unidragon's torso, trying to lift her.

Dracuni's legs slipped weakly against the hard ground, unable to stay upright.

Riony snatched up her sword without stopping, dragging it as she raced on. The heavy edge clattered and chipped along the rock-hard ground. She traced a finger over the rune without looking, eyes ahead as she tried to ignore the stabbing pains in her stomach and sting in her arms.

She had to get to Lyrrin and Dracuni in time. She was too far away and the dragon too close.

Aishena got there first. "Let go!"

"No!" Lyrrin screamed back.

Aishena was stronger, pulling Lyrrin down into a tackle, rolling beneath the sharp talons that cut through the air. The wide purple wings thrust outward, slowing the dragon's dive.

Dracuni bleated, snout drooping, paws scrambling weakly as the purple etherdart collected her into the cage of its huge claws.

Sister, help!

"Dracuni!" Riony's bare feet slapped over stone.

She had no armor on, and as her sword glowed into life, lifting weightless in her hands, the purple light shimmered across a fresh spill of blood from her waist. Cold sweat broke out over her forehead and neck, and she bit her tongue as though that could help her ignore every other pain.

They had Dracuni. They had her. She couldn't stop.

The dragon banked around again, hovering low across the ground as its wings worked hard to raise it into the air. From the saddle, Kife grinned down, clapping his hands in a slow rhythm as though in appreciation of a performance.

Riony expected to see the same smug expression on his sister as well, but she only looked pale and small, crouched behind Kife.

They were still close enough that Riony could see a deep frown etched between Kess's brows. Still close enough to reach.

With a mighty cry, Riony launched from her sprint into a flying leap. She put every bit of strength she had into her legs, her feet, springing from the hard ground. The magic of her sword carried her, higher and higher than she'd ever been able to jump on her own.

She angled the sword as she flew, ready to direct it into a slashing cut across the dragon's front legs. She would make it drop Dracuni. Maybe she could bring it down entirely.

But then the dragon beat its wing and it swept through the air, blocking Riony's soaring path. The sword stuck into the filmy leather, slicing a thin slash and tangling into the tissue.

Riony hit the thick, muscular structure of the wing across her middle, bending in two from momentum, and lost her grip on her sword. She screamed at the impact against her already aching wounds.

Then the wing lifted in a powerful motion, flicking Riony and her sword free.

Riony tumbled in the air, a heavy weight bound to

gravity with no magic to soften her fall. Before she could even tell what side was up or down or think *oh sparks, I'm falling, how far am I—*

Her back hit the ground. The impact shuddered up through her spine and her head lolled back, cracking on the bare stone of the quarry.

Riony gasped through the daggers that filled her chest and the darkness that filled her eyes. Her head throbbed and swirled, and acid stung her throat.

Her sword clinked lightly down somewhere behind her.

The dragon beat its torn wing, rising slowly, awkwardly, higher and higher. It flew up into the sky above and the candle-lit stars that sprinkled through the dusk, and it took Dracuni with it.

When smoke rose from the direction of the village, Kess's stomach dropped.

She'd been lying on her back, feigning sleep despite it being too early, despite the war of emotions in her head keeping her starkly awake.

Maybe Kife wouldn't notice. Maybe ...

"Hey, do you see that?" He sat up from his reclined position, hand over his forehead as he squinted into the sky.

"It's probably just a nearby rev burn." Kess's heart beat too fast, and her voice caught.

Her decision not to get rid of Riony at the waterfall would amount to nothing if the idiot had gone and lit a massive fire. Kess didn't want to go and find out what was burning. It couldn't be good.

"It seems to be coming from the village. I'm going to check it out."

He was up and climbing into the saddle before Kess could object.

"Wait for me." Kess scrambled, hugging Griskin as the wolf pulled them both up off the ground in a fluid roll.

She raced Griskin over to the dragon's side. Kife already had the dragon's wings stretched and beating as she clambered up into the seat behind him, gasping at the effort.

"Don't leave Griskin!"

"We're not going far."

Kess was about to buckle herself to the saddle but instead made a show of reaching for one of her knives. "Bring him."

Kife rolled his eyes as he brought his flight goggles down. "Yeah, yeah, I'll bring your smelly mutt."

They flew, and as they soared over the forest and the village came within sight, it was clear what was burning.

"It's a funeral pyre," Kess yelled over the wind.

For whom? Who'd died? Who had Riony lost that had left her so broken?

Would anyone ever feel that way if they lost me?

"Who cares? There's the creature!" Kife pointed.

In Kess's wind-blown eyes, the figures below were blurry smudges, but she could see the silvery rainbow scales sparkling in the firelight.

Kife aimed the dragon down.

"What are you doing? We can't attack now. It's a funeral!" Kess hissed. "Where's your honor?"

"We can have all the honor we want after we have the silvernix-bleeding creature!"

And then they had her. They had Dracuni in the dragon's clutches, and it was over.

Kess's breath came in short, desperate pants.

Kife had dropped Griskin from far too high. Riony had struck the dragon's wing—*the fool! Why did she throw herself into the air like that? Against a dragon?*—and had hit the ground hard.

But they had Dracuni.

But it didn't feel right.

But what could she do?

They had Dracuni but it felt like everything she wanted was being lost.

"You can't ... You can't leave Griskin behind!" Kess

cried out.

The dragon hovered for a moment just above the ground, torn wing working hard.

"The wolf? It doesn't matter. We don't need the dumb dog anymore." Kife smiled over his shoulder, then turned halfway around in his saddle. "And now that I think about it, I don't need you anymore either."

No. Kess scrambled for the strap holding her to the saddle that she hadn't done up in their brief flight.

With a sweep of his arm, Kife shoved her and she tumbled off the dragon's back.

Again. Thrown away by her brother again, but this time it came as no surprise. She'd expected this betrayal from the start. And as she rolled down the length of the dragon's outstretched wing, she felt as though it was everything she deserved.

The wing lowered, and Kess clawed at the leather through sheer self-preservation, then slid off the wingtip.

There was a moment of free fall before she rolled across the ground, elbows and hips knocking in the tumble.

The dragon lifted into the sky, taking Kife and Dracuni away with it, and leaving Kess at the mercy of all those she'd betrayed in turn.

She didn't even bother lifting herself from the ground.

There was crying, yelling. The kid Riony called her

sister was fighting with the Hjelzahn girl. The younger brother tried to hold her back. The pyre still burned.

It wasn't long before an imposing length of glowing crystal was pointed at her.

"You did this!" Riony stood above Kess, her face pale and twisted with ferocity. The sword wavered in her grip then steadied.

"I know," Kess replied.

Riony shook her head, wincing her eyes closed for a long moment.

"You ..." She grunted. "Why didn't you ... You were at the waterfall?"

"I'm sorry," Kess said.

"Sorry?" Riony sounded like she'd been told trees grew gold.

She flicked her head again, as though she were trying to shake water from her ears. "I told you! I told you he would do this. You're only getting what you deserve."

"I know."

"Stop saying that!" Riony roared.

There was a low growl nearby and more shouting. "Keep it back!"

Kess turned her head from where she lay. *Griskin.*

He pounced from side to side, snapping at the glowing blades and crystal-studded staff holding him at bay. He

favored one side, hurt but alive.

He'd survived. That was all Kess needed to know. And he would continue to survive, and he'd be better off without her.

"I'm sorry," Kess said again, eyes on her wolf.

She would have liked to have said goodbye properly, told him to leave and get away before he was also punished for her mistakes. But those two words would have to be enough.

"He took Dracuni!" One of Riony's legs went out from beneath her, and she pulled herself back up again quickly.

The falter brought the tip of the sword right up against Kess's neck, and she swallowed.

This was it. This was what all her dreams and scheming and battles had come to. Never destined to fly. Never deserving, for all the pain she'd caused along the way in pursuit of what she'd thought was owed to her. How did she ever think she belonged in the sky?

It seemed right, after all, to die at Riony's hands. At least it wasn't Kife who'd ended her.

"Do it," Kess said. "Do it and be rid of me. Do it, *Pony*."

Riony screamed, and it came out as a harsh scratch of air. Her hands around the sword tightened and the blade lifted.

The bright-eyed, pale-skinned child was there. Not Riony's real sister but loved more than Kess ever had been.

She grabbed at Riony's arm. "Don't! It won't fix anything."

Riony's head swayed from side to side, lolling freely on her neck. "She'll never stop, Lyrrin. She'll never ..."

"You're bleeding!" Lyrrin's voice was high and crackling. "Put the sword down, please! Just stop."

Kess saw it then too. Twin dark trickles, running down Riony's neck from her ears. The thick bloom staining her shirt at her waist, growing rapidly larger.

Riony shook her head again as though refusing, denying the reality of everything around her, and the sword lowered in her grip.

Then her eyes rolled back to whites, and she folded into a limp pile on the ground.

TWENTY-SIX

Kess couldn't see whether Riony was alive or dead as her body was immediately surrounded by four others. Kess tried to move forward, but the fear that she would see Riony lifeless and gone locked her joints, and the cold grip of death seemed to wrap around Kess's own heart.

"What happened?" The woman that Kess didn't know the name of blocked the view with her curvy back.

"She hit the ground really hard. I heard her head crack," Lyrrin said in a high, whining pitch. "And she's bleeding, a lot."

Through a small gap, Kess saw the Hjelzahn girl pressing splayed fingers across Riony's neck and skull. "Oh no, oh no."

"What is it?" the boy asked.

"It's not good." Aishena laid Riony's head carefully back onto the rocky ground again, then straightened her body into a more comfortable position and pushed the large sword to the side.

As she lifted the bottom hem of Riony's shirt, her chest heaved up and down. "She's tough though. She could make it. She's going to make it."

Still alive then. But maybe not for long.

"What do we do? We don't ... we don't have Dracuni." The curvy girl whispered the last part despite everyone being close enough to hear.

A soft snout brushed Kess's ear, her own chest heaving with ragged breaths as well. Drawn like a lost traveler to a guiding light, Kess reached her arms around Griskin's fur in a subconscious reflex while her eyes remained locked on the others. The wolf's body was low to the ground beside her, and she hefted herself up into the saddle.

"We should have kept some, bottled some of Dracuni's blood, just in case," the Hjelzahn boy said.

"Riony would never have allowed it." Aishena's eyes flitted across the multitude of scratches and flowing wounds, and she had her fingers clutched around one of Riony's wrists. "We have bandages, herbs. We can try ... to make her comfortable."

From her raised position on Griskin, Kess could look

down at those kneeling on the ground and the motionless body of Riony between them. Still and far too pale. The blood from her ears had smudged into a red streak across her cheek from Aishena's hands. She wasn't responding to the little sister's constant calling of her name.

Kess brought Griskin a step closer.

The curvy girl snatched Riony's sword, still glowing, off the ground and waved it in the air between them. "Get back!"

"I can—"

"What? Gloat? Betray us again? Which of us are you going to kill next?" She advanced, swinging the sword with each thrust of her words.

Griskin dodged back. "I'm trying to—"

"Nisk! Bandages. We need them now if we're going to stop this bleeding!"

Nisk grunted fiercely at Kess, a final warning, then turned and ran for a building nearby where a few packs were piled together.

Kess reached into the small hidden pouch under the front of her saddle and moved around toward the gap that Nisk had left. "I have—"

"Stay back, Kess! We don't have anything left for you to take from us." Aishena glared up at Kess and Griskin, unflinching despite her proximity to the wolf's mouth. "Be grateful that we don't have time for you or the vengeance

you have coming your way."

Yellow light illuminated in one of her hands, a glowing knife, like the one Kess had used to slice through stone. She and Griskin dodged back again.

This was ridiculous. Riony was running out of time. Bandages and herbs weren't going to do anything. Kess had seen a guard fall from the walls of Heithorn estate once, seen the bleeding ears, seen the soft spot on the back of his head. He'd been dead before they could even debate if it was worth opening the family vault to save him with silvernix.

Nisk returned with a bundle of gauze, and she knelt across from Aishena, shuffling around the others to get closer to Riony's middle.

The sister stood up to give Nisk more space, and with a huff of desperation, Kess spurred Griskin into a pounce.

In a flash of fur, she had the child pulled up against the side of the wolf, a slim bone dagger to her throat.

"Stop and—"

"Let her go! Don't you dare hurt her." Aishena sprung from the ground, tracing her feet across the ground into a fighting stance.

"I'm not going to! I'm trying to get you to listen so—"

"Let go of me!" The girl shrieked and wriggled. Her hands lashed at Kess's grip.

The tips of her fingers dug and sliced into the thick hide

bracers around Kess's forearms, snapping free the throwing daggers held there. They clattered onto the ground.

Razed earth, how are her fingers so sharp? Kess hissed but didn't let go.

Nisk circled around behind Griskin, Riony's glowing sword held high. "What cruel trick are you trying to pull now? Did your brother leave you behind to finish the rest of us off?"

She was being surrounded, and Riony was still bleeding.

Raising her voice over the accusations and interruptions, Kess bellowed, "I have silvernix!"

A silence followed, dark glares and confused faces all around until Kess held the tiny vial up for display.

She was glad she'd stolen it back from her brother late one night. Even then, she knew he'd betray her, so it only made sense to betray him in advance and take back what was hers.

"Hand it over," Aishena commanded.

"Not going to happen." Kess closed her fist back around the miniscule bottle.

She wasn't trusting anybody else with this. She couldn't.

Aishena's face became more furious than before. "I hope you're ready to trade your life for it then because we have nothing left you'd want to trade."

"The only thing I want is for you to *get out of my way!*"

Kess pushed the child free from her grip and marched Griskin forward.

It seemed as though Aishena was determined to play chicken, holding her ground until the last second before swearing and stepping aside.

Riony still hadn't moved. Kess's chest clenched like it was being squeezed with a dragon's claws at the thought it might be too late. She slid down off Griskin and sat beside the wounded woman.

"What if she's just getting close to finish Ri off?" Nisk asked. "This has to be some kind of trick."

Aishena circled around, keeping a close eye on Kess. "Don't try anything."

"If I wanted her dead, all I'd have to do is wait." Kess touched two trembling fingers to Riony's neck and found a struggling pulse. She sighed shakily.

"Well, if you were going to help her, you could have just said so," the sister glowered.

"If any of you had listened to me, maybe I wouldn't have had to point a knife at a child." Kess glowered back and carefully cracked the seal on the tiny vial.

"I'm still not sure I believe you are going to help her," Nisk snarled.

Kess ignored her, turning her face to Riony's. She wasn't entirely sure she could believe it either.

But sacrificing her silvernix for this felt like only a trivial loss amongst many when Kess already had so little left. No dragon, no wealth. No hopes, no dreams, no goals. No family, no friends, no love.

Saving the life of the only person who'd ever shown her even the dawning light of kindness or caring was the least she could do, after every suffering Riony had taken on her behalf. After all Kess's mistakes.

Kess tipped the vial, letting the single, glistening drop of iridescent fluid spill onto Riony's lips.

The bickering and threats turned to silence as everyone watched and waited.

A flush of starlight glow glimmered over Riony's bronzed skin. Her eyes remained closed, but her mouth opened in a silent gasp and then a roaring wail.

Her back arched up suddenly and her chest collided with Kess, still bending over her. Kess pressed her hands onto Riony's shoulders as she bucked and writhed. She wasn't strong enough to keep the larger woman pinned, so she slid her hands beneath Riony's head to stop her from cracking it on the hard stone ground all over again.

Kess knew that the pain of being pulled back together by that magic was almost as great as the original wound.

Brilliant light shimmered all around them, pulsing through Riony's flesh as the unicorn blood mended every scratch and gaping hole, every bruise and fracture.

With her hands scooped around the wild hair and small pigtail at the back, Kess was close enough to see the few strands of silver spreading through the red.

How many times had Riony come close to death and been healed by silvernix now? In the dragon's nest cave, in the glass factory, now ... Any other times?

Enough that it was starting to show just as Kess's hair was streaked with the stains of her parents' attempts to fix her.

Too many times.

Slowly, the light dimmed, and Riony stilled.

Kess suddenly found she was terrified, shaking and sweating and far, far, far too close to this woman who only moments ago had been going to kill her. A woman who could probably snap her in half if the desire took her.

But before she could back away, Riony's eyes snapped open.

Taking in Kess's close proximity, Riony's expression was of pure horror. "What in the starless depths is going on?"

Kess sneered. "You idiot. You almost killed yourself. You always act too ready to die."

"What? Why do you care?"

"Because *you* have people who don't want you to die." Kess shifted her weight off Riony and gestured to the four standing around them.

There was a rush of agreement and then a flail of limbs as the little sister flung herself in first, right onto Riony's lap, toppling her back down again as she tried to sit up. Aishena and Nisk helped pull Riony upright again, then wrapped their arms around her in a hug as well.

The boy patted Riony awkwardly on the knee before she grabbed him by the scruff of the neck and dragged him into the huddle too.

Kess turned to Griskin, her only anchor to life, and pulled herself into the saddle.

There was a flurry of low voices behind her, blending into one long string of sound, half the words lost under others.

"Kife took Dracuni."

"I know. I remember."

"Wasn't sure. Your head—"

"You should have treated the other wounds earlier."

"—brain is still feeling weirdly squishy. What did Kess—?"

"Lucky she had some—"

"Did you force—?"

"No, it wasn't like that."

"Then she grabbed me but—"

"You're kidding me. Why?"

Kess looked over the rocky ground, turning lilac and gray with the falling light. The pyre still burned down near

the shore, and Kess wondered again who it was for since everyone she knew that had been traveling with Riony was there, alive still.

All except for Dracuni. She was long gone now, in that dragon's clutches. And everything felt over.

Kess leaned toward Griskin and whispered, "Come on. Let's go."

"You trying to make me regret not dying?"

"It could be the only—"

Riony and her little sister argued in hushed tones.

"It won't—"

"It could!" the small girl pleaded.

There was a low, disgusted grunt and then chasing footsteps pounded toward Kess.

Riony stopped in front of her, expression closed, eyes roaming as if searching for the answer to questions she hadn't asked. "Where are you going?"

"Away."

Blood still marked Riony's face like stripes of war paint, and Kess found she couldn't look at it for long.

"If you're going after Dracuni again—"

"I'm not. I'm done. It's over."

"You're giving up? Now?" Riony laughed without any humor. "Why? Because you got your feelings hurt? Betrayal stings. We both know that, and I *warned you* ..."

Kess leaned away from Riony's words as though they were blows from a sword.

"And now your malevolent turd-breath brother has Dracuni, and you're just going to roll over and let him win? Who even are you? Not Kessara Heithorn, that's for sure."

"What else do you expect me to do?" Kess urged Griskin to continue toward the gate in the palisades.

Riony matched their pace. "What you always do, you relentless, selfish gremlin! *Go after Dracuni* and don't stop until you've got her back!"

"Why would you want that?"

Riony gave a long-suffering sigh. "Because what I was going to say before you interrupted me was if you're going after Dracuni again, we're going with you."

Kess and Griskin stopped.

She couldn't form a response, could hardly comprehend what Riony was saying.

The sharp-clawed sister, the Hjelzahn siblings, and Nisk joined them, flanking Riony with wary expressions.

"With me? Why would you trust me?" They couldn't. They shouldn't. And she couldn't trust them either.

"We don't need a reason." The small girl lifted her hood up to cover her head, and Kess saw her hands more clearly, the sharp, long nails almost as blue as her eyes. "We're just choosing to."

Riony's voice was a low grumble, her eyes averted. "And you saved my life. You didn't have to do that. It earned you ... something. One last chance. Don't sparking blow it this time."

It felt like a trap. Kess could see the wire of the snare laid bare and glinting before her but couldn't turn away. The bait had her transfixed.

One last chance.

For what? What exactly was on offer here? The increasing race of her heart beat a rhythm of hope, but she knew the truth. It was one last chance to be used by this group of people to retrieve the prize, the same as she'd been used by her brother. And then discarded.

"That only sounds fair," Kess muttered.

"So will you help us, then?" Lyrrin asked, almost brightly.

"We have more of a chance of getting Dracuni back with you. Help us save her." Riony looked like she was swallowing a spinerat covered in manure. "Please."

That one word shook Kess. She knew Riony was desperate to get her dragonling back, but why all of this? Why was she even standing here, asking Kess for help instead of charging off like a battering ram?

The young girl's eyes flickered down to Griskin, giving him a gentle look, much kinder than the way any of them looked at Kess.

Kess's heart seemed to turn to stone and drop into her stomach. That was it. They wanted Griskin. Only Griskin. They needed a way to move faster. A way to track. They didn't want her.

It didn't matter. But it still hurt with a sharp, all too familiar pain.

"Fine. I'll help," Kess agreed, knowing she was answering on behalf of her wolf.

And they would help. They'd both do what they could.

But even with Griskin's speed, how were they going to catch up to a dragon?

TWENTY-SEVEN

Riony was filled with more emotions than she knew what to do with, and they were each screaming for her attention.

Her mother's body still burned in the dwindling embers of the pyre.

Dracuni had been taken. She was already too far away to hear her thoughts, but Riony could still *feel* her and her panic, like a string tied between their hearts pulled taut.

And Riony had almost died. And although that didn't seem very novel anymore, it was still freshly terrifying each time. She'd thrown herself bodily at her problems again and been swatted by a dragon. She should have known better. Her luck was going to run out at some point. But *Dracuni was taken.*

And it seemed somehow, in a complete slap in the face to reason, that it was Kess who had saved her, and through all the other noise in her head, Riony couldn't work out the angle. Did Kess just think she needed Riony to achieve her goals and no doubt also revenge on Kife? Just as Riony now awfully needed Kess if she wanted a chance of saving Dracuni?

But even with the wolf on their side, a rescue seemed hopeless.

"What do we do? How can we catch up to a dragon?" Lyrrin asked, as though voicing the same concern.

"It depends where they will be heading. Where would your brother go?" Aishena snapped at Kess like an interrogation.

"He has a home at Skaellakeep."

Benjin took Aishena's map, checking their shrine locations. "That's the other side of Elundrae, and we don't have any gateways open near there yet."

Riony cleared her throat menacingly as Kess tried to look at their map.

Returning her dull gaze to Riony, Kess said, "But I don't think he'll go there. He couldn't get there in one trip—not with the dragon's wing injured. That's going to slow him down."

"Where then?" Aishena asked.

"He's going to want to tame Dracuni as soon as he can and then probably hole up somewhere, make plans on what to do with his new wealth and work out how to protect that wealth as he builds up a supply of silvernix."

Riony's heart clenched, and she narrowed her eyes at Kess. That must have equally been Kess's plan. "So how can we get to him before he can hurt Dracuni? He could land anywhere and do it."

He could be doing it right now.

Kess shook her head, and a glint of her usual guile showed. "He can't. He doesn't have what he needs for taming. I took the stake and silvernix off him."

Riony and Kess's eyes met as the unspoken words hovered between them—that was the silvernix that had saved Riony's life. Kess looked away first, and Riony stared a moment longer, trying to understand.

Aishena rubbed a finger over her bottom lip and paced. "He may not need silvernix, not with Dracuni, but he will need a stake. He'll try to find somewhere to get one, within flying distance on an injured wing."

"Wouldn't he"—Lyrrin swallowed, her face paler than usual—"use Dracuni's blood to heal his dragon?"

Kess scoffed. "No. He wouldn't even think of it. He doesn't care about the dragon at all. He'll probably keep flying it until its wing is shredded before considering healing it for his own convenience."

"And how long would that be? Where can he get to in

that time? Where is he *going?*" Riony's voice grew louder and faster, frantic with everything taking too long.

She picked up her dropped belongings from the ground and pulled her boots on, trying to be prepared and at the same time feeling as though there was nothing she could do.

"He has maybe a few hours' flight. And there's one place he could get to in that time where he might find taming stakes—a place that he knows is otherwise abandoned." Kess kept her eyes averted from Riony's and continued. "Heithorn estate."

"Abandoned?" Riony whispered to herself as she strapped on a bracer.

"Where is that?" Benjin held their map, with its markings and notes on the shrines they'd activated or had settlements at, right up close for Kess to see.

Riony sucked in an annoyed breath but they had to do anything that could hasten retrieving Dracuni, and consequences could be dealt with later.

"There's a shrine right there!" Benjin nearly shouted.

"But we haven't activated it," Lyrrin reminded him.

"Oh. Yeah."

"I suppose it might make sense he'd go that way." Aishena continued her thoughtful ramble.

She took the map herself, narrowed eyes darting over it. "He couldn't risk going to a keep, trading outpost, or smugglers

for a taming spike with Dracuni in tow and untamed. He'd be seeking somewhere isolated. But it's still a big assumption. He could equally go somewhere like the glass factory, keep Dracuni in a cage while he sought what he needed."

Riony glanced over the map too and tried to get her bearings, turning herself in the direction of the estate.

It was the direction the dragon had flown. And it was the direction she could feel Dracuni's weakening sense of panic pulling from.

Riony stilled as Niskina helped her to buckle the final strap of her remaining shoulder guard. "We should try the estate, as much as I'd rather pull my eyeballs out and vomit on them than go back there again. But he could be there in a few hours, and it would take us days to get there on foot from the nearest gateway. We'd be too late."

"Just how close is the shrine to Heithorn estate?" Aishena stopped pacing, her brows furrowed deeply over her dark eyes.

"Directly behind the hatchery," Kess answered.

Riony threw her hands up. "It doesn't matter how close it is. It's not activated."

Aishena held up a finger to Riony and kept her interrogation of Kess going. "Would he go to the hatchery to find a taming spike?"

"Probably. Why?"

Aishena turned to Riony then. "Because the gateway could *become* activated."

"Oh." Riony sighed out the word.

Because Dracuni activated the shrines, and Dracuni was being taken to the shrine. Or at least, close enough to it that it might work. The larger Dracuni got, the farther away her effect on empowering the shrines seemed to be.

"That's it then," Aishena said firmly. "We'll split up. Kess will get you to the nearest shrine as fast as possible. Then you'll know soon enough whether Kife is at the estate with Dracuni. And you can travel through and save her."

Kess's eyes narrowed, but she didn't question the hows.

Riony had plenty of questions though. "Me and Kess? Kess and me? You're coming too, right?"

"I've tried to look at this from all angles. My gut is telling me that speed is the most important factor for this mission. It doesn't matter how many of us get there if we get there too late. We need our strongest to get there as fast as possible, and that's you, on the wolf, without any extra weight. The only faster way would be if Kess didn't—"

"No," Kess cut in.

"As I thought." Aishena gave her a sharp glare. "This is the best plan I can think of. Unless there are other ideas, if anyone else wants ... No, I think this is it. We should do this."

Riony took in the hard edges around Aishena's mouth,

the tight lift of her shoulders, the worried flicker in her eyes. Aishena, who had distrusted Zade from the start. Who'd known the glass factory was a mistake. Who'd questioned her ability to lead or make decisions despite having the best instincts of all of them.

"It's a good plan. And if you think it will work, it's going to work." Riony took one of Aishena's hands and gave it a squeeze.

Kess made an ugly, unimpressed sound.

"Do you have a better idea?" Riony snapped back. "No? Right. Then we're going. Now."

Lyrrin dashed over, blocking Riony's path to the wolf. "But why? Why does it have to all be on you? More of us should go."

She turned to Aishena, pleading. "I know she's strong but it's too much. We're not supposed to put everything on her anymore, remember?"

"It's not all on Riony. It's her and Kess," Aishena said. "They are both our best options for fighting a dragon and rider. It's not just Riony and her strength and her sword that have a chance of beating Kife. It's also Kess's knowledge of the estate, insight into her brother, and her aim."

Everyone turned to stare at Kess then, and the wolf-riding miscreant seemed unsure whether to shrink and hide in Griskin's fur or show them just how good her aim was.

Lyrrin stepped in front of the wolf, closer than Riony approved of, and glared up at Kess. "You'd better actually help. It's up to you to bring my sister and Dracuni back safe. And if I lose either of them, I will personally make you regret it."

Kess stared down for a long moment before she nodded once. "I don't doubt it."

"Okay, go, and go fast," Aishena said.

Niskina handed Riony's sword to her, still glowing. "We'll keep the kids safe—don't worry. Go and get our Dracuni back."

Riony left the sword activated and strapped it to her back. Griskin lowered down for Riony, and she threw a leg over to slide into the saddle behind Kess. The wolf raised back up, his strong legs tensing and ready to run.

"Wait!" Lyrrin said and raced to Riony's side. She pressed a pulsing stone into Riony's hand. "So I know you're okay. And can you at least *try* not to almost die again?"

"Promise." Riony held her sister's hands in hers for a long breath as she took the paired crystal from her, feeling the beat of her sister's small heart.

Then she tucked the crystal down her shirt so she could keep feeling that thumping rhythm.

"Don't worry." She tilted her head toward Kess and pulled a face. "At least one impossible thing has already

happened today, so we've got that on our side."

Then, without a command from Kess that Riony could discern, Griskin burst into motion.

They were at the palisade gates before Riony knew it, and she glanced back one last time at the home she'd lost then returned to, and was leaving again. The fiery glow of sunset lit the cottages as though each of them was a pyre. And she found she was no longer sad—only determined.

She'd lost what she'd lost, and it was the people she loved amongst that loss that mattered, and she didn't want to lose any more. She was going to do anything to get Dracuni back, and the very fact she was on this wolf and riding into battle behind Kess was proof enough of that.

She didn't trust Kess as far as she could throw her, although she enjoyed wondering just how far that might be for a moment.

But Griskin was fast. Even with how he seemed to be favoring one side of his body, he dodged and weaved through the trees faster than Riony could have run. With Riony's sword activated, her weight on the saddle was practically nonexistent. She only had to hold on as Kess sped them toward the shrine.

"Could you maybe scooch forward a bit more?" Riony asked in Kess's ear.

There was no response, but from Kess's silence and the

hard angles of her back, she seemed as comfortable with this whole experience as Riony was.

The dwindling thread of panic coming across a great distance from Dracuni kept Riony on edge, but it also settled her. Despite knowing the plan, it felt like they were going in the wrong direction, away from that tugging string. But the sensation also meant that Dracuni was still herself, still thinking. Not yet tamed.

"If this isn't working, I could ride in front. It will make it easier for you to stab me in the back when you're ready," Riony offered.

No reply again. Not even a bite. That disturbed Riony almost as much as the rest of the situation.

Then Kess said, "Duck," and it took Riony almost too long to work out why, barely getting under the low branch that flashed by. They were already out of the woods of thin, straight trees and into a grove of drooping branches and prickly, waxy leaves.

She doesn't really care whether I get a log to the face. She just needs me to open the gateway, to distract her brother while she runs off with Dracuni.

Riony would be ready for the betrayal this time. She wouldn't be blindsided like she had been in the Alderkin depths.

But the way Kess had lain on the ground where she'd been pushed from the dragon's back, the way she'd seemed so ready for death—that had felt real.

Riony leaned close, muttering into Kess's ear, testing, "How did it feel when Kife left you behind again? Did that hurt more or less than knowing I was right about what he'd do to you?"

Again, nothing, even from words so cruel Riony's stomach churned at saying them. There was an almost imperceptible increase in tension across Kess's shoulders, maybe, but it could have been imagined.

Even Riony was furious Kife had left Kess to die a second time. He'd coldheartedly left her in the hands of her enemies to do with as they wished.

Nobody deserved that. Riony hadn't been thinking clearly at the time—half her head had been mashed to pulp, after all—but if she hadn't almost died, Kess would have suffered from her brother's betrayal at Riony's hands.

And Kess hadn't seemed to care.

Once, when they were kids, Riony had snapped. Gotten Kess by the throat. Even if she'd thought she could have gotten away with being a slave that murdered the Heithorns' only daughter, she hadn't really considered *killing* Kess. She'd just been angry and dumb.

And then Kess had told her to do it. She'd almost begged her to do it.

That lapse passed as quickly as it came. Both of them

were somehow so horrified at those few moments of wild, brokenhearted fury shared between them that there was an immediate, unspoken agreement to pretend it had never happened.

This time seemed different. The girl riding in front of her on the wolf seemed like an entirely unknown entity. Riony had never known Kess to be without a persistent, driving goal to win no matter what, by her own means, to her own ends.

Riony didn't push her again. They rode in silence as night darkened the world around them. Griskin foamed and panted, stopping once by a small stream to drink before racing on. Kess leaned forward a couple of times, brushing encouraging hands over his ears in a way so tender that Riony again wondered who this person she rode with was.

Their way was brightened only by the glow of Riony's sword, but Griskin moved with confidence. It felt like both mere moments and an eternity passed as they rode. Still, that far away sensation of Dracuni's emotions called out across the distance, giving her hope. And Lyrrin's heartbeat pounded next to hers.

And then the standing stones of the shrine came into view and then the crumbling building within.

Griskin leaped between the tall pillars of crystal-streaked stone and into the central structure. The geode stood before them.

Riony slid off the wolf and crouched over the rune, tracing it quickly and out of sight of Kess. The gateway shimmered to life, all the symbols of other gateways they'd unlocked before lighting up around the ring.

And no new ones.

"What if he went somewhere else?" Panic clutched Riony around the throat.

"He might not be there yet. We made good time." Kess brought Griskin closer on soft paws.

Riony flinched away, but with an expressionless face, Kess pointed to a sigil halfway up the geode. "It would be this one."

"How do you know?"

"Each shrine is marked with their symbol." Kess looked at her like she was an idiot. She pointed to the doorway where, above the archway, the symbol for this gateway was carved in amongst etchings of unicorns and lilies.

Riony felt like an idiot. She'd never noticed. No wonder Kife and Kess had been able to track them so easily.

"Then we wait for that one to light up." Riony focused back on the geode, as though if she stared hard enough, she could will it to activate.

"If it doesn't soon, we should consider our next—"

"It will." Riony paced, turning her head to keep her

eyes locked on the symbol. "Aishena is right as often as she's hot."

"Never?"

Riony threw her a sardonic look. *That* got a bite out of her?

She was going to see how deep she could rub that salt, but when she turned back to the geode again, her breath caught.

The symbol flickered, then lit with a glow as bright as the others.

"Yes! I told you!" Riony crowed and slapped the symbol. Light washed over her and the view through the jagged oval changed.

Heithorn estate.

Riony stepped one leg through. Kess didn't join her.

Frowning, Kess patted Griskin's ears again. It seemed like a subconscious action, as comforting to her as to the wolf. "Is it safe?"

"You've seen me go through plenty of times."

"You choosing to do something isn't a signifier that it is safe."

"Would I have taken Lyrrin and Dracuni and the others through if it wasn't?"

Kess seemed to chew over that like a piece of gristle, then moved to follow Riony through the magical portal.

They stepped out together on the other side.

Griskin sniffed at the air and gave a low growl.

"They're here. Can you make that ridiculous sword less bright? We should approach carefully," Kess said.

Riony pulled her sword into her hands and brushed her finger over the rune to deactivate it, and the purple glow faded away to nothing.

The Alderkin shrine on Heithorn estate was much like Riony remembered it. The simple stone building had shelving against every wall, packed with old farming tools and moldy canvas.

The back wall of the hatchery ran right up against the Alderkin structure on one side, the entryway opening out onto a small field within the estate's walls.

"Are you as excited as I am about the harm we're about to inflict on Kife?" Riony whispered as she followed Kess and Griskin, prowling carefully around to the hatchery entrance.

"Shh!" Kess scolded, then looked her up and down disapprovingly. "Can't you move any quieter?"

As they rounded the corner, it didn't matter how quiet they were being. Kife was being loud enough to cover any approach.

The dragon-sized front doors to the hatchery stood wide open. Riony and Kess slid into position beside them, daring quick glances around the edge.

A fire burned in a brazier in the center of the barn, creating a flickering dance of light and dark.

Kife had his back to them. He pulled a drawer out of a storage cupboard and tipped the contents onto the ground, then tossed the drawer after it, the timber smashing.

Swearing loudly, he swiped an arm across a shelf, searching and clearing as he went, knocking metal canisters and feed bowls down in a clanging chorus.

His dragon loomed over him, a foreboding backdrop staring blindly toward the door, and at its feet lay Dracuni.

She was on her side, legs and snout wrapped roughly in old rope.

Kife turned, and Riony ducked back behind the wall again.

I'm here. I'm here! Riony tried to force her thoughts through to the unidragon.

Sister? The returning thought was weak, but it came through. It was a reply. Dracuni had heard her.

You'll be safe again soon. *Somehow.* Riony hoped Dracuni didn't hear that last part of her thought.

Hurts.

Riony edged around to look again.

And she saw it—two knives lodged into Dracuni's front leg at opposing angles, spreading the skin beneath them, and a glass bottle tucked into the rope beneath them, slowly filling with shimmering liquid.

Riony's own blood turned cold. Dracuni was already weak from flaming. She couldn't take this. There was no way Kife could know that, but to bleed the dragonling at all drove Riony into a frenzy. She didn't even realize she was marching forward until Kess grabbed her by the shirt and pulled her back behind their cover of the wall.

"He'll see you!" Kess hissed. "There's too far to go. He'll see you before you reach him, and if he orders his dragon to flame, we're done!"

"He's bleeding her!" Riony rasped back. She glanced quickly around the open door again, seeing the dragon aimed directly for them.

Kess snatched her hand reflexively away from where it was still clutching Riony's shirt. "We need to do something about the dragon first while Kife's not on it. He hasn't found a stake yet. We've still got time to work out a plan."

"Aha! Finally!" Kife bellowed. He pulled a thin spike of shining steel from a wooden crate and flipped it in the palm of his hand.

Lifting a mallet from a pile of tools on the ground, Kife strolled toward Dracuni, whistling a Taen anthem of triumph.

Riony drew and activated her sword. "We just ran out of time."

TWENTY-EIGHT

Riony had seen a taming ceremony before, and there wasn't much *ceremony* about it. A steel stake was hammered into a dragon's skull, and that was that. Dragonlords only called it a 'ceremony' to make themselves feel special about the barbaric process.

And Riony only had however long it would take Kife to walk from one side of the hatchery to the other to work out how to stop him from doing that to Dracuni.

Kife on his own didn't worry Riony. He was a fair swordsman but was only human. It was the purple etherdart, sitting idle and tame, awaiting his orders that was the problem.

She and Kess were about as far away from the dragon as Kife was.

At least they had the element of surprise. Kife had no reason to believe they could get there as fast as they had. He remained completely casual and unalert as he pulled a bottle from his pocket and doused the end of the stake in iridescent liquid.

Staring at Dracuni, Kife muttered, "You're such a weird and ugly little dragon. It doesn't matter, though, when your blood is so very beautiful."

He'd already filled another bottle? *Dracuni, I'm so sorry.*

Riony gauged the distance between her and the unidragon and the way the big dragon was aimed right at them and could burn them the second Kife spotted them. She could race to get to the dragon first. But what then?

Riony had an idea that made her question how well silvernix repaired injured brains.

But she was out of time. She had to act, now.

"Sparks, this is the worst idea I've had in my life. Are you ready?" Riony reached over and wrapped one arm around Kess's waist, lifting her off Griskin's back into a close hold against her chest. She adjusted her grip on the glowing sword in her other hand.

"What ... what are you going to do?" Kess balked, going rigid in Riony's hold.

"I'm going to give you everything you ever wanted."

Riony turned away too quickly to know for sure

whether Kess's cheeks flushed a deep red. And she had no time to consider any horrific ramifications behind that reaction. She burst into motion, bringing the two of them into the hatchery in a dash.

Kife's stroll became a disjointed stumble as he spotted them. "How in the razing ...?"

Riony ignored him, sprinting toward the purple etherdart. Then, with a roaring cry, she kicked off the ground with a strong thrust of her legs, and she and Kess flew. The magic of the sword lifted them, and they sailed in an arc through the shadowy hatchery.

The moment of confusion passed, and Kife sprung to action. "Fire! FIRE!"

His dragon's chest and neck convulsed, and its jaws dropped open. The crackle of fire rushed forth as it spewed a blazing sphere straight ahead.

Riony pulled her knees up, bringing Kess's legs with them, and the flames licked across her toes as they hurtled over the blaze. At the barn doors, Griskin whined, ducking low, and the fireball shot over him and out into the night.

Riony and Kess sailed over the dragon's head, and in a clatter, landed unevenly on its back. With her hands full, Riony braced her thighs around its scaly spine to stop them from slipping right back off again.

Then she lifted Kess and placed her into the dragon's saddle.

Kess made a face like an owl. "You ... you want me to ...?"

"You *can* control it, right? Oh, sparks. Don't tell me you've wanted a dragon all this time but don't know how to ride one!"

It was a risk, a huge one, giving Kess control of a dragon. If Riony had the first idea how to control it herself, she'd be the one in the saddle, snatching Dracuni and flying off without either of the terrible Heithorn siblings. But Kess in the dragon's seat was infinitely better than Kife.

The thin bridge of Kess's nose scrunched, and she spat, "Of course I know how!"

"Then congratulations. It's all yours. Please don't kill me in return." Riony flung her leg over from where she'd straddled the dragon's back and slid down the scales of its shoulder, landing with a soft thunk at its feet.

Dracuni was only a few steps away. Kife flung the stake and hammer down and raced toward the dragonling. Riony ran to beat him there. He drew his sword. Riony blocked his path with hers. Metal clanged against hardened crystal.

Kife's face was distorted with fury. "How did you even get here?"

"Easy." Riony shielded a strike toward her heart with the flat of her sword. "I just rode here on your mother."

Kife faltered, staring at her like one would a rabid bovin. Riony only had a split second to glance down and check on Dracuni. The unidragon lay on her side, wings twisted and pinned uncomfortably beneath her, and chest heaving up and down. The bottle strapped into the bindings of her leg beneath the knives was overflowing. Sparkling blood soaked the dirt floor. Her lilac eyes fluttered.

"You're as mad and disgusting as you ever were, slave."

"And you continue to lack any sense of humor. Just one way you're worse than your sister."

Kife struck again, a thrust to the left, then the right. He was fast and precise, flicking the length of steel like lightning around Riony's cumbersome weapon.

Unbalanced from the flurry of attacks, Riony didn't expect Kife's boot to hit her ribs, and she stumbled back across the floor.

"Fire!" Kife bellowed again.

Riony spun around to see the dragon's head aimed right at her and golden light erupting up its throat.

Then its neck swayed, swinging the other way, and the fireball exploded against the far wall of the hatchery. A mound of grayed straw caught in a flash of sparks and smoke.

"Too close, Kess! Can you get that thing out of here?" Riony checked to make sure the back of her shirt wasn't on fire.

The dragon stepped a full circle on the spot, its tail smashing into shelving. Griskin had slunk inside as well,

prowling and dodging around the dragon's feet.

Kess's voice growled in frustration. "I don't exactly have a lot of experience! I'm trying to make it work."

Riony smirked and angled the tip of her sword toward Kife. "That's exactly what the girls say you cry during sex."

Kife came at her, swinging wildly. "You think my useless sister has any chance of controlling that dragon? I should have smothered her in her sleep instead of leaving her to the revs."

Despite it being Kess he spoke of, a defensive streak flared inside Riony. "Sparks, were you born evil or was it being less desirable than dragon farts that drove you there?"

"Left, left! Fire!" Kife snarled. He disengaged, leaping backward.

The dragon's head swung left, bringing it in line with Riony again, then kept swinging. The fireball whooshed over Riony's head and spilled its flames across the thatched ceiling.

"You're going to burn this whole place down if you don't shut your mouth!" Kess leaned forward in the saddle, hands on the dragon's neck in the same position she held them when she rode her wolf.

"You've no right to be up there!" Kife yelled another command and Kess pressed her own through touch, and the dragon strained, legs moving one way and neck going the other.

Its tail swept a low arc across the barn, knocking down the brazier and scattering coals across the floor. The searing rocks skittered beside the tied up unidragon.

"Watch out for Dracuni!" Riony tried to get to the unidragon again, but Kife blocked her path with a swift jab toward her throat.

"Gris!" Kess gave a low whistle and pointed to Dracuni. "Get her out of here before this whole place goes up!"

The wolf bounded in, sniffed at the ropes and bleeding wound and Dracuni's blinking eyes, then wrapped his teeth around her tied up back legs.

A jolt of the unidragon's fear knocked Riony sideways.

"Careful!" she yelled.

But the wolf seemed to be as careful as he could be, pulling from the lashed rope. He could only drag the unidragon a little at a time, since she was limp on the ground and almost as big as he was. Dracuni bumped through the still red coals, and the larger dragon's claw came down right where she'd been a moment before.

Above them the thatched roof burned, filling the air with smoke. From some command of Kess's or Kife's or the dragon's sheer confusion, it beat its wings once, cracking into the ceiling above it and fanning all the flames.

They needed to get Dracuni out fast, but Riony didn't like that the dragonling was at the wolf's mercy. And as

soon as he had her outside? Kess would take that dragon out as well and leave Riony without them.

Distracted, Riony only saw Kife's lunge of his sword too late. She turned her shoulder toward the blow, forgetting that her guard on that side had been lost and left behind.

The blade cut in. It seared through muscle and nicked bone. Riony snarled, breath hissing out through clenched teeth.

Kife grinned, admiring the color at the tip of his sword. "That's just first blood, slave. I'll have you strung up and bled out soon enough."

Riony had been swinging the sword with both hands but released her grip and let her right arm hang. She blocked his next attack clumsily with her left, then swung her sword in a wide arc, making Kife give ground.

She kept up the onslaught, backing him up across the burning floor.

Even when faced with the sweeping might of the huge, glowing chunk of magical crystal, Kife didn't slow down, dodging and striking between the gaps.

He no longer shouted 'fire'—there was plenty of that already—but he yelled other things. Down. Up. Sweep. Bite. Each was a command Kess had to counteract.

Riony tried to angle around, following Griskin as he dragged Dracuni out, but Kife kept her trapped as much as she kept him busy.

As relentless as his bloody sister.

There was a desperation there, too, that concerned Riony, and the back and forth between them had already wounded her. Smoke stung her eyes, and the blood dried and cracked on her arm under the searing heat.

She'd promised Lyrrin she'd try to not almost die this time and she already felt off track in that goal. She had to attempt something new. What would Lyrrin do? What would Lyrrin want her to do?

Groaning a short sigh, Riony offered, with all her sincerity, "Put your sword down, Kife, and we can all get out of this alive."

"Are you getting tired with that stupidly big blade of yours? Because I'm not stopping until your whole body is the color of your hair and that sister of mine is off my dragon. Sweep!" he yelled again.

The dragon was no longer bucking and twirling, the thump of its footsteps stilling behind Riony.

Has Kess finally worked out what she's doing?

Huh. So that's what relief and utter terror combined feel like.

"Come on, Kife," Riony offered again, because the only other option was continuing to throw herself into their deadly battle. "You're outmatched, and this place is a bigger burning trash heap than your life. Give it up."

He lunged again in a forward thrust of his sword, and Riony cut back, knocking him stumbling into the wall behind him.

And yet he smiled.

"Fire!" he screamed rabidly.

And Riony saw the dragon's teeth right over her shoulder.

In the moment it took her to gasp what might have been her last breath, the purple head lifted, and the fireball thundered past her ear, singeing her cheek.

It erupted against the wall around Kife with so much force that the stones shifted and tumbled. The roof came down with it, crashing in a fiery tide of sparks and embers right where Kife had been.

Right where Riony would also have been if she'd gone and engaged him in battle again.

I bet you're feeling my heart racing now, Lyrrin. And it's still beating, thanks to you.

The hole in the roof grew larger, cinders raining down. Dracuni and Griskin were still only halfway to the door.

After quickly strapping her sword to her back, Riony dashed across the room to their side.

"Let's get you out of here." She knelt behind Dracuni.

Griskin stared up at her with piercing eyes from where his teeth were still tight around the ropes.

Riony stared directly back. Somewhere between a sigh

400

and a challenge, she said, "Don't make me fight you, pup."

Through the roar and spit of fire came a soft whistle, and Griskin let go.

He vanished on soft paws toward the purple dragon as Riony scooped her arms under Dracuni's limp body and neck. She hadn't lifted the dragonling in weeks, maybe months. But there was no way under the stars she was leaving her there.

"Okay. On three. One, two, THREE!" She heaved, arms burning, bringing the deadweight of the unidragon up to her knees, then waist, then over her shoulder.

She stood on shaking legs and took a step toward the doors.

Then the huge teeth of the purple etherdart filled her vision.

From her high perch on the saddle, Kess glared down with a fierce intensity.

TWENTY-NINE

Riony sat with her back against the cool, flat edge of a standing stone, staring at the remaining ribbons of smoke tangling their way into the brightening sky, and wondered how she was still alive.

Dracuni lay half in her lap. Still. Sleeping. Riony stroked a hand down her long neck, the velvety scales warm and steady pulse beating beneath.

"It's okay. It's okay. You'll feel better soon."

Lyrrin would be feeling the unidragon's heartbeat too, with the paired crystal lying on Dracuni's chest. It was Riony's way of sending back a message to the others. *I have Dracuni. We're safe.*

Riony could still barely believe it, hours later, as the

darkness of night yielded to a lilac luminance so much like the unidragon's eyes.

Safe. And as of yet, no more betrayal.

Dracuni was desperately weak from blood loss but seemed stable.

Riony didn't want to move her too far. She *couldn't* move her too far and refused to let Kess carry Dracuni with the dragon.

Kess had offered to when Riony had been struggling to lift the young dragon, and the offer had felt so much like a trap that Riony refused.

But Kess hadn't pushed, hadn't tried to take Dracuni from her despite how Riony had stumbled out of the burning hatchery, barely keeping herself and the growing dragon upright. Kess had only put the dragon's wing out above Riony, sheltering her and Dracuni from the fire and falling building.

Riony had stopped just outside the shrine, just far enough away from the fires that were rapidly spreading to every building of the estate, and there she and Dracuni had remained ever since.

With a fountain of apologies and fumbling fingers, Riony had removed the blades that had been pinned into the dragonling's leg to keep the wound open and bleeding. Dracuni's wound had closed quickly then.

Riony had stoppered the bottle of silvernix Kife had filled, glowered at it, and put it away. Despite the unforgiveable reason it existed, even Riony couldn't consider wasting it. And Riony's arm had been healed, too, when she couldn't avoid getting that magical blood on her hands.

Not far from them, across in the open ground between still smoldering buildings, the purple dragon sat idly, seemingly unaware of anything going on around it, with no rider in the saddle to give it commands.

Riony shook her head at it. *I can't believe that selfish goblin didn't roast me and fly off on her new dragon already.*

Kess didn't even stay on the dragon.

Once she'd maneuvered it outside, she'd slid down from the saddle and back onto Griskin without a word, and the two of them had skulked away.

As the stars wheeled overhead, Riony remained watchful, eyes locked on the dragon, wary that Kess could return at any moment and take Dracuni.

Why wait? Why not take the advantage with the dragon? Why did she leave? Why, why, why?

The questions alone kept Riony awake all night. Then as the sky brightened, she spotted the silhouette of Kess and Griskin high atop the stone walls that encircled the estate, watching as it burned.

A couple of times during the night, overcooked revenants

shambled out of the flame-gutted buildings and collapsed.

Abandoned, Kess had said.

Abandoned to revs, much like Riony's village had been. A twang plucked at Riony's rib cage as she stared at the silhouetted wolf girl.

Now, finally, as the first bright rays of gold pierced the smoky air, most of the buildings were ashy rubble. The Alderkin shrine, made of solid stone and crystal, remained.

"It worked. This must be it!" Lyrrin's voice came from the interior of the shrine.

It roused Dracuni, and Riony turned and saw the glow of the gateway shining from within.

"We're out here!" Shifting Dracuni's head off her lap, Riony tried to stand only to find every one of her muscles had cramped from so long holding the same position. She grabbed her sword and used it to prop herself up.

Aishena came out first, athames in each hand at the ready.

"We're okay, I think." Riony groaned and stretched her back.

Lyrrin pushed through from behind Aishena and ran to Riony's side across the long grass, ash and dew smattering her legs. "You didn't almost die!"

She hugged Riony, then pulled back and gave her a questioning side-eye. "Did you?"

"I kept myself a very reasonable distance from imminent

death. You would have been so proud."

"We came as quick as we could, on foot as we were, kids and all since they refused to stay behind," Aishena said, warily putting her athames away.

"What in Elundrae happened?" Benjin stepped out of the shrine along with Niskina, both turning to take in the idle dragon, the burning estate, Dracuni blinking awake, and the distinct lack of Kess.

Riony tried to summarize. "Fire, mostly. Kife is somewhere under all that char and ash. Dracuni is okay."

Hungry, the unidragon thought sleepily.

"And hungry." That seemed like a good sign.

"What happened to the awful wolf-girl? Did you have to—" Niskina made a squelching sound with her mouth and drew a line across her throat with her finger.

"The awful wolf-girl is still here," Kess muttered, emerging from a foggy drift of smoke.

Griskin padded up beside the purple etherdart, keeping a decent distance from the others.

Lyrrin gasped, then whispered, eyes sparkling, "She didn't betray you?"

"Not yet anyway," Riony murmured back.

Eying the wild girl and her wolf, Riony leaned on her sword and called over, "Are you going to take your dragon and go? Or do we have a problem?"

Aishena and Niskina flanked Riony, the kids and Dracuni behind them, standing opposed to Kess and the dragon.

"It's not my dragon."

"It could be," Riony offered, warily.

Aishena leaned in, whispering, "Is this the deal you came to? Are you sure it's a good idea letting her have a dragon?"

"If it means she's satisfied and leaves us alone forever, she can have the dragon *and* three of my teeth if she wants," Riony said.

"No," Kess exhaled the word. "I don't want that."

Riony pointed at her mouth with a frown. "They're good teeth, and I don't have any other body parts I'm willing to give you."

Kess closed her eyes in a slow, long-suffering blink. "The *dragon*. I don't want it."

"You don't *want it*? I'm sorry, *what*?" Riony's voice rose dramatically, and a hysterical burble built within her.

Maybe she had broken her head irreparably because she couldn't understand a thing coming out of Kess's mouth. Where was the girl who had spent every waking moment of her life working toward having her own dragon to ride?

It was only the awkwardly sincere contortions of Kess's face that stopped Riony bursting into manic laughter. She waited for Kess to say she wanted Dracuni instead. She waited for knives to be thrown. But Kess remained still,

staring at the small flurries of ash swirling across the ground.

"It's Kife's dragon, and it just feels ... wrong. Broken. Riding it ... it wasn't what I'd thought it would be like. It felt like riding something already dead, like a primitive machine. It was nothing like ..." Kess's hand rubbed up through Griskin's fur and over his ear. "I didn't like it."

"You still can't have Dracuni if that's what you're angling for."

Behind Riony, the unidragon snorted agreement.

Kess shook her head and said nothing.

"You really don't want it?"

"After everything I've seen, no. I don't want a tamed dragon." Kess looked at Dracuni then with a hint of longing that made Riony grip the hilt of her sword. But she said, "I don't think being a dragonrider is what I'd thought it would be. What I wanted it to be."

Riony smirked. "A sport for the violently psychotic? It's perfect for you."

Kess met Riony's gaze, the icy blue-gray of her eyes flashing like a wolf's in the rays of sunrise, then she looked away just as fast.

Riony's smile dropped. There was something so lost, so shattered in that brief glance that it made Riony's heart stutter and mouth go dry.

Kess really had given up. Riony believed it now.

And she had no idea what it meant.

She frowned, taking in the lumbering weight of the etherdart sitting before them. "Soooo ... what do we do with this, then?"

Aishena paced around the dragon, inspecting the stationary beast. "We can't leave it here alone. It would die of starvation without being provided for."

Riony raised an eyebrow. "Can *you* ride a dragon?"

"I've had training, yes. But I don't think having a full-grown dragon with us is a good idea. It will attract more attention than it's worth."

"If reading *Rebel Riders* taught me anything," Niskina added, "it's that the dragonlords really don't like rebels having their own dragons."

"That's what you got from it? I was reading it for the sex," Riony whispered back.

"Can we—" Kess spoke up, seemed to choke on her words, swallowed, and started again. "Is there any chance we could free it?"

"Free it? Free the dragon?" Riony asked.

Aishena shook her head, confused at the question. "It can't survive on its own. You know that."

Kess placed a hand on the dragon's shoulder. "I mean, is there any chance we could *untame* it. Reverse the taming. *Free* it."

Riony's eyes widened. She sought the glint of metal amid the purple scales on the etherdart's forehead. "Reverse the taming?"

"Would that even work?" Lyrrin asked.

"I don't know if it's ever been attempted before," Aishena said.

Big dragon could think again? Dracuni lifted her head, neck wobbling.

"I suppose we could try," Riony said. "Would we just ... take the taming spike out?"

"Might need silvernix to heal the wound again. Otherwise, it may not survive the process," Aishena replied, tilting her head toward Dracuni.

I help. Want to help big dragon friend.

"I've got silvernix. Kife ... collected some, and I have it," Riony said, and then thought, *No more helping for you, Dracuni. You need to recover.*

Dracuni huffed and laid her chin back on the ground again.

"Let's try it!" Lyrrin practically squealed.

"It might not work, and it could be dangerous." Riony gestured at the huge creature's talons and teeth. "I didn't love my last run-in with a wild dragon."

"It deserves to be free," Kess said flatly. "Will you help or not?"

Everyone was in favor of attempting to untame the dragon.

They made a rough plan. Aishena cut the dragon's saddle, harness, and bags free, dumping them on the ground out of the way. She used her cutting athame to carefully remove the heavy steel collar around its neck.

Then she took the bottle of silvernix and waited for the moment it would be needed. Niskina, the kids, and Dracuni moved into the shelter of the shrine, just in case.

Kess tapped the dragon's shoulder, getting it to bring its head down low to the ground.

Moving around to get a position with good leverage, Riony ended up with one knee on the dragon's snout. The steel spike seemed so small compared to the bulk of the dragon's head, stuck there between its brow ridges since it had been a dragonling.

Riony cringed as she worked the tips of her fingers beneath the flat head of the spike until she had a solid grip.

She looked down at Kess. "Last chance to keep it for yourself. Are you sure about this?"

Kess brought Griskin around beside Riony, staring up with sad eyes at the dragon. "I will not shackle another life to mine without its consent."

Riony's fingers slipped from the hammered end of the spike, and she had to get her hold on it again. *Sparks! I'll deal with whatever* that *was about later.*

"Okay, let's do this." Riony pulled.

She braced her knee against the hard skull of the dragon's snout and tensed her back, every muscle in her arms straining. Her fingers locked around the stake, the metal biting into them as she refused to let her grip slide a second time.

Slowly, slowly, the spike eased out from between the scales and bone it had melded into. Then, as the thicker section detached and only the tapered end remained, the rest came free in a rush and Riony toppled backward, landing on the ground in a puff of ash.

Aishena stepped in with the silvernix, placing a few drops on the resulting hole and thick, dark blood that spilled from it.

There was a sizzle, and a flicker of light from between the dragon's dusky scales. The hole closed over.

And the dragon didn't move.

"Is it okay? Did it work?" Lyrrin took a step out of the shrine.

"Stay in there." Riony warned her as she got to her feet, brushing off the soot, but she was so covered in blood and ash it really didn't matter. Standing again, she was far too close to the dragon's teeth for comfort and she backed away, watching for movement.

Aishena joined her at the doorway to the shrine. "Maybe it's had the stake in too long. It might not recover."

Kess remained at the dragon's side, stroking its cheek. Gusts of smoke from the smoldering buildings drifted by.

And then something else, dark and smoky, fluttered in the air around them. Like a trail lifting from an extinguished candle but in reverse, a black, shadowy substance drifted down from the sky and into the dragon's healed wound.

And the dragon shivered.

"What in the stars was that?" Riony hissed.

Even Kess backed away from the beast then. "I've seen that before, sort of. In tamings. When the spike is hammered in, there's a sizzle and rise of dark smoke."

Riony and Aishena nodded, having seen it too. Riony had assumed at the time it was literal smoke, that the stake and silvernix somehow burned.

But this? They were seeing it happen now in *reverse*.

If that shadowy substance was just smoke, why would it *come back*?

Riony didn't have time to think about it as the dragon shook itself again, eyes rolling in their sockets. Hot air huffed in ragged pants between great swords of teeth.

It loosed a deafening, pained roar that ended in a whimper, then raised its head high, glaring down. It wavered side to side, eyes on Kess, its mouth opening.

Riony's toes tensed against the ground, ready to tackle the stupidly immobile wolf-girl away from a fireball or the snap of teeth.

The dragon roared again, and a great wash of emotions flooded forward—questioning, accusing, confused—and the group gasped as it hit.

Is everyone feeling this?

Then massive purple wings, all healed, snapped outward and pressed down. Kess and Griskin crouched low to the ground as a torrent of air rushed over them, swirling their clothes and fur, and the dragon lifted into the sky. As though learning again how to fly, its motions were stiff and awkward.

But it was free.

THIRTY

Have I made the biggest mistake of my life? Kess watched the purple etherdart fly away until it was nothing more than a smudge of memory against the shell-pink morning sky.

There were cheers and celebratory embraces and happy waves of goodbye from the others. A dragon freed. Perhaps it was a thing to celebrate, but Kess couldn't stop shaking.

I had a dragon. The thing I always wanted, all I ever wanted, and I let it go.

She'd wanted to let it go in the end.

While tracking Dracuni's mother, Kess had seen the unfettered glory of a free dragon. While hunting Dracuni, Kess had seen the compassion and loyalty of a free dragon.

A tamed dragon was a lame, faded substitute by comparison. Kess could find no honor in owning such a creature. And now, all Kess's goals and dreams felt equally diminished.

Want felt like a distant concept, and even further removed again from *having* that it would be simpler to ignore the possibility of either.

"Do you think it will be okay?" the Hjelzahn boy asked.

"It seemed to come back to itself and was able to fly unaided. Hopefully it will be able to hunt and stay safe too," his sister said.

"What was the weird smoky stuff that went into it?" he asked again, full of questions.

"Yeah, that was weird, right? It looked ... are we all thinking what I'm thinking, or have I lost it?" Riony replied.

"You know what it reminded me of?" Lyrrin said softly, almost too low for Kess to hear from where she remained separate. "The shadowdragon."

"So it was clear to people without head injuries too. Good to know."

Kess had thought so too. The swirling darkness, the faint sense of mourning that had emanated from it. She'd seen the shadowdragon enough for it to have felt familiar.

"I've been wondering about that lately. Since seeing the mural in the Alderkin depths. Since seeing the site of the first taming..." Niskina turned her face to the sky, shaking her head as though unable to voice the end of her thought.

Riony finished for her. "That the shadowdragon isn't an Alderkin curse? That the shadowdragon is the result of taming dragons? Yeah, I've been wondering the same thing."

A long silence followed.

Kess stared at the taming spike, lying discarded on the ground. Dark, tar-like blood coated the end from where it had been lodged deep in the dragon's brain.

Could it really be the tamings that had created the shadow dragon? She imagined how many dragons there were across Elundrae with similar stakes in their skulls, the wisping smoke from every taming, rising into the sky, joining together into that one malevolent entity.

"We should clear up and get Dracuni out of here, go someplace where she can recover," Aishena said. "Somewhere safe, in case all of this has drawn attention from the living or the dead."

The unidragon lifted her head to Riony, and Riony whispered something back. Kess's lip twitched and she looked away.

There had been a moment, hidden between the flutters of her heartbeat, when she'd hoped that maybe, maybe once freed, the dragon would choose to remain. That it might choose her.

A truly ridiculous thing to hope—that anything would choose to be with her. Only Griskin ever had, and that was more than she deserved.

"Where should we go then?" Nisk asked brightly. "Where do you want to go, Ri?"

"Anywhere I can wash all this smoke and blood out of my clothes and sleep for a week sounds good to me."

Kess fussed with her saddlebags, checking the contents, pretending she had any reason to remain a moment longer.

Nisk slung an arm over Riony's shoulders. "We don't have to go back to your village. Any of the shrine enclaves will have us at least for a while. They feel like they owe us for helping get them somewhere safe from revs."

Kess frowned. Was that why people were congregating around the shrines? Were those ruins somehow protected from revenants?

And Riony had been helping people get there—saving people, all over Elundrae. While all Kess had done was chase and terrorize her, Riony had been the hero that Kess had always wanted to be once she got her dragon.

"How about Myrwa's?" Aishena said, her gaze casting over Riony with a tenderness Kess hadn't seen from the grim young woman before.

"Yes, please. That would be really nice." Riony sighed. There was so much relief in her voice that it stung

Kess to the bone.

"I want to see how big Kellae's baby is now!" the sister squealed. "And I want to keep helping people. Do you think we can? Keep traveling around and making more shrines safe for people?"

Riony pushed the girl's hood down and brushed her hand through her hair. "Yeah, that sounds pretty good to me."

"Let's move then," Aishena said. Her brother went into the shrine, and the glow of the magical gateway lit from within.

All of them were filled with joy and peace because they weren't being hunted anymore. Because the suffering Kess had inflicted upon them had ended.

Nose stinging and eyes hot, Kess nudged Griskin, leading him away along the smoky path through the rubble of her family home.

Behind her, there was a squabble in low voices between Riony and her sister, then Kess rounded the corner of what remained of the hatchery walls and could hear no more.

"Hey, butt face!" Riony loped over. A thick gust of smoke blew up around her as she stood, eying Kess with a crease between her brows. "I'm still waiting."

"For what?"

"The vicious betrayal."

"So sorry to disappoint." Kess pushed Griskin on again.

Riony called after them, "You really were just going to leave? No more games, no tricks, no treachery? No final shot at stealing Dracuni?"

Kess glared over her shoulder and said nothing.

"Where are you even going?"

Kess tensed, the squeeze of her fingers halting Griskin. Where was she going? She had no idea. She growled back. "Does it matter? What's with all the questions?"

"I'm curious, okay? Consider me confounded. I thought I knew … *you*. But nothing is making sense anymore. Why did you help save Dracuni if you weren't doing it to take Dracuni for yourself afterward?"

"Dracuni saved my life. I repaid the debt."

Riony's shoulders lowered, and more quietly, she asked, "And why did you save me? You used your silvernix. You didn't owe me—you had nothing to gain. What possible reason could you have had for that?"

Kess snapped, "Maybe you're just *worth saving*!"

The words shocked them both to silence. Their eyes met through the smoky glare. Heat flushed up Kess's face and she turned away, swallowed by shame.

There was a mumbling of curses, and then Riony called out from behind her, "You don't have to go."

A long, rattly shiver ran up Kess's back. Had she misheard?

"You don't have to be alone anymore. You could … come with us." Riony's words were strained, but real.

Want resurfaced within Kess like verdant new growth from beneath melting snow. She tried to shake the wanting away, but it clung with aching force to her bones. "Did your 'sister' put you up to this?"

"Nooo. Okay, yes. Sort of."

"Tell her I don't need her pity."

Riony ran both hands through her tangled red hair, tensing the muscles in her arms and looking at the sky. "It's not … *just* her."

"I don't need yours either."

"No, I mean … *sparks*." Riony turned around, staring back the other way, then she hung her head. "I'm tired, Kess. I'm tired of fighting, tired of loss and pain, and worrying that is all we can have from life."

Kess turned Griskin around, watching Riony's back as she took deep breaths between her words. She remembered Riony's back, scarred and washed in blood and the water of the falls, and how she'd cried those deep, mourning sobs.

And Kess knew exactly what Riony meant. She was tired too.

After another long inhale that lifted her shoulders, Riony said, "I just want people to be nice to each other, help each other, because that's what makes this blighted world livable. Even good, sometimes. And I know it might be a stupid dream, but maybe we can start making it real. We could start with the two of us."

"Us?" Kess repeated in a whisper. Griskin growled a soft warning, but she didn't react, unable to look away from Riony.

Riony turned her head to the side, still not looking back, almost as though she was too scared to face Kess. "What do you think?"

Kess didn't know what she thought. Half her insides were screaming this was a trap, to run, to strike first, and the other half *wanted* in a way that eclipsed any want she'd ever known before.

Kess tried to calm her breathing enough to reply as a waft of smoke puffed around her again. The heady scent burned through her nose, different to before, overwhelming, a soapy and peppery fragrance.

Kess's eyes widened in recognition.

Morass mercy.

She tried to call out, but her throat had gone numb, and she gave only a rough grunt.

"I don't mean you have to stay with *us* exactly." Riony shrugged, head hanging forward again.

Griskin slumped beneath Kess, crumpling in a limp puddle of fur. Kess fell over him, arms flailing weakly,

slipping, losing all control.

"We could take you somewhere you want to be—one of the shrine enclaves. Anywhere."

Kess slipped off the saddle, landing on her side on the ground. A figure stepped up, looming over them in the thick smoke.

Kife?

Kess's head swirled as she looked up at the ghost of her brother. Except a ghost wouldn't need a scarf wrapped around the bottom half of his face to block the smoke thick with sedative.

He survived. He survived. Riony!

Kess wanted to scream, but darkness tugged at her and all she could do was fight to remain conscious.

Riony mumbled, "Or if you did want to travel with us, maybe it wouldn't be absolutely awful."

Kife's eyes smiled as he dumped a burning pile of morass mercy in front of Kess, then leaned down and pulled one of her bone-throwing daggers from her bracer. Kess's fingers twitched, trying to stop him, fight him. Her throat croaked in protest.

How did he survive?

Kess's whole body seized. Silvernix. He'd had a bottle of silvernix on him when the fireball had knocked half a building down on top of him.

No.

They should have checked. They should have dug him up and made sure he was gone.

Was he going to kill her now with her own dagger?

After one long, hard look at Kess, Kife stepped away, rushing on silent feet down the stretch toward the woman with her back to them.

Riony. Riony!

"Kess, are you going to say *anything?* I'm trying ..." Riony groaned, starting to turn around.

Kife grabbed her by the shoulder with one hand and with the other, plunged Kess's dagger hilt deep into the center of her back.

Kess felt as though her own heart stopped.

No. No. Come on, Riony. Fight back. Fight. Scream. Call for help. Come on!

Riony took one stumbling step forward and then fell like a stone, face-first onto the ashy ground. The dull white of the dagger sticking from her back was stark against a growing spread of blood.

Horror flooded Kess, and she couldn't scream, couldn't cry. She couldn't even blink or turn away.

Kife stalked back up the long path to her, dusting off his hands.

"Wasn't that a bit of fun, little sister? This is just the

first of the suffering I have planned for you to repay you for what you did to me." He grabbed her by the wrists, pulling her the rest of the way off Griskin.

"Although you did do one favor for me—leaving my saddlebags behind when you *let my dragon* go. At least that let me get to my supply of this wonderful herb." Kife kicked away the last of the fuming morass mercy.

Kess was barely listening to her brother's tirade.

Riony. Move. Move. Please.

She didn't move.

"You're coming with me. And you're going to watch as I get myself a new dragon, and then I'll get the silvernix-bleeding creature again and get everything back that you took from me. And we'll make sure every one of my triumphs hurts you as much as possible."

One thin, gritty tear spilled from Kess's frozen eyes. Darkness encroached from every side.

A low rumbling built into a harsh growl, and Griskin surged back to his feet. Wavering, legs buckling and wobbling beneath him, he swung his snapping jaws at Kife.

Too slow, too dazed. Kife stepped back with ease, then lifted one leg and thrust his boot into the wolf's flank. Griskin went stumbling, crashing through a gap in the tumbled-down walls of the hatchery and falling in a puff of ashes beyond.

Kife followed him in, stepped over the prone wolf, and picked up a rock, lifting it high.

"Say goodbye to your dumb animal."

Kess prepared for her heart to be shattered beyond repair, hoping only that the damage wouldn't be survivable, hoping it would be the last time.

A voice floated from around the corner. "This is taking too long. I'll go check."

Kife snarled and let the rock drop on the ground. He rushed back to Kess, snatched up her wrists again, and dragged her roughly along the ground. The world twisted and warped in Kess's locked eyes and she drifted in numbness and gloom.

They were just around the next corner when a cry rang out.

"Riony!"

"What did Kess do?"

"Help me lift her. Go, go! To the gateway!"

There was a long, wailing moan.

"She's not breathing. Aish, she's not—"

And all the light in the world went out.

To Be Continued
in
Blood of the Dragon Throne

GLOSSARY

Including pronunciation guide

CHARACTERS

Riony Eyfarr (Ree-OH-nee AY-far) – Rolanian, Daughter of Eylin and Farrad, born when servants to the Gyrstein Dragonlords, then sold on as a family to the Heithorn Dragonlords, and since living as fugitive slaves. Trained as a midwife and herbalist. Sword enthusiast.

Lyrrin Eyfarr (Li-rin AY-far) – Daughter of "The Guest", an unknown dragonlord woman, and an unknown father. Taen and Elgarthan? Has some unusual features. Likes animals and magic.

Kessara Heithorn (Kess-AH-ra High-thorn) – From the once wealthy Heithorn dragonlords with strong dragon riding traditions, estranged. Taen. Rides a wolf.

Kife Heithorn (K-eye-f High-thorn) – Elder brother to Kessara, dragonrider. Taen.

Dracuni (Drak-YOU-nee) – Unique hybrid between unicorn and dragon, created from the use of silvernix on a broken dragon egg, and something more?

Griskin (Griss-kin) – Large gray wolf, male, for some reason abides Kess's company.

Aishena Hjelzahn (AYSH-en Hyel-zarn) – Delver, Middle sibling of three (remaining), fifth generation heir, grayglim in training. Taen.

Yoskar Hjelzahn (Yoss-kar Hyel-zarn) – Delver, Eldest sibling of three (remaining), fifth generation heir, Alderkin rune expert and academic. Taen.

Benjin Hjelzahn (BEN-jin Hyel-zarn) – Youngest sibling of three (remaining), fifth generation heir. Taen.

Kverra Hjelzahn (Kv-errar Hyel-zarn) – Grayglin warden and wife to Vori Hjelzan, fourth generation heir to the Dragon King. Taen.

Brishan Ulfaran (Brish-arn OOLF-ah-ran) – Taen ex-grayglim, Master of the delvers.

Niskina Ulfaran (Nissk-EE-nah OOLF-ah-ran) – Half Taen, half Rolanian. Brishan's daughter.

Yeonard Draekhan (Yeh-nard DRAKE-arn) – Dragonking, ruler of Elundrae. Taen. First to tame a dragon.

Sir Butterfur Spelunkychunks – A cave otter. Food motivated.

Myrwa (Meer-wa) – Rolanian leader of an aboveground community.

GENERAL

Alderkin (ALL-der-kin) – a secretive and powerful race of elven humanoids. Masters of rune crystal magic. Extinct.

Alderkin Depths – Massive underground cities once inhabited by the Alderkin. There are five known Alderkin Depths across Elundrae.

Alderkin Runes – Magical symbols carved into crystal items, which, when somehow charged, allow for a range of magical functions. The runes must be traced in the right sequence and direction of strokes in order to be activated and deactivated.

Alderkin War – A twenty-year war between the Alderkin and the Dragon King's forces, ending thirty years prior to the events in these books. Prompted by the human's slaughter of unicorns, and the Alderkin's attempts to protect them.

Athame (Ah-Thahm-Ay) – A dagger of varying size, made from crystal, and powered by various Alderkin runes for utility or combat.

Breachers – Undercity dwellers who brave the aboveground world to scavenge resources, highly dangerous but sometimes required.

Delvers – Undercity dwellers who brave the dangers of the Alderkin depths to salvage useful artifacts to be sold in the undercity. A risky but lucrative profession.

Dragon Glass – Glass manufactured with the use of dragon's fire to melt the base ingredients.

Dragon guards/riders – Those trained to ride dragons, generally for combat purposes. Either born to or hired by Dragonlord families who own the dragons.

Dragonhold – A building with multiple facilities for dragon keeping and raising, including hatchery, stables, and training areas.

Dragonkeeps – Walled in cities protected by dragons. The Dragon King has built and gifted a dragonkeep to each of his first generation heirs.

Dragonlords – Those who have the riches and resources to own their own dragons. Not necessarily royalty.

Elgarthans – A sea-faring race, pale skinned, they will visit and trade with Dragonkeeps for the riches of steel and glass provided through dragon labor, but rarely remain in Elundrae due to the dangers.

Elundrae (Ell-Un-Dray) – The continent in which the story takes place. Nearest neighboring country being Elgartha, across the seas to the East.

Rebel Riders – Title of a popular serial fiction, published and distributed in chapters.

Revenant/Rev/Shadow Revenant – Any undead creature raised by the Shadow Dragon's curse. Generally defeated by fire or dismemberment.

Rolanians – Once ruling large cities throughout Elundrae, most Rolanian settlements were destroyed as the Shadow Dragon curse spread through the land. As very few Rolanians became dragonlords, they had to buy into protection from those who had dragons, often at the cost of their own freedom. Generally presenting with a warm array of darker skin tones, and hair ranging from blonde, through reds and browns.

Shadow Dragon – a cursed and mysterious creature of smoke and sadness that brings the undead blight to the land of Elundrae. Wherever the Shadow Dragon touches ground, the dead rise.

Silvernix – Unicorn blood. Miraculous healing qualities, a single drop can cure a body from near death. Can only be stored in dragon glass, otherwise loses potency within minutes. Opalescent liquid.

Taens – Generally dark-haired and light-to-mid-brown skin-tones, Taens were once a warrior like clan of horse-riders, taking residence through the north-west of Elundrae. When the Dragonking rose to power, Taens became favored and more likely to become dragonlords, and soon became the dominant race across the land.

Taming – The ceremony in which all dragons are subjected to in order to be domesticated, similar to a lobotomy. Performed not long after birth on dragons bred in captivity. Utilizes silvernix in the process.

Undercity – A human settlement, established in the large upper cavern of the Central Alderkin Depths, as a refuge from the dangers of the aboveground world.

Unicorns – Ethereal, horned horse-like creatures. Driven to extinction in the race for the riches of their blood.

Herbs

Carrowmy – culinary.

Corpsefoot – used for contraception, dangerous in high doses.

Genjermint – sleeping tea.

Hennen – for hair dye.

Morass Mercy – powerful sedative with bad side effects.

Plumeberry – tart, seedy berries, poison detox.

Shillgrue – to condition leather.

Tinctoria – for hair dye.

Weftweed – a sticky (both in appearance and sap production) antiseptic.

Dragons

Natural subspecies

Etherflame – Plains dragons. Golds and reds, large size. Fire breathing for clearing grasslands/cooking herds, and big wings for hovering. Blood itself is flammable and is aerosolized in breath weapon. Most common dragonrider mount.

Seasong – Sea dragons. Silvers, greens, blacks, largest size, big lungs creates big surge of air/sound to stun schools of fish, and bigger mouth for feeding. There are tales they once sang, but never have in captivity or once tamed. Mostly used for interbreeding and beasts of burden.

Snowshimmer – Mountain dragons. Whites-blues, medium-sized, fast build for snatching up rare prey. Big talons, lightning breath attack, rare and solitary. Used in industry for power and interbreeding.

Treedart – Forest dragons. Yellows, browns, purples, camouflaged scales. Smallest type, with concentrated fire bolts for individual prey. Considered pretty basic by breeders and dragonlords, mostly used for interbreeding. Main/only dragon still in the wild because of size.

DRAGONS
Interbred selective breeding species

Etherdart – Etherflame/Treedart cross. Medium size, tough but slow, big fireballs. A basic combat dragon.

FlameSongs – Etherflame/Seasong cross. Largest size, high-capacity fire-breathers, used mostly for industrial uses, not used as mounts because they can spontaneously explode.

Seashimmer – Seasong/Snowshimmer cross. Large size, cold, icy breath used in ice making and food storage industry.

Shimmerdart – Snowshimmer/Treedart cross. Small size, with small ball lightning darts, dangerous for single targets but not great against mass undead, bred for speed as scouts/communications/assassinations.

Snowflame – Snowshimmer/Etherflame cross. Medium-large size, white "liquid" fire, fast, considered a great dragonrider mount, but short lifespan as breath weapon deteriorates their health fast.

Treedart/seasong – don't interbreed successfully.

ᴀNIMALS

Bantam Ferrets – Mouse sized ferrets.

Bovin – A large (twice human height) buffalo or yak style creature, docile, used to be in large herds that supported wild dragons. Moved into farming for captive dragons.

Carrion Birds – Massive scavengers with a cry like a wolf's howl.

Cave Otters – A large sized otter with specially adapted claws that allow them to climb sheer walls easily, pale colors to match limestone surroundings.

Cave Spiders – Head-sized spiders, nonvenomous.

Dreer – Deer with Armadillo like scales, that grow as large as giraffes. Also popular prey for wild dragon populations in the past.

Glowflies – firefly-like bugs, finger sized, live in large swarms and light up when disturbed.

Mouse Deer – Cat sized deer with fangs.

Olm – Just like real olm, but larger than human size and carnivorous.

Owlettes – Cave dwelling owls that feed on small rodents and insects within the caves, the size of a small hand.

Rope Worms – Just a worm, but much larger. Delicious when fried.

ALDERKIN RUNES

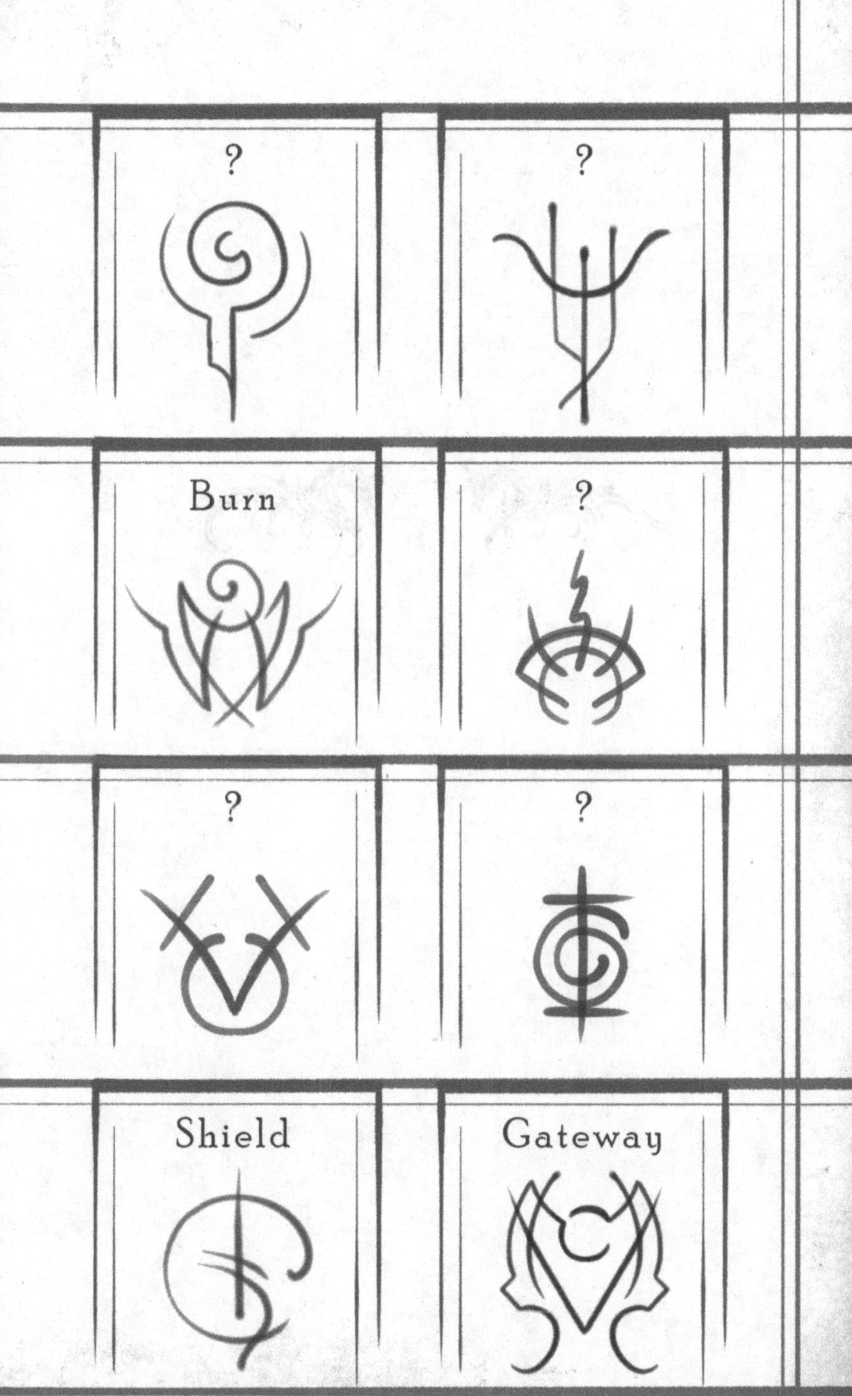

?
?
Burn
?
?
?
Shield
Gateway

Tree Dart
Sea Song
Snow Shimmer
Ether Flame

About the Author

P ROFESSIONAL DAYDREAMER, SELINA A. FENECH writes "adorably dark" Epic and Urban Fantasy for teens and adults. Filled with sweet and quirky characters, laugh out loud moments, and perilous adventures, her magical worlds are perfect for readers who love daring twists and happily ever afters.

A cancer survivor determined to live life to the fullest, she is an escape room enthusiast, avid gardener, foodie and self-proclaimed geek, residing in Australia.

In addition to literature, Selina applies her unique take on the dichotomy of light and dark as a professional fantasy artist working under the name Selina Fenech and has published many illustrated books, oracle decks, and colouring books.

Find Out More About Selina

OFFICIAL WEBSITE: www.selinafenech.com

Memory's Wake Trilogy

A modern girl lost in and hunted in a fairy tale world.
An illustrated young adult portal fantasy with
Arthurian and Victorian themes.

Empath Chronicles

Teenagers with superpowers fueled by emotions ... what
could go wrong? A young adult superhero romance.

MORE BOOKS BY SELINA A FENECH

Beshadowed

You have been lied to. Werewolves, vampires, ghosts …
they aren't what you think. What is really lurking in the
dark? A spooky urban fantasy.

Heartsblood

Her blood is irresistible, but is it worth the cost? A
vampire romance for adults.

9 781922 390912